"You want me."

Constance stroked a hand over Robert's falls, her touch as bold as polished brass. "You desire me."

For the rest of my life. "You don't seem surprised," he said. Or shocked or horrified.

"Intrigued." Constance wrapped her hand around Robert's nape and partook of his mouth. "I could be more familiar with your person, right here, right now, Your Grace. I'm not some sheltered blossom with no experience of the world."

"*I* am a sheltered blossom," Robert replied. "I want more from you than a tumble against the orchard wall. Much more."

She stepped back, expression disgruntled. "Right, you want a portrait, some landscapes. I can do that, though posing you—"

"Constance Wentworth." He took both of her hands in his, lest she march off down the hill, leaving him alone and—ye gods, what a day—*aroused*. "I'm not much of a bargain. I will doubtless be declared incompetent before the year is out, and all manner of scandal will result, but as it is yet within my power to marry, and we are well disposed toward one another...should I go down on one knee?"

"You are proposing to me? Proposing *marriage*?"

"I thought I'd made it plain that I was proposing rather than propositioning."

She raised her hand as if to worry a nail, then brushed her fingers through his hair instead. "You could do both."

PRAISE FOR GRACE BURROWES AND THE ROGUES TO RICHES SERIES

"Grace Burrowes is terrific!"
—Julia Quinn, #1 *New York Times* bestselling author

"Sexy heroes, strong heroines, intelligent plots, enchanting love stories.... Grace Burrowes's romances have them all."
—Mary Balogh, *New York Times* bestselling author

"Grace Burrowes writes from the heart—with warmth, humor, and a generous dash of sensuality, her stories are unputdownable! If you're not reading Grace Burrowes you're missing the very best in today's Regency Romance!"
—Elizabeth Hoyt, *New York Times* bestselling author

A DUKE BY ANY OTHER NAME

"All of Burrowes's secondary characters shine with wit and personality, and her sensitive development of two characters living with disabilities in the unaccommodating Regency era is particularly notable. This sparkling romance does not disappoint." ***—Publishers Weekly***

"A standout in the historical romance subgenre but is also a powerful story all on its own... Highly recommended."
***—Library Journal,* starred review**

FOREVER AND A DUKE

"Another smart story from popular Burrowes. Fans of

Amanda Quick and Brenda Joyce's Cahill mysteries should enjoy this."
—***Booklist***

"Delightfully geeky and warm . . . an excellent continuation of a very strong series."
—***Publishers Weekly***

WHEN A DUCHESS SAYS I DO

"An unusual pair of smart and worldly but reticent lovers; a modern sensibility about themes of consent, class, and disability; and a surprising and adventurous plot make Burrowes's latest Rogues to Riches Regency satisfyingly relatable nerdy escapism . . . will warm readers' hearts to the core."
—***Publishers Weekly*, starred review**

"Readers will root for these two wary people as they learn to trust each other with their foibles and their truths. With revealing dialogue, games of chess and subtle sensuality, this romance sings."
—***Bookpage***

MY ONE AND ONLY DUKE

"Skillfully crafted and exquisitely written, Burrowes' latest is pure gold; a brilliant launch to a promising series."
—***Library Journal*, starred review**

"Burrowes is a writer of towering talent."
—***USA Today* Happy Ever After**

ALSO BY GRACE BURROWES

The Windham Brides Series

The Trouble with Dukes

Too Scot to Handle

No Other Duke Will Do

A Rogue of Her Own

Rogues to Riches Series

My One and Only Duke

When a Duchess Says I Do

Forever and a Duke

A Duke by Any Other Name

THE TRUTH ABOUT DUKES

A Rogues to Riches Novel

GRACE BURROWES

FOREVER
New York Boston

This book is a work of fiction. Names, characters, places, and incidents are the product of the author's imagination or are used fictitiously. Any resemblance to actual events, locales, or persons, living or dead, is coincidental.

Forever

Hachette Book Group

1290 Avenue of the Americas, New York, NY 10104

read-forever.com

twitter.com/readforeverpub

First Edition: November 2020

Forever is an imprint of Grand Central Publishing. The Forever name and logo are trademarks of Hachette Book Group, Inc.

The publisher is not responsible for websites (or their content) that are not owned by the publisher.

ISBNs: 978-1-5387-0033-4 (mass market), 978-1-5387-0035-8 (ebook)

Printed in the United States of America

OPM

10 9 8 7 6 5 4 3 2 1

To those with "invisible" ailments

Acknowledgment and Author's Note about Terminology

One of the prominent topics in this little tale is mental health as it was understood in the Regency era. Regarding terminology, I faced something of a quandary. At the time, *idiot* was a term of medical art, not to be confused with *lunatic*. Lunacy or insanity was potentially curable; idiocy was on the order of a birth defect and considered permanent. I don't like using words such as this, or madhouse, madness, lunatic asylum, insane, and so forth, but to dodge off into less fraught modern terms would introduce an element of anachronism.

Members of my family are diagnosed with mental and neurological illnesses. I don't choose the period-appropriate terms lightly. I use them because they make the story more historically accurate, and a better reflection of what Constance and Robert had to overcome as they won the battle for their happily ever after.

Which they did. *Handily.*

And before we begin our story, I must emphatically thank writin' buddy and sister author Louisa Cornell for her generous assistance with the legal details regarding mental incompetence proceedings. She walked me through the relevant arcanities, and pointed me to a very useful period primer on the whole business. For storytelling purposes, I simplified a few aspects of the process, but the basic ideas—accusations of mental incompetence could come from anyone, and thc judgment rendered was from a legal commission without any medical expertise—are accurate. If you want to have a *really* interesting conversation, ask Louisa about the commissions (note the plural) convened to consider the Duke of Portland's mental fitness. My, my, my…

THE TRUTH ABOUT DUKES

Chapter One

Constance Wentworth's task was simple: sidle along the edge of the ballroom, looking like a forgettably plain woman making a discreet exit. The safety of the archway lay a mere two yards distant when Robert, Duke of Rothhaven, turned his gaze in her direction.

Surprise flashed in his green eyes, as fleeting as distant lightning on a summer night.

Bollocks and bedamned, he *recognized* her. He lifted his glass of lemonade in a gesture of acknowledgment.

More than ten years later, and he still knew Constance at sight, as she had known him. She'd had half an hour to adjust to the shock of seeing him, a paltry thirty minutes to reconcile the current man with memories formed years ago.

Rothhaven's height was striking, but so was his sense of focusing utterly on the object of his attention. He'd had the same quality as a much younger man. His entire being came to a still point, then he aimed every sense exclusively and intensely on who or what had caught his notice.

He was worth noticing too. Deep-set emerald eyes, dramatic brows that gave him a slight air of inquisitiveness at all times. High forehead, dark hair pulled back in an old-fashioned queue. Features that blended Nordic power and Celtic ruggedness with just enough Gallic refinement that his portraits would be stunning even into old age.

Once upon a time, Constance had contented herself with sketching his hands. Given the opportunity now, she would be far more ambitious with her subject.

She inclined her head, for it would not do to snub a duke, much less a duke who held sizable acreage in the neighborhood. That he'd completely misrepresented himself to her years ago, that he'd at one time been a friend, that he was hale and whole and not ten feet away made her steps as she wove through the crowd more urgent.

Which is why she nearly ploughed into him, though his reflexes, as always, were uncannily quick.

He bowed correctly. "Lady Constance, a pleasure."

With the whole ballroom watching, Constance could only curtsy in return. "Your Grace."

"You are looking well." No emotion colored that observation, and Constance *was* looking well compared to when he'd known her previously. She had made it a point to look well and dress well since then, though never *too* well.

"Thank you, and Your Grace appears to be in good health." When she'd first met him, he'd been a wraith, pale, mute, watchful, and bitter.

"I have my dear brother to thank for my improved health. Shall we enjoy the evening air?"

He offered his arm and Constance had no choice but to take it. Her very own sister, Lady Althea Wentworth, was the hostess at this ball. Her brothers, Quinn and Stephen, were on hand, and as far as the family knew, Constance and Rothhaven were at best distant neighbors with only a passing acquaintance.

Would that it were so.

The goggling crowd that hadn't allowed Constance through a moment before parted like sheep for Rothhaven. His pace was leisurely, and he rested a gloved hand over hers, as if he knew she struggled not to flee.

"The quartet is in good form," he said. "I do fancy Mozart done well."

"Do you still play the violin?"

"Rarely. Do you still paint?"

"Every chance I get." He'd taught her to paint, though all he'd had at the time were oils, which ladies were dissuaded from attempting.

"I rejoice to know that something of lasting value came from our association, my lady."

They reached the doorway to the back terrace. "May I slap you now, Your Grace?"

"Best not. Your sister as hostess deserves to command all eyes this evening. Then too, your brothers might take a notion to remedy any insult done to you. I could end up a very dead duke."

"Again."

"Let's step outside, shall we?"

Constance allowed that, because she loved to look at the night sky. Rather than lead her to the balustrade overlooking the garden, His Grace escorted her to a bench along the outside wall of the house. Music and conversation spilled through open windows, and torches flickered in the evening breeze. The terrace itself, though, was blessedly deserted.

"How are you?" Rothhaven asked, taking the place beside her. He sat a bit too close for propriety, but his proximity meant Constance could speak quietly.

"I am well. I paint, I attend the social activities I'm told to attend. I dance, I drop French phrases into my conversation, I read but not too much. I have become a portrait of a lady. And what of you?"

"The tale is complicated, and I will happily regale you with it at another time. For the present, might we agree to behave as if we are two cordial people acquiring a family connection through our siblings?"

"We *are* acquiring a family connection through our siblings, more's the pity. Your brother and my sister are in the advanced stages of besottedness." How had that happened, when Althea had given up on polite society and Nathaniel Rothmere famously shunned company of every description? That he even *had* an older brother sharing Rothhaven Hall with him was quite the revelation to local society. All and sundry had taken Nathaniel as the titleholder, believing Robert to have died prior to reaching his majority.

"Can we manage the cordial part?" Rothhaven asked. "I would like to try." He sounded sincere. He had always sounded sincere.

"I don't know what I can manage where you are concerned."

"Your ladyship is honest, as ever. Your forthright nature is one of your most appealing qualities."

"As if I give a hearty heigh-ho for your good opinion of me." Constance rose, abruptly at the limit of her patience. "I wish you a pleasant evening."

Before she'd taken a single step, Rothhaven had risen and manacled her wrist in a firm grip. He did not hurt her—he was the last person to inflict physical harm on another—but neither could she leave.

"You will please not abandon me to the darkness, my lady."

"Why not? You are a duke, of sound mind, in good health, and the worst that can befall you on this terrace is that one of the Weatherby sisters will try to get herself compromised with you."

He changed his hold so his fingers interlaced with Constance's. "You must not leave me alone out here, because I am generally terrified of the out-of-doors."

Constance's first inclination was to laugh, scornfully, because Rothhaven's comment sounded like a pathetic attempt at flirtation, but the quality of his grip on her hand stopped her.

"You are serious."

"I am entirely in earnest. If you would assist me to return to the ballroom, I would be much obliged. I should never have assumed I was up to the challenge of wandering about an unwalled terrace under an open sky, even at night."

Constance had been angry with this man for half of her life, but that tirade could keep for another time. He was entitled to his fears, and she liked the notion of having him obligated to her. She took his arm and re-joined the crowd in the ballroom, and before her thinking mind could stop her, she agreed to partner His Grace through the ordeal of the supper buffet as well.

* * *

Sensory perceptions assaulted Robert—the scent of the beeswax dripping down the chandeliers, perfume and pomade in a gaggingly thick cloud, incessant conversation that beat at his ears like angry hornets, the stomping and gliding of dancers' feet against the chalked floor…

I will kill my baby brother.

The thought was unworthy of a duke, but Nathaniel's behavior—abandoning Robert amid the ballroom crowd—was heinous. Robert had ventured forth from Rothhaven Hall for the first time in years only because Nathaniel's courting aspirations had required a show of familial solidarity.

Robert had been about to excuse himself in the middle of a conversation with no less personage than Quinton, Duke of Walden, when he'd spotted a woman weaving through the crowd. She had slipped between the other guests like cool water trickling past mossy stones, and the quality of her movement—graceful, silent, efficient—had stirred Robert's memory.

He knew those blue eyes, he knew the curve of that jaw. Constance Wentworth was older, of course. Her figure was quite womanly now, and she was attired as befit the daughter of a wealthy and titled house. The subtle wariness hadn't left her, though, and probably never would.

She'd done Robert the great courtesy of greeting him civilly, and now she had—true to her nature—allowed him the additional kindness of her company at supper. If she thought it odd that he all but clutched at her hand and sat nearly in her lap, she kept that sentiment to herself.

He held out an empty plate to her as they waited in the buffet line.

"I believe, Your Grace, the standard approach is for you to hold the plates while I fill them."

Because a lady should not have to carry even a plate. "Of course. My apologies." Growing up isolated from all proper company had left gaps in Robert's social vocabulary as vast as the Yorkshire moors. Even if he'd wanted to dance with Constance—which, of course, he did not because he *could* not—the time and the place were wrong.

Constance could drop French phrases into her conversation in a proper Parisian accent. Robert's French was that of Provence, and he hadn't realized there was a difference until Nathaniel had asked him about his odd inflections.

"What shall you have to eat?" Constance asked. *Lady* Constance.

The buffet presented another ordeal, for Robert's palate was quite particular. "I favor fresh fruit and cheese, a bit of bread and butter. Meat served without sauces." Peasant fare, oddly enough, was the best diet for minimizing the effects of his illness.

"That appeals to me as well." She had them through the line a few moments later, their plates only half full. "Come with me," she said, leading him into a side passage. "I cannot abide to eat in a crowd. I am afraid somebody will steal my food."

Her comment reassured him that she was still the same blunt, self-possessed, make-no-apologies female he'd met years ago.

"Are you tempted to steal food that belongs to others, my lady?"

"Not anymore." She opened a door and preceded him into a cozy parlor. "My sister won't mind us using her private sitting room when the alternative would be to make a scene before the neighbors."

Robert set the plates on a writing desk angled near the window. "My grasp of proper manners is shaky at best, but should we be alone here?"

"You are safe with me, Your Grace."

"But are *you* safe from the Mrs. Weatherbys and Lady

Phoebes?" he asked, naming the most malicious of the neighborhood gossips.

Constance closed and locked the door, then pulled the draperies shut. "*We* are safe from them. They are all too busy gawking at Althea and Lord Nathaniel."

"Did you close the drapes out of concern for our privacy or out of consideration for my peculiarities?" In either case, Robert was grateful. Constance was thinking clearly, while he was nearly overwhelmed with the need to be back at Rothhaven Hall.

"Both. Let's eat, and then you will answer my questions."

He owed her that. "Will you answer some questions for me as well?"

"Perhaps." Her ladyship took a seat at the desk, handling her skirts as gracefully as a princess managed her ermine robes. She set about applying butter to her bread, her hands competent and mannish.

Robert adored her hands. He'd missed much about her, especially her hands. She still wore no rings, not that such details mattered to a man longing for another five years of relative solitude.

"What questions have you, my lady?"

"Eat first, Your Grace."

Robert wasn't hungry, or didn't think he was hungry. His minders at Dr. Soames's establishment had controlled everything he'd eaten for years, and he'd learned to separate himself from bodily appetites. Then five years ago, Nathaniel had fetched him home to Rothhaven Hall, where the kitchen's efforts were so indifferent that food remained a means to an end rather than a pleasure in itself.

"I still have the falling sickness," he said, accepting the butter knife from her.

"I wasn't aware it could be cured."

"One can outgrow it, or it can abate in adulthood. With me..." He considered his bread and butter. "I am not as prone to fits, but they still plague me on occasion. I also have staring spells, or so Nathaniel tells me."

Constance considered a deep red cherry. "You don't know for a certainty?"

He *knew*, more's the pity. "I lose track of conversations. I see a certain look on Nathaniel's face and grasp that he's trying not to appear worried. Occasionally, I can hear everything going on around me, but I cannot speak or react to it. Sometimes my vision will blur."

The list of symptoms from that point grew long and strange: blurred *hearing*, though explaining what that meant was beyond Robert's powers of articulation. Forgetfulness that was in itself temporary. Strange lights in his field of vision, a sense of having over-imbibed despite not taking spirits, and crushing fatigue.

A veritable buffet of miseries, and no pattern to which ones befell him when.

Constance tossed the cherry into her mouth. "But what does it *feel* like when you are staring off into space like that?"

In all the years Robert had been locked away out on the moors, nobody had asked him such a question. "Sometimes anxious, like when you've forgotten something, but you aren't sure what. Sometimes blessedly peaceful."

"You aren't in physical pain, then?"

The same curiosity that allowed Constance to plunder his privacy as an epileptic made her a ferociously talented painter. Robert was surprised that she'd held on to her inquisitiveness, given her family's recently exalted circumstances.

"I am not in physical pain," he replied, but not carefully

enough, because Constance regarded him across the desk, her expression disgruntled.

"I want to be furious with you, but here you are, still frail in a sense, and all brave and honest about it. I cannot be as angry with you as I'd like, though no gentleman ignores correspondence from a lady. I violated every rule of propriety to write to you, and you never wrote back. I'm glad you are no longer in that awful place."

Robert still had her letter, still read it from time to time. Sometimes he simply held it in his hands or traced the pretty loops and curls of her penmanship. As long as he'd been out on the moors, he'd forbidden himself to think of her. Since coming home to Rothhaven Hall, he'd tormented himself with reminiscences.

"Are you glad you aren't there either, my lady?"

"Only a fool would long to be confined in such a place. The cherries are an exquisite choice with this Brie. Althea's cook is a mage of the kitchen, even when all he's doing is concocting a menu. The man has powers beyond human explanation."

She ate with such obvious pleasure that Robert did as she suggested and tried the Brie and the cherries.

"This is…good." The flavors and textures contrasted, which made a bland cheese and simple orchard fruit more complicated, more interesting. "I will request this pairing at Rothhaven."

She munched another cherry. "Is that where you've been hiding?"

"I thought the interrogation wasn't to start until we'd finished eating."

She laughed, a soft chortle that illuminated her features with a rare and breathtaking warmth. "*Touché, vieil ami.* You were never frail of mind, were you?"

Old friend. The closest thing to an endearment Robert had heard in years. "I am invariably disoriented after a seizure. Nathaniel is concerned that I will be declared mentally unfit by a hostile court, and all our lands and wealth will fall into the hands of crooked trustees."

Robert was terrified about the same possibility.

"You still seem frightfully astute to me. Do you share your brother's concern?"

"When I can be rendered insensate for hours, forgetful of even the words coming out of my own mouth, I must acknowledge the validity of Nathaniel's worry."

Constance stabbed a piece of cheese with the butter knife and held it out to him. "Then you must have a plan in place for dealing with an attack on your mental competence. What have you in mind?"

What Constance said made sense. Nathaniel had fallen in love with Lady Althea Wentworth, older sister to Lady Constance. A life of peaceful seclusion for Robert at Rothhaven Hall would be impossible to maintain without Nathaniel holding the reins. Another plan was needed, and quickly.

"For the present," Robert said, "I plan to enjoy my supper and your company. Perhaps you have a few ideas?"

* * *

Stephen Wentworth reserved his most difficult conversations with his ducal brother for when he and Quinn were on horseback. His Grace of Walden rode with easy competence, and thus his attention when in the saddle was not commanded by the horse. Quinn chose sensible, sound mounts, up to his weight, and not given to fidgets or strongly stated opinions.

Stephen, by contrast, was a passionate equestrian. On the back of a horse, he was the equal of any man—or woman. He needed no canes, no inordinate caution. He traded his own unreliable leg for the horse's four sturdy limbs and enormous muscle. In the saddle, he was free from physical pain. In the saddle, he sat as tall and straight as any dragoon.

In the saddle, and there alone, Stephen was superior to his brother in skill, fitness, and confidence.

The other reason for bracing Quinn on delicate matters when he and Stephen rode out was practical. Quinn was seldom alone. Jane and the children claimed his heart and as much of his time as he could give them, particularly when His Grace wasn't wreaking havoc in the House of Lords or terrorizing his bank managers.

If Quinn walked in the park, he took his older daughters with him or wheeled the baby in her pushchair while Jane sashayed along at his side.

If Quinn enjoyed a drink before dinner, he often did so while playing simple card games with the children on the rug in the family parlor.

If he sat reading in the garden, Jane brought her embroidery to the same bench.

Stephen's brother was awash in domestic bliss, and seemed to have no clue how much difficulty that posed to any sibling seeking a private word with him. Stephen thus proposed a ride around the acreage of the Yorkshire property Quinn had earmarked for Constance to manage.

"Constance has done a good job here," Quinn said, giving his horse a loose rein to negotiate a winterbourne. Mungo popped over the trickling stream while Stephen's horse, an un-confident five-year-old with more potential than sense, danced around on the near bank.

"Constance takes management of her property seriously," Stephen said, "as Althea has done with Lynley Vale." Stephen, by contrast, trusted to good managers and spent little time ruralizing at his estate.

His horse rocked back on its quarters as if facing a dragon determined to snack on equine delicacies.

"Give the ruddy beast a proper swat," Quinn said, watching this display from the far bank. "If he makes this much drama out of a tiny stream, he'll unseat you the instant he's faced with anything truly challenging."

The horse danced back, then took a tentative step forward while Stephen remained passive. "He's gathering his courage, Quinn. To force him now means I don't trust him to sort out the puzzle for himself. The problem with a tiny stream like this is that the poor lad can hear it and smell it, but when it's barely a rill running between tussocks at his feet, he cannot see it."

As if to emphasize Stephen's words, his horse—Beowulf—craned his neck, raising and lowering his head.

"For God's sake," Quinn said, "he's dithering for the hell of it. You'll ruin him by indulging these histrionics."

This advice came from a man who'd never given *any* of his children a *proper swat*, who'd never raised his voice to them, who had never once been heard to publicly express opinions differing from those of his duchess. He'd spanked Stephen exactly once, nearly twenty years ago and for a serious transgression. Quinn doubtless still felt guilty over it.

"Your tone of voice, Your Grace, is not helping the poor fellow to locate his courage, or me to maintain my patience. Walk on, please, and Beowulf will vault the dreaded chasm rather than be separated from Mungo."

Quinn obliged, and Beowulf—from a near standstill—

gave a mighty leap to clear a stream a puppy could have gamboled over.

"Good lad," Stephen said, patting the horse soundly on the neck. "Well done, young man. Well done."

Beowulf trotted forward as if parading before the royal standard, then kicked out behind in an exuberance of high spirits.

"I will never understand why you prefer ill-mannered youngsters to settled mounts," Quinn said as the horses resumed walking side by side. "You, of all people, know what an injury can mean."

"I, of all people, know what a severe blow to one's pride and confidence can mean, and when I see a young horse condemned to a life of misery by poor training, I intervene where I can."

"And then a year later, you sell them for less than they're worth."

Quinn understood money the way Constance understood portraiture and King George understood lavish self-indulgence. Money was to Quinn what grass was to a horse. The *sine qua non* of all noteworthy endeavors, the intuitive metaphor for any undertaking.

Though sometimes, Quinn's grasp of finances made him blind to other truths.

"I find my horses suitable homes," Stephen said, "and price them according to the owner's means. I am compensated, the horse is well situated, and the new owner is thrilled with his or her purchase. I am not thrilled with the acquaintance forming between Constance and the neighborhood duke."

Quinn glanced back in the direction they'd come, though Stephen had raised this topic early in the ride, before Quinn could challenge him to a homeward gallop.

"Constance and Rothhaven shared supper, Stephen. They appeared to chat amiably. Given that Rothhaven has all but hidden from polite society for who knows how long, I don't see how he and Constance could be acquainted. She was merely being sociable."

"Constance is never sociable, Quinn. She is polite, she is agreeable, she is so unrelentingly well mannered she could be wallpaper in some vicar's guest parlor."

Quinn glanced over at Stephen. His Grace was the taller sibling by at least two inches, but Stephen had the taller mount and the better seat, thus putting him at eye level with his brother.

"That is an unkind thing to say about your own sister, Stephen."

"Bugger kindness, I speak the truth. Althea tried very hard to gain society's approval and got a lot of gossip and spite for her efforts. Constance has perfected the art of being ignorable. Two nights ago, she all but monopolized the company of a man every matchmaker in England will be fascinated with. Why? Rothhaven is a dry stick who apparently suffers a serious unwillingness to leave his own property."

And that version of events glossed over the more titillating facts. As best Stephen could pry the tale from Althea, the current duke—Robert—had been declared dead in his minority by his own father, who dreaded the notion of an heir with the falling sickness. The younger brother—Nathaniel—had taken up the title without realizing his older sibling was not only alive, but housed in some private madhouse out on the Yorkshire moors.

That Robert, as firstborn, was now willing to take on the title and the station of a duke would occasion attention from the sovereign himself—surely the king would have to formally reinstate the correct duke in place of the younger brother?—and talk at all levels of society.

"You fail to note," Quinn said, "that a connection between Rothhaven's house and ours has formed through Althea and Nathaniel. Constance's cordiality toward Rothhaven makes sense. He has a retiring nature; she has learned to be unassuming. A crooked pot needs a crooked lid, if only to endure a long and difficult evening."

Beowulf shied at nothing at all, a dodge sideways that might have unseated a lesser rider.

"Steady on." Stephen gave the horse a nudge with his knees. *I'm still here, lad. I'm not ignoring you.*

"Steady on to the knacker's yard," Quinn muttered. "If that horse causes you further injury, I will shoot him myself."

I love you too. "Rather how I felt about your duchess when it became apparent she had married you in earnest."

"You felt murderous?"

"Protective, Quinn, not *quite* the same thing. Just as I am feeling protective where Constance is concerned. You talk about pots and lids while I am focused on Constance's happiness. She has become all but invisible, a figure in a shadowed corner of her own paintings." Damned skilled paintings they were too.

"What a pity we can't all be like you, commanding attention for the sheer deviltry of it."

"I am no longer seventeen and full of ill temper, Quinn. Please attend the topic at hand. Invisibility served Constance when Jack Wentworth was swinging his fists, but thank the infernal imp of hell, our father is dead and gone. Have you never wondered who or what Constance hides from now? Why a duke's sister courts the next thing to anonymity?"

Mungo grabbed a mouthful of leaves from the low-hanging limb of a locust tree.

"Leave our sisters alone," Quinn said, making no move to correct his mount's rudeness. "If Constance wants polite society to view her as a boring cypher, she doubtless has her reasons. I'll race you to the stile beyond the orchard."

For Quinn that was an awkward change of topic, which only reinforced Stephen's conviction that nothing good could come from this acquaintance between Constance and the reclusive duke next door. Constance apparently had reasons for remaining in the shadows, reasons Quinn knew or suspected, but had decided to keep to himself—for now.

Stephen nonetheless allowed the subject to drop, and instead focused on beating Quinn to the stile by a margin that allowed an older brother to call the defeat a very near thing indeed.

Chapter Two

"Althea and I will wed by special license, I think," Nathaniel said, spearing a mushroom sautéed in brown sauce. "We'll wait the usual interval and hold the ceremony in Rothhaven's chapel. It's about time the old place got a thorough airing."

Robert did not care for food served with sauces. The sauce could hide an off flavor—or medication—and more bothersomely, sauces made separating the various types of food on one's plate nearly impossible. He lacked the heart to complain about the kitchen's efforts, though, when the Rothhaven staff had been so stoutly loyal for so many years.

"Aren't the specifics of the wedding the province of your bride?" Robert asked, choosing the smallest mushroom first.

Nathaniel beamed at his mushroom. "What a lovely phrase—*my bride*. Of course I will discuss every detail with Althea, but as regards the special license, I am confident she won't want a long engagement. More wine?"

"No, thank you. When do you intend to speak your vows?"

"Althea's family is here now. We might as well hold the ceremony soon."

Robert drove his fork into the next smallest mushroom. "A date, Nathaniel. I am asking for a date."

Out of long custom Nathaniel sat at the head of the table, Robert at his right hand. The staff had spent years supporting the pretense that Nathaniel was the duke, and they had done so at Robert's insistence. As far as polite society knew, Robert had only recently returned to Rothhaven Hall, when in fact, Nathaniel had brought him home more than five years ago.

The man reclaimed from the asylum had been the furthest thing from a duke. Robert wasn't convinced the years at Rothhaven Hall had seen all that much progress in a ducal direction either.

"What difference does the date make?" Nathaniel spread a pat of butter on his bread and took a second pat. "You aren't the lucky fellow looking forward to your wedding night."

In all the time Robert had been at Rothhaven Hall, he and his brother had never once quarreled. They discussed, they even debated in a theoretical sense, and one of them occasionally made an abrupt change of subject, but they'd avoided a true difference of opinion.

That feat was doubtless a testament to fraternal guilt on both sides.

"I am not looking forward to a wedding night, true," Robert said, selecting the next smallest mushroom from among those on his plate. "I am instead facing responsibilities you have shouldered for years. I must meet with tenants who have long presumed me dead. I must deal with the awkward moments when somebody asks where I've been all these years. I must at all times present myself to be of sound mind, despite a lamentable tendency to stare off into space when I'm not twitching and shaking on the floor."

Nathaniel put down his bread. "You are angry. I am sorry. I know that taking up the reins here will be a challenge, but you are ready for it."

Whether Robert was ready or not, Nathaniel was too deserving of happiness to be denied a future with Lady Althea.

"I need a plan." Lady Constance's words had not left Robert's mind since she'd uttered them. "Five years ago, you devised a plan to give me the time I needed to heal from *that place*, and I thank you most sincerely. I need another plan now, one that frees you to jaunt down to London and take your new wife shopping. Have you considered where you and Lady Althea will live?"

Nathaniel stabbed a third pat of butter, then beheld his bread and set the knife down, the butter still on it.

"I had assumed we'd dwell at Lynley Vale. Althea's property is well appointed and shares a boundary with Rothhaven Hall."

"I suggest you bide at Crofton Ford for at least part of the year." Robert had given the matter much thought, and though the words were painful, Nathaniel looked intrigued.

"Crofton Ford is a good twenty miles from here," Nathaniel said.

"I suspect a new bride wants a home she can consider her own. Not a property allotted from her brother's ducal holdings, but her own hearth and haven. You hold the deed to Crofton Ford outright, it's comfortable and closer to York. If your bride's charitable projects take her into the city with any frequency, Crofton Ford is the more convenient property."

Nathaniel poured himself more wine. "Are you banishing me, Your Grace?" The question was offered with a smile.

"Yes, in a sense. I have put more demands on you than any brother in the history of brothers, and you have never failed me. Go forth and be happy, Nathaniel. Provide me with lots of little nieces and nephews I can spoil and tell tales about your wicked childhood. Have the life you were meant to have before you learned that I was moldering away among the lunatics."

"Two days ago, you did not want to attend Lady Althea's ball. Now you're holding the door for me and wishing me off on my wedding journey."

Oh, God, the wedding journey. "Have you made those arrangements yet?"

"Althea has only just agreed to be my wife." Another smile, even more fatuous than the last. "The wedding journey hasn't been a priority. She'd probably enjoy Paris."

Paris wasn't too far away, not as far away as Rome, Lisbon, or Greece, for example. "If you are leaving on that journey in a mere few weeks, you had best begin planning it. These mushrooms are actually quite good. How is that possible?"

Their cook, a venerable relic from the last century, had neither skill in the kitchen nor any ambition to acquire same, but he'd never betrayed the family's privacy outside the estate. That had mattered more than fancy dishes or an interesting selection of wines.

"Althea's Monsieur Henri paid a call here yesterday," Nathaniel said, "and I'm told some cooking and trading of recipes was involved by way of professional recreation."

"*Our staff* is receiving callers now, Nathaniel?" For years, the house staff had rarely so much as gone into the village for a pint, lest awkward questions be asked about *the doings up at the Hall*.

"We'll be receiving callers here soon too," Nathaniel said gently. "Althea will come by frequently and I daresay the vicar will be close on her heels. The floodgates will open after that, but I will be here to help manage the neighbors."

Exactly what Robert did *not* want. "You will be planning your wedding journey. You will be wooing your bride. You will be taking her for a visit to Crofton Ford, because that will become her home. I must learn to manage the neighbors."

Even saying the words held no appeal. Good God, going to divine services loomed as an ordeal though the church was not two miles away.

"You needn't, you know." Nathaniel tore off a bite of bread and sopped it in his sauce. "Simply put it about that the Hall is still not receiving guests. I eschewed the tea-and-crumpets drill when I was presumed to be the duke, and a lack of social obligations allowed me to accomplish much in the course of a day."

I haven't the luxury of following that example. "A little socializing will be necessary to appease the curious."

"I'm glad you feel that way," Nathaniel said, finishing his wine. "I've accepted an invitation for us to enjoy luncheon at Lynley Vale tomorrow. His Grace of Walden, ably assisted by his duchess, will want to interrogate me and start the settlement negotiations."

"They can interrogate you all they please, provided they do so politely, but when it comes to the settlements, Walden will address himself to me."

Nathaniel looked up from his wineglass as if a loud crash had come from the direction of the warming pantry. "I beg your pardon?"

"I am the nominal head of this family now, and even in my infirmity, I have managed our investments. If we assume I am sane and sound enough to uphold the duties of the title, one of those duties is negotiating marriage settlements."

"So…it…is." Nathaniel spoke slowly, like a man blinded by the approaching glories of holy matrimony to the true ramifications of setting aside the ducal role. He put his empty glass to his lips, then set it down. "You haven't touched your wine."

"I don't care for that vintage with this dish. This sauce wants a good claret."

"You never notice the wine pairings. You never even seem to notice what's on your plate."

Robert held the largest mushroom up on his fork. "I am a duke now. I must notice many things that I paid no heed to before."

Whether I want to or not.

* * *

"The courtship dance has moved on to the second phase," Rothhaven said, offering Constance his arm. "The engagement is a *fait accompli*, and now Nathaniel must pass muster with the lady's family. I do believe he relishes the challenge."

They strolled the Lynley Vale portrait gallery, a long,

narrow room along the back of the manor. The gallery faced west and enjoyed abundant afternoon light. Constance pretended to study a portrait of some old fellow in a ruffed collar and sagging hose, but she'd seen this painting a dozen times before. The Elizabethan gent wanted restoration, though even if he were brightened up, he'd be an unremarkable specimen as both a subject and a painting.

"Does Althea face a similar challenge where you're concerned?" she asked. "Must she meet with your approval?"

"She meets with Nathaniel's approval. Who am I to question my brother's choice?"

"You are the Duke of Rothhaven." But who was he really? Rothhaven looked more at ease than he had the night of Althea's ball, though he'd said little at lunch. Jane had begun probing around the edges of Nathaniel's plans for married life, and Constance had been taken aback to learn that Althea happily anticipated moving to some property twenty miles distant.

"And if I disapproved of Nathaniel's choice of wife," Rothhaven said, "do you think he'd reconsider marrying your sister?"

"Not for an instant." Nor would Althea reconsider her choice of husband. "One feels a bit dismayed by such confidence. Althea is no Puritan, but her experience of men has been limited mostly to ballroom flirtations, fortune hunters, and idle speculations. Now she is engaged to a fellow I hardly know, and soon they'll take up residence someplace I've never been. I had thought they'd bide here at Lynley Vale or with you at Rothhaven Hall."

Rothhaven stopped before the next picture, an informal rendering of the previous Duke of Walden in his youth. His Grace had apparently been an approachable sort, for the artist had captured him leaning on a fence, his hand outstretched toward a leggy bay colt. The Dales in all their green glory undulated to the horizon, and a sky worthy of the Low Country masters billowed with fluffy clouds.

The image should have been one of bucolic joy, but Constance saw menace in the dark tree line bounding the pasture, and loneliness in the young duke's hand, outstretched to a wary beast.

"Might we continue this conversation someplace less... empty?" Rothhaven asked.

"Empty?" The gallery was full of light and quiet as well as of pictures and elegant conversational groupings.

"Your ancestors stare from their gilt frames," he said, gaze on Constance's hand resting on his arm. "A different pair of eyes regards us every few feet, and yet the room echoes. The windows let in abundant light, but they also allow anybody with a spyglass and access to the fishing cottage to peer in. I would rather be someplace else."

"You were serious when you said being out-of-doors makes you uncomfortable."

"And I assure you, my lady, I am serious now."

He was also avoiding looking at any of the paintings. "You were watched, at the hospital." Constance turned toward the door, her arm still linked with Rothhaven's.

"I was observed. I wasn't supposed to find the spyholes the good doctor had bored all over the walls of my chamber. When I did find them, I could not cover them up or he'd simply drill new ones and chide me for being ungrateful. I learned to tarry behind my privacy screen and drape towels in unusual locations."

"You were ungrateful, to want the smallest measure of privacy?" Constance forgot to allow her escort to hold the door for her.

And Rothhaven apparently forgot to hold it for her. They left the gallery nonetheless, Constance scooting through the door ahead of him.

"The doctor observed me for my own safety," Rothhaven said, "the better to treat my illness."

"Except he didn't treat your illness, did he? He simply poked at you as if you were a lizard in a jar."

"A ducal lizard, so he poked carefully. Where are we off to now?"

"My sitting room. It's on the east side of the house, so we'll have less sunshine at this time of day, and nobody can spy in the windows. Why are you allowing Nathaniel to hare off to Crofton Dike, or whatever the place is called?"

Rothhaven would not be hurried, though Constance now felt a sense of urgency about their destination. Quinn, Jane, Althea, and Nathaniel were strolling in the garden, which was a polite way to say Jane was offering Nathaniel private instructions on the proper behavior of a husband toward his beloved wife. Once that lecture concluded, Rothhaven would be expected to accompany his brother back to the Hall.

"Nathaniel's estate is Crofton Ford, a pretty little cottage of twelve bedrooms that came to him through a maternal aunt."

"And are you banishing him to this cottage? Not very gracious of you, Rothhaven." She led him into her sitting room and drew the curtains closed. "The couch will do."

Rothhaven stopped two feet inside the door. "I beg your pardon?"

"The couch." Constance waved a hand at the emerald velvet upholstered settee. "The green will pick up the color of your eyes, though all I have to work with at present is a pencil. If you take that end"—she nodded toward the corner—"you'll be half in shadow, which will give me an interesting challenge for a three-quarter profile."

Rothhaven remained right where he was. "Does one or does one not typically ask a subject's permission before sketching that subject?"

"Sometimes I do, sometimes I don't. If I'm sitting in the park, a sketch pad open on my lap, and a pair of dowagers are feeding ducks ten feet from my bench, I don't bother the ladies with a request to continue sketching. I will give you any drawing I complete, and you may do with it what you please."

The point of the exercise for Constance was to better understand the second duke to whom she would have a family connection. One ducal title had cost her severely. A second was a daunting prospect.

"Very well," Rothhaven said, "I consent to sit for your sketch. Do I understand that you would rather your sister set up housekeeping closer than twenty miles away?"

He took the indicated corner of the sofa and positioned himself so he was caught in both light and shadow. The effect was intriguing, for the illuminated portion of his face conveyed a detached aristocratic mask. Dignified, a little impatient, like Wellington eager to return to his troops.

The shadowed portion of Rothhaven's countenance was more complex. He looked out on the world with not merely a sense of disappointment, but rather, with the certain knowledge of betrayal. Sadness, anger, possibly resignation…

Constance's pencil began to move, and she bestirred herself to recollect Rothhaven's question. Conversing with a subject was a skill most portraitists developed of necessity, and he'd asked about…

"I never thought to be parted from Althea at all," Constance said. "We are allies, comrades in arms—or in ball gowns. Nobody in the whole of London knows exactly what leaps and stumbles I've made to arrive where I am, save Althea." Even Althea did not know the whole of the tale, but she hadn't needed the details. She'd had the rough sketch, and that had been enough.

"So how is it," Rothhaven asked, "that your sister tarried in Yorkshire long enough to capture Nathaniel's heart while you went to London for the usual social whirl?"

His eyebrows were intriguing. The slight swoop gave him an air of expecting answers even when no specific question was on the floor.

"Althea indicated that she no longer needed or wanted my companionship. We spent the Yuletide holidays together at my home, Thorndike Manor, where Althea passed most of the time reading in her room. She was visiting me less and less, and extending fewer invitations for me to visit her. I knew something was afoot when she declined to go shopping with me in York as the New Year began. Then it became apparent that she needed me to go to London."

"*Needed* you to go to London? Does anybody ever need to go to London?"

Such disdain, from a man who'd likely never left Yorkshire, and yet, his question was insightful too.

"Althea needed me to make the journey south without creating a fuss, to arrive at Quinn and Jane's home in the usual course, pretending that Althea's choice was of no moment. As it is, they didn't leave her alone for long, did they?"

His eyes...a mere pencil sketch would never do justice to a gaze that complicated. Rothhaven was both calm and turbulent. Distant and intensely present. To study him made Constance thirsty for a glass of wine—or something stronger.

"Your sister will not depart for Crofton Ford out of any distaste for your company, my lady. I all but told Nathaniel to leave the Hall."

His nose was easy. A proud beak, worthy of his title. The line was straight—no boyhood breaks or brawling—and gave his features an implacable quality. Rothhaven would be polite, even considerate, but he would not back down from a fight.

What had he . . . ? "Why send away the brother who loves you so? Why not allow him to make those choices?"

"Because Nathaniel loves me so."

His mouth was another challenge. Not quite grim, particularly not with the slight ironic quirk he gave it now.

"You sent your brother away, because he would never abandon you, given a choice."

"He would stay by my side out of guilt, because the falling sickness can run in families—my father was apparently prone to it—but Nathaniel is free from it. His is the guilt of any family member faced with an afflicted sibling. He sees my suffering and cannot put his own interests first."

Constance had to make several tries to get his lips right, and still . . . Lord, she wanted a glass of wine, or—how long until sunset?—brandy.

"Is it Nathaniel's guilt you are managing or your own, Your Grace? You cannot help an infirmity that has afflicted you since boyhood."

"True, but I can help the extent to which that infirmity casts a pall over my brother, at least for the present. He deserves a few happy years."

Constance had been studying her subject long enough

to attempt his chin and jaw in one smooth line. More resolution here, and maturity. Rothhaven was not a boy, not a pretty youth, and yet he was attractive.

"Why only a few happy years?"

A bleakness came over Rothhaven's expression, quickly chased off with that ironic smile. "I was hidden away for more than a decade because my condition makes me unfit for the title. When some impecunious distant relation or meddling neighbor decides that my father was right to remove me from the line of succession, Nathaniel will find a way to blame himself. He will take up his mantle of misery, and likely never again set it aside."

Constance wanted to tell Rothhaven to be quiet, to stop distracting her, but the purpose of conversation was to distract the subject. To aid him to remain still and relaxed while being closely studied.

She erased her first attempt at his chin. "You are clearly sane and hale. Who could declare you unfit?"

"I am sane at present, but what about five minutes from now, when you address direct questions to me and I simply stare past you—what then? When I cannot sit a horse for fear of a shaking fit overcoming me in the saddle—I have nightmares about that. When I refuse to take strong spirits for fear that too will increase the frequency of my seizures?"

He had barely sipped his wine at lunch, and Constance had been tempted to drink it for him.

"But you come right," she said. "You soon regain your composure and your mind is unaffected. There are no perfect peers, Rothhaven. I've danced with enough of them to know. They limp, they suffer megrims, they go blind. His Grace of Devonshire is all but deaf. The king's gout is so bad he can barely walk. Your primary burden appears to be one of guilt, which makes no sense to me at all."

Rothhaven turned his head slightly, so more of his features fell in shadow. "No sense at all, Lady Constance? Truly?"

The craving for a brandy tried to take over her concentration, but just as His Grace battled an ailment of long-standing, so too had Constance learned to deal with the temptation of the decanter.

"You moved," she said. "Please resume your previous posture."

He paused a telling beat before complying. Perhaps he knew how intimately acquainted she was with the sticky weight of guilt. More likely he was making shrewd guesses and letting innuendo do the work of certainty.

His Grace might be prone to seizures, but his mind remained quite sound. Perhaps it was his heart that refused to come right, another affliction with which Constance was too well acquainted.

* * *

"Will Lord Nathaniel *do*, Your Grace?" Quinn asked his wife, as Althea walked with her swain at the foot of the garden.

"They humor us, Quinn," Jane replied, taking a seat on a wooden bench. "Those two will marry, whether we approve of the match or not."

Quinn came down beside her, wondering what Jane saw when she gazed at Lord Nathaniel and his intended.

"They seem compatible. He's loyal to family, and Rothmere land marches with ours. I want to object to this betrothal, but my only grounds would be that Althea grew up when I wasn't looking, and I wasn't done cosseting her myself."

Jane laced her fingers with Quinn's, which had become a habit somewhere between the first and second babies.

"Is Nathaniel loyal to family, or is he deceptive?" Jane mused. "Nathaniel knew for five years that his older brother was alive. He allowed all and sundry to continue to think Robert dead, as the previous titleholder intended, when Robert had instead come to live at the Hall. I wonder if Nathaniel didn't enjoy playing the duke."

"Babies make you introspective." Quinn rested his arm along the back of the bench, for when Jane was expecting, his need to touch her, to hold her close and protect her from all perils, was constant.

"Babies make me bilious and tired and weepy. This baby is turning me into the Duchess of Unscheduled Naps," she said, smoothing her hand over the slight rounding of her belly. "I wish we knew Lord Nathaniel and his brother better."

"We likely will, in time. I can tell you this: Nathaniel's version of playing the duke, rarely leaving Rothhaven property, never socializing, neglecting his seat in the Lords, looks a lot like brotherly devotion to me. I suspect brotherly devotion is also why Rothhaven himself supports this match. I don't think anything less than a strong fraternal bond would drag that man from his estate even to take a meal with his nearest neighbors."

Jane laid her head on Quinn's shoulder. "Is that why you asked Constance to show His Grace the portrait gallery? Because Rothhaven has a retiring nature?"

"Not retiring, Jane, reclusive. Nathaniel claims the falling sickness is most of the explanation for Robert confining himself to the Hall for years on end. No man wants an audience when he has a shaking fit."

"And the rest of the explanation?"

"I can only speculate."

Jane sat up and peered at him. "You know something you're not telling me. Constance and Rothhaven appear to have a prior acquaintance. How can that be, when he's a recluse, and she has been tucked safely under your wing since Jack Wentworth's death?"

Early in the marriage, Quinn had deceived Jane. Out of misplaced consideration for his new wife's delicate sensibilities, he'd kept a few plans to himself—and nearly got himself killed in the process. Death would have been an acceptable result of such foolishness, but disappointing Jane had been nearly unbearable.

She had forgiven him. Quinn did not make the mistake of presuming he would be granted such clemency twice.

"Constance hasn't always been tucked safely under my wing, Jane."

"You worked," she said, patting his arm, "as a youth. I know. You took any paying job, and you were a footman for a time, though you sent wages home for your siblings."

As dearly as Quinn loved his wife, as much as he trusted her, this tale was still difficult to recount.

"After Jack Wentworth died, I became a clerk at a bank in York. The owner of that bank bequeathed me some means and many useful connections. My situation began to improve, partly because I was willing to travel—to Scotland, to London, to the ports, and thus I left my siblings in the care of tutors and governesses from time to time. When Constance was fifteen, I came home from negotiating a loan to a Birmingham gunsmith and found my sister had fled the premises."

"Fled the premises? *Fled*, Quinn?"

Leave it to Jane to seize on a telling detail. "That was

my sense. I searched for her everywhere, hired runners, questioned every neighbor, offered a reward, took out advertisements, posted spies at every coaching inn and quay, but she had vanished. We knew her flight had been premeditated because she took some old clothes and a bit of money."

"Did she elope with a tutor? A curate? A connection from her former life?"

"That was my first thought, but Althea said Constance positively loathed her music teacher and her French tutor, that she had no use for the riding instructor and even less for the dancing master. My bank staff never frequented my home, and our neighbors tended to be older couples with grown children. She ran off alone and she was gone for more than three months."

At the foot of the garden, Althea was standing much too close to Lord Nathaniel—or he to her. Was Constance watching this scene from the gallery, and if so, what did she make of her sister's sudden engagement?

"Constance excels at hiding," Jane said. "When I first married you, I thought she would be my greatest challenge. Althea confronted me directly about my intentions where you were concerned; Stephen did so even more overtly. I kept waiting for Constance to question my motives or test my resolve, but she never did. She was polite and quiet, no trouble at all, but to this day I have the sense she will pounce if I ever serve you a bad turn."

"She caused a great deal of trouble when she was fifteen."

"Many of us are troublesome at that age, Quinn. Where did she go?"

"I still don't know the whole of it. When I eventually found her, she was handling the rough work in the kitchen of a private hospital in the West Riding."

Good God, Althea had just kissed her fiancé's cheek. The kiss had been chaste enough, but Quinn's heart still lurched at the sight.

"Why would a girl who knew how dangerous the streets could be run off like that, Quinn? Why turn her back on safety, security, and loving family?"

The lovebirds wandered up the walk, arm in arm, meandering back toward the house.

"Constance was initially unforthcoming about the why of it. When I brought her home, I had to promise that I'd not question her, or make a great to-do, or call anybody out. She would have gone right back to scrubbing potatoes if I'd so much as raised my voice."

"She has endless self-discipline," Jane said, smoothing a hand over her skirts. "All four of you do, Stephen most of all."

Self-discipline was not a characteristic Quinn would have attributed to his brother. Stephen was self-indulgent to a fault, but also inhumanly determined on his objectives.

"There is more to the tale, Jane, but I'll save it for when I'm not mustering my resolve to impersonate a gracious, doting older brother."

Jane kissed him, much as Althea had kissed Nathaniel. "You are a gracious, doting older brother. You suspect Constance encountered Rothhaven when she worked at that private hospital?"

"I can't think when they might have met otherwise." Did not want to think of how they could have met otherwise.

"You still don't know why Constance ran away?"

"That's the part of the tale that must keep for another day." Quinn rose and extended a hand to his wife. "Constance leaves the room if I so much as hint that I'd like to discuss her past."

"She figured out early how to manage you." Jane slipped her hand through Quinn's arm and by subtle changes of posture and expression, became the gracious duchess beaming at a prospective addition to the family.

God above, where would he be without her?

"You are the only woman who knows how to *manage* me," Quinn said, as Althea and Nathaniel drew closer, "and that will ever and always be true."

Chapter Three

Robert found that indulging Lady Constance Wentworth's urge to do some sketching was oddly restful. Her sitting room was small, which soothed a few of his sundry anxieties, and she herself was a distraction from those same worries.

He did not know if the locking mechanism on the door worked from both sides, for example. Had no idea if the windows were locked or merely fastened. Did the adjoining bedroom have its own door to the corridor? How, precisely, was her balcony situated?

To investigate those factors—they were *not* details—would have been the behavior of an eccentric. Her sitting room was carpeted—always a fine thing, when a man might fall to the floor insensate at any moment—and her sofa plush and comfortable.

Her lips were plush too. They were an extravagance

in an otherwise spare and serious countenance, though she pressed her mouth into a line as she concentrated on her drawing. Behind a practiced, blue-eyed guilelessness, her gaze was still wary. She'd done her hair in a simple chignon worthy of a chambermaid, and she wore a plain blue afternoon dress, only a touch of lace at the collar and a dash of white embroidery at the cuffs.

Lady Constance was trying very hard to appear unremarkable, a wren among the Wentworth peacocks, and yet in the intensity of her focus, in her quiet, in her studied plainness, she begged for further study.

"What happened to you?" Robert asked.

She spared him not even a glance. "I went home, as you apparently did, eventually."

"You left home of your own volition, while I did not. Did your family receive you decently?"

He'd worried for her, for years he'd worried whether the soft-spoken, blue-eyed maid had found safety. She'd shown courage, ingenuity, and kindness in a place those virtues had all but deserted. When she'd left, he had not dared reply to her letter for fear his epistle would get her in trouble.

Then too, slipping another letter past Dr. Soames's watchfulness would have been tempting fate.

"Chin up half an inch, Your Grace. My family was excessively understanding." She made the word *understanding* into something burdensome, a quality that induced both guilt and resentment.

A combination Robert knew all too well. He tipped his chin up. "Shall we make explicit an agreement not to discuss our former association?"

Over the top of her sketch pad, she aimed the most fleeting scowl at him. "I do not violate confidences, and if

I know anything about you, it's that you don't either. My family has no idea that we've met, and I prefer they remain in that blessed state of ignorance. They would speculate. Chin *up*."

"Nathaniel has never asked about conditions at the hospital. Some of it, he saw for himself. Some of it, I described for him to explain my otherwise unexplainable behavior. I would not want my brother to learn the whole of it."

This glance was different, a little bleak, a little curious. "I don't *know* the whole of it, Rothhaven. I wasn't there that long, and I had the sense you'd learned much about managing your situation before I arrived. You had newspapers, the other residents generally did not. You had that violin, you had books."

She fell silent, her pencil pausing. Then she took up her eraser.

"Are we agreed, my lady, that our present acquaintance will appear to be one of first impression?"

"You are a duke with a known illness. That your father, born in a less enlightened age, hid you away to keep your falling sickness a secret will make a certain sense to those who learn of it. They will pity you or they will derive mean satisfaction seeing a man of high station afflicted. What explanation can there be for a duke's sister plucking chicken carcasses and chopping leeks?"

She considered her sketch, then bent close to the paper and resumed drawing. "Why would a girl raised in dire poverty," she went on, "actively seek out the lowliest employment in the most scandalous place she could find, once that girl's station in life had considerably improved? Such stupidity has no plausible explanation. The scandal would be ruinous, and I owe my family too much to bring that down upon them."

She fell silent, curling that full lower lip under her top teeth.

Robert reminded himself that the girl who'd run from her improved station hadn't known her brother would become a duke. She'd had no idea at the time that nieces would come along whose options could be foreclosed by a scandalous auntie.

She had known, though, where she could blend in, where her family would never think to look for her. She'd been clever, that girl—and desperate.

"You have my word," Robert said, "nobody will learn of our prior acquaintance from me."

"Nor from me, though mind you, my siblings are abominably clever. Stephen in particular likes to solve puzzles, but Jane and Althea notice details too."

"And what of His Grace?" Robert asked. "How did he react to your return?" If Quinn Wentworth had hurt his sister in any way, Robert would hurt him back. To betray trust when a prodigal came home broken in spirit and exhausted in body demanded punishment.

"Quinn was all that is decent. He's always decent, because Jane expects it of him. Jane married him because he expects decency of himself. Here." She sat up and tore the page free from the sketchbook. "It's rough, but not a bad start. You are an interesting subject."

Robert took the sketch with a sense of foreboding. He saw himself in mirrors, and when a man lived a reclusive life, his turnout became a low priority. He wasn't exactly going to pot, but he did not ride, he did not fence, he did not—as Nathaniel did—strip off his jacket and cravat on occasion and join in with the laborers mending wall or clearing a drainage ditch.

On this occasion, though, Robert had donned company

attire and acquitted himself as much like a duke as possible. That had been a challenge. His only pattern card for how a duke behaved had been an arrogant, self-interested father willing to consign his firstborn to hell for the sake of appearances.

Robert studied the image on the page in some surprise.

"Well?" Lady Constance asked, setting aside her sketch pad and pencil. "Will you sit for me again or have I given offense?"

The man on the page was a bit haughty, also proud—the sketch found the difference between justified pride in an ancient lineage and aristocratic arrogance. He shaded toward the first, but not entirely. He was no boy, this fellow, and he exuded a man's physical self-possession and intelligence. He might not be precisely handsome—what mattered handsome?—though he would give a good account of himself in any debate.

The last, most intriguing aspect of the portrait was a hint of humor lurking deep in the eyes. An acceptance of life's absurdities gained through firsthand experience. A man with that quality could be a tolerant friend, if somewhat irascible.

"You have turned me into a duke."

"An accident of birth did that. I sketched the person who sits before me."

Constance was an accomplished artist, but then, anything she undertook—from a disguise, to a sketch, to the study of pianoforte—would be done well.

She also knew how to respect a silence, how to remain still and quiet so an inspiration could steal forward from the shadows in a man's head.

"You said I need a plan, my lady, for when an assault is made on my legal competence. You have given me a glimmer of an idea." Robert needed solitude and time to work out the details, but he could feel them swimming in the depths of his imagination. Patient focus could lure them to the surface, and he was nothing if not patient.

"That's good, then," she said, a smile dawning in her eyes, only to disappear when Jane, Duchess of Walden, appeared in the doorway.

"I should have known this would happen," Her Grace said, marching right into the room and peering at Robert's sketch. "Constance is talented, and we thwart her artistic impulses at our peril. Your Grace, my husband is asking for a word with you in the family parlor. I believe the marriage settlements are to be discussed."

She wiggled her eyebrows as if sharing a bit of gossip. Robert had no idea if the duchess was poking fun at her husband, at the topic of marriage settlements, or at the notion of a man who'd not left his property in years negotiating finances with a wealthy banker.

"I'll show you to the parlor," Lady Constance said, "and I will leave the sketch on the sideboard in the foyer. I did promise you could have it, after all."

The duchess claimed she needed to confer with the nursery maids, meaning Robert had Lady Constance's company to himself as they descended the main staircase.

"I have never negotiated marriage settlements before," he said. "I likely will never negotiate them again."

"You won't marry? Won't *see to the succession* as all titled men must?"

"I have the falling sickness. Or had you forgotten?"

"And does this illness render you incapable of siring children?" She put that hopelessly blunt question to him at the foot of the steps.

"It does not, but the illness can run in families. I have some evidence suggesting my father was afflicted."

"And yet nobody recalls him as anything but a highly effective, self-possessed duke. How odd."

Robert again had a sense of innuendo escaping him. "Are you *teasing* me?"

"Yes, I am. I expect I will commit the same transgression regularly. Best learn to tease back, Your Grace. Now, about these settlement negotiations: The issue isn't money. Althea's portion is generous and earning good interest. Quinn respects a fierce negotiator. He will expect you to be accommodating and generous because the aristocracy believe in appearing gracious to each other, but instead you must be a staunch advocate for your brother's welfare."

She drew him along the corridor, pausing outside a room from which masculine voices rumbled. "Don't give too much too easily," she went on. "Demand that every detail be in writing—every detail. Quinn will leave something out of the first draft to test you. It's a favorite tactic with him. Good luck."

"Thank you," Robert said, for he could not recall another occasion when anybody save Nathaniel had so clearly taken his part.

Her gaze became a tad wary. "For the sketch?"

"For the sketch, for the advice. For..." *For not ending up dead at the age of fifteen.* "For teasing me." He yielded to impulse then, probably for the first time in months, and bent to kiss her cheek. Very forward of him, despite the fact that their families were soon to be connected.

Very bold.

Constance kissed him back, also on the cheek. "Remember to be fierce."

Then she sashayed up the corridor, leaving Robert feeling a little dazed, a little bemused, and perhaps even—possibly?—a little fierce.

* * *

"This is monstrous," Lady Phoebe Philpot said. "Monstrous, Mr. Philpot, and as a solicitor, society looks to you to uphold the decorum and dignity of the realm. You must *do something*."

What Neville Philpot longed to *do* was take up his newspaper and leave for the stable, where a man could find a sunny bench, a pint of summer ale, and some dignity of his own. Painful experience told him Phoebe would only work herself into more agitation if he left her to fret, and when her ladyship was agitated no sunny bench in all of England was safe from her dramatics.

"I rather thought the sovereign was charged with upholding the dignity of the realm," Neville replied, pretending to sort through his correspondence, "or perhaps the military, though they do a wretched poor job of it."

Phoebe stomped across the library, her footfalls thumping on the new carpets. "Do not jest with me, Neville, not on a topic of this magnitude."

Neville had yet to figure out *what* exactly that topic was. Phoebe had summoned him home from York several days ago with a cryptic note. He had only that morning been able to leave his legal duties and return to his country seat. On occasion, Phoebe's tempers blew themselves out if she was left to her own devices for a few days.

This was apparently not such an occasion.

"Dearest wife, for a lowly solicitor much pre-occupied with the press of business, please do explain which monstrosity has you in a pet now."

She bowed her head, the picture of feminine martyrdom. Phoebe had married down all those years ago. An earl's daughter accepted the suit of a promising young solicitor only if enormous pots of money were involved. The pots of money were more or less intact, mostly because of Neville's abilities as a lawyer, but with each passing year, Phoebe's irritability grew.

Afternoon sun caught the dusting of powder on her cheeks, intended to hide the approach of middle age. He'd seen her pulling a gray hair from her head last week, and she spent enough on creams, tinctures of youth, and restorative lotions to beggar a sultan. Phoebe was not yet forty, but to Neville she was taking on the qualities of a bitter old woman—and he knew not how to make her happy.

"We have all been deceived," Phoebe said, gazing off at some vast horde of aggrieved innocents that existed only in her imagination. "The lot of us, from the lowest potboy at the posting inn to the neighbors, very likely to Vicar Sorenson himself. The Duke of Rothhaven allowed us all to believe his younger brother—Nathaniel—was the titleholder. I expect you to see the family prosecuted for perpetrating such a monstrous fraud."

Neville refrained from laughing only from long experience dealing with clients. They wanted the impossible for free, they expected miracles for a pittance, and most of them believed any injustice they suffered was the worst outrage ever to befall mortal man or woman.

"Phoebe, might we think this through?" Neville considered pouring himself a brandy from the decanter on the sideboard, but the hour was early, and Phoebe would disapprove. "We have our standing in the community to consider, and whoever the real duke might be, he is a *duke*."

"What matters our standing in the community when an outrage of this magnitude will go unpunished?"

Insight dawned as Neville studied Phoebe's pinched

features and glittering gaze. She'd been a pretty young woman and was still an attractive lady, but she had borne him no children, and—to give credit where due—not for lack of trying. She'd miscarried twice and delivered a stillborn son at seven months.

That a ducal family's supposedly deceased heir should pop out of the bushes as casually as a hare returning to his favorite clover patch would affront her sorely.

"I understand your concern," Neville said, "but we must think of our Sybil. Your niece is on the verge of making a very advantageous match thanks to your good influence. Lord Ellenbrook would hardly look with favor upon Sybil's connections if I took up a suit against His Grace now." And what would the cause of action be? Aristocratic eccentricity was hardly grounds for a lawsuit.

The fire in Phoebe's gaze dimmed, her lips pursed. "Ellenbrook would not break an engagement. You could sue him for breach of promise if he did."

"But he has not proposed, has he?" Ellenbrook had followed the proper steps in the proper order: impressing Sybil with his agreeable company, approaching Neville to ask if addresses might be paid, and then resuming the impressing-and-agreeable-company part.

Last week, Ellenbrook had departed for his hunting box some miles to the west. He was due to return in a fortnight or so, and the household—the female part of the household—expected a proposal would follow.

"You must trust me on this," Neville said, taking Phoebe's hands. "I have seen too many young people fall out of love once the settlements come under discussion. I can do my part for Sybil, and I'm sure her dear papa will do his, but Ellenbrook's family might regard our efforts as insufficient."

Phoebe had such lovely hands. Graceful, soft, not so much as a freckle to mar their perfection.

"I want to argue with you," she said. "I want to shout and pace and behave in a most unladylike manner, but you raise a valid point. Ellenbrook looked kindly on Lady Althea—he very probably pitied her that harum-scarum family of hers—and now she is to marry Lord Nathaniel."

Phoebe's gaze became speculative. More than once she had seen how to settle a difficult case on the basis of social standing, family pride, or some other non-legal consideration. She had a streak of guile, did Phoebe, and Neville truly admired that about her.

"Missing heirs have seven years to challenge an inheritance," Neville said. "The previous duke died less than six years ago. That means the older Rothmere son still has time to officially challenge his younger brother for the title."

"Lord Nathaniel—I don't like even speaking his name—made it clear at Lady Althea's ball that he has no interest in keeping the title. Had himself announced with only the courtesy title, presented his brother to us all as the duke. I suspect that dreadful woman is to blame for this scandal."

The current *dreadful woman* was Lady Althea Wentworth. A succession of similarly unfortunate females had suffered Phoebe's opprobrium over the years, including, occasionally, her closest acquaintances.

"Let's take some time to reconnoiter the situation," Neville said, kissing the backs of his wife's hands. "You excel at that, and Ellenbrook must come up to scratch before your concerns draw any public notice. I will set the clerks to researching missing heirs, while you make the appropriate overtures to the new duke."

She withdrew her hands and he let her go. Phoebe was

not an affectionate woman by nature, which was appropriate, given her breeding, but she was loyal and shrewd and Neville loved her dearly. His business had prospered in large part because she knew everybody in the local surrounds worth knowing and knew their secrets as well.

He would never burden her with a declaration of his sentiments—she'd be horrified at such vulgarity from her own husband—but he also knew she blamed herself for their lack of children.

A complicated woman, his wife, much like the law was complicated.

"We must not wait too long before we act, Neville. The shock of this great deception will wear off, people will go on with their lives, and a significant injustice will become so much old gossip."

The significant injustice was that Phoebe had been forced by circumstances to marry into an untitled family for money. She'd been denied children, and she'd ended up presiding over the squirarchy of rural nowhere. Now the further injustice of advancing age approached, and of all things, not one but two ducal families were usurping Phoebe's limited consequence.

"Tell me, my lady, who exactly will be made to pay for the deception that sits so ill with you?" Neville asked. "Are you wroth with the false duke? The real duke? The lady who is marrying into the Rothmere family? With the Wentworth family members for so badly overstepping their humble origins? Who is the opposing party in this case?"

Phoebe should have been a general, leading troops into battle on the strength of her military posture alone. "The lot of them, Neville. I want the lot of them to pay."

He bowed. "Then pay they will."

This earned him a smile. "I knew I could count on you."

"Always, my dear."

He meant to leave her in the library, among the rare books, precious porcelain, and venerable landscapes he'd purchased in an effort to provide for his wife in the style she deserved. If fate were kind, Phoebe would become absorbed in preparing for Sybil's wedding to Lord Ellenbrook, and this vengeful impulse would join the numberless indignities her ladyship could summon into a conversation at will, like lines of memorized poetry.

By the time Ellenbrook and Sybil had spoken their vows, some other little intrigue or taradiddle would have arisen to affront Phoebe, and Neville would be spared the distasteful challenge of bringing suit against—God have mercy, was Phoebe *daft*?—a duke, on grounds that would make Neville a laughingstock among his peers.

"When your clerks are doing their research," Phoebe said, her tone once again merely conversational, "have them look up that bit about impersonating a peer."

Neville paused, turned, and regarded his wife. "I beg your pardon?"

Phoebe gazed around the library, as if puzzled as to how all those books had collected on all those shelves.

"I had some time on my hands, so I did a little reading. Anybody who thinks to ape his betters by pretending to hold a title is committing a criminal act. The peerage has significant privileges over the common man, and as a spare impersonating the titleholder, *Lord Nathaniel* has clearly broken the law. The current duke apparently conspired in this crime, wouldn't you say? Your cousin is the magistrate, and I trust he won't tolerate such wrongdoing simply because the offenders are members of a ducal family."

"I will task the clerks accordingly," Neville said, before he all but bolted out the library door.

He paused in the corridor and took a substantial nip from his pocket flask in the vain hope of calming himself. There was no calm to be had, for—damnation and doom—*Phoebe had been reading law again.*

Chapter Four

"We must help Rothhaven become accustomed to his new situation," Althea said, tying her bonnet ribbons beneath her chin. "He is family now, and Nathaniel will fret endlessly if Rothhaven doesn't reconcile himself to holding the title."

Constance plunked a straw hat on her head and opened the front door, earning her a slight lowering of the brows from Strensall, Althea's butler.

"Sorry, Strensall."

"No apology needed, my lady. Of course you are eager to call upon Lady Althea's intended."

The staff was obnoxiously pleased with Althea's betrothal to Lord Nathaniel. Monsieur Henri could be heard singing from the kitchen and Althea's companion, Millicent McCormack, was planning an extended visit to Paris "after the happy event." Nathaniel's mother was already visiting old friends in France, though she would doubtless hurry home in time for the nuptials.

If this tidal wave of joy was occasioned by a marriage, what would the reaction be when Althea conceived a child? When she bore her husband a son and possible ducal heir?

Constance descended the front steps and scraped those thoughts from her mind, as she'd scrape paint from a failed attempt at a landscape.

"Come along, Althea," she said, climbing into the gig, "or Lord Nathaniel will think you were carried off by Vikings."

"Not Vikings." Althea came down the steps at a more decorous pace. "Jane, intent on shopping for my trousseau. She has an eye for well-made goods, also for a bargain. The merchants in York will long recall her in their prayers."

Engagement to Lord Nathaniel had lightened Althea's spirit in some intangible way. She laughed more, she smiled almost constantly, like a woman who knew a delicious secret.

She *glowed*, dammit, and Constance—who had spent years observing people and rendering their likenesses on paper and canvas—knew that glow would be impossible to catch in anything but oils.

"Is it hard for you," Althea asked as she took the place beside Constance and gathered up the reins, "being back in Yorkshire at this time of year?"

"Don't be ridiculous." Being in Yorkshire at any time of year was hard. Being away from Yorkshire was harder.

"Crofton Ford is lovely, Con. Nathaniel has kept it up and the staff is wonderful. I've always wanted a little cottage of my own."

"A cottage with twelve bedrooms?"

Althea clucked to the horse. "Compared to Lynley Vale, it's a cottage. Compared to Rothhaven Hall, it's a farmhouse, but we will be happy there."

Lovely, wonderful, happy... these terms peppered Althea's speech like cheerful colors dotting a still life.

"I am glad you have found a man who deserves your affection, Thea. I will miss you."

Althea bumped her shoulder against Constance's. "I'm going a mere twenty miles away, not far at all."

No, but in a significant sense, Althea, who was Constance's closest ally, had already departed, never to return.

Time to change the subject. "Has Nathaniel heard anything from the solicitors?"

"Yes. They are optimistic that Robert need only present himself as a missing heir, one who did not realize until recently that the old duke had gone to his reward. The letters patent can be reissued to ensure the title remains in his hands."

Was that what Robert wanted? Had anybody thought to ask him what his wishes were? But then, as Constance well knew, titles were unruly beasts, rampaging across family trees like famished dragons obedient exclusively to the terms of the documents giving them life.

"You're wishing we had walked," Althea said, as the walls of an old orchard came into view.

"Of course I wish we'd walked. The distance isn't but a mile and the countryside is beautiful."

"You cannot be trusted under a sunny sky, Con. You'll get out your pencil and sketch pad, and neither hunger nor thirst will pluck them from your hands. You will be agog at Robert's walled garden. He's spent years there, and his plots are magnificent."

Constance would have to sketch the duke in his garden to wrap her mind around that notion. She could still picture him as a younger man, gaunt and deathly pale from years indoors, his drapes always closed, the candles in his room always lit. He'd put her in mind of a hibernating wolf, except that wolves never hibernated, no matter how cold and dark the winter.

"His Grace enjoys gardening?" Constance asked.

Althea turned the horse up a long, weedy drive. "I don't think Robert loves the flowers so much as he loves creating patterns and watching them emerge. You seem to have an easy acquaintance with him, considering he hasn't moved in society."

So that was what this invitation to pay a call on the Hall was about. Rothhaven had sensed family would pry, while Constance had been confident that nobody would dare allude to her youthful mistakes.

"His Grace is restful company," Constance said, which was the absolute truth. "He doesn't put on airs, he's exceptionally well read, he is tolerant of human failings, and a good conversationalist."

The gig hit a rut, tossing Constance against her sister.

"Is he, Con?" Althea said, when the horse was again trotting along. "Yours might be the minority opinion in that regard. Rothhaven can be unreasonably stubborn. Nathaniel says he's had to be."

Nathaniel says, Nathaniel thinks, Nathaniel, Nathaniel, Nathaniel...who did not know the half of his own brother's past.

"Stubborn?" Constance replied. "Imagine that, a stubborn duke. I know of only six or seven others, our brother among them. Good heavens, could this façade be any more bleak?"

Gray stones could be made cheerful by flowers, greenery, gracefully curving arches, or pretty mosaics, but Rothhaven Hall was devoid of those touches. Lichens encroached on the wall supporting the front terrace, weeds added to the neglected air, and moss climbed the corner where the north and west walls joined. Every curtain was pulled closed despite the fine weather, and the brass lamps on either side of the front door were tarnished.

"The neglect served a purpose," Althea replied. "A bleak façade discourages callers. The past five years have not been happy at the Hall. That can change now."

She drew the carriage to a halt, and no groom appeared to take the horse.

"Let's drive to the stables," Constance said. "The staff is apparently out of the habit of watching for guests."

The day was sunny, but Constance's mood was increasingly dark. How could anybody thrive in surrounds like this—negligent staff, desolate grounds, no beauty or grace to be seen? Especially for a man burdened with a chronic affliction, such a setting was all wrong.

Althea gave the reins a shake. "I know you are entitled to your privacy, Con, but I have to ask: If you are acquainted with Rothhaven from some previous situation, does that make him unfit company for you now? I can say something to Nathaniel—something vague—and you need not deal with Rothhaven again."

Protective family was a blessing—also a curse. "His Grace and I are cordially disposed toward one another, as people with a prospective family connection should be. Stop worrying, Thea. Spinsterhood is almost within my grasp and I will be fine."

Much to Constance's surprise, she was looking forward to seeing Rothhaven again. He'd taken the sketch she'd left for him after their previous encounter and sent a polite thank-you note. That note was in her jewelry box, the first thank-you note she'd ever received.

An older fellow of diminutive stature shuffled out of the stables as Althea drew the horse to a halt.

"Mornin', your ladyships. Fine day, is it not?"

"A fine day indeed, Mr. Elgin," Althea replied, climbing down. "We will stay for luncheon, and we might walk home."

"I'll await your orders, your ladyship." He touched the brim of his cap and led the horse away.

The stable was in better condition than the Hall, the whitewashing fresh, the ground raked. Half barrels of heartsease sat on either side of the barn doors, and the earthy smell of equine wafted on the breeze.

"You will not stay here and sketch," Althea said, taking Constance by the arm. "You do know if Quinn ever finds out that you ran away to elope with some man, and that man broke his word to you, Quinn will see the fellow held accountable?"

Perhaps for Althea to move twenty miles away was not entirely a bad thing. "Ancient history, Thea. I will say this once, and not speak of it again: I did not run away to elope with anybody. Nobody need be held accountable." Not quite the truth, but as good as.

Althea remained silent all the way to a door set into a high wall at the back of Rothhaven Hall. "If you ever—"

"Cut line, Althea. It's old business, and you are starting a new life. I am fine, I will be fine." *Fine* being a relative term.

"But, Con, I've been thinking, and—"

"No *thinking*. My past is not yours to think about." Constance shoved the door open harder than necessary and stepped through ahead of her sister. She stopped after two strides, Althea crowding her from behind.

"This is heaven," Constance murmured. "This is absolute, perfect, eternal heaven."

Before her stretched a sea of fragrant, bobbing flowers, mostly irises and tulips. Colors blended, white to pink to red to purple, and then a contrasting bed—vibrant yellow—drew the eye. Everything, from the height of the blooms to the planted patterns of the beds, showed a loving hand and a lively imagination given freedom to experiment and indulge.

A statue of Saint Valentine presided over the whole, with two stone Cupids shouldering ceramic clamshell birdbaths. White walkways of crushed shells brought more geometry and light into the garden, and old wooden benches added the perfect final touch.

I could be happy here. The thought was unexpected and far from rational, but it made Constance smile. *I could be so happy here.*

"Lovely, isn't it?" Althea said. "Nathaniel claims as the season progresses, the garden becomes spectacular. I cannot imagine anything more spectacular than this."

Across the garden, Rothhaven stood on the terrace. He was bareheaded and coatless, his cuffs turned back at the wrists, his waistcoat of blue paisley another dash of color in this luscious retreat.

He waved. He did not smile—no grin, no flash of teeth—but his eyes, oh, his eyes…Even at this distance, Constance could tell he was pleased to see them.

Pleased to see *her*. "The garden is impressive," she said, moving forward so Althea could join her on the walk. *But I see a sight more impressive than all these lovely flowers.*

* * *

"Nathaniel informed me that I must expect callers," Robert said, shrugging into his coat. "He did not warn me that you and Lady Althea would lead the procession today."

Lady Constance had again dressed for comfort rather than to impress. She wore a plain rose walking dress, a discreet swath of purple velvet facing at the collar. The hem was decorated with a bit of purple and green stitchery, and the whole ensemble had not a single flounce or ruffle. Her shawl was a simple white crocheted affair, and on her head sat a plain straw hat with a wide, floppy brim.

"Why must you entertain callers?" Constance replied, taking his arm as Lady Althea went in search of her intended. "I want to bide endlessly in this garden. The fragrance alone . . ." She closed her eyes and inhaled through her nose. "You will be besieged with visitors once word of this garden reaches the village."

This prospect apparently annoyed her. It moved Robert close to panic. "As long as you are among their number, I will bear up under the strain. Let's gather a bouquet, shall we?"

"You needn't be gallant with me, Your Grace. I will be more than content to sit out here and sketch."

Robert leaned closer, as if old Saint Valentine might overhear. "I am not being gallant with you. I am sparing myself the torment of keeping company with the happy couple. They have lost all pretensions to decorum. The staff is in transports, and I alone am left to uphold the dignity of the house—of all the limitless ironies. The irises are coming in early this year, and I'm particularly impressed with some varieties I ordered from Antwerp last autumn."

Lady Constance watched him as if he were speaking in a foreign language familiar to her and getting every fourth word wrong. He wondered if perhaps he'd had one of his spells, though usually when they struck, he could hear and see everything about him, he simply could not reply or move for a time.

"I am sure the irises are spectacular," Lady Constance said, falling in step beside him. "So was my ire, when I beheld Rothhaven's front drive. Such neglect will not do, Your Grace, unless you are determined to return to your reclusive eccentricities."

"You were angry at a few weeds?"

"Weeds, ruts, the clogged drainage ditch, the flagstones cracking on the terrace. I understand your brother sought to guard you from an unkind world, but why not simply put a gate across the foot of the drive? You deserve a pleasant home, a place of refuge and repose, not some mausoleum for living ghosts."

"You are annoyed on *my* behalf?" He had to ask, because his dealings with women had been limited, his dealings with women of rank non-existent.

"Of course I was annoyed on your behalf. A gate isn't that expensive, but instead Lord Nathaniel, light of Althea's soul and gentleman without compare, decided to make a wreck of your ancestral seat. Stephen has a similar flair for drama. I suppose you can handle the grounds as you please now, but I do hope repairing the drive is near the top of your list."

Repairing the drive hadn't been *on* his list, mostly because he hadn't got 'round to making a list. "You inspire me to rethink my plan." They'd reached the irises, which had the most delicate fragrance, hardly a fragrance at all. Simply a sweet note on the air. Robert took out his penknife and sliced off a deep purple bloom about a foot below the flower. "Mind the petals don't bleed on your dress."

"Thank you." Constance took off her gloves and accepted the flower. "I would like to put this in water so I can—"

"—sketch it," he said, cutting another four stems. "We'll find water and a vase in the library."

"What plan did you refer to, Your Grace?"

"My plan for appearing mentally competent for as long as possible." He added three yellow tulips to the bouquet.

"You are mentally competent."

"At times, I can be. Come." He led her to the experimental bed and knelt to cut off one last stem. "Now your sketch will be a little more interesting." He rose and presented her a tulip with variegated petals of pink and white.

"I have never seen a tulip like this before except in Dutch paintings."

"Some people think the bulb has been tainted with a hereditary flaw, others think the color comes from crossing strains. The color reproduces, though, so I lean toward the first explanation."

She took the final bloom. "Having more individuality than other flowers is not a flaw. You should plant these on the front drive for the whole world to see, not hoard them here for your private delectation."

"You scold me?"

"I give you something to think about. Nathaniel likely tiptoed past your every whim and sniffle. These flowers need water."

And I need you. Robert came to that conclusion as if he'd been working through a geometric theorem. The answer sat at the bottom of the proof, patiently awaiting the student's deductions.

But was it the correct answer, or merely a relic of a young man's fondness for an even younger female?

"This way," he said, turning back toward the house. "I would normally take you through the French doors, but love is in the air. For all I know, love is in the library, taking shocking liberties on the desk, so we will use the corridor and knock loudly."

"Are you jealous?"

"What a question." *What an insightful question.* "Are you?"

"I am, and I'm not. Althea has always wanted a family, a home of her own where she can take care of others and be taken care of. She will have her heart's desire, and I do envy her that."

"Have you a similar long-cherished dream?"

Lady Constance paused on the garden steps, the bouquet held before her. The picture she made was lovely—also lonely.

"To study art in Paris and Rome, I suppose. In a few years, I'll be able to talk Quinn and Jane into allowing that. Stephen might be willing to share a household with me, at least for a time."

"You *suppose*? This is your heart's desire and you only *suppose*?" Robert *supposed* his guest was dissembling, giving him an acceptable answer rather than an honest one.

She preceded him into the house. "When one has nightmares, one avoids dreaming altogether. I would enjoy a year in Paris. What of you, Your Grace? What is your heart's desire?"

"To see Nathaniel happy. He has suffered much on my account, and he deserves to be free of the burdens I've placed on him."

"I understand fraternal loyalty, but what about you? What is your dream *for yourself*?"

Robert rapped loudly on the library door. "That is my dream."

"Then you need more dreams, Rothhaven. You need dreams that include you in them, rather than painting a lovely picture full of other people." She smote him gently on the chest with the flowers. "More dreams, happier dreams. Selfish, wild dreams. You're a bright man with a fine imagination. Come up with something besides good wishes for a devoted sibling."

The door abruptly opened and Nathaniel, looking a tad disheveled, stood on the other side. "Yes?"

A flushed and rosy Althea sat at the desk, not a book or a letter to be seen on the blotter.

"We need water for my flowers," Constance said. "Have you no other place to disport than a public room, you two? What if we had come in the French doors? You are as bad as Quinn and Jane." She flounced past a sheepish-looking Nathaniel and continued on to the sideboard.

"Perhaps," Robert said, "Lady Althea would like a turn about the garden before luncheon. You could check on the seedlings in the potting shed."

Nathaniel ran his hand through his hair. "The potting shed?"

"The one with the lock on the door." Robert held open the French door. "We'll see you when the kitchen bell rings."

Althea rose from the desk and took Nathaniel by the hand. The happy couple scampered from the library without another word, and within two seconds, Constance was snickering, then giggling, then overcome with hilarity.

"The potting shed," she managed, some minutes later. "The one with the l-locking door. My next niece or nephew will be named for a p-potting shed. Sprout, perhaps. Seedling Rothmere. You are very naughty, Your Grace. Very naughty indeed."

"Nathaniel is *carrying on* in *my* library with *your* sister and you say *I* am naughty?"

She dabbed at her eyes with a handkerchief and beamed

at him. No careful, ladylike smile, but rather, a mischievous grin that did odd things to Robert's insides.

"Nathaniel is very lucky to have you as a brother, Your Grace. My brothers would have barged in without knocking and enjoyed themselves thoroughly at my expense."

"I did enjoy myself." Robert was still enjoying himself, and that peculiar fact captured his attention.

He had realized in the past few days that Lady Constance Wentworth had trod a path he had yet to travel. She had traversed the difficult terrain between absolute social obscurity and general acceptance by good company. She had left her employment at the asylum, and years later, she was an unremarkable fixture during the London Season, while Robert dreaded travel by coach, and felt uncomfortable under open skies.

He needed to know what she knew, needed her insights and skills, her instincts and wisdom, as he attempted to take his proper place in the world. He hadn't figured out how to entice her into sharing those challenges with him, but he was nothing if not tenacious with mental puzzles.

Hearing her fill his library with laughter, though, watching her scold Nathaniel within an inch of his handsome pride, seeing her arranging the flowers on the sideboard, Robert came to another conclusion:

He needed her, if he was to make a convincing adjustment into the role of duke.

More than that, though—and this astounded a man who'd parted ways with astonishment years ago—*he desired her.* He still desired her.

Chapter Five

For Constance, paying attention to her surroundings had originated not from artistic curiosity or a romantic fascination with nature, but rather, from the sheer compulsion to stay alive. Jack Wentworth had been both the sole beacon of safety in his children's lives and the greatest threat to their well-being.

Constance had learned to notice differences in Jack's tread outside the door—was he tired, drunk, seething, jaunty, or—most dangerous condition of all—sober? Did he come home bearing a whiff of cheap perfume, or did the brisk approach of his steps signal a new scheme afoot, a run of good luck with the cards?

She had paid attention to Jack for the same reason a sailor took note of the wind and a farmer studied the sky. Life and death had turned on Jack's moods. More than once, she'd wakened Althea and Stephen to hustle them out the window as Jack fumbled at the door. By the tone and vileness of his curses, she'd known he was determined to once again take gambling losses out on those unable to defend themselves.

Now she paid attention to Robert, Duke of Rothhaven, who had created a spectacular garden at the very edge of the bleakest moors, and who had made her laugh until her sides ached.

"You are easily amused," he said. "In life, that quality has to be an asset. We have a portrait gallery in the duchess's wing, if you'd like to see it while we're waiting for our meal."

"Perhaps another time. I'm tempted to spy on your potting shed instead."

"You are being kind. Let's take a stroll on the drive, shall we?" He headed for the door, opened it, and waited for her.

"I thought you didn't care for the out-of-doors."

"My relationship with the natural world is complicated. As a boy, I wanted nothing so much as to be outside, away from my tutors and very especially away from my father. He watched me as if he knew I was about to disappoint him, as if sooner or later, I would stumble or give an incorrect answer. Then I realized he *wanted* me to disappoint him so that he could correct and rebuke me. Calculating how short of perfection I needed to fall and how often became my consuming burden. The only time I felt free was when Nathaniel and I were truant."

Rothhaven Hall could be a pretty home, in Constance's opinion, but it wanted fresh air. A breeze stirring the curtains. The sound of birdsong piping through an open window. The place was clean enough for an enormous dwelling with an aging staff, but the house was not *alive*.

"So you escaped to the out-of-doors as a boy," Constance said as they approached the foyer. "What about now?"

"Now..." His Grace peered out the window at a beautiful sunny day, his expression suggesting he beheld torrents of sleet. "It's difficult. When I was sent away, Dr. Soames realized that if I was to be made amenable to his various regimens and experiments, he needed to manipulate the things I longed for most. He withheld from me the privileges of the yard, and after a time..."

"The yard came to symbolize his power, not your freedom. What a hideous man, to pervert your joy into fear and rage. I knew I detested him for good reason. So why are we going outside now?"

Rothhaven was no longer studying the sky, but rather, regarding Constance. "Because it is time I reclaimed my joy, or at least put the rage and fear into the past. You are dangerously perceptive, my lady."

"Dr. Soames was a dictator, as was your father. Dictators teach those beneath them to be alert." She marched onto the terrace and waited for the duke to join her. He again glanced up, then scanned the front drive and the overgrown park on either side of it.

Constance beckoned to her host. "I have yet to see any giant birds swooping through the Yorkshire sky, ready to devour unsuspecting dukes. Nor have any French patrols been spotted in the environs. Come along, sir. We must make a list."

He stepped outside and pulled the door closed behind him. "Perhaps we should have spied on the potting shed instead. My driveway is not a very cheering prospect, is it?"

"If your efforts in the walled garden are any indication, you have a capacity for establishing order that will soon address the neglect I see here. The drainage ditch would be my first priority."

To Constance's delight, Rothhaven made an actual list—took pencil and paper from an inside pocket and jotted down notes as she strolled with him to the foot of the drive and back. At some point between bickering over the need for a gatehouse and arguing over the best place to install a ladies' mounting block, Constance began enjoying herself.

Organizing a painting was all well and good. An image full of accurate renditions and appealing colors could still fail as a work of art for lack of sound composition. Organizing the approach to a stately home was a more compelling challenge. One couldn't simply scrape away the paint and start over. The project had to be thought through down to every detail first.

"What about goats?" Rothhaven said, scowling at the weeds separating the parallel ruts of his driveway. "If I run goats through here for a few weeks, the groundsmen will have much less work to do scything the verges and breaking sod for the plantings."

The longer they talked, the less His Grace glanced at the sky, the more his stride had relaxed. He'd fairly jogged up the steps of the terrace, and he stood outside the front door, hands on hips as he surveyed marble steps besieged by weeds, lichens encroaching on his balustrade, and flagstones heaving as a result of winter frosts.

"Althea uses sheep to keep her lawns in trim," Constance replied, as Rothhaven made another note and tucked the pencil and paper back into his pocket. "Goats would do a more thorough job."

"Would goats be an eccentric choice, though?"

Constance was framing a response along the lines of efficiency being more important than appearances when a coach-and-four trotted over the hill a half mile from the foot of the drive. She turned to Rothhaven to inquire whose carriage that might be and found herself standing quite alone on the sunny front stoop.

* * *

"I scarpered," Robert said, regarding the fool in the mirror. "Dodged straight in the front door and closed it behind me. Lady Constance will never call here again."

Beside him, Nathaniel was still lathering his hands over the breakfast parlor's washstand. "You decided you'd had enough of a pretty spring day and took yourself back inside?"

Robert pulled a yellow leaf from Nathaniel's sleeve. "*I ran.* I heard the wheels of a heavy coach off in the distance and bolted like a cat dodging under the porch when a dog trots across the yard. I am not ready for this. Not ready for callers, not ready to wander around out of doors, casual as you please, making a complete, utter, absolute, *hopeless* jackass of myself."

"So why did you do it? Why make the attempt?" Nathaniel batted at his hair, which a trip to the potting shed had put in even worse disarray.

"Carry a damned comb," Robert said, passing over his. "Potting sheds can leave a man looking tumbled." He buried his face in a damp length of toweling and considered Nathaniel's question. "I went outside because I needed to inspect the drive if I'm to take it in hand. Rothhaven Hall must acquire the appearance of a ducal residence. I thought having Lady Constance at my side would distract me from...things." From the anxious weight of a wide blue sky, from the feeling of being watched from all directions, from a worry that had no source and no solution.

And she *had* been a distraction. Her ladyship had a way of cocking her head, like a sharpshooter closing one eye to sight on a target, before she delivered her pithy conclusions. She smelled of goodness—roses and sun-warmed linen—and she could follow a conversation that leapt about from the gatehouse to the dry fountain to the best way to discourage lichens from defacing an ancestral pile.

"What about an approaching coach unnerved you?" Nathaniel asked.

"The sound of the wheels."

"Why?"

Nathaniel was simply curious, simply trying to be helpful, but thank the angels who took pity on lunatic dukes, the ladies arrived at that moment, both of them looking cheery, tidy, and in charity with the world.

"I have worked up an appetite," Lady Althea said, beaming at her intended.

"If you don't cut line," Lady Constance muttered, "I will take my meal with His Grace in the garden, and you two can dine in the potting shed."

"A picnic sounds lovely." Lady Althea serenely took the seat Nathaniel held for her. "I do adore a friendly meal al fresco."

Lady Constance sent Robert a glance that communicated both humor and long-suffering. Nothing about her demeanor suggested he'd disappeared from her side not ten minutes before, without warning, explanation, or excuse.

"His Grace may ask to borrow some goats from Lynley Vale," Lady Constance said. "The Rothhaven drive is to be reclaimed from the wilderness. I will pass on the soup. Lentils do not agree with me."

The conversation at lunch was about Crofton Ford, this year's crop of spring lambs, and the looming ordeal-cum-celebration of shearing. Robert listened with half an ear, then caught Nathaniel watching him with the guarded expression that suggested Robert had missed part of the conversation.

"I beg the pardon of the ladies, I was woolgathering." Trying to fashion an apology for a reaction that had no rational explanation. *Why* had he run from the sound of coach wheels? Robert needed to understand that moment if he was to prevent himself from repeating it.

The meal concluded seven eternities later, with Nathaniel declaring that he wanted to show Lady Althea plans for landscaping Crofton Ford. Robert was once again thrown into the company of a woman before whom he'd committed a serious faux pas.

"I must have a tour of your walled garden," Lady Constance said, rising. "I'd like to spend the rest of the season out there painting the joy you've created."

"I will not abandon you in my flower garden, not unless you'd like to be abandoned. I am sorry."

Nathaniel and Althea had all but sprinted down the corridor for the library, and thus Robert's apology was made privately.

"I would like to be very abandoned in your garden," Lady Constance replied. "With pastels, oils, watercolors, even charcoal. I could have an orgy out there with mere pencil and paper, as you've had an orgy with your flowers."

She was being polite, giving him an opportunity to avoid further mention of his odd behavior. From her, he did not want that courtesy.

Robert escorted her ladyship into the corridor, glad to be away from the cozy parlor. "I was not allowed out of doors for several years at one point. I look like my late father, and Soames was concerned that some gardener or village child might see me and note the family resemblance."

"He told you that?"

"Of course not. His only explanation was ever and always concern for my *terrible condition*. One of the attendants made a comment about my resemblance to my father, another resident made another. I reached the obvious conclusion based on available evidence, though Soames wasn't above withholding basic pleasures for the bloody-minded hell of it.

"As the old duke aged," Robert went on, "Soames and I negotiated various truces. This began not long after you left. I was eventually allowed out for short periods, but only into the walled garden—the small walled garden, not the kitchen garden—and only for short periods. At the sound of carriage wheels, I was to return to my room immediately. We all were, or we would lose the privileges of the house."

He ushered Constance out onto the back terrace, trying to view the irises, tulips, and daffodils before him as an orgy. Perhaps a riot of color? But no, he'd planned the color scheme of the garden very carefully.

"'Privileges of the house' meaning," Lady Constance said, "the right to leave your rooms?"

"And to dine in company, though meals were to be silent but for basic requests. 'Pass the salt,' 'May I have the butter.' Soames purported to believe calm kept the seizures at bay."

Lady Constance stood at the top of the garden steps and took in a deep breath. "Did it? Keep the seizures at bay?"

"Nothing keeps them at bay." Robert wanted somebody to know that. Nathaniel never asked, and Mama's timid and vague questions never ventured close to that topic.

Lady Constance slipped her arm through his. "Walk with me. Does anything bring them on?"

As Robert wandered the paths with his guest and stopped to sniff the occasional bloom, he explained to Constance what he had learned about his affliction: Calm and order did seem to help, insofar as they guaranteed regular and ample rest, regular and modest meals, a very limited intake of spirits, and only modest exertion at any one time.

"Gardening is perfect, then," Lady Constance said. "It's physical, but doesn't result in all-out sweating and panting like fencing or hill running. You might enjoy riding horseback for the same reasons. One can daunder along, enjoy a canter, or exhaust oneself in a hard gallop."

"I do not ride."

She stopped with him beside a bed of rosebushes still more thorns than leaves. "But you could."

"And if a seizure occurs while I'm in the saddle, then I take another fall, suffer another injury to my head. I had never had a seizure until I came off a damned horse as a boy."

She patted his lapel. "So fierce. Stephen can teach your horse to halt the instant you begin to tremble, and he can show you how to fashion a brace, such that you cannot fall from the saddle. He needed that brace to learn to ride, and now he's happiest in the saddle. It's very discreet. A belt around your thigh." She drew her hand across the top of her leg. "Here, where your riding jacket obscures it."

He seized her by the wrist because he could not conduct a proper argument when she was petting him, much less mentioning *thighs*.

"My lady, it's not that simple."

"It's not that complicated either."

"I cannot ride in a walled garden. You saw me on the drive. A common, everyday sound, one heard a dozen times a day in any village, and my dignity deserted me."

They had not put their gloves back on after their meal, and thus when Lady Constance laced her fingers with Robert's, he and she were hand in hand.

"From what I can see, Your Grace, your dignity is still very much intact. Your instinct for survival is too. They simply need to learn to converse on different terms."

With anybody else, even with Nathaniel, Robert could have continued the argument. *You have no idea what you're asking of me. You speak from well-intended ignorance.* Constance, however, had survived the slums, survived a violent father, survived months away from the sheltered life her family had eventually been able to give her.

What else had she survived?

"I'm not ready to ride," Robert said. "I might never be."

"Fortunately, one need not ride to be a duke or to be happy. Tell me where you acquired these gorgeous tulips, the ones with the interesting variegation? I find the usual tulip rather boring, but these catch my eye."

They meandered along, talking about flowers, until they returned to the statue of Saint Valentine at the foot of the steps.

"Conversation tires you," Lady Constance said, smoothing a hand down the saint's granite robes. "Talk tires me too. Some people have the knack of monitoring a discussion with half an ear, dropping in and out as they would call upon a neighbor of long-standing. I cannot do that."

"There's something Lady Constance Wentworth cannot do? I am agog at the very notion."

"There's much I cannot do, but I noticed your attention wandering at lunch. I do the same thing. If the conversation is trivial—and other people's flirtations are always trivial—my imagination instead fixes on some bouquet that died a week ago. I see how the pattern of the plaster molding and the paisley of a lady's shawl echo each other. I have a reputation for being not very bright as a result."

"You like that reputation." Robert set aside the intriguing possibility that his periodic inattention was not always a symptom of illness.

"Boring people are left in peace."

Lady Constance was not boring, and yet in her company, Robert did feel a certain peace. More than anybody, she knew what his imprisonment had been like. He loathed that she knew, and he was tremendously relieved to have had a witness to his suffering.

Unwitnessed suffering could come to feel like imagined suffering, after all.

"You have divined my plan for assuming the duties of the dukedom," he said, watching her hand on Saint Valentine's cold stone robes. "I will be boring. I will look like a duke, talk like a duke, and comport myself like a duke. I will do nothing to draw attention to myself or to my household."

"You will be a wallflower duke?" She surveyed his garden, awash in color and imported blooms, appointed with trellises and espaliered greenery, not a wallflower to be seen. "Good luck with that. I am happy to aid you."

"I was hoping you would be, but you must tell me what I can do to aid you in return. Perhaps something to do with the dream of your heart, the one dearer than a year spent painting in Paris?"

She turned her blue-eyed gaze on him. "How do you know I aspire to anything more ambitious than pursuing my art in Paris?"

Because in some way, he knew her. Not from long acquaintance, but from shared experience. "I was hidden away, lest my family be shamed by my condition. For at least a brief time in your youth, you hid yourself away. I was hidden because my father's dreams for me as his heir turned to dust. What lost dream sent you into service at a private madhouse?"

"We weren't to speak of that. We agreed."

No, they hadn't. They'd danced around an overt pact, and agreed not to acknowledge the past when others were present.

"People who dwell in the shadows have dreams," he said. "We need them or we go truly mad. What is your real dream, Constance? The one you never allow to see the light of day?"

She paced away, taking a seat on the old wooden bench between the Cupid birdbaths. "I have spent years in London on the edges of ballrooms, at the backs of the theater boxes. I have watched polite society as one watches a pantomime and I have noticed something."

She had doubtless noticed far more than anybody would ever realize. "What have you noticed?"

"Much of what happens in polite society is based on connections, on who is neighbors with whom back in Shropshire, whose auntie went to school with whose mama. The Wentworths have few such connections."

Robert took the place beside her. "You want a connection with me?" The notion flattered, it did not please. "I have some influence through my mother, or I will if she ever returns from France. I am happy to exert—"

"No." Constance sat up very straight and appeared to become fascinated with the rosebushes across the walkway. "I want a *friend*, Rothhaven. I want somebody who is truly my friend. Not a sibling, not a fellow wallflower, not another artist seeking to curry favor with my wealthy brother. I want a friend of my own."

Her ladyship was clearly poised to flee, and for less provocation than the sound of approaching coach wheels. The wrong word, the wrong smile, and she'd withdraw as surely as if she'd removed across the water to Paris, never to be seen again.

Robert studied the roses, the jewel in this little floral crown, though they looked like so many angry weeds now. "How curious that you should harbor that aspiration, for as it happens, I am in need of a friend too. I am once again in need of a friend."

He had embarked on that reply meaning to appease her worries, to assure her that her request was reasonable and welcome. He'd completed those few sentences wishing with all his heart that he could be the friend she longed for.

They sat side by side in a comfortable, introspective silence. When Nathaniel and Althea came laughing out onto the terrace from the library, Robert was still sitting beside Lady Constance—beside his friend—in the sunshine.

The ladies left shortly thereafter, electing to walk home with Nathaniel as their escort. Robert remained in the garden pondering, for he was certain that Lady Constance, for all her honesty, had not yet confided to him the dream of her heart.

* * *

"Rothhaven likes my sister." Althea made that observation while watching Constance stride off down the path to Lynley Vale's stables. "I am amazed."

Nathaniel tugged Althea by the hand away from the front drive and around to the side of the house where the formal garden lay.

"Why amazed?" he asked. "Constance seems likeable, if a bit..."

"Exactly. She *seems* likeable. She's perfected the art of seeming. Seeming sweet, biddable, agreeable...but with her family, she can be quite blunt and often is."

"Can't we all?"

As soon as they were around the corner of the house, Althea pulled Nathaniel in close for a kiss. The sheer wonder of being free to share affection with a man she desired, the glory and joy of it, left her with a sense of chronic inebriation.

"We must be married soon," she said. "Promise me."

Nathaniel made no reply, but instead held her a moment longer.

"What is it?" She drew away enough to study him as she hadn't studied him in the library, the potting shed, or over lunch. "Something troubles you."

"A detail, merely a detail. I'm sure it will soon be sorted out."

"You are sure of no such thing. Tell me, Nathaniel."

He took her hands. "You know I love you."

"And I love you." Althea had never said those words to anybody else, not to her siblings, not to her reflection. She said them to Nathaniel as often as she could without sounding foolish.

"I love you and I will marry you as soon as possible, but Rothhaven has pointed out a potential issue. He raised this issue with His Grace of Walden, and your brother is in agreement that the problem must be resolved before we speak our vows."

"A pair of dukes are deciding when you and I will be married?"

"I suspect a duchess was also consulted. I can ignore my

brother's good intentions, I could probably reason around your brother's inherent caution, but Her Grace of Walden has been brought into the discussion."

And all of this had transpired without anybody speaking a word to the bride? Althea stepped back.

"The news must be terrible indeed if you discuss the situation with your brother, my brother, and my sister-in-law, but not with me."

"I am discussing it with you now. I am not the Duke of Rothhaven."

"God be thanked."

"But the proper duke, the real duke, has not yet observed the usual courtesies involved with a titular succession, nor can he."

Althea sank back against the cold granite wall of the manor house. "Robert cannot observe the courtesies because he cannot heed the parliamentary writ of summons. He nonetheless can and has succeeded to the title." Why must polite society be afflicted with so many inane rules?

"*I* succeeded to the title as well. In error—because I believed Robert dead—but I did. If the wrong names and titles appear on our marriage lines, our union could be invalid. Our issue could be illegitimate, and assuming Rothhaven has no sons, the title could revert to the Crown."

"This is tedious." Frustrating, infuriating, and bloody stupid.

"That's all it is—tedious. Walden is using his influence with the College of Arms to address the matter. He's already sent a pigeon south, with directions to send another north when a decision has been made. The king is usually quite attentive to matters involving the peerage."

"My happiness rests in the hands of a self-indulgent, lazy, supercilious..." Althea let the tirade die aborning, because beneath her temper lay the more honest emotion. "I am afraid, Nathaniel. I finally find you, I wade through years of arcane social conventions, and yet another pointless convention stands in my way. I know who you are, you know who I am. What do I care if at the time of our wedding you are still officially wearing some dusty old titles that have nothing to do with us?"

He kissed her, a swift, "That's my Althea" sort of kiss. "I want the matter resolved for us, but also for Rothhaven. If he ever thinks to marry, his union must be unassailably legal."

"I would like to know Robert has a companion in life," Althea said, running her fingers through Nathaniel's hair. "She'd have to be a woman of extraordinary tolerance."

"Or she'd have to be extraordinarily in love. It happens, you know. The most unlikely people—"

Althea smacked his arm. "If Rothhaven is to take his place as duke, he needs the dullest, most blue-blooded, unremarkable, conventional duchess ever to wear a tiara. His past must fade under a cloud of boring decorum and his illness must become an insignificant footnote at the bottom of a monotonously ducal life."

"I believe you have divined his strategy, or part of it. He's already set about creating a proper façade and front drive for the Hall, and I expect he will soon be receiving callers."

Althea pushed away from the wall and prepared to bid her fiancé a temporary farewell. "And where will he find that dull, conventional, unremarkable duchess, Nathaniel? Yorkshire society is not exactly awash in blue-blooded young ladies."

"I know of at least one who excels at *seeming* conventional and biddable. She also happens to be the sister of a duke."

Oh, dear. Oh, no. "Nathaniel, we must not let that happen. Constance isn't suitable, and Rothhaven isn't either."

"We weren't suitable, Althea, and if they make each other happy, who are we to gainsay them? Kiss me, and then send me on my way, please."

Althea kissed him—and he kissed her—and all thoughts about unsuitable dukes and even more unsuitable sisters flew from her head.

Chapter Six

The undersigned invites your ladyship to a meal al fresco to discuss a project of mutual interest. I remain, your most obed serv,

R

Was the *R* for Rothhaven or Robert? His Grace had not overtly offered Constance leave to use his given name, but he had used hers. *What is your real dream, Constance?* Perhaps someday she might tell him. Today she would join him for a meal al fresco.

A ducal picnic. Her first, and probably his first as well.

"You look pretty." Stephen made that observation as if puzzled by his own conclusion. "Rose is a good color for you."

Constance selected a plain straw hat from among the

choices hanging on pegs in the foyer. "Thank you. Are you about to follow up with one of your damning-by-faint-praise insults?"

"Such as, what a shame your fancy has been caught by a man who doesn't often leave his own property?"

She fashioned the bow of the bonnet ribbons off-center, then untied the ribbons and left them trailing. "What a shame my younger brother is a snob. Could you teach a horse to stand whenever his rider trembles in the saddle?"

Stephen shifted his grip on his cane—he was using only one today, a sign his leg wasn't paining him too badly. "Of course. It would take a few days, possibly a fortnight, and the right horse, but I could do it. Why should I?"

"Because you are bored, because doing a good turn for a neighbor is gentlemanly, because I ask it of you."

He slouched back against the wall. "That last part gives me pause. You never ask for anything, Con. You simply take what you need, do without, or demand your due. You are *asking* on Rothhaven's behalf. This troubles me."

Stephen was being protective, for which Constance wanted to smack him with her reticule. "He will never ask for himself. He's too much like you."

That salvo merited a raised eyebrow. "Stoic? Long-suffering? Self-sufficient? He's cowered behind his castle walls for years, needing his brother to play the dress-up duke in his stead. We are nothing alike."

She tried angling her hat the other way. "Some people need walls to feel safe, some people lean on a sword cane for the same purpose." She pulled on her gloves, then took them off again. One did not call upon a duke with one's bonnet ribbons trailing.

"My bad leg isn't my fault, Constance."

"Your lame leg is only part of your problem. Jack

Wentworth is the other part. What if Jack hadn't been your father, but rather, your jailer, and your own father put you into his keeping and then had you declared dead? Would all the walls in England be enough to keep you safe?"

"They would not be enough to keep me *sane*," Stephen said with uncharacteristic gentleness. "Rothhaven was kept at that asylum for more than a decade, Con. A place for crazy people."

Althea must have let that slip. Unwise of her. "Where do you think I went all those years ago, Stephen? A nunnery?"

He became fascinated with the painting hanging behind Constance's left shoulder, a dull landscape of sheep and hills under a sky of puffy white clouds.

"You went to finishing school," he said. "Young ladies from well-to-do families attend finishing schools."

"I went to finishing school after I came back. Where do you think I was when I went missing?"

A hint of the vulnerable adolescent showed in Stephen's eyes, though he was well past twenty years old. "Quinn said you could take care of yourself, and you apparently did."

Quinn would investigate Rothhaven simply because Althea was marrying into the Rothmere family. Constance could save her brother a bit of time and provide Stephen some worthwhile intelligence.

"I did not *take care* of myself. I could not. I'd been too long away from the streets and I'd grown too well fed and well kept. My instincts dulled, my looks improved. I found work as a maid at a private madhouse. Rothhaven *took care* of me."

The consternation in Stephen's gaze was as gratifying as it was rare. "He *kept* you?"

"Do men think only of swiving? *He kept me safe.* He

warned me which staff to avoid, when to stay off the back steps, how to hide my coin. He played the violin when he knew I was faltering. He read to me. Poetry, drama. He was barely sane himself but he kept me sane until Quinn found me."

"But how did you...?" Stephen's gaze narrowed. "You were a maid at the private hospital out on the moors. Rothhaven was apparently an inmate of the same establishment where you were a menial. You worked from dawn to midnight, slept in a cold garret on a straw pallet, and nearly starved. Why? I don't understand why."

And Stephen must understand every puzzle even if he had to destroy the puzzle to find its secrets. "Will you teach a horse to stand when the rider has a shaking fit in the saddle?"

"Give me a fortnight."

"Thank you." She tied her ribbons off-center, pulled on her gloves, and prepared to dine al fresco with a gentleman for the first time.

"Does Quinn know about Rothhaven's role in your past, Con?"

"He will have guessed. You can confirm his hunches, or not." She marched over to Stephen, looked him squarely in the eye, and deftly pried his cane from his grasp. He was braced against the wall and in no immediate danger of toppling, but his eyes filled with veiled panic.

"How you feel now is how Rothhaven feels, all the time, every waking and sleeping moment. No canes for balance, no handy weapon, no means of safely crossing so much as an empty room, and yet he asks no quarter of anyone. He can be felled at any moment by a foe no one has ever vanquished, with no warning, no parlaying terms. You don't know what he's endured. You and anybody else in this family mock him at your peril."

She held Stephen's cane between them at eye level for one more moment, then shoved it at his chest and let herself out the front door.

* * *

Nathaniel was off admiring the figurative potting shed at Crofton Ford with his intended, and Robert had seized the opportunity to be unsupervised with Lady Constance. This was doubtless not the done thing. An unmarried lady on a neighboring estate, even a lady with whom Robert was acquiring a family connection, should reject an invitation to dine with him privately.

Lady Constance would not come because he'd asked her to, she would come for his garden—if she came at all. Robert paced before the hearth in the library, ignoring the stack of correspondence piled on the blotter. For the first time in his adult life, he was listening for the sound of coach wheels with something like anticipation.

Though as rutted and weedy as the drive was, how could a coach or even a gig navigate the path?

A tap on the door had him almost jumping out of his skin. "Come in."

"Lady Constance to see you, Your Grace." Thatcher pulled off that bit of formality very creditably.

"Thank you, Thatcher. You may tell the kitchen we'll have our luncheon within the half hour." Thatcher bowed, jacket for once neatly buttoned, the tufts of white hair at his temples combed.

"My lady." Robert remembered to bow. "Welcome."

Lady Constance strode into the room. "No lovebirds in the library today?"

"Nathaniel took Lady Althea over to Crofton Ford,

where they will doubtless spend every moment on such pressing matters as landscaping, wallpaper, carpet, and furnishings."

She'd worn a soft rose walking dress that fell in graceful folds from an embroidered bodice. The hems swished a little as she examined the room's paintings one by one.

"Our siblings will spend every spare moment on a bed, you mean," she said, pulling off her right glove. "And who is this fine fellow?"

"That's Great-Uncle Ingleby. He was a favorite with the ladies but he never married."

Her ladyship swiped a finger over the artist's signature and leaned closer to the frame. "Was he fond of drink? His nose is a bit too red."

"I have only a few memories of him. I believe the pigmentation to be accurate. Without a wife to moderate his appetites, he might well have been a sot."

Lady Constance turned the same inquisitive gaze on Robert. "Did he have the falling sickness?"

"I do not know." Though Robert had speculated about every relative whose portraits graced the ancestral walls. "If he was epileptic, that might explain why he never married."

She looked away, as if noticing a fortune in books for the first time. "I did something."

Robert waited. Whatever she'd done, it had made the quietly dauntless Constance Wentworth uncertain.

"I asked Stephen to train a horse for you. A steady, sensible mount who will stop if the rider trembles in the saddle."

"Thank you." Robert would never so much as sit on the horse, but her impulse had been kind.

"You're not offended?"

"I am *epileptic*. I must accommodate myself to that fact or risk aggravating the condition needlessly. If I were ever to climb on a horse again, only such a mount would do."

He'd apparently passed a test of some sort. Her ladyship's posture relaxed and she tugged off her second glove.

"I did something else."

"You've been busy." He opened the French doors and gestured her toward the garden.

She crossed the library and stood before the open door. "I like to stay busy, but this was... I told Stephen I'd met you at Soames's hospital, that I'd been a maid there. He will ponder that revelation for a few days, then tell Quinn, which means Quinn will tell Jane."

"You had a reason for this disclosure?" For himself, Robert didn't care if Nathaniel's in-laws were privy to the whole sordid Rothmere family tale, but Constance's privacy mattered. She had been so young and so upset. So alone.

She stepped out onto the terrace, and Robert followed her.

"I wanted the truth known on my terms," she said. "Quinn will pry into your family's past. There aren't that many private respites in the West Riding. He will recognize the name of the facility where you... stayed."

Where Robert had been imprisoned. "There are more asylums, spas, and walled estates out there than you think. Some for females, some for consumptives, some for the violently insane. My father researched them all, and I have read his diaries."

"He *researched* them?"

"Not pleasant reading, but enlightening. To the old duke's credit, he sought a facility that purported to treat the falling sickness and other mental disorders, not merely warehouse cast-off relations. My malady has no cure, of course, but one cannot blame even a rotten father for hoping."

Lady Constance scowled at him. "You are more forgiving than I will ever be. He had you declared *dead*, he deceived your family and all of society, committed fraud upon the Crown. If he were still alive, would you yet be in Soames's institution, playing your violin and reading holey newspapers?"

How ferocious she was. "You would recall that."

"As if week-old articles about York's latest society ball could upset anybody's humors. Walk with me to the orchard."

Across the terrace, two new footmen were setting up the noon meal, aided by a very young kitchen maid. Staff generally did not like employers hovering, and new staff were probably even more self-conscious.

"I have not been to the orchard in years." Robert inventoried his reaction to this prospect, and found dread, anxiety, and resentment. Next to those predictable nuisances was a growing impatience with his own limitations. "I might well fail to complete the journey."

"This time you might not, but eventually, you will." Lady Constance marched to the end of the garden where the door in the wall had once upon a time loomed in Robert's mind like a portal to the edge of the world.

She kept right on going, and once again, he followed her. Months ago, on a foggy autumn morning, he'd begun experimenting with what lay beyond the garden door, navigating as far as the river. He left the garden only when the mist was so heavy as to obscure anything like a horizon. The thicker the fog, the better he liked it.

A world where he could see only a dozen feet ahead—and could not be seen himself beyond those dozen feet—

had suited him splendidly. This sunny spring day, with damned birds chirping and an arrogant hare loping off toward the river, had no appeal at all.

"Come," Lady Constance said, extending her hand. "We will speak of the project you invited me here to discuss."

Robert winged his elbow at her—that was the conventional gesture offering escort, if memory served—but she instead took his hand in hers, her grip warm and firm.

"We have missed the cherry blossoms," she said. "But the plums should be in their glory. Tell me of your project."

Constance was humoring him, jollying him into taking the first few steps on the path to the walled orchard. Robert knew it, she knew it. He went with her anyway, because he had at least as much right to be on that path as the wretched hare did.

Make small talk. Distract yourself. "I would rather return to the garden. We can discuss the project there."

"I would rather wear breeches. I often do, when I paint. Skirts get in the way."

Picturing Constance Wentworth in breeches was, indeed, a distraction. "I have decided that if I'm to be the Duke of Rothhaven, I must behave as a duke. I must look like a duke, speak like a duke."

"Quack like a duke?"

"Don't be impertinent." He failed utterly to suppress a smile. "I can no longer indulge my eccentricities, confident in the knowledge that my brother will carry on in the ducal role. A duke sits for the occasional portrait."

The path angled up slightly, which slowed Constance not one bit. "You'd like me to recommend a portraitist for you? Somebody who will mind his own business and not turn your nose purple?"

"No, thank you. I do not need a recommendation."

"Then you'd like me to confirm the choice of portraitist you've already made. Offer reassurances that he—for only the male gender is suited to rendering portraits, of course—is passably competent."

Constance picked up the pace as they climbed, and Robert had the sense she was annoyed. He did not turn loose of her hand, but rather, lengthened his stride to keep pace with her. She was by no means a tall woman.

"Passably competent will not do. This portrait must convey to the world that I am in every way appropriate to execute the duties of my station." The traveling coach had been sent into York for a complete refurbishment for the same reason.

Appearances mattered.

"You *are* competent to execute the duties of your station," her ladyship retorted. "Let us not belabor the obvious. That you have handsome features, a compelling gaze, and a fine masculine figure means any half-skilled apprentice could fashion a decent likeness of you."

"Do you mean that?"

"Perhaps not an apprentice, but anybody half skilled. You'll probably let him talk you into painting you wearing coronation robes, the usual castles and churning seas in the background. He'll try to suggest you have blue eyes instead of green, but you must stand firm. Eye color is not a detail and your eyes are *lovely*."

They had reached the orchard gate, which her ladyship yanked open and charged through.

Robert stood for a moment outside the walls.

"Well?" Constance said, holding the gate open. Her question, a single syllable, demanded something—an explanation or justification of some sort, for the human condition, for the evils of the day, for the imponderable mysteries of life itself.

Robert knew he ought to dash through the gate, slam it closed behind him, and refuse to budge until the comfort of darkness descended. Instead he marveled at the view of the Hall amid the fields below. The dread and resentment and whatnot were still lurking in his mind, but they slept like winded hounds, and let him look on his home—his *home*—from a distance for the first time since he'd been sent away.

"Rothhaven is not so dreadful when seen from this perspective." The Hall looked peaceful, in fact, mellow old stone settled on a quilt of green. "Not so bleak."

Constance re-joined him just outside the gate. "It's a fine old place. Perhaps whoever does your portrait would be willing to paint a few landscapes. The portraitists are a snobby lot, generally, but we all pass through a landscape phase, once we leave the still lifes behind."

He took her hand this time, a very bold overture on his part. *She* was not terrified of the out-of-doors, after all.

Though at the moment, neither was he. Uneasy, a bit anxious, possibly even agitated, but not terrified.

"I would like to leave my still-life phase behind," he said. "What could I offer you that would induce you to paint my portrait?"

Constance studied him in that serious way of hers. "Do you mean that? You want *me* to paint your portrait?"

"I'm told as subjects go, I'm not hideous. I want no strangers under my roof strutting about and acting artistic. You are beyond half skilled, and I know you won't turn my nose purple. I am offering you a commission to paint the portrait of the present Duke of Rothhaven."

In Robert's mind, until that moment, the Duke of Rothhaven had been his father, or a role inhabited by Nathaniel.

He, himself, had been Robbie, or to old familiars, Master Robbie. Soames had called him Robert, for last names were discouraged at such an establishment.

Watching Constance inventory his features, her gaze roaming from his brow to his nose, to his mouth, to his hair, he felt himself becoming the Duke of Rothhaven. Standing a little taller, adopting a slight air of hauteur the better to withstand her perusal.

"Sitting for a portrait is boring," she said, brushing his hair back from his temple. "You will grow testy." She eased a finger under his cravat and ran it around his neck. "I will grow testy." She gently steered his chin a half inch to the left, then a half inch to the right. "We will disagree."

"I trust your judgment." He would somehow trust himself to withstand her touch too.

She smoothed his lapels, fluffed his cravat, and made another adjustment to his hair. Her smile said she knew his compliment extended beyond her ability with paints and brushes.

"Let's have a look at the trees," she said, leading him through the gate. "I adore the scent of plum blossoms."

She prattled on, about light and seasons, how many different types of green could shine forth from a single tree branch, and why coronation robes were too trite to be endured. Then she shook a branch and showered herself with petals, and Robert knew himself for a doomed duke.

She adored the scent of plum blossoms, and he adored her. He simply, completely adored her.

* * *

"I am making a fool of myself," Constance said, as the last of the petals drifted down from the branch above her. "Acting like a child."

His Grace stood just inside the orchard walls, the gate open beside him. Constance knew she ought to be saying something more, *making conversation*, but she'd never seen quite that expression on a man's face before.

Rapt, sweet—there was a word for this sort of regard, just as there was a color for every object to be rendered on canvas. Rothhaven's gaze was respectful, also intimate. His eyes conveyed...She searched her mind for the term that applied, a sort of rosy, soft, deep word. A special word not often used out loud.

"So what if you are acting like a child?" he said. "You were never allowed to *be* a child, or not allowed to be enough of a child. I at least had ten years of genuine childhood, and they stood me in very good stead."

Constance brushed plum blossoms from her sleeves. "Childishness stood you in good stead? In *that* place?"

He approached, a man who always moved quietly, who even thought quietly. How on earth should she paint him?

"Not childishness, though I indulged in much of that, particularly at first. Childlike-ness, perhaps. My saving grace became my mind, which is ironic when an illness of the mind landed me there in the first place."

"Explain yourself." The green of his eyes alone would take much consideration, much experimentation, though mixing pigments was not an enjoyable aspect of Constance's art. Some of the colors were toxic, others volatile, and yet, from those dangerous concoctions could come great beauty.

"A child is curious," Rothhaven replied, "to the point of folly sometimes. Because I was curious about Pierre's accent, I learned French, albeit from a footman. I did not understand that it was a farmer's version of the language, but I can read the proper kind now because I was curious then. I was curious about the stars—they were visible to me even in a walled garden, even through a locked window. I thus learned astronomy and how to navigate by the heavens. If and when I escaped that place, I would need that skill."

His room had been filled with books, maps, and strange gadgets, becoming a sort of lending library for the other residents, not that anybody had let Soames know about that.

"You thought of escape?"

He came a few steps closer. "For about the first five years. I filled my head with fantasies. Perhaps Papa did not know that John Coachman had left me at the madhouse instead of at school. Papa would come fetch me when he realized the error. Papa had died and Mama was searching for me. I wrote letter after letter, which Soames dutifully sealed and addressed for me. He put them in the boot boy's sack, and when my back was turned, took them out and tossed the lot of them into the fire—after he'd read them."

Rothhaven regarded the rambling old pile at the end of the weedy drive. "I gave up on Nathaniel last, and that took more years."

"How did you not go mad?"

He closed the distance between them, gazing down at her as if she were the subject to be painted.

"I did, for a time. I was completely…the ice baths, the lashings, the lack of decent food, the confinement, seeing the other residents part with what reason they'd had when they arrived. I was contemplating an escape of a very permanent variety when along came a new maid. A serious, watchful girl who kept her eyes open and her mouth shut. Soames was allotting me just enough food to keep me perpetually ravenous. This maid, so quiet and so bold, managed to sneak a wedge of cheese to me between the clean linens she brought for my bed."

Constance indulged in another brush of her fingers through his hair. "At first I thought you were slender by nature, then I realized Soames was starving you."

"He was manipulating my diet to see if any particular food brought on seizures and, as it happens, his theory had merit. Too many sweets, too much alcohol, tobacco, strong tea, or coffee aggravate my condition, as does a lack of regular, adequate rest."

"He did not need to starve you to test that theory. An occasional bite of cheese, a few slices of ham, fresh apples…" She'd brought Rothhaven whatever she could pilfer from the larders, and had done the same for the other epileptic resident subjected to Soames's vile science. She'd sneaked books to Miss Sophie—nobody had a family name at that wretched place—and *accidentally* allowed the cat into Miss Helen's room as often as possible.

"You saved my life, Constance Wentworth. Saved my life and also my sanity, the one being occasionally exclusive of the other."

Rothhaven stood directly before her, and Constance was reminded that this was not the gaunt young man who'd watched her with such rage in his eyes when she'd come to sweep his hearth. The first three days she'd undertaken that chore, he hadn't spoken a word to her. The fourth day, he'd *thanked* her.

Nobody thanked a char girl for hauling ashes, and Constance hadn't expected thanks. Even as Miss Constance Wentworth of Highlane Street, York, nobody had thanked her for anything.

"I viewed it as a game," Constance said. "Whatever

misery Soames inflicted—forcing a patient to bide alone in her room, depriving her of diversions, keeping decent food away—I plotted to thwart him. I wasn't always successful."

"For which you were caned by the housekeeper."

"Never very hard. She did what she could too. Compared to Jack Wentworth…"

Constance fell silent, her attention arrested by Rothhaven's gaze. The furious, brilliant, half-mad youth yet lurked somewhere inside him, but that younger man had learned to manage his confinement. Not to make peace with it, but to tolerate a cease-fire.

"I didn't want to leave," Constance said. "I did not want to go with Quinn when he showed up that morning. I still have no idea how he found me. I worried for you so when I left, worried for all of you." She hadn't had the luxury of worrying only for them, though. "You received my letter?"

"You addressed it to the housekeeper, and she kindly let me have it. I was not in a position to reply."

Constance let that admission pass unremarked, for now. "And after I left, then what?"

"We managed. You taught us much. When Soames kept us apart, when he pitted us against one another with his false friendship and fleeting approval, we all suffered. When I shoved a book under Miss Sophie's door, when I saved some of my bread to pass along to Alexander at prayers, when I slipped Miss Helen a deck of cards so she could play solitaire, we all benefited. I bought the place, you know."

Rothhaven was tall and strong now, also confident in a way a man who'd been spared that hell could never be. Even Quinn didn't have quite this much…what?

Awareness of self? Self-possession? Gravitas? Whatever it was, Constance wanted to paint it.

"You bought that awful, nasty…you *bought* it?"

"When Nathaniel found me, taking ownership of my prison was one of the objectives that motivated me to leave, to learn to live in the world again, albeit a world nearly as circumscribed as a hospital. In that larger world, the letters I sent reached their destinations. I had coin and influence, even without leaving the Hall. My very signature had power."

He relished that power now, and Constance was glad he had it. "What did you do with the hospital?"

"Eventually, I closed it. With the exception of Miss Sophie, we weren't mad, and she was certainly not violent."

"She was violently convinced Napoleon had married her during the Peace of Amiens."

"And that he was coming for her any day. Where is the harm in such a fantasy? She's living with a niece now, writing letters almost daily to the deposed emperor. He writes back sometimes, courtesy of the local curate's epistolary talents. For Miss Sophie, the Corsican has not yet gone to his heavenly reward."

"That is…marvelous." Brilliant, in fact. "And Mr. Alexander?" A shy, slight fellow also given to the falling sickness.

"In Leeds, teaching maths at a boys' school run by Quakers."

"Perfect. Miss Helen?" She'd been such a sad, quiet young lady. Even at meals, she'd had an air of alone-ness.

"Married to Alexander. I gave her my violin, and she became very proficient. She teaches music at the same school. They have a pair of boys, both rambunctious, both saddled with the middle name Robert."

Rothhaven was quietly pleased to report that, very quietly, very pleased. As he rattled off the whereabouts and professions of the three remaining residents Constance had known, she realized that Rothhaven had done what few people ever do—made dreams come true for others.

"I want to shake the blossoms from every tree in this orchard and dance for joy," she said. "I want to shout my delight to the heavens. This is better than I could have dreamed of, a triumph for the ages."

"It's a half dozen people finding the lives that should never have been taken from them, Constance, but thank you. Nathaniel was very much the duke when he and I were reunited, and I was very much...not myself. I needed a project, he needed time to accommodate the notion that I was yet alive. When I had everybody settled, I realized I had yet to settle *me*, and thus I began my work in the garden."

This conversation was extraordinary for so many reasons, not the least of which was the sheer gladness Rothhaven's news brought Constance. The lot of Soames's patients were all safe and sound, all reasonably happy. The families who'd tried to wash their hands of inconvenient relatives, the villages relieved to see a difficult person "sent off for a respite" hadn't had the last word.

Not at all.

Rothhaven brushed a few plum blossoms from her shoulders, once again giving her that bemused, contemplative look he'd turned on her previously.

"Do you recall how you felt when you found that cheese wrapped in linen among your weekly allotment of clean bedding?" she asked.

The last few petals clinging to her shoulders, he blew away. "I was intoxicated with hope, with glee, with the certain knowledge that somebody saw my circumstances and was outraged enough on my behalf to take action. The power of that, of being seen and cared for by a person with the courage *to act*, made all the difference in the world."

She took him by the lapels. "That's how I feel when I'm with you, Rothhaven. Seen, cared for, by somebody with great courage and integrity. I am full of good, powerful feelings. May I kiss you?"

"No," he said, his lips quirking. "I have earned the right to kiss you first." He brushed his mouth over hers, and even in his kiss, Constance tasted joy and sweetness and—yes, *that* was the word—*tenderness.*

Chapter Seven

Robert had spent years longing to return home, imagining that beautiful day, and conjuring explanations to excuse his father's betrayal. In his mind's eye, he'd seen the ducal coach-and-four pulling up to the front door of Rothhaven Hall, the servants lined up to welcome him home. His parents would stand at the top of the terrace steps, beaming proudly and a little awkwardly, for they would have much explaining to do.

He'd seen himself as the wronged party, welcomed home with open arms.

He'd eventually replaced that fantasy with a return of the conquering hero, victor over many tribulations and injustices, worthy of the title awaiting him. For in that version of events, the old duke had died, and very likely been sent to perdition for treating his firstborn so disgracefully.

In reality, Robert had little memory of his exodus from captivity. At his own request, he'd been dosed with laudanum, the better to fortify him for the ordeal of leaving the premises. By then, fear of the out-of-doors, of being touched, of varying his routine had all held him in a powerful grip.

He'd insisted on a night journey, lest the sight of the open sky relieve him of his remaining wits. Nathaniel had half carried him into the Hall under cover of darkness, and Robert had hidden in his rooms for months thereafter.

Standing in the orchard with Constance, watching her eyes light with rejoicing over confidences Robert had never shared with even his own brother, all the imaginings and daydreams about returning to the Hall faded away.

Those dreams had served their purpose, and now that Constance had taken Robert by the lapels and asked to kiss him, those dreams would never be needed again.

He touched his lips to hers, his heart full of reverence for the moment, so unlikely and perfect, for this was *home-coming*. This was reunification with a past he was proud of, and a foundation for a future shared with someone he cared for deeply.

Constance Wentworth, of all the women in all the world, had seen him at his worst and taken his part. She'd grasped how to survive against long odds, and better still, how to not simply endure, but to triumph.

He kissed her with all the gratitude in him, all the passion channeled so carefully into learning and self-control, and, may the Deity hold her forever in heaven's most benevo-lent light, she kissed him back with equal fervor.

"Purple and orange," she murmured against his mouth, "with bright greens, like the tropics. Exotic, brilliant, delicious..."

"Silk and flannel," he replied, "softness and warmth, precious spices and mountains of pillows."

She drew away half an inch, smiling like a houri. "*Pillows*, Rothhaven? Shall I paint you as a pasha?"

He rested his forehead against hers. "I'm not describing a painting, Constance."

She drew back farther, her brows knit. "You want me." She stroked a hand over his falls, as bold as polished brass. "You *desire* me."

For the rest of my life. "You don't seem surprised." Or shocked or horrified. That terrible childhood had taught her much of value.

"Intrigued."

She repeated the gesture and Robert had to close his eyes. Watching her explore his responses was too much pleasure.

"Surprised. Pleased. We are behind four sturdy walls, Your Grace."

"If you're that familiar with my person, might I be Robert to you?" And what had walls to do with anything?

Constance wrapped her hand around his nape and partook of his mouth while he fisted his hands at his sides and tried to think of chess puzzles.

"I could be more familiar with your person, right here, right now," she said. "I'm not some sheltered blossom with no experience of the world."

He opened his eyes, which was unwise, because now he was fascinated with the curve of her lips and the curve of her waist.

"*I* am a sheltered blossom," he said. "I have experience of women—some—but I want more from you than a tumble against the orchard wall. Much more."

She stepped back, expression disgruntled. "Right, you want a portrait, some landscapes. I can do that, though posing you—"

"Constance Wentworth." He took both of her hands in his, lest she march off down the hill, leaving him alone and—ye gods, what a day—*aroused*. "I want everything with you. I'm not much of a bargain. I will doubtless be declared incompetent before the year is out, and all manner of scandal will result, but as it is yet within my power to marry, and we are well disposed toward one another... should I go down on one knee?"

Perhaps he was daft after all, because proposing to Constance had previously hovered only at the edges of his mind, another fantasy in a head full of them—though a pleasant fantasy. A lovely dream in fact that had turned into erotic pleasure late at night behind the locked door of Robert's imagination.

"You are proposing to me? Proposing *marriage*?"

"I thought I'd made it plain that I was proposing rather than propositioning."

She raised her hand as if to worry a nail, then brushed her fingers through his hair instead. "You could do both."

"I am proposing to you now. We can discuss the other later. One wants pillows for such a momentous undertaking. Wouldn't do for the Rothhaven heir to be conceived while my duchess's comfort is thwarted by a disobliging tree root."

She glanced at the place below his waist. "If I am conceiving your heir, I suspect I will be oblivious to anything so paltry as a tree root. Are you sure, Rothhaven? I will come to the supper table with smears of paint on my sleeves, smelling of linseed oil and turpentine. I am no sort of hostess and never will be. I don't keep a regular schedule, and my family can be troublesome."

Why was she trying to talk him out of handing her a tiara? Robert was certain that his malady meant nothing to her, on the order of being left-handed or having a poor memory for numbers. The world did not share her opinion. She knew exactly what the world thought of men who became insensate without warning and dramatically lost control of their limbs.

"I know that you love your art," he said, "and I'd be dealing with your family anyway because of Nathaniel's marriage to Althea. Is there another reason why you hesitate, Constance?"

She looked around the orchard, a beautiful place, now that Robert had stopped longing to return to the Hall. The cherry trees were leafing out in a gauzy green canopy to the left, the plums were in full bloom overhead, while the apples waited their turn to the right. Spring in all its glory imbued the hilltop with light and hope, and the promise of succulent fruit in a few months' time.

"I do not hesitate on my own behalf," she said. "I am surprised, is all. We have known each other in some ways for but a very short time."

"And in other ways," he said, holding out his hand to her, "I know no woman better than I know you. I esteem no woman more highly than I esteem you. Be honest with me, please. I have been precipitous, I know, but my regard for you is genuine and time, unfortunately, is of the essence. If you cannot be happy with me, say so, and we will remain friends."

He'd keep that promise, somehow. Constance deserved every happiness and he was asking much.

She took his outstretched hand. "I will be happier with you than I could be with anybody else, but please give me three days to contemplate the question. I expect I will accept, but I have learned caution, and I must be certain my choice is not a triumph of selfish impulse over consideration for a man I esteem greatly."

She didn't want to take advantage of him. *Of all the outlandish*... "You are concerned that *you* are somehow inadequate to marry *me*?"

She gave a terse, self-conscious nod. "I am no bargain, Your Grace. I lack charm, I lack...much."

"And have I any charm to speak of?" Robert paced away and marched back to her. "Do I command any respect in the Lords? Am I a host of any renown? I cannot waltz, I have no small talk, I will not drink a full glass of port to save myself, I have never driven a dog cart, much less a high perch phaeton, nor have I sat a horse since childhood. Some duke I am, but I will make it my life's work to ensure that we suit. I promise you that."

He kissed her then, really, truly kissed her, wrapping her in his arms and silently vowing that he would make her happy, that he would make her dreams come true...once she confided to him what those dreams might be.

* * *

"Are we going shopping?" Althea asked. "Or am I spending most of the morning on my own, then meeting you at the coach and pretending you never left my side?"

A fair question, considering Constance had asked exactly that of her sister any number of times. Beyond the coach window, the outskirts of York went by in the usual procession of drab granite edifices and cramped cobblestone lanes.

"We will shop, but I have an errand to see to first," Constance said. "Whenever I return here, I always fear I will see Jack Wentworth lounging outside one of the disreputable inns, trying to look handsome and rakish, and mostly looking evil."

"I try not to think of Jack Wentworth at all."

Constance considered her sister, who'd returned from yesterday's outing to Crofton Ford quite late and humming Handel. "Have you succeeded in evicting Jack from your mind?"

Althea became fascinated with the dreary shops beyond the coach window. All the bright sunshine in the world could not make York look less medieval.

"I'm doing better lately," Althea said. "Better at putting the past behind me. I've told Nathaniel about a lot of it. About Jack, the begging. The men. I thought telling Nathaniel the particulars would bring it all back, but instead…It's like I handed over a heavy burden to my intended, and he was able to set it aside for me. There are good people in the world, Constance. Lots of them."

Sometimes, goodness was not enough. "But where were those good people when Jack Wentworth broke Stephen's leg? When Jack told us to be nice to his men friends?"

"He hadn't any friends."

"You know what I mean. We were children, Thea. Nobody was outraged enough *to do anything* for us. I can grasp that Jack was broken in his soul, mad somehow, but nobody sent him away where he couldn't hurt us, did they? Whether we lived or died was of no moment when the alternative was to insult a poor man *down on his luck*."

Rothhaven had also been sacrificed to his father's fragile arrogance, oddly enough. This discussion helped Constance understand part of why she'd been such a disobedient maid at Soames's hospital. Why she'd grasped the situation there without anybody having to explain it to her.

"You think Jack was mad?" Althea asked, shifting on the padded bench. "A lunatic?"

"When Stephen was in his worst difficulties, I did some reading regarding the legal aspects of mental competence. One measure of mental fitness is whether a person knows the difference between right and wrong. Jack surely failed that test. Right was whatever benefited him; wrong was whatever annoyed him. No judge would approve of Jack's definitions in a civilized society, but those same judges would never regard Jack as mad. I conclude that society itself is mad in some respects."

The neighborhood had improved as the coach rolled along. The houses were grander, the window boxes full of bobbing tulips.

"By your definition," Althea said, "half the peerage and most of the wealthier cits are legally unfit. Everything under the heavens exists for their pleasure, women especially. I hear you inspired Rothhaven to walk to the orchard yesterday."

"Subtle, Thea." Though Constance gladly abandoned the topic of Jack Wentworth and society's complete indifference to the evil he'd wrought. "The only way you could have heard about our stroll to the orchard is if Nathaniel paid you a visit sometime between moonrise and dawn." Assuming Rothhaven had told his brother about the outing to the orchard, and had not been spied upon by his own servants at that brother's request.

"Perhaps Nathaniel sent me a note to read with my morning tea."

He most assuredly had not. Constance's room was immediately adjacent to Althea's. Shortly before midnight, soft voices had drifted from one balcony to the next, and that was *after* the happy couple had spent the entire day together.

"Aren't you worried about conceiving a child, Thea? Sorting out the title could take some time."

"Sorting out the title will be the work of a moment. Quinn's consequence is a good thing for once. Besides, unless Rothhaven marries, ensuring the succession will fall to Nathaniel and me. Fortunately, all I've ever wanted is a family of my own. Tell me about your trip to the orchard."

Not bloody likely. "Rothhaven would like me to paint his portrait."

The coach slowed to take a sharp corner, the streets in York lacking the open grandeur of their much younger Mayfair counterparts.

"Are you considering accepting the commission? You need not, not on my account. Rothhaven can be difficult company."

How little Althea knew. The idea that the ever-competent, never-hesitant older sister was dealing from a paucity of information pleased Constance more than it ought to.

"Rothhaven never asked to be the duke, Thea. Nathaniel promised Robert he would not have to assume those responsibilities when he brought Robert home. Now the ducal title is thrust upon him, in part so you and Nathaniel can spend all of your waking hours *seeing to the succession*. Criticize Rothhaven to me at your peril."

"Robert," Althea said, making the two syllables distinct. "And you have agreed to paint *Robert's* portrait. What are you truly about, Con? Nathaniel says Robert could be declared mentally unfit at some point, and that will be painful enough without you becoming entangled in the situation."

Why must the coach move at such a sedate crawl? "You are being protective. I am growing impatient with my siblings' protectiveness. I would also appreciate it if you could close your balcony door when you are entertaining callers in the middle of the night."

That had the desired effect of shutting Althea's mouth, at least temporarily. When the coach drew to a halt in the yard of the George and Charlotte, Althea paused before getting out.

"Nathaniel and I mostly talk, you know. He hasn't had anybody to talk to for years."

"He's had his brother."

"And I have had you, but it's not the same, Con. I can tell Nathaniel anything. He tells me anything. We are in some way more friends than lovers, but that's not entirely accurate either. Perhaps we are truly lovers, rather than merely trysting partners. I don't know how to describe what has bloomed between Nathaniel and me, but I hope someday the same wonderful intimacy befalls you. I feel as if I have found a missing part of my heart."

The words were painful, so very painful, to hear. "Then I am happy for you, Thea. I will meet you here at noon."

They parted at the coach, Althea sailing off in the direction of her favorite modiste, two footmen in tow. Constance went the other way, back toward the smaller shops and older houses. When she came to a nearly shabby two-story stone building on a slightly tired side street, she pushed her way inside without knocking.

The sign on the door said simply INQUIRY AGENT, BY APPOINTMENT ONLY, though Constance had long since passed any need to make an appointment here.

"My lady." The trim older woman at the desk rose. "Good day."

"Miss Harper, good day. Is Miss Abbott in?"

Miss Harper was a master at hiding her emotions, but Constance always saw pity in those calm gray eyes.

"I have standing instructions that for you, my lady, Miss Abbott is always in. Please have a seat in the parlor and give me a moment. Shall I have a tray brought up?"

The ladies did a good job of creating a sense of normalcy for clients dealing with desperate situations, as if a tea tray could turn heartbreaking business into a social call upon a trusted old friend.

"No tray, thank you."

Miss Abbott joined Constance in the parlor two minutes later. She was tall and substantial, and she dressed in severe good taste, usually in gray or some other half-mourning color. She often carried a cane, an affectation many women adopted only when substantially older than Miss Abbott. Most would call her handsome rather than pretty, though she was pretty. Constance had seen that within seconds of meeting her. The skill Miss Abbott used to disguise her feminine appeal had weighed in favor of retaining her.

Heaven knew, the men Constance had hired previous to Miss Abbott hadn't had expertise sufficient for the task they'd been paid to do.

"Good day, your ladyship," Miss Abbott said, taking the second wing chair. "I will be direct. I have not found her, but neither have I found her grave."

"No progress, in other words." Exactly what Constance had been expecting and dreading to hear. "Will there ever be?"

Miss Abbott looked at her hands. They were pale, not a ring or a bracelet upon them. The lapse in composure was small and telling.

"After five years, my lady, I would be misleading you if I said I expect to find her. I will not stop looking until you tell me to, but these days... Young women immigrate, they move to the cities in search of positions or husbands, they follow the drum when they find those husbands. She could be anywhere in the world by now."

Constance had embarked on this search nearly ten years ago, the very day after her pin money had become hers and hers alone to spend. When Quinn had acquired a title, the task had become more difficult for requiring utmost discretion. Constance was tempted to give up, to admit defeat, but the object of this search was still young enough that Miss Abbott's conjectures regarding marriage were premature.

"Keep looking. I expect I will soon become engaged to a man of considerable standing, and my efforts must become even more discreet, but do keep looking. She's out there, and we will find her."

Miss Abbott's gaze was kind. "I would not blame you if you made another choice. Nobody would, particularly if you are about to acquire a husband *of considerable standing*."

The scent of considerable scandal hung unacknowledged in the air, but guilt outpaced even that worry. "I would blame myself if she needed me and I failed her. Keep looking."

"Of course, my lady."

Someday, Constance would have to explain this situation to Robert, but when years of searching had produced no result, that day was not soon.

* * *

"You did *what*?" Nathaniel came half out of his chair to roar that question.

Robert hid his smile behind a sip of cider. "I do believe that is the first time you have raised your voice to me—

truly shouted—since we were boys. I am touched, brother. Please pass the salt."

Nathaniel set the salt cellar down so hard the silver spoon bounced. "You *proposed* to a woman you barely know? I grant you Constance Wentworth is a formidable female, but what on earth possessed—"

Nathaniel's gaze became hooded. His word choice had been unfortunate, for demonic possession was the usual explanation for epilepsy among the less enlightened.

"Why propose marriage to a near stranger?" Nathaniel asked. "Lady Constance has no idea how your affliction manifests, and she will not be pleased to learn of it after the wedding."

"That you are concerned for the lady is another compliment to my improving health, is it not? Two months ago, you would have assumed Constance was taking advantage of me."

Two months ago, Constance would not have been permitted to set foot on Rothhaven property, so unrelenting had been Nathaniel's protectiveness toward his older brother.

Nathaniel crossed his arms. He uncrossed them. He picked up his wineglass, then put the drink down untasted. "You are making progress, if you can walk to the orchard in the broad light of day with no ill effects."

"I have traveled off the property by coach, Nathaniel. I have hired new staff. You haven't troubled yourself over the correspondence in weeks, and need I remind you, your figurative boot applied to my arse was what inspired these feats of normalcy on my part. This beef is surprisingly good."

"Althea's cook has been making regular visits belowstairs. How can you sit there, calm as a Quaker at his prayers, and tell me in one breath that the roast agrees with you and in the next that you've proposed marriage to a near stranger?"

Nathaniel was not only puzzled, in his eyes lurked a hint of worry, as if Robert was evidencing a new and troubling symptom not of epilepsy, but of all the quirks and eccentricities that being incarcerated for years had produced in addition to the seizures.

"Calm yourself," Robert said. "I trust you will keep my confidences even from your intended, at least for a time. Constance and I have a prior acquaintance from years past. She has seen the extent of my illness as clearly as you have, though my more recent crotchets had yet to fully develop when last she knew me. Do eat your steak before it gets cold."

"To hell with my steak. Althea suspected the two of you knew each other, but how could Constance have known you? You were gone to that place, thirty miles from civilization."

Thirty-two miles, actually. "Your word, Nathaniel, that you will not whisper this tale to Lady Althea, for it is not entirely my tale to tell."

Nathaniel nodded—grudgingly, in Robert's opinion.

"In her youth," Robert said, "Lady Constance was not a lady. She was the younger sister of a banker intent on making his fortune as quickly and successfully as possible. You know the situation prior to that. I gather that in Constance's adolescence, a falling-out occurred with her older brother, and Constance decamped for independent employment. She took a post as a maid of all work in the facility where I was kept. We struck up an acquaintance."

Nathaniel swirled his wine, peering at Robert over the rim of his glass. "How old was she?"

"A very self-possessed and savvy fifteen, or thereabouts."

"You didn't—?"

"She was *fifteen*, Nathaniel. Clearly from decent family. I was young enough to have untoward thoughts, but what did I have to offer her? Madness and obscurity? That makes a fine dowry. Her brother found her after a few months, but in that time, she and I became friends."

An understatement and the truth.

"And now you want to marry her?"

"I have asked her to marry me, and I await her reply. She knows quite well that at any point, some meddling busybody who comes upon me in a shaking fit will decide I must be returned to the care of other meddling busybodies. Between you and the Wentworth family, I hope a judge can be persuaded to allow me to remain here at the Hall. My estate will nonetheless be managed by guardians, and they will doubtless leave my finances the worse for their efforts. His Grace of Walden will know how to protect the lady's portion from such plundering."

Nathaniel cut into his beef, which had to be cold. "Why do this, though? If you want a woman's company, there are friendly widows who'd put no demands on you. Why complicate your life?"

That a man so clearly besotted would ask that question suggested that Nathaniel still saw his older brother primarily as an invalid.

"Because if I do not marry now, before my competence is brought into question, then I will not ever marry, will I? Lunatics are presumed incapable of knowingly taking nuptial vows."

"You assume you will be found incompetent. You're a duke, for God's sake. Who will think to attack you?"

How quickly Nathaniel had gone from being an over-vigilant protective sibling, anticipating every possible threat, to a man convinced of life's benevolence. The shift in Nathaniel's perspective felt to Robert like a minor abandonment and a major relief.

"Anybody with a grudge against our dear father could attack my legal fitness," Robert said. "Anybody in need of substantial coin. Anybody with a grudge against Althea's family or against you. I am a duke, but I am also afflicted. I was incarcerated for nearly half my life due to that affliction, and I am not entirely well as we speak. Nor will I ever be. One must face facts, Nathaniel."

On this subject, Robert had become the elder, the head of the family. He took an odd satisfaction from that, though not a happy one.

"You have no need to rush into marriage simply to produce an heir. Althea is more than willing to accept that responsibility with me."

"How very generous of you both." Also a trifle arrogant. The Almighty alone decided which couples had male children and which did not. "Does it not occur to you that I might want a wife, somebody who accepts me as I am and will advocate for me as fiercely as you have? Might I not represent companionship that suits Constance better than what a more socially prominent, self-important man could offer her?"

"Crooked pots and crooked lids, Robert? Althea is cross with me when I use that analogy."

"I am not cross with you. I will merely point out that we are all crooked pots, to one degree or another. Assuming Lady Constance accepts my suit, will you stand up with me?"

Nathaniel, to his credit, did not hesitate. "Of course I

will. What do you take me for? I would ask one thing of you, though."

"Name it."

"Find out exactly what sent Lady Constance fleeing her brother's household. She would have known how dangerous a course she set for herself when she left, and to accept employment as a maid of all work...Something went seriously awry, Robert. Something that might yet be amiss. Ask her about it. You don't want Walden or Lord Stephen as an enemy, and some affront to one of them might lie behind her flight."

Sound advice, if a bit cautious.

"I can do that. You should take Lady Althea to the orchard, you know. The plum blossoms have a lovely, delicate scent."

Nathaniel looked like he wanted to say something more, then apparently thought better of it and went back to sawing away at his cold slice of beef.

Chapter Eight

"You are not to shout at me," Constance said. "You are not to pace about like a caged hyena. You are not to clench your jaw as if biting back every foul oath you learned before the age of ten."

She'd chosen the nursery for this confrontation—for this discussion, rather—knowing the sleeping baby would keep Quinn quiet. The infant would also ensure Constance did not lose her resolve.

"A hyena?" Quinn began lining up the books on the shelf in order of height. "A peer of the realm, a duke no less, and you liken me to a hyena."

"You're putting the books out of order, Quinn. Althea arranges them by title alphabetically, so she can find the story she wants without having to hunt through the whole shelf."

He continued putting shorter books to his left, taller to his right. "Now she'll have to actually peruse her collection of tales for a change but without having to endure the sight of disorder. What tale are you about to tell me?"

"Your promise first." Constance could withstand a raised voice from anybody except her brothers.

"I will not shout," Quinn said, jamming *Robinson Crusoe* next to *Pilgrim's Progress*. "I will not pace about as the hyenas in the royal menagerie do when feeding time approaches. I will not clench my jaw like a man striving to spare his dear sister bad language. Satisfied?"

"Thank you." Constance stood behind a stout rocking chair, though putting furniture between her and her brother betrayed how nervous she was. Damn Jack Wentworth for that.

"I have reason to believe Rothhaven will approach you about offering me his addresses."

Quinn left off dis-arranging the storybooks. "I *beg* your pardon." Quinn alone of Jack Wentworth's children had never begged anyone for anything. He wasn't begging now.

Constance met his glower, having endured the same fusillade many times before. "I am well past marriageable age, His Grace is of an appropriate station, and his suit will be agreeable to me."

"Rothhaven is half mad, Constance. Bad enough that our sister is marrying into such a family."

She shoved the chair aside. "You snob. *You perishing hypocrite.* Don't make me ashamed of you."

If she'd slapped him, Quinn could not look more surprised. "I seek to protect you from an unfortunate union, and you insult me for it?"

She wanted to do much more than insult him, but the moment called for reason. "You and Jane are tolerated because of your titles. Doors must open to you, but everywhere you see judgment, veiled censure, and hostility—from people who don't know you at all.

"Those people know the gossip about your upbringing," Constance went on. "*They nearly killed you with their determination to cling to petty prejudices where you're concerned.* They have never exchanged a word with you. They nonetheless think you unfit to break bread with them because once upon a time—*to survive*—you did honest work with your bare hands."

She'd crossed the room to face Quinn directly, lest he evade her by moving away.

"Go on."

"All of society judged you unfairly, Quinn, even as they trusted you with their fortunes and called upon you for loans. No matter how brilliantly you manage their wealth, they will nonetheless judge your children and your grandchildren. For yourself, you don't care, but what about for your daughters? And now you judge Rothhaven, having barely any acquaintance with him. You deem him *half mad*, putting more credence in gossip and ignorance than in the evidence of your own perceptions."

Quinn set aside *Grimm's Fairy Tales*. "Rothhaven has fits, Constance. He's afraid of a sunny sky. His own brother has said as much. Rothhaven won't imbibe but a single glass of spirits at a time. He has no friends, no connections. He's never been to Town and he likely will never go, not even to make the acquaintance of his sovereign. That much coach travel would un-man him. Is this the sort of father you seek for your children?"

She nearly did slap him for that, but Quinn had spoken quietly, pleadingly.

"Rothhaven is honorable and kind. He is intelligent and well read. He cares for his family, his staff, and his tenants.

If he's afraid of a sunny sky, his courage is sufficient to overcome his fears, for he escorted me from the Hall to the orchard and back again without incident." And he'd proposed to her in that lovely, sunny orchard, and kissed her and kissed her and kissed her.

Quinn took a stuffed bear down from the bookshelf and sniffed it. "But could he have escorted you to York yesterday?"

"Stephen dreads that assignment, Quinn, and you never censure him for shirking it."

"Stephen cannot walk from shop to shop all day. Rothhaven could if he pleased to."

"Because an ailment of the mind is less real than a lame leg? When Stephen's problem was melancholia rather than lameness, did you dismiss the malady as of no moment?" Quinn had not, in fact, taken effective measures in Stephen's case until the situation had become dire.

The baby stirred in her bassinette, and Quinn was immediately tucking the blanket up around her.

"We should take this discussion elsewhere," he said, placing the bear at the baby's feet. "We must not wake the princess or her mother will somehow know of it and cut short her own nap."

We will finish this discussion here and now. "If you fell prey to shaking fits tomorrow, Quinn, would you love your daughters any less? Would you be less of a father to them, or would your disability make you even more devoted to their welfare?"

He gave the blanket one last twitch. "You should have been a barrister, and that is not a compliment. When I am a feeble old relic, half blind, deaf, and toothless, I will love my family with the last of my breath and the ferocity of a dragon, but Constance, you deserve peace, a man who can give you contentment, not a fellow who has demons of his own to battle."

What worthy man or woman didn't have the occasional demon to battle?

"I met Rothhaven when I ran away. He is more formidable than you give him credit for, Quinn. Most people consigned to a madhouse for ten years wouldn't live to tell the tale, much less recount it coherently."

Quinn gestured to the rocking chairs before the hearth. "One suspected you and His Grace were not strangers. As asylums go, that place was commodious."

Constance took a seat with a sense of relief. Quinn was no longer trying to evade the topic, meaning he'd found a means of reconciling himself to the situation.

"That hospital was only commodious on the outside, Quinn, and that was by design. Soames fancied himself a physician of the mind, and used his patients to experiment on, but the worst torment those people suffered was shame and rage that their own families had put them there."

Quinn leaned his head back and closed his eyes. In his profile, Constance saw both the handsome, determined youth he'd been, and the fierce old fellow he'd become, but she also saw her brother. A good man, not perfect, but well worth loving.

He set the chair to rocking slowly. "One of the worst torments I ever faced was coming home to find that my baby sister had left my house. Rothhaven's father discarded him, you discarded us. You discarded safety itself, and while I can guess at some of your reasons, I've never asked you why."

"I was upset." The grandest of understatements. "I was afraid."

Quinn turned his head to gaze at her. "Of me?"

Oh, Quinn. "Not of you, Quinn. Never of you. Of what would follow. I was not thinking clearly. You might say I was addled."

The silence that bloomed was a little sad, but mostly peaceful. Constance could have this conversation with her brother now because Quinn was a father and a husband, no longer a young man ruthlessly determined to build his fortune and damn anything and anyone who stood in his way.

"If you are thinking clearly now," he said, "you will agree to two conditions. I know you can marry Rothhaven without my blessing, but that would disappoint Jane. Let's avoid that if we can, shall we?"

"I'd rather not disappoint anybody." *Ever again.*

"First, with respect to the settlements, I will ensure your money remains in trust outside the ducal estate. Rothhaven will understand why."

"Because you think he's half mad."

"Because I don't know him, but at any point, somebody could decide an inquiry must be made on behalf of the Crown regarding his fitness. If a guardian of Rothhaven's property is required, I will of course offer my services in that capacity, but generally, the more disinterested a prospective guardian is, the more likely he is to be appointed. I could conceivably inherit some unentailed property from Rothhaven through a deceased sister, for example."

Men and their machinations. "Not if his will says otherwise."

"Valid point. Nonetheless, Lynley Vale marches with Rothhaven Hall, and thus I am not disinterested in Rothhaven's estate. I could divert his water for my benefit, allow my flocks onto his fields, and so forth. I want your money protected, in part because it might be the only money you and His Grace can claim."

"I see your point." Quinn had a gift for strategy, and he was right: Rothhaven would understand this measure and agree to it. "What else?"

Quinn rose. "You must tell him about the situation that sent you fleeing to the moors, Constance. He deserves to know the whole tale, and before he takes the public step of courting you."

Constance remained in her seat because she did not trust her legs to hold her up. "Of all people, I thought you would understand why discretion is in order. It was nearly half my life ago, Quinn. In all the years since, we've heard nothing. No breath of scandal, no hint of repercussions."

Quinn prowled over to the bassinette again and peered down at his youngest daughter, his expression unreadable.

"Jane and I did not have an auspicious beginning as husband and wife. I was condemned to die, she hadn't a groat to her name, and her father was more of a worry than a comfort. We were not at our best, but we agreed to be honest with each other. We agreed to show each other that much trust and respect. I did not keep my side of the bargain very well at first. My motives were above reproach, but I disappointed the woman who'd trusted me with the rest of her life."

He left the infant dreaming her baby-dreams and headed for the door. "If you value Rothhaven's esteem, if you truly mean to have a marriage with him and not simply a union of convenience and appearances, then you must put your situation before him in all its details. Whatever else is true about Rothhaven, he's honest. You say he's no coward, and I believe you, but neither are you a coward, Constance. Far from it."

He waited, hand on the door latch, as if Constance was supposed to say something to such an odd, touching, back-handed compliment.

"It's old news, Quinn. Years old."

"If it's of so little import, then telling your prospective husband should make no difference. The hardest lesson I had to learn when I married Jane was to match her for honesty and courage. My duchess is awake, and I must convey this development to her, if that's allowed?"

"Yes, you may tell Jane, but please don't mention this to Stephen yet. I'll tell Althea, though I suspect Nathaniel is already aware of the situation."

Quinn aimed a look at Constance, half over his shoulder. "Do you *like* him, Con?"

"Very much. We argue, we discuss, we plan....I like him very much, Quinn."

That seemed to satisfy Quinn for the moment. He slipped through the door, closing it quietly, leaving Constance to the company of the sleeping baby. She was tempted to pick up the child and steal a snuggle, but waking a sleeping baby was never well advised.

Instead Constance put a question to her small, dreaming niece. "How did Quinn know that Jane was awake?" Because he had known. Somehow, he'd known.

* * *

The cat, a long-haired black monstrosity named Monteverdi for his operatic tendencies, was acting oddly. This did not bode well for Robert's plans, but Monteverdi often acted odd when the lady cats in the stable were feeling amorous.

"I am feeling amorous," Robert muttered, scratching the cat's furry shoulders.

Monty yawned and padded across the library desk to lick Robert's chin.

"My, what foul breath you have."

Another lick. Then a chin-butt. Robert gently pushed the cat to the side of the desk and, for the fortieth time in twenty minutes, consulted his pocket watch.

"She's late." Though only by five minutes, which was nothing, but was Constance more likely to be late when she was accepting a proposal or when she was rejecting that proposal? Robert rose to admire the view of the garden—not to pace—and Monty leapt from the desk to nearly trip him.

"Go to the stables, you wretch."

The cat batted gently at Robert's boot and let out a yowl.

"None of that." He'd picked up the beast, intent on turning it loose in the garden, when Thatcher tapped on the open door.

"Company, Your Grace. Lady Constance Wentworth to see you."

Robert held the cat away from his body in the vain hope that no black cat hair would find its way to his attire. Lady Constance appeared at Thatcher's elbow before this awkward posture could be remedied.

"I told Thatcher he needn't announce me. What a splendid kitty." She sidled past Thatcher, whose stoic expression hid the pain of a man too long denied the office of announcing callers. Lady Constance wore her old straw hat again today—Robert was becoming fond of that hat—and dropped her gloves on the sideboard.

"The splendid kitty is demanding attention," Robert said, opening the terrace door and nudging Monty out of doors with his boot. "He'll enjoy a call on the stable. Thatcher, that will be all."

"No tray, Your Grace?"

Constance put a sizable reticule down on the blotter. "No tray, and His Grace and I do not wish to be disturbed."

Was that good news or bad news?

Thatcher bowed and drew the door closed behind him as he left.

The past three days had revealed that Robert's patience, a skill he'd honed with bitter intensity over years of confinement, was out of practice. He'd told himself to set aside the issue of his marital prospects. He'd made his offer, and the lady would agree or not. He'd tried to focus on plans for repairing the drive.

On his mother's plans for refurbishing the dower house, though those plans would doubtless change when Her Grace returned from Paris.

On reviewing the settlements negotiated for Nathaniel and Althea.

On the growing stream of correspondence offering him awkward congratulations for not being dead—without putting it quite like *that*.

He might as well have been in a protracted staring spell for all he'd accomplished since bidding Constance farewell.

She brushed a glance over him, a fulminating look that presaged loaded verbal cannon and fixed bayonets. The cat *mrrrralphed* outside the door, batting a paw at the glass.

"I have considered your offer," Constance said. "I am inclined to give you leave to pay me your addresses."

"I am pleased." Also relieved as hell, though Robert also knew a conditional acceptance when he heard one. "Do go on."

Yooooowl. Bat...bat...bat.

"Perhaps we should join him in the garden." Her ladyship picked up her reticule and made for the door. "The light is better out there anyway."

Robert retrieved her gloves from the sideboard and met her at the door. "Whatever else you have to say, Constance, just tell me. A long engagement, a special license, that year in Paris…Tell me, and if it's within my power to accommodate you, I will."

"You'd come to Paris with me? Travel by coach and ship and so forth?"

"Yes." Robert had given this some thought, when he was supposed to have been laying out annual beds for the drive. He and his duchess could sail from Hull to Le Havre and cut out some of the overland travel.

"You will be my wife, the woman who has forsaken all others to stand by my side. I traveled thirty-two miles by coach with Nathaniel when I was in worse health than I am now, albeit I was drugged at the time. I would need to keep the shades pulled in the carriage, and I'd rather travel at night under a waning quarter moon, but yes. I would come to Paris with you."

"London?"

Robert considered the question as the cat batted away at the glass. They could sail almost all of that distance, and for some reason, the prospect of a coastal seascape was less intimidating than the prospect of parallel ruts undulating endlessly over the English countryside. Perhaps the sound of coach wheels was to blame.

"I will journey with you to London, if I must. As my wife, you could well risk your life in childbed. I can face the horrors of the capital to show my face at court." That was hope speaking, uncharacteristic optimism.

"I detest London. I like you."

I more than like you. "The sentiment is assuredly mutual in both regards, and yet, you hesitate to give me your answer."

"I want to sketch you." She swished through the door, across the terrace, and down the steps.

Robert followed, bemused. Constance hadn't said no to his proposal, but she certainly hadn't said yes. Perhaps this was a taste of married life, learning to read a sort of uxorial code.

"Will the bench do, my lady?"

"The bench will do nicely." Constance fished a sketch pad from her reticule, stuck one pencil behind her ear, brandished another—brandished, that was the word for it—then took the far end of the bench. "Have a seat and think ducal thoughts."

Robert had no sooner done as she'd bid him—thinking of his prospective duchess was very ducal—when Monty popped up onto the bench.

"Shameless beggar."

Constance fell silent as Monty circled on Robert's lap, purred, demanded to be scratched, and otherwise spoiled the moment.

She took up her pencil and made a few passes at the page. "I told Quinn that you would ask him about paying me your addresses. He was reasonable, considering he was surprised. Cat, settle or I will sketch you with horns."

The cat walked across Robert's lap and dug its claws into his thigh.

"Shall you have a long courtship with all the trimmings, Constance? I'm already steeling myself for the ordeal of divine services. I could flirt with you in the churchyard, share a hymnal, the usual silliness." Though how much better if he could waltz with her at an engagement ball or even at a local assembly? How much more impressive if he could take her out driving in a fancy gig?

Maybe someday.

"I understand why a shorter engagement makes sense," she said, "and I don't need any silliness. What ails that cat?"

"He's lonely, I suppose." Or he sensed a seizure in the offing. Nothing to be done about it if that was the case. Robert picked up the cat and cradled him against his shoulder, which seemed to be what the dratted pest wanted.

"Quinn will arrange the settlements so that my portion is safe from any meddling." Constance wrinkled her nose and squinted at her sketch.

"Prudent on your brother's part. He should do likewise regarding Lady Althea's funds as well. If Nathaniel should pre-decease me, God forbid, her finances and the ducal estate should be as separate as possible." The bench was hard, the cat was hairy, and this was not how Robert had envisioned this discussion going.

"Quinn said you'd understand about that part."

"Is there another part?"

"Yes."

She went digging into her reticule again and came up with an eraser. "I am to tell you how I came to be a maid of all work."

"You had a falling-out with your family." She'd told him that years ago. Everybody condemned to Soames's establishment had also had a falling-out of some sort with family.

"Not exactly. Keep looking at whatever you're looking at. I was unhappy." She glanced up as if to make sure Robert hadn't moved. "I was wretched, in fact. I'd been raised until a certain age as Jack Wentworth's get, good for nothing but the gutter, headed for a brothel or worse. Then Jack died, Quinn's prospects improved, and without warning or explanation, our situation changed."

"But did your situation *improve*?"

"Not to my way of thinking. Instead of freedom to roam where I pleased, I was confined the livelong day. My feet were stuffed into pinch-y little slippers that I was forever losing. My hair was trussed up in braids and ribbons and infernally uncomfortable pins. My time was spent incarcerated in a schoolroom, where I was supposed to cram ten years of learning into two. Quinn was never home."

And of all the tribulations she listed, that last was probably the most bewildering.

"He was off pursuing his dreams," Robert said, "while you were imprisoned with governesses and elocution teachers."

"Quinn was worried about Stephen, and with good reason. Then we started spending much of the year in London—the financial capital of the world, to hear Quinn tell it. The more Quinn's purse thrived, the more miserable I became."

She bent to her sketching, and Robert let his imagination roam over the plight of a street urchin being made over into a young lady. All of her freedoms taken away, her friendships ripped asunder, and should she have the temerity to question her good fortune, she'd be told, as Robert had been so often told, "It's for your own good."

Were there five more presumptuous, pontifical, preposterous words in the language?

"You had no friends," he said. "Your servants kept you at arm's length, and your brother lost sight of you when he was home." Robert knew what was coming, in the same way that an odd, detached sort of anxiety or peculiarity of vision sometimes told him a seizure was on the way.

"I had no friends, but as we bided in York the summer I was fifteen, I engaged the affections of a handsome fellow whose parents owned the house across the alley from ours. The parents were traveling in the Low Countries, and Quinn was away for weeks at a time. The young man and I would meet in the mews. We talked about everything, and we traded notes that became increasingly ridiculous. He left me flowers, I gave him an embroidered handkerchief, and the inevitable soon occurred."

Robert's heart broke for that quiet, serious, lonely girl. "Your brother found out?"

"Nobody found out. I was careful, and people see what they want to see. I never had tantrums as Stephen did, never suffered the temper that plagued Althea. My governess told Quinn I was finally settling down and making peace with my lot." Constance used the side of her pencil, scraping it against the page in a rapid back-and-forth motion. "I was planning to elope."

Scotland was much closer to York than it was to London. "But you were fifteen. The age of consent even in Scotland is sixteen." The young people of England, by contrast, were not of age to marry until they turned one-and-twenty.

"I know *now* that eloping to Scotland would have been pointless. Matters never reached that stage. Before I could run off with my handsome cavalier…"

The pencil ceased moving. The cat leapt to the grass, and Robert risked a glance at Constance. "Before you could elope…?"

She looked down at her sketch. "I didn't think reciting ancient history would be difficult. It's very difficult. This is not a story I've told to many."

"You need not tell it to me now." Though he hoped she would.

"I promised Quinn, the blighter." She clutched her

sketch pad against her chest and bowed her head. The moment became painful, even before she spoke. Robert slid closer to her, wanting to stop whatever unhappy words troubled her, knowing he must not.

"Whatever you have to say, Constance, I want only for you to be happy." What an enormous relief, to mean that, to be utterly committed to somebody else's well-being and safety. A healthy man had those aspirations, a man competent in his mind and whole in his heart, if not his body.

Constance looked out over the garden, eyes bright with unshed tears. "There was a child, Rothhaven. Somewhere, I know not where, I have a daughter, and I cannot find her. I have searched and searched, for years I have looked for my darling girl, and I cannot f-find my daughter."

Chapter Nine

Maybe a seizure was a little like what Constance endured on that hard, sunny bench. Rothhaven took her in his arms, and try as she might, she could not maintain her composure. The tears had come, silent and messy, then loud and messy, and then in quiet shudders.

Before Constance was through, her face ached, her nose stung, her eyes burned, and Rothhaven's handkerchief was a damp ball of hopelessly wrinkled linen in her fist. Her dignity was a cause so lost she doubted she'd ever recover it.

"I never cry," she said, voice raspy. "I abhor tears." A legacy from a father who'd delighted in tormenting any daughter stupid enough to let him see her cry.

Constance sat beside Rothhaven on the bench, his arm around her shoulders, the solid, warm bulk of him against her side. Her straw hat had ended up on the grass along with her sketch pad, reticule, and pencil, and the cat was crouched beside her effects, chewing on her eraser.

"I hate that you have suffered," Rothhaven replied. "I gather the bounder never meant to marry you." His hand stroking Constance's hair was beyond gentle, while his tone presaged protracted torture for *the bounder*.

"I told him everything, about Jack Wentworth, growing up without shoes, Quinn digging graves....He listened so sweetly, called me his wild rose. When I told him I had conceived, I thought he would share my joy and we would tell our families of our impending nuptials."

Rothhaven remained silent, silence being one of his gifts. He was a quiet, patient, kind man, and Constance vowed to make him the best duchess she could possibly be.

"He laughed." For the first time, Constance recalled that memory with rage rather than sadness. "He laughed and asked me why I'd spread my legs if I hadn't expected to conceive a bastard. Girls *like me* were supposed have ways of preventing *that sort of thing*, and he wasn't about to be trapped by a streetwalker in muslin and velvet. In his version of events, I'd thrown myself at him, and he'd never breathed a word of marriage much less made me any promises. I'd also picked his pocket while plying my trade, stolen his dear grandpapa's gold watch."

Her lover had threatened her with hanging, something Constance would likely never tell Quinn.

Robert's hand on her hair paused, then resumed its slow caresses. "I'm a fairly good shot. I practice in the gallery when the winter megrims threaten. Something about the loud noise revives my spirits. Even wounding this fellow would put me in a positively jolly humor."

"You are so dear." Constance snuggled closer, while the cat curled up on her reticule and closed its eyes. "He died at university before the baby was born. I suspect somebody's irate husband or brother called him out. The family put it about that he'd fallen prey to a sudden illness."

Robert kissed Constance's temple, as if they'd been married for years. "Were you cured of your infatuation by then?"

"By then, I had spent two months in a private madhouse on the moors, working as a maid for people who had lost much, but who yet retained their dignity. By the time Quinn found me, I had been cured of my infatuation and even of some of my self-pity. I explained to Quinn what was afoot, and he arranged for me to bide with a widow in the Nottingham countryside until my confinement had passed. I was at finishing school, as far as the world knew, and the experience did nearly finish me."

"A difficult lying-in?"

"No, as those things go. I was young, strong, in good health, and had good care. I had a month with my baby. Only a month, and then, the day after she was christened, the couple who'd agreed to raise her came to take her from me. I kept her baptismal lines, and they are my most prized possession. Nothing, nothing you can conceive of on this earth, will ever be as hard for me as that day."

Though telling the tale from start to finish, no delicate evasions, no glossing over the details, came close.

"I wanted to do what was best for my baby and for my family. I had no idea how hard that would be or how quickly I'd come to doubt my decision."

Rothhaven drew in a breath, and Constance realized she was breathing with him. The same slow, calm, in-and-out rhythm.

"Walden insisted you share this truth with me. I'm not sure how I feel about that, for even the memories hurt you.

I honor you for your honesty, though, and for the trust you place in me."

An enormous weight of self-doubt lifted from Constance's heart. Quinn had been right to insist on this confession, not that Constance would tell him so.

"I respect you, Rothhaven. I care for you. I want a real marriage with you rather than a superficial arrangement. I am no paragon, and you should know that in time to withdraw your proposal."

"Withdraw my proposal?"

"I am not chaste, far from it. I have engaged in scandalous behavior. I have a bastard child, and I want very much to know where she is and that she's well and happy. I am willful and hardheaded, stubborn and—"

Rothhaven kissed her. "You are ridiculous. Will you marry me, Constance?" He hugged her one-armed against his side, the gesture both gently chiding and endlessly affectionate.

Rothhaven had no reason to dissemble. He likely had no *ability* to dissemble, and thus his scold-cum-proposal did what reason, debate, and hope could not accomplish.

He gained Constance's trust.

"Yes, Robert, Duke of Rothhaven, I will marry you."

"Good. We'll get that part dealt with, see Althea and Nathaniel marched up the church aisle, wave your meddling brothers on their way, and then we will find your daughter. Tell me her name."

If Constance hadn't fallen in love with Rothhaven before—and she had—she fell in love with him then. Such happiness coursed through her, a deluge of warmth and joy as torrential as the sorrow and anger that had come before.

She recounted for him every detail she recalled about

her daughter—perfect fingers and toes, a mop of bright red hair, and prodigious health, God be thanked—and every emotion and dream she'd carried for that small person, wherever she might be.

The sun dropped behind the garden wall, the cat scrambled up over the gate, and still, Constance stayed in the arms of her beloved, sharing her dreams.

* * *

"Explain to me the nature of your illness," Quinn said, closing the door to the Lynley Vale estate office. Because Althea ran the property, the office was not as imposing as Quinn preferred a business venue to be. A bouquet of fading tulips sat on the sideboard, the curtains were lace rather than somber, heavy velvet. Worse yet, the color scheme was a cheery pink, green, and cream rather than a more imposing burgundy and blue.

Quinn would have preferred to conduct this interview from behind an enormous mahogany desk of venerable pedigree. Instead he and Rothhaven shared a damned tufted pink sofa awash in green tasseled pillows, a delicate Sèvres tea service on the tray before them.

Rothhaven took a leisurely sip of plain gunpowder. "I am epileptic. I have shaking fits and staring spells. The first of those occurred when I was ten, some days after I fell off a horse and took a severe blow to the head, the second such injury in the space of a week. In the nigh twenty years since, the seizures have never abated for more than a few months."

"And the most recent seizure?"

"The most recent shaking fit was over a fortnight ago. The staring spells are harder to judge. I sometimes don't know one has occurred."

A fat black cat emerged from beneath the sofa and sniffed at Rothhaven's boots. His Grace had arrived at Lynley Vale in a carriage, all the shades drawn, though the distance between manor houses was only about a mile across the fields and the afternoon weather was gorgeous.

"How can you not know that you've been staring off into space? Schoolboys are caught daydreaming, and Headmaster ensures they have occasion to avoid a repetition of that behavior."

Rothhaven set his tea aside and extended a hand to the cat. "Trust me, Walden, if corporal punishment could extinguish my staring spells, they would no longer afflict me. As it happens, a passing inability to attend a conversation bothers those around me more than it inconveniences me. I can often hear, see, smell, and otherwise perceive everything happening at the time. I'm simply incapable of reacting to it for a bit. What is his name?"

At first Quinn thought Rothhaven's mind had stuttered. *Whose perishing name?* Then he realized his guest referred to the presuming cat.

"I have no idea. The beast does not belong to me."

"He belongs to your sister and to this house. He has privileges abovestairs, and he's certainly friendly."

Though Rothhaven spoke mildly, Quinn sensed a reproach in the words, or perhaps teasing?

"One doesn't want to be indelicate, Rothhaven, but can you *function*?"

Quinn did not trust cats, though his sisters favored them. He preferred dogs, and his duchess's canine—a great black beast with lots of teeth and a properly intimidating growl—made a nice addition to an outing in the park.

Cats, though...They slunk about, silent and hungry,

pouncing from dark corners when they weren't leaving hair—or worse—on every upholstered surface.

Althea's cat licked Rothhaven's hand and then leapt into his lap.

"Get down," Quinn said, using the voice that made bank clerks wish they'd joined the overseas diplomatic corps.

The cat squinted at Quinn and put two paws on Rothhaven's chest, touching its nose to the duke's.

"Cats and siblings," Rothhaven said. "Both intractably independent. To answer your question, I am capable of those acts which generally result in procreation. That said, if Constance marries me, I will doubtless embarrass her in public from time to time. In the churchyard, in the middle of the high street, or over dinner with guests, I will produce a spectacular fit with little or no warning. Then I will be dull-witted for a time, even sleepy. Nothing prevents the seizures, but intemperance, exhaustion, tobacco, and strong drink seem to aggravate them."

Quinn was torn between sympathy for the person bearing the affliction and frustration that his sister would marry herself to such a one. Rothhaven was deserving of every happiness, but both he and his wife would be the butt of whispers and curious glances.

"So you avoid the churchyard," Quinn said, "the high street, and dinner guests. Do you expect Constance to join you in this self-imposed exile?"

The cat batted at Rothhaven's chin. That rudeness was rewarded with a gentle scratching behind the beast's ears.

"Walden, if you think avoiding church, the village green, and rural dinner parties is exile, your imagination is wanting. Exile is not seeing your only brother for more than ten years, never receiving a letter from family in all that time. Exile is being told at the age of eighteen that you will never again see your sibling or the only home you've known, and that this deprivation is *for your own good*.

"Exile is being denied access to the out-of-doors, never feeling the fresh Yorkshire wind on your face, never hearing a human voice raised in song lest it over-excite your *delicate nerves*. Try a few years of that, no privacy, no freedom, no manly exertions to work off your temper or your dismals, and then we will discuss what constitutes exile."

That recitation was made all the more alarming for the half-amused tone in which it was delivered.

"Constance does not have epilepsy," Quinn said, resisting the compulsion to toss the damned cat out the door. "She deserves to entertain callers, attend services with her neighbors, and frequent the busiest streets in Mayfair if she pleases to."

"Marriage to me precludes none of that." Said patiently, as if the veriest dolt should understand the liberties a married woman enjoyed. "As your sister, however, the lady was made to endure each of those penances, will she, nill she. Her ladyship has told me about the child. What have you done to aid her to find her daughter?"

Quinn was so absorbed watching the cat lick its paw, all the while perched on Rothhaven's shoulder, that the question nearly eluded his notice.

"Find her daughter? The point of the exercise, Rothhaven, was to ensure that the child never became a source of worry or embarrassment. Matters were dealt with appropriately, and Constance resumed the normal life of a young woman anticipating a bright future." That much, at least, Quinn had been able to do for his sister.

Rothhaven took up his teacup, sipped placidly, put the cup down, as if every proper duke took tea with a cat sitting on his shoulder.

"Constance has been using her pin money for years to hire investigators. Because *you* insisted she dredge up her past for my benefit, I assumed you knew this. Am I mistaken?"

When had Quinn lost control of this conversation?

"You are mistaken." While Quinn was reeling. This Duke of Fits and Faints, this interloper who claimed to have met Constance years ago, was privy to a secret Constance had kept to herself for *years*?

"She's hired investigators? Without telling me? Why wouldn't she tell me? Why not seek my aid? I'm a bloody duke, for God's sake."

"A bloody duke—now—and a bloody banker then. Would the idle and titled of the realm have entrusted their fortunes to you if it became known you couldn't even keep your sister safe? The blighter dallied with her for weeks while you were away in service to mammon. Then too, what if you'd said no? You refuse to lend coin to some of the most powerful families in the land when they are facing utter ruin, and your reputation for dealing exclusively in logic rather than sentiment precedes you. Had you known of Constance's search and disagreed with its objectives, you could have thwarted her easily. Your forbidding nature aside, I suspect the whole business came down to Constance not wanting her past to reflect poorly on you or her other siblings."

Quinn didn't bother taking offense at Rothhaven's observation, for Quinn *had* failed to keep Constance safe.

"You are saying that Constance has been trying to protect me with her discretion? Trying to spare me from gossip?"

"From gossip, and—siblings are ever so well intended at the worst times—guilt, would be my guess."

Rothhaven sat there swilling his tea, as placid as a dowager at her tatting, while Quinn wanted to…What he wanted was to turn the clock back fifteen years and be a better brother to his siblings.

"What Your Grace seems to be experiencing now," Rothhaven said, "is very likely how a staring spell feels to me. The words make sense, the sentences all have meaning, but the internal fulcrum that meshes the gears of thought and action refuses to turn. One sits, mind agape, as it were, and gropes about for even a thought. Drink your tea. It's a lovely blend."

Quinn needed to kick something—perhaps his own backside—and bellow profanities until he was calm enough to put this situation before his duchess.

He picked up his teacup instead. "Constance has been trying to find the child?"

"Searching for your niece, Artemis Ivy Wentworth."

The teacup shook slightly in Quinn's hand, why he could not say. "She named her daughter Artemis?"

"For the goddess who protects young girls. Ivy, as in 'I will cling to her as ivy clings to the oak.' If you are awash in self-recrimination, Walden, I will leave you to your guilt, but I will also tell you that the reason I alerted you to Constance's whereabouts all those years ago is because I was falling in love with her. She was too young for me then, of course, but more significantly, *I* was also too young and had nothing to offer her. I was a prisoner of my father's arrogance and my own self-pity. Do close your mouth."

Quinn's teacup went clattering to its saucer. "*You* notified me that she was at that dreadful place? *You* sent that note?"

"By that point, I was permitted to read a redacted version

of the York newspaper. Dr. Soames carefully excised most social news, but he forgot how absorbing the personal advertisements could be. I saw your advertisement. I connected your description to the young woman responsible for preventing my starvation. I had no idea if she was your sister, but she fit the description and was clearly more educated than any chambermaid ought to be."

The cat climbed down from Rothhaven's shoulders, stretched luxuriously, and crossed the sofa to sniff at Quinn's knee.

"You found her for me," Quinn said. "You could have kept her there, but you sent her home. Does she know about this?"

"Not yet. The revelations regarding Artemis were of greater moment. I will of course let Constance know the truth in due course. I recall his name now."

Whose bloody bedamned—? "The cat?"

Rothhaven rose and swatted at his breeches. "Septimus, because he came from a large litter, according to Constance. I've prepared a draft of my proposal regarding her settlements. The arrangement takes particular care to leave all of Constance's funds under your jurisdiction or Lord Stephen's should anything untoward happen to you."

"Because you are a person who suffers from epilepsy?"

"Because I am a reasonable man, and the less enlightened among us still regard my condition as evidence of demonic possession. I am in a mental fog after a bad seizure, and if my own father had me put away at the onset of my illness, somebody else might try to have me committed again, for my own good, of course."

Rothhaven stroked the cat's head, which occasioned purring.

"Not committed," Quinn said. "I won't allow that. You

and Constance can live out your days in relative obscurity at Rothhaven Hall, and I will manage your property if necessary to keep the courts happy, but you won't be exiled again."

Rothhaven withdrew a packet of papers from his coat pocket and set them on Althea's escritoire.

"Very kind of you, Walden, but if the courts become involved, the judge will appoint the guardian of his choice. With not one but two sisters married into the Rothmere family, your objectivity regarding my circumstances is questionable. The courts like to appear above petty influences like ducal consequence. Your attempts to meddle might actually make my situation worse."

Quinn rose before the cat could appropriate his lap. "It won't come to that."

"It came to exactly *that* for nearly half my life. I'll bid you good day." Rothhaven bowed very correctly. "You need not see me out, and no, I didn't omit a material term from the settlement agreement in some inane cat-and-mouse game between prospective family members."

That rebuke—for it was a rebuke—merited a riposte, but Quinn was still coping with the interview's other revelations.

"One question before you climb into your hearse and return to your mausoleum: Why tell me how to find my sister? You were confined under miserable conditions, she befriended you, and yet you sent her home. Why?"

Rothhaven's lips quirked. "I had nothing to offer her at the time, so let's call it a fit of conscience, shall we?" He withdrew, leaving Quinn to the dubious company of the cat.

* * *

"Am I allowed to be pleased that you attended services on Sunday?" Constance asked, twining her arm through Rothhaven's outside the solicitors' office.

She had waited to raise the topic of Sunday services until after some legal papers had been signed for a youngish Mr. Cranmouth, nephew to the present senior partner in the firm of Cranmouth and Cranmouth. The documents had something to do with selling a patch of ground, and Rothhaven had been determined to see them signed.

Althea and Nathaniel had strolled off, intent on sharing an ice at a shop around the corner. From thence, the plan was to meet at the livery in two hours, giving Constance time to introduce Rothhaven to Miss Abbott.

"You are too easily pleased," he replied, scowling at Lord Nathaniel's retreating form. "The Almighty saw fit to leave the church roof in place, so we must conclude my presence in the family pew was a matter of indifference to Him as well."

What little conversation Rothhaven had offered today had been irritable, understandably so. The journey into York on a sunny morning had to have tried his nerves. He'd said little for the entire distance other than "Curtains down, please," and "How much farther?"

Now he stood on the walkway before the offices of Cranmouth and Cranmouth, looking ready to hurl thunderbolts.

"Your neighbors bowed and curtsied out of respect, Rothhaven."

The duke had waited until the moment before the first hymn had begun to have his coach deposit him at the foot of the church steps. He'd stalked up the church aisle and taken his place beside his brother, but not before every person in the church had risen. For the yeomanry and laborers, no pews were provided, but for the gentry and the merchants, Rothhaven's arrival had created a stir.

Every soul present had acknowledged his arrival, and the singing had been glorious. A duke returned from the dead was cause for rejoicing, apparently. Vicar Sorenson's sermon had been on the prodigal son, and some of the older ladies had sniffed into their handkerchiefs for most of the service.

Rothhaven had darted right back into his waiting coach before the final notes of the recessional hymn had ended.

No matter that he hadn't stood about making small talk in the churchyard. Attending services at all was a start, a leap rather than a step in the right direction. Constance's joy had been profound. Two days later he'd sent a note asking her about a trip into York to meet with Miss Abbott.

What difference did churchyard pleasantries make, when a man so clearly understood what mattered most to his intended?

"How far is Miss Abbott's office?" he asked, scowling at a perfectly beautiful blue sky after he'd completed his business with the lawyer.

"Several streets that direction," Constance said, tipping her chin. "It's a pretty day for a stroll, and she is expecting us."

Rothhaven pulled on his gloves—one did not wear gloves when signing documents—and tapped his hat onto his head.

"Let's be..." He shook free of Constance's grip. "I need the coach. *Now.*"

His tone was so abrupt, Constance mentally recoiled. "But we can walk, Rothhaven. I would like to stretch my legs, in fact, and I daresay—"

"Get me the damned—" One moment, Rothhaven had

been standing before her, muttering foul language, the next, he slipped downward, his hat tumbling into the street.

"Rothhaven?"

He curled onto his side, his limbs twitching spasmodically as passersby either stopped to gawk or hurried past as if appalled. His boots scrabbled against the cobblestones, his watch fell from its pocket, and his walking stick was trapped at an angle beneath his body.

Constance knelt beside him, feeling helpless, angry, worried, and stupid. "Rothhaven?"

The seizure took an eternity that in all likelihood consumed less than a minute. When he lay still, eyes closed as if he'd died, Constance looked up to find a circle of strangers staring down at her.

"Lord Nathaniel Rothmere should be at the ice shop around the corner," Constance said. "Somebody please fetch him."

Nobody moved.

"*Fetch Lord Nathaniel now*," she snapped, rising. "And please have the livery at the corner send the Rothhaven coach on the instant."

Mention of the family title sent a young man scurrying around the corner, while a small boy kicked at the sole of Rothhaven's boot.

"Be he dead?"

Constance nearly swung her reticule at the lad, whose mother had yanked him up by the arm.

"His Grace has the falling sickness. He will be better in a moment or two. Please stand back."

Rothhaven would never be better. He had tried to convey that to her, but the magnitude of the burden he carried was only now becoming real to her. To be unable even to walk down the street…

"Your Grace," Constance said, kneeling beside Rothhaven. "Can you sit up?"

An older fellow in knee breeches and a worn brown jacket came down beside her. "He'll come right soon enough. M'wife had the falling sickness, God rest her. We bled her and bled her, and nothing helped. There now, he's waking up."

Rothhaven tried to push to a sitting position, his movements as clumsy as a drunk's.

"Easy there, Your Grace," the older man said, helping Rothhaven to brace his back against a lamppost. "Don't want a bump on the noggin in addition to your other woes. No need to hurry."

The crowd began to drift away as a nattily dressed fellow bustled out of the solicitors' offices. "What's this? Has His Grace been set upon by ruffians? What is the world coming to? Daylight robbery, of all the insults. You lot, move along. Miss, give the man some air, please. I am His Grace's solicitor. I cannot believe—"

Constance glowered up at him, and something about her expression must have penetrated the lawyer's well-developed self-esteem, for he fell silent.

"His Grace has had a seizure," she said, standing between Rothhaven and his lawyer. "He will be well in a moment. You may return to your office."

The solicitor, who resembled the young Mr. Cranmouth, craned his neck to peer around her. "But if His Grace is in need of aid, then I must send for a doctor. Ebenezer Cranmouth, at your service, miss."

Another man came up on Cranmouth's right. "Somebody get into a brawl right outside your office, Cranmouth? What sort of clients are you represent— I beg your pardon, Lady Constance."

Neville Philpot doffed his hat and bowed. Constance knew him only in passing from local assemblies. His wife, Lady Phoebe, was a notorious gossip and had been a thorn in Althea's side.

"If you'll excuse me," Constance said, turning to help Rothhaven get to his feet.

Philpot tried to intercede, but Rothhaven shied from him so violently as to nearly lose his balance again.

Constance inserted herself between Philpot and the duke. "I have him, Mr. Philpot. It's quite all right."

The man in the brown jacket was actually doing much to support Rothhaven's weight, and just when Constance was about to tell Philpot to bugger the hell off, Nathaniel and Althea trotted around the corner.

"Seizure?" Nathaniel asked, relieving the older gent.

Constance nodded. "Of no great moment, but more than a little inconvenience. Mr. Philpot, if you would *please* excuse us."

"Yes, do," Althea added, picking up Rothhaven's walking stick and crumpled hat. "The situation is in hand. Thank you for your concern." She swept a glance at Philpot and Cranmouth, who remained by his office door, looking ghoulishly curious.

The coach pulled up before Constance could launch into a lecture about gawping imbeciles impersonating lawyers, and Nathaniel helped Rothhaven inside. Then they were pulling away, the last of the onlookers finally leaving the scene.

As the coach rounded the corner, Constance caught a glimpse of Cranmouth and Philpot, heads bent in conversation as they disappeared into Cranmouth's offices.

"Sorry," Rothhaven muttered. "Not very dignified."

Nathaniel looked like he'd speak, but Constance silenced

him by taking Rothhaven's hand. "It doesn't matter, as long as you are unhurt. Perhaps you'd like to nap now?"

For most of the distance home, Rothhaven slouched against Constance's side, dozing quietly. She tried to sort out her feelings as the miles rolled by, but she got no further than admitting that the suddenness of the seizure had disconcerted her and the reaction of the crowd had angered her.

Althea sat on the opposite bench, fingering the crumpled crown of Rothhaven's beaver hat, and that added another emotion to Constance's pile of feelings.

Rothhaven had fallen on the walkway. Had he gone two more steps in the direction of the street, his head rather than his hat might have been crushed beneath the coach wheels. That realization was frightening, and explained, if only a little, why the old duke might have sent his son to an asylum on the moors, rather than watch day by day as one danger after another befell an innocent young man.

Chapter Ten

Neville Philpot waited until after supper to discuss the day's events with his wife. Lady Phoebe's sensibilities were refined, and the scene outside Cranmouth's office had honestly been upsetting even to Neville, whose profession had inured him to human foibles.

"I have never seen anything more pathetic," he said, passing Phoebe a portion of elderberry cordial for her digestion. "A peer of the realm, a duke, a man who should be in his prime, twitching like an inebriate in the last throes on the walkway. Cranmouth was quite overset. Rothhaven is his client, and that unfortunate drama took place right outside the poor fellow's office."

"I'm sorry you happened upon such a situation," Phoebe said, settling into the wing chair by the fire. "You say the Wentworth sisters were on hand?"

Neville poured himself a brandy—the subject called for it—and took the second wing chair. "Lord Nathaniel was present as well as Lady Althea and Lady Constance. Lady Constance was trying to manage the situation, but how could she? She's merely a neighbor to His Grace, and a woman."

The brandy was good—illegally good, as it happened, as all the best brandy tended to be. Still, Neville would be an old man before he forgot the sight of Rothhaven, helpless and addled on the ground.

"Lady Constance is a Wentworth," Phoebe said, touching her glass to her lips. "They think only about money, and if Lady Althea has her hooks into Lord Nathaniel, then you can bet Lady Constance has set her sights on Rothhaven."

"God pity the woman if that's the case."

"Pity her? Husband, your charitable sentiments do you credit, but Lady Constance was raised in the vilest of circumstances. Her concern for Rothhaven is doubtless motivated entirely by self-interest."

In Neville's experience, self-interest was not limited to the lower orders, at least not among his clients.

"Her ladyship was ready to gut anybody who interfered with Rothhaven," he said. "Wouldn't let Cranmouth near him." Smart of her. Cranmouth was a notorious gossip, which in a solicitor was a fatal failing. Old Man Cranmouth had been the genuine article, to be trusted in all matters, a lawyer of discretion and tact. The nephew wasn't a bad sort either.

"Cranmouth says His Grace is selling off some property in the West Riding." Hardly a sensitive matter, but still, Cranmouth ought to have kept his mouth shut.

"If I owned property in the West Riding," Phoebe said, "I'd sell it as well. God has created no drearier corner of the realm, particularly in winter."

Neville thought the Dales rather beautiful, but he was loath to contradict Phoebe. "Rothhaven cannot be long for this earth, my dear. He was in a terrible state when I saw him. Could not speak, could not stand unassisted."

Phoebe frowned at the crystal glass in her hand. "You weren't attempting to pass the time of day with him, I trust?"

"Of course not. I tried to assist him to stay on his feet, and he cowered away from me so violently he nearly overset himself again."

"You are a good man, Neville. If His Grace has taken leave of his senses, that is not your fault. I heard he tried to attend services and made a complete hash of it."

The brandy was working its magic, as was Phoebe's sense of calm and good sense. "How can one make a complete hash of attending services, short of a loud case of the wind during the sermon?"

"Neville, I despair of your humor. Rothhaven arrived at the last minute, said not a word to anybody, and left before the organist had concluded the final hymn. He looked neither left nor right, greeted nobody, and kept his coach waiting right at the foot of the steps. Very odd, if you ask me."

Very pragmatic. The biddies in the churchyard would gabble until sunset with a new duke to torment.

"He was pale," Neville said, thinking back over a situation that would not leave his mind. "Rothhaven, when he tried to get up. Looked like a shade."

"Clearly, attending services was the limit of his ability, and then those women had to drag him all the way into York, parading him about as if he's some sort of oddity. What can you expect from a family of *bankers*?"

As bankers went, His Grace of Walden had a spotless

reputation. Quinn Wentworth hadn't been among the cabal that had financed Napoleon's Hundred Days, for example. Another set of London bankers had helped the fledgling United States buy the Louisiana Territory from Napoleon, providing an enormous infusion of cash into the emperor's coffers.

In Neville's opinion, most bankers were economic parasites. They made money off of other people's hard work or misfortune. Solicitors might not be gentlemen in the strictest sense of the word, but at least they earned their coin fairly and in exchange for honest services rendered—in theory.

"Lord Nathaniel arrived as His Grace's fit was passing," Neville said, taking a fortifying sip of his brandy. "He seemed to know what to do."

Phoebe set aside her cordial. "And that makes it better, that the same brother who all but imprisoned Rothhaven was abetting His Grace's public torment today? First, poor Rothhaven is kept hidden away like some disgusting secret. Then they drag him around to the Wentworth entertainments. Now they force him to attend services and haul him clear to York. Of course Rothhaven's wits went begging. It's a wonder he didn't strike you with his walking stick or flail at you with his fists."

Phoebe fell silent, hands folded in her lap. She didn't often lose her temper, but in this case, she had a point.

"Rothhaven wanted to be away as quickly as possible," Neville said slowly. "That much was obvious." Though the man had been in possession of a stout walking stick, stout enough to do damage if wielded like a weapon.

Phoebe spread her fingers, the firelight catching the gemstones and gold of her rings. Another woman would have tossed out a few recriminations or a succinct *I told you so.* She merely sat, ladylike and composed, while Neville's conscience and his legal instincts wrestled with a puzzle.

"We don't know Rothhaven is being run ragged by his brother. We don't know whose idea it was for him to attend services. We don't know that a trip into York wasn't at His Grace's bidding. He called on Cranmouth. The old duke retained Cranmouth's father, and I'm fairly certain Lord Nathaniel did as well."

Though come to think of it, Cranmouth never mentioned meeting with Lord Nathaniel in the years when the true duke—Robert—had been away from the Hall. All very curious, that. The timing of Robert's re-emergence at Rothhaven Hall was never discussed in any detail, not in the circles Neville frequented.

"Do we know when Rothhaven re-joined the household at the Hall?" he asked.

"We do not," Phoebe replied. "I've probed gently, strictly out of concern for the duke. As best I can tell, Robert simply did not interest himself in affairs at the family seat. He wasn't aware his father had died, which again suggests a man of unusually eccentric sensibilities. How can a parent's death be a matter of indifference to a son in line for a great title?"

Neville was about to say *They aren't like us, my dear*, but Phoebe was an earl's daughter. She placed herself firmly on the *them* side of the us-and-them divide, and Neville forgot that distinction at his peril.

"The old duke had Robert declared dead," Neville said, "suggesting the family crotchets aren't limited to the present generation. More cordial, my dear?"

"Thank you." She passed over her glass. "One doesn't want to borrow trouble, but I do fear Rothhaven's situation will require legal intervention, Mr. Philpot. Between Lord Nathaniel and those Wentworth women, His Grace is without allies, and too much is being asked of him. The falling sickness can be fatal, you know, and I would not want it on my conscience that Rothhaven was being hounded literally to death by selfish meddlers while I stood by and said nothing."

Neville replenished her drink and topped up his own. "No man is above the law, or so we're told, but Rothhaven is a duke. Walden's sisters command ducal standing. Lord Nathaniel is a duke's son, and there's tremendous wealth in play. A mere lowly solicitor charges at that windmill only after very careful consideration. Have we heard anything from young Sybil's swain?"

Phoebe's smile was an echo of her youthful beauty. "Lord Ellenbrook sent a lovely note to me yesterday, including his good wishes for our Sybil. He expects to be passing back this way early next week. I am encouraged, Mr. Philpot. I am very encouraged."

The change of subject had served its purpose, restoring Phoebe's good humor, and allowing Neville to finish his second and third brandy in a better frame of mind. Rothhaven's situation was troubling, to be sure, but without proof that the duke was being ill treated by his family and neighbors, the matter was not any of Neville's affair.

Not, at least, until Sybil and her young lord became engaged.

* * *

The inevitable had occurred sooner than Robert would have liked. Constance had seen him in the middle of a great fit, convulsing on the ground like a bovine in its final throes at some knacker's yard. And then what had he done? Had he offered her conversation, reassurances, any semblance of normal interaction?

"I slept most of the way home. Slept in a moving coach, and I detest coach travel."

Nathaniel regarded him with a slight, maddening smile. "Isn't that progress of a sort, that you *could* sleep in a moving coach at midday?"

"No, it is not progress." Robert sat back on his heels, the walled garden for once providing no solace. "I could not have stayed awake in the coach had I wanted to. I could not prevent myself from having that seizure. I sensed trouble approaching, but I hadn't enough notice to turn the coach around."

Nathaniel twirled one of the last of the red tulips by its stem. "How do you sense trouble approaching? Can you anticipate a seizure?"

"Not reliably, and not for want of trying." The flower bed had bloomed and faded, but Robert believed in allowing the foliage to die back naturally, at least for a few weeks. The appearance of the declining bed was too wretched to be borne, so he folded the leaves to the stalks and tied the lot into tidy bundles. "After yesterday, I must offer Lady Constance the opportunity to cry off."

"Are you formally engaged already? Fast work, Your Grace."

Nathaniel sounded a bit envious, which brightened Robert's outlook marginally.

"Constance is the sister of a duke, the proprieties will be observed. We have an understanding, or we did." He tied off the last forlorn, pale plant. "Constance needs a man who can support her in all endeavors, not some graceless invalid who embarrasses her in public."

"Bit late for that, isn't it? You knew you had epilepsy when you courted her favor." Nathaniel sat on the gardener's rug beside Robert, knees bent, feet spread, *twirling his tulip* and gazing across the garden like some damned philosopher.

Robert had seen the looks on the faces of the crowd around him in York. He'd felt the swift blow to the sole of his boot delivered by a lad more curious than appalled. *Be he dead?* Those words had lodged in his memory, along with the recollection of being unable to roar back: *No, I am not dead.*

"People are still unenlightened when it comes to epilepsy, Nathaniel. For myself, I will cope with the hand I've been dealt. Having seen one of my seizures firsthand, Constance should be given an opportunity to decline having to share my lot."

"If you send Constance packing," Nathaniel said, rising and stretching, "I will be disappointed. She cares for you, and you care for her. The rest can sort itself out if that foundation is in place. Shall I have a look at the correspondence?"

How casually he made that offer, how kindly. "I've already gone through the day's mail, and I'm caught up, thank you. Take some catmint to go with your bouquet. Damned stuff comes back twice as thick for being pruned."

"You have as well," Nathaniel said, scooping up the jar. "Thus far, every time life has tried to prune you, you've found a way to thrive despite all. I admire that. Looks like we have company." He sauntered off toward the garden door to greet Lady Constance, who'd apparently tossed propriety to the wind and parted from her sister on the drive.

Brave woman. Dear woman. But was she brave enough?

Why should she have to *be* brave, given what life had already put on her plate? Robert pulled off his gloves, ran a hand through his hair, and prepared to have a difficult, necessary conversation with his intended.

Nathaniel went whistling on his way, bouquet at the ready, leaving Robert alone with the woman he might soon part from.

Again. "Good day, my lady." He bowed.

She gave him the sort of look she probably reserved for difficult portraiture subjects. "It won't wash, Rothhaven. The formality, the courtesy. I understand that you need your dignity—heaven knows I have need of mine—but that won't serve for what I have to say."

Oh, dear. Oh, damn. "What will serve?"

She stepped closer. "I wanted to kill them all, every one of them, all but that old man who was so calm and helpful. I wanted to brandish a sword at them and breathe fire upon them. They dared look at you with less than respect, and I wished them all to perdition."

How easy she was to love. "Did you, now?"

"I wished them to perdition in my thoughts." She stalked away, pivoting at the Cupid birdbaths. "We are born flawed. Why does that surprise people? Stephen has an injury. I fell in love with a bounder. Quinn can be rigid, and Jane can't sing to save herself. Why is anything less than perfection cause for judgment and curiosity? I am overset. I didn't mean to explode like this. I had planned to be articulate and self-possessed, as your future duchess should be."

"Should she?"

Constance's path brought her back to him. "Of course. *You* are dignified and self-possessed, when not in the midst of your affliction."

She patted his cravat, which he'd tied in a quick, simple mathematical because he'd craved the comfort of his garden.

"Do you recall our little hike to the orchard, my lady?"

Another pat, or more of a caress. "I relive that encounter in my dreams."

As did Robert. In his fondest, wildest dreams. He slipped his arms around Constance's waist. "Do you recall kissing me?"

She linked her fingers at his nape. "Yes, and I recall you kissing me too."

"Was I dignified and self-possessed?"

The question occasioned a frown. "At first. You have self-restraint, Rothhaven. Buckets and bales of it. I do not."

Robert drew her close, slowly, gently. "All those years in the schoolroom learning proper deportment when you wanted to go barefoot and paint nature. All the hours spent repeating French phrases you had no use for. All the years of hiding your sorrow as a mother from even your family." He kissed her temple. "You have self-restraint, Constance. Buckets and bales of it, but I hope you have little need of it with me."

She let him have her weight on a soft exhalation. "Althea said you might set me aside. She said you are accustomed to being alone and that your attraction to me was too precipitous to endure. I'm a novelty."

"My attraction to you began years ago. There's nothing precipitous about it. I set you aside once before, and now that the moment is upon me..."

She peered up at him. "Explain yourself." Then she bundled closer, as if settling in for a long, comfy snuggle.

And that—the trust, the affection, the desire—decided

that last of Robert's uncertainty. "Now I know I can never let you go." Then he kissed her, with no self-restraint *whatsoever*.

* * *

"How are you not angry all the time?" Constance asked Rothhaven when she'd recovered from his kisses. "How are you not mad?"

"Oh, but I am." He kept his arm around her shoulders and walked her toward the garden door. "You've seen it for yourself. I am uneasy under an open blue sky, I dread the company of strangers, and I can barely abide to ride in a coach, though I've done some thinking about that."

The man beside her now was a relaxed, even chatty fellow compared to the man who'd managed that coach ride into York.

"But you did travel into York. You will again."

He paused before the garden door, arms linked around her shoulders. "When my father put me into the traveling coach all those years ago, it was a sunny, lovely day. I thought I was going off to school, as the ducal heirs had gone off to school for generations. Mama was crying, poor thing, and Nathaniel was trying to be brave, but I was confident that my life as a young man of the world was about to begin.

"I would have adventures," he went on, "I would make friends, I would excel in my studies. I would finally make Papa proud of me, and the disapproval I'd felt from him since birth would evaporate into paternal rejoicing at how wonderful I was."

Oh, God. That poor boy. That poor innocent boy. "You were betrayed. When your father put you into that coach and sent you on your way, knowing full well what your destination would be, you were betrayed."

Rothhaven held the door for her. "There's more. I finally figured this out as I so rudely dozed on your shoulder yesterday. Soames at one point in my early years would run me into the village by coach to study Greek with the local parson. We'd leave early in the morning, when the sun was low. The light flickering through the trees could start me shaking. Soames was delighted to observe this, though it took me eons to connect a cause and an effect."

"Light through the trees caused a seizure?" What manner of brain ailment reacted to light?

"When a coach moves down a wooded road and the sun is at a low angle, the intermittent obstruction of the tree trunks causes the light to flicker. I realized that I never had a seizure on the journey home. If he switched my appointments to the afternoon, I had no seizures either going or coming. If he drew the shades, no trouble befell me.

"Time after time, if I was made to sit gazing out at the trees for one of those early morning journeys, I would succumb to my malady. Soames never made the connections, but I soon did, and I refused early morning or late afternoon outings if I could."

Constance hurried through the door, wanting to be away from the garden walls and from the eyes of anybody observing from the house.

"I hate Soames. Hate him with an unrelenting fury. He had better be dead, or I will be tempted to make him dead. To torture a boy like that and call it science...No wonder you dread travel, no wonder you abhor coaches and sunshine. Why are we out here?"

She would return to the house with him, she would shut

herself up in that house with him, if that was what his condition required.

"I wanted to enjoy the plum blossoms with you before they fade."

Oh, this man. This dear, wonderful, man. "Will you kiss me again? I've a notion to more than kiss you. I came over here to tell you that Quinn has heard from the College of Arms. King George has kindly signed some letter or modification or parliamentary whatever and the honors of your station have been restored to you. George is quite the Tory these days, and he expressed sympathy for the offspring of so *difficult and devious* a man as your papa."

She had taken Rothhaven's hand in the midst of that babbling. His calm was contagious, a balm to a troubled soul.

"Do I owe Walden more than my thanks for this bit of political sorcery?"

What did he—? Oh. "Quinn did not raise the topic of money. You fellows can sort that out if necessary. I suspect money did not change hands, it being only just that you assume the title that never should have been denied you. Quinn has no patience for bribes."

They reached the orchard, though rather than pass through the gate, Rothhaven stood at the top of the hill, gazing upon his family seat.

Constance slipped an arm around his waist. "You are considering how to explain what you said earlier, about having set me aside once before. That was at the hospital, wasn't it?"

"Yes. You were too young; I was too ill for more than friendship."

She rested her head against his shoulder. "You were my friend, though. You sought nothing from me, and after what I'd been through with that bounder...I did not believe a male to whom I was attracted could be a friend."

He continued to gaze at the house nestled on the undulating green fields below, and the silence took on a peculiar vacant quality. Rothhaven's gaze was vacant as well, as if his focus had gone not merely inward, but elsewhere entirely.

"Rothhaven?"

He appeared not to have heard her. Before alarm could take root, Constance realized this was a staring spell. He'd had them when she'd known him before, and they always passed. A subtle shift in his posture a few moments later suggested the interlude was over.

"As I was saying," she began, "I did not believe a male to whom I was attracted could be a friend."

"Your trust had been violated too." He kissed her brow. "I just went away, didn't I?"

"You fell silent. The lapse was momentary, not half a minute. We were discussing our earlier association, at the asylum."

He enfolded her in an embrace that invited her to hide her face in the crook of his neck.

"You will be angry with me," he said. "All those years ago, I notified your brother of your whereabouts. I saw his advertisement asking for information regarding a dear relation gone missing from York. You fit the description. I sent word to him anonymously—Alexander risked much to abet that effort—that a young lady matching the particulars had taken up employment at a facility familiar to me. Your brother replied within a week."

Constance took in his words, knowing that in all material regards, Rothhaven was honest to his bones.

"*You* alerted Quinn to my whereabouts?"

"I did. While I was prohibited from sending mail, Alexander had limited correspondence privileges. He was happy to do me that favor. I did not feel I had the right to impose on him again when it came to answering your note to me some weeks later. Nothing could have come from a correspondence between us in any case. You may explode now if you like. I won't blame you."

Constance did not want to explode, exactly. She wanted to *understand*. "When you contacted Quinn, you took a risk with my welfare. You assumed my family would be kind to me, that they were not the reason I was on my own."

Rothhaven stepped back and took her by the wrist, leading her into the orchard, then closing the gate behind them.

"I assumed your family was part of the reason you sought a position in service in a corner of the world the Almighty Himself preferred to forget. But we are not at our most rational when aggrieved at the age of fifteen, and the ad had been appearing in every paper I read for weeks. I demanded assurances from your brother that you would be well received, without recrimination or punishment. He provided those assurances by return post. You admitted to missing your family, to regretting that you'd caused them worry."

Rothhaven walked off a little way and slanted a look at her over his shoulder. "How I envied you a family who worried about you. I concluded that if I raised the topic of your brother's search with you, you might well disappear again, perhaps even take ship. Surely the care of a concerned family was preferable to that outcome? As I said, I can understand if you are in a temper with me over this revelation, but I did not want a lie by omission between us."

"We are in accord in that regard. Is there anything else I need to know?" How different this discussion was from the passionate kisses they'd shared in the garden, and yet, both were intimate. Both required trust and courage.

"Yes, in fact." Rothhaven brought a branch heavy with pink blossoms to his nose, sniffed, then let it go. "I sent Miss Abbott a letter this morning apologizing for missing yesterday's appointment and explaining that I became abruptly unwell. I informed her that regardless of any further developments in my situation with you, I was prepared to stand any expense involved in locating your daughter. *Any expense, any effort*. The search is to proceed with all due haste to a happy conclusion, whether you and I wed or not. I have meddled in your personal affairs. I believe that brings to three the total justifications you have at present for exploding."

Any expense, any effort. Constance heard those words, heard the absolute determination in them, and had to focus on the fading blooms overhead lest she turn into a watering pot.

"You sent that letter?"

"By express courier. I am determined on two objectives, Constance Wentworth. The first is becoming the best husband I can be to you. The sooner we speak our vows, the better, if you'll have me. My second objective is to find your daughter so that you may be assured of her well-being, and decide on the best course going forward."

"Artemis is a by-blow. I don't expect to be able to acknowledge her openly."

Rothhaven approached, his green eyes lit with some emotion Constance could not fathom. "Peers have by-blows as regularly as King George has fevers. If the child is happily situated, and you are content to dote on her from afar, so be it. If her circumstances lend themselves to her joining our household, then she will join our household. If you aren't comfortable claiming her as a by-blow, I happily will. I prefer that option, actually, as it will lend the girl more consequence, but you are her mother, and your wishes must be controlling."

You are her mother. *You are her mother.* Said with such conviction, such certainty. "I am her mother." Constance threw herself against Rothhaven, her *heart* exploding. "I am her mother, and I will be your duchess, and the very best wife I can be to you. This, I vow."

Chapter Eleven

A man in love was willing to endure many hardships for the sake of his beloved. Witness, Nathaniel was enduring this chess match with Althea.

"I love flowers," she said, gaze on the bouquet Nathaniel had arranged on the windowsill of his sitting room. A lone tulip nestled among the last of the irises, the best he could do on short notice. "They make me sad too, though. Their beauty fades so quickly. A whole year goes by before they bloom again, assuming they can withstand our winters."

Nathaniel moved his rook. "Would we appreciate them as much if they were ever-blooming? I think half of what gets Robert through the winter is planning his flower beds, inspecting the ground to see if the bulbs are coming up, and fretting that they'll come up too soon. Our siblings have left the garden."

The last time Nathaniel had looked out the window, Robert and Constance had been in a shocking embrace at

Saint Valentine's feet, which left a younger brother torn between relief—Robert was long overdue for some shocking embraces—and concern.

"You aren't attending the game," Althea said, shifting a bishop halfway across the board. "Check."

Nathaniel had no interest in chess whatsoever. Althea was suffering the female indisposition. She'd announced this before he had bowed over her hand. That she'd share that information so baldly, and with such a disgruntled air, presaged an intimate and interesting marriage.

Though how was a doting fiancé to receive such news? "You have me," he said, knocking over his king with one finger. "Where do you suppose Robert and Constance got off to?"

Althea caught him by that finger. "They are of age, courting, and sensible. I hope they are admiring the wonders of the potting shed."

"As do I, but it's an adjustment, to go from worrying every waking minute about my brother, and knowing he's somewhere within a very narrow range of possibilities, to being dismissed by him as if I'm a nosy footman."

Althea came around the card table to perch on Nathaniel's knees. "I worry about my siblings. They aren't eccentric to the same degree Robert is, but they have vulnerabilities. He's making great strides, though, and Constance will be a ferocious ally."

The feel of Althea in Nathaniel's lap was already familiar and comfortable. She curled up like a large, contented cat, and some of Nathaniel's anxiety ebbed.

"Constance was ready to plant Neville Philpot a facer," he said. "Cranmouth was lucky she didn't draw his cork." The sight of somebody else ready to do battle on behalf of Nathaniel's afflicted brother had been heartening and disconcerting. Even Althea's participation in that drama had been an adjustment.

"And yet," she said, "neither solicitor truly yielded Constance any authority over the situation, did they? When you showed up, matters began to sort themselves out." Althea traced Nathaniel's features with her index finger, her touch as soothing as birdsong on a summer morning.

"You are worried about Philpot?" Nathaniel asked. Lady Phoebe Philpot had taken Althea into extreme dislike, mostly because Lady Phoebe was perpetually bitter, and the daughter of an earl had to yield socially to the sister of a duke. Such a pity, that.

"I am worried because you are worried," Althea said, "and because Philpot and Cranmouth looked thick as thieves as the coach horses trotted 'round the corner. Constance and I—our whole family—will do what we can for His Grace, but Rothhaven will always need you too."

"And I will always worry that I'm inadequate to defend my brother's interests." Which could not be helped. Nathaniel kissed his intended, for courage, for luck, for the sheer pleasure of kissing her, and because speculating about what mischief Philpot might get up to was depressing in the extreme. "When can we be married?"

Althea had brought the wonderful news that the king was being reasonable regarding the confusion over the title.

"Constance says that I am the older sister and thus I must speak my vows first. I think she likes the idea of being courted by a duke."

Althea gently bit Nathaniel's ear, and he resigned himself to temporary, unrequited arousal, a lovely problem to have.

"I didn't think Constance set much store by titles."

"She doesn't, but she very much enjoys watching Quinn

and Stephen at a loss. You and Rothhaven are their equals, socially, intellectually, and otherwise. Consternation on the part of the Wentworth menfolk is too delicious not to be savored. My lord, I do believe you will soon be in a state."

"I will be perpetually in a state married to you. I'm looking forward to it." Nathaniel was not looking forward to another blasted game of chess.

Althea began setting up the pieces in their starting positions. "I love chess, but you really must try harder, Nathaniel. No gentlemanly scruples about seizing my queen, if you please."

He set his king back in position. "If you say so, my lady. Perhaps you'd like to be white this time?"

"That would be splendid."

She turned the board around, her hand brushing his, and Nathaniel resisted—barely—the urge to throw the board against the wall and howl.

* * *

Robert held his intended, loving the sturdy feminine curves of her body, the robust energy of her mind, and the ferocious passion of her heart. How on earth, how on God's beautiful, green, lovely earth, had no other man caught Constance Wentworth's fancy in all the time she'd been apart from him?

But then, he knew how. Artemis Ivy Wentworth accompanied her mother everywhere, waking and sleeping, a living presence carried in the heart by love, worry, and determination.

"Shall we return to the house?" Constance asked. "I don't want to overtax you."

Robert rested his chin against her crown—her hat had gone tumbling to the grass. "It's not like that. I had a seizure yesterday, then I napped thoroughly. By the time I handed you down from the coach, I was myself again. That seizure could have been a week ago for all it affects me today, and I might not have another incident for a month."

She stepped back. "Or you might have one twenty minutes from now. This affliction is diabolical. What is that?" She kept hold of his hand and led him around a row of plum trees. "You arranged a picnic? *For me?*"

"I hoped to share a meal with you, even if in parting. One wants pleasant memories." *One* wanted so much more than that, with a hunger that made Robert's heart ache. The pain was sharp and sweet, like a soldier's longing for home. To hurt like this was to be fully human, inviting life to roll forward in all its messy glory.

Truly, spring had arrived to Yorkshire and to Rothhaven Hall in the person of Lady Constance Wentworth.

"One wants a midday meal too." She dropped to her knees on the blankets. "Althea put me off my breakfast. I suggested she speak her vows before I do, mostly so she won't big-sister me all the way to the altar. I hope that plan is acceptable to you. What a lovely effort you went to."

"The kitchen went to. I took the liberty of consulting Monsieur Henri."

"Althea's cook is a marvel."

Rothhaven knelt on the blankets with her, a large wicker hamper between them. "Do you ever draw self-portraits?"

Constance paused, a corked flask of lemonade in her hand. "I do, not often lately because I have other, more interesting subjects to work on. Why?"

"If I were a better artist, I'd sketch you as you are

now, midday sun bringing out the red highlights in your hair, your curiosity and vitality in equal evidence." *I love you.* He tried those words out mentally, knowing them to be true.

She set aside the lemonade and went diving for treasure again. "I wonder if Artemis kept her red hair. She got that from her father, but a baby's hair can change. Her eyes were blue. I'm told with babies, eye color can change too. Within a year, green or brown hues can emerge. Oh, this is Monsieur's luncheon bread."

Robert said a silent prayer that Constance would always discuss her daughter with him so casually, so trustingly. That she would discuss everything with him so easily. Nathaniel all too often tiptoed through a conversation for fear of upsetting the invalid.

A younger brother could have worse failings. Far worse.

"I guessed at your appetites," Robert said, "and having sampled Monsieur's efforts, I thought you might enjoy them al fresco."

The luncheon bread was made from dough pressed flat and covered with chopped ham, cheese, and spices, then rolled up, baked, and sliced. Monsieur had been apprenticed to a cook in the army and had concocted that bread as a meal for men on the march.

Constance set aside the bread and crawled around the basket. "There's something else I'd enjoy al fresco." She kissed Robert's cheek and remained near enough that he caught the scent of her soap—orange blossoms with notes of clove and cinnamon. Warm, sweet fragrances apparent only in intimate proximity.

"You are feeling frisky today, my lady." And God help him, so was he. Robert was always aware of Constance as a woman, aware of her in ways he didn't permit himself with any other female. He'd greeted her today prepared to be set aside as a bridegroom, and all that he'd lose if she cried off had been painfully clear.

Mostly, he would have lost her—lost her companionship, her lively mind, her humor, her energy. But he would have lost as well the hope of a degree of intimacy that went beyond bodily urges. He'd never experienced that blessing and longed desperately to share it with her.

Only with her, always with her.

"I am feeling more than frisky, Rothhaven," she said, starting on the knot of his cravat. "If there's something I need to know about an epileptic man's intimate needs or limitations, tell me now before I become too…"

"Aroused?"

"Eager. Is a mathematical all your valet can manage?" She drew off his cravat and began on the buttons of his shirt.

"I don't use a valet. The first footman tends to my clothing. I tend to me. To answer your question, I am unaware of any limitations on my ability to please a lover, at least as a function of my illness."

"You aren't just saying that?" She ran her fingers inside the collar of his open shirt. "I can handle disappointment, you know."

"You are also adept at handling *me*." By virtue of a loose hug, he started undoing the hooks at the back of her dress. "Some believe that sexual congress or onanism invites seizures. My experience of the former is limited, but based on my exhaustive familiarity with the latter, I can confidently refute that theory."

She rested her forehead on his shoulder. "Even your naughty talk is ducal. We will be so happy."

Because she believed that, he could believe it too. He could hope for happiness, not mere contentment, and even hope for joy. The magnitude of that gift, a future unlimited by infirmity or secrets, made his kisses luxurious, his hands cherishing.

"I seem to have misplaced my clothing," Constance said, some minutes later. Her smile assured Robert the errant articles were not much missed.

"Shall you remove your shift?" Robert was down to his breeches and hoped to part with them momentarily.

"I leave that up to you," she said, lying back on the blankets. "I have always loved the scent of plum blossoms, and now I will have precious memories to go with their fragrance. Thank you for that. I knew I could find a man willing to overlook my origins—I am the sister of a duke and my settlements are generous—but I never thought I could find a man who could accept…" Her smile faded as she reached for him.

"Not merely accept," Robert said, coming down over her. "God spare us from the paltry consolation of mere acceptance. I love you, Constance Wentworth, *madly*, forever. Love you especially for who you were, and love you with equal devotion for who you always will be. You love with your whole heart, and with you I am helpless to do anything save follow your example."

Constance loved Robert with her whole body too, wrapped her arms and legs around him, explored his every muscle and sinew. Her touch awakened him from a long, lonely sleep into a blazing rapture, and when he joined his body to hers, the pleasure nearly overcame him.

But not quite. He clung to the last shred of his self-restraint long enough to bring her with him into that place of transcendent joy. She matched him passion for passion, then demanded more, until he was wrung out, a man done in by glorious satisfaction.

"You are a wonderment." He whispered that, probably incoherently, as he slipped from her body.

Some bright soul who was not the Duke of Rothhaven had thought to put her handkerchief on top of the wicker basket. Passing that handkerchief to Constance taxed the limit of Robert's strength. He rolled to his back and Constance snuggled against his side, her contented sigh breezing across his shoulder.

She kissed his biceps. "We might have a large family."

"Yes, love." The notion of having children terrified Robert, for childbed was a dangerous place, but Constance was not afraid. She apparently wasn't afraid that their children would have the falling sickness either, and for that Robert would have loved her even more, except he already loved her to the limit of his soul.

He opened his eyes to see a mosaic of pink blossoms against a perfectly blue, sunny sky, and all the beauty and peace that sky could hold flowed into him. *She* had done this, given him back the sun, the sky, and his own heart.

Whatever Constance needed of him, whatever he could do for her in return, he would do, and do joyously. He drifted off into the sweetest, most contented rest he'd ever known, while Constance slept at his side.

* * *

"How is Rothhaven's steed coming along?" Quinn asked, swinging into the saddle. From long habit, he made a production out of straightening the horse's mane, adjusting the reins, and otherwise averting his gaze while Stephen clambered onto a solid gray gelding.

"We'll see," Stephen said, sliding his canes into the scabbard on the right side of his saddle. "Revanche is a good fellow and he's up to Rothhaven's weight. So far, he's been quick to grasp what's expected of him, but this will be our first outing beyond the paddock. What have you learned of Neighbor Rothhaven since he made off with Constance's common sense?"

Her common sense and apparently her heart. "We know he has the falling sickness."

Stephen tugged on his hat brim and kneed Revanche away from the mounting block. "Yesterday's incident was apparently nothing short of spectacular. What of his finances?"

Mungo fell in step beside Revanche without Quinn having to steer him. "Rothhaven's skill when it comes to investing is spectacular as well. Apparently when a man has little to do other than read newspapers from every corner of the realm and as far away as Boston and Rome, his investment decisions bear abundant fruit."

"High praise from you."

The horses clip-clopped along, and while part of Quinn was enjoying an outing with his brother, another part was concerned for Jane. She'd managed little more than dry toast at breakfast.

Again.

"Rothhaven is a thinker, Stephen. He ponders and conjectures and sees connections that only emerge when a situation is studied with equal parts insight, information, and imagination. His father was apparently a plodder, and Lord Nathaniel did what he could with the estate finances. Rothhaven took on the investments five years ago and has worked miracles."

"Miracles?" Stephen turned Revanche left at the foot of the drive, in the direction of Rothhaven Hall and the village.

"Fortunes can be won or lost when a nation is at war," Quinn said, "as you well know. Rothhaven has made several fortunes, and in a very short time. He knows when to buy corn and where to sell it. Knows what the Americans want before they want it. He grasped exactly what France would need to rebuild—seed, seed drills, ploughs, bullocks, brick molds, *paintbrushes, for God's sake*—and set about quietly buying it up and cheaply shipping it. He could open a bank and do very well for his customers."

"You are saying he's brilliant with money."

The day was lovely, a harbinger of summer, though by tonight—this being Yorkshire—the sky could be hurling down sleet. Had Stephen not asked Quinn to join him, Quinn would probably have spent the afternoon indoors, poring over some damned ledger. That was a recipe for premature aging, also foolish, and Rothhaven had been kept away from fresh air for years.

What did that do to a man?

"I get the sense," Quinn said, "that Rothhaven isn't even trying when it comes to money, Stephen. He was cooped up indoors day after day. He amused himself with investing based on voracious reading and prodigious mental speculation. He's some sort of investing savant. Whatever else is true, Constance and Althea will be lavishly provided for."

"This is not particularly good news, is it?" Stephen asked, urging his horse into the trot.

"What could possibly be wrong with abundant settlements?"

"If Rothhaven is fabulously wealthy, his fortune could lure the unscrupulous into scheming against him. I will now imitate a man having a fit."

Stephen shook the reins first, then wobbled his body,

then made his limbs tremble as the horse slowed from a trot to a walk, then shuffled to a halt.

"Is that what Revanche is supposed to do?" Quinn asked.

"No," Stephen said, sitting up and patting the horse's neck. "He was supposed to come to an immediate stop and stand like a statue, but I purposely did not practice in the arena first, nor did I give him any verbal command to stand. We practiced this morning, then I put him away. This was an unannounced exam. He did well, he needs to do better. How's Jane?"

Jane was expecting, a situation in which Stephen took an inordinate interest. Never had a man longed as fervently for a ducal nephew as Lord Stephen Wentworth apparently longed for one.

"She will be intermittently miserable for the next five months. I will be unrelentingly worried."

"I know not what inspires more dread in me: Jane's condition or the ongoing courtships of our sisters. Evidence of present or impending marital bliss faces me on every hand."

Stephen, who was obnoxiously intelligent, sounded genuinely dumbfounded.

"It might be contagious, that bliss," Quinn said. "Constance succumbed almost as soon as Althea brought Lord Nathaniel up to scratch. You'd best return to London posthaste, lest the ailment afflict you too."

Stephen shot him a peevish look. "Hilarious, but if you think I will abandon our sisters before they are securely ensconced in the state of holy matrimony, you have spent too long impersonating a bear in the nursery. Neville Philpot saw Rothhaven's seizure yesterday, and I beg leave to doubt that Philpot's solicitude was motivated entirely by Christian charity. Philpot has something of a reputation."

"You are, as usual, creating drama where none exists. Philpot will gossip with his confreres, and Lady Phoebe will loudly remember His Poor, Infirm Grace in her endless prayers and small talk, and nobody will take any note of either of them."

Stephen remained silent, urging his horse back up to the trot. That Stephen would let the matter drop proved nothing. Rothhaven might be a genius at spotting lucrative investments. Stephen, of a certainty, could smell trouble in the wind. That he would subject himself to not one but two courting swains and a duchess on the nest suggested trouble was indeed approaching.

* * *

"His Grace of Rothhaven is no more insane than you are, Philpot," Cranmouth said. "One doesn't accuse a duke of mental incompetence and come away unscathed."

"One does not," Neville replied, taking a sip of excellent claret, "unless the duke is incontrovertibly afflicted. Then one is taking on a thankless and necessary public duty." Phoebe's words, though they had sounded more convincing when she'd spoken them.

Neville had chosen to have this discussion with Cranmouth over a superb rare steak at the club frequented by most of the solicitors and men of business in York. The Dalesmen premises weren't as busy at midday, and thus the conversation was private.

"Rothhaven is *my client*," Cranmouth retorted, leaning across the table. "I cannot be seen to betray the interests of my client."

Neville refilled Cranmouth's wineglass and topped up his own. Reasoning with Cranmouth was thirsty work.

"Now there you raise an interesting question, Cranmouth. Is your client the man—Robert Rothmere—or the duchy of Rothhaven as embodied in that man? If your client is the duchy, then a duke who cannot manage his own affairs is a threat to his own duchy, wouldn't you say?"

"You know nothing," Cranmouth muttered. "The old duke—Duke Alaric—nearly ran the whole business into the ground. Mistresses, hunting parties, royal court pomp, and Paris fashions. He was old-school, if you know what I mean. Papa used to dread his summonses, and not because it meant a journey into the countryside. The old duke had no head for business, and he wasn't willing to be educated."

"True of most dukes, from what I gather." Not that Neville truly knew any dukes.

"The old duke died, and the surviving son—the fellow we thought was the *only* surviving son—Nathaniel, stepped into his shoes. Immediately, matters began to come right. Expenses slowed to a trickle, the foolish investments stopped, the books were brought up to date."

Neville took another bite of excellent beef and made a do-go-on gesture with his fork.

"Shortly thereafter, a year or two at most, I began to receive more detailed guidance regarding the investments. Sell this, buy that, ship the other. Some of the instructions were quite odd—buy nails, in quantity, tons of them, for example. After Waterloo, the Birmingham gunmakers stopped consuming every available ton of iron and steel. The nail manufactories were thrilled to have a bulk order from any quarter, and the Continental markets were eager to buy those nails at very competitive prices."

Nails? Who would have thought something so simple could rebuild a fortune, but then, most of Europe needed rebuilding, and nails were necessary to that undertaking.

"All quite enlightening, but what does this have to do with a man twitching on the street in broad daylight?"

"I suspect," Cranmouth said, lowering his voice, "the guidance regarding the rebuilding of the Rothhaven fortunes came from Robert, not Nathaniel. Nathaniel let the house go to ruin. Busied himself tending the estate, and seldom bothered to call on me. How would he have come across a scheme to enrich the family coffers by brokering nails, lumber, and the like?"

"Lumber?" Lumber, especially hardwood, was scarce in England. The ever-growing cities and towns wanted quick construction, not the more expensive stone variety, and what didn't end up in housing had long since been impressed into service in the Royal Navy.

"Rothhaven bought lumber in America," Cranmouth said, "where they literally have trees to burn, and let the wood finish seasoning as it traveled across the sea, thus reducing the time the inventory needed to be stored at its origins. These are not the behaviors of a lunatic."

"But until recently, Nathaniel was the duke of record, so the cleverness must be attributed to him. Of Robert, we know only that he grew up away from his family, likely in a madhouse, and only recently returned to Rothhaven Hall."

Cranmouth glanced around. "Lunatics do not amass fortunes in only a few years' time."

"You have no proof that the investments were Robert's doing, Cranmouth. Sensible people are not relegated to madhouses."

Cranmouth sat back, wineglass in hand. "Sensible people are sent to madhouses every day, Philpot. You know that as well as I do. Inconvenient wives, carping aunties, simpletons with no harm in them whatsoever…They can all be quietly incarcerated for a modest sum, and if they aren't barmy when they arrive at those places, they will be by the time a doctor comes around on an annual visit."

If any such visit was ever made. "As best I can determine, Robert Rothmere would have spent at least a decade in a private madhouse. He was sent off somewhere as a boy, we know that much, and if you did a very thorough review of the old duke's ledgers, you could probably ascertain where. Add the falling sickness to his afflictions, and you doubtless have a man of very frail mental faculties. You saw him, Cranmouth. When his fit was over, he couldn't speak, and he could barely stand. Anybody could have served him a bad turn in such a state or made off with him bodily."

Cranmouth grimaced and took a sip of his wine. "It was awful, no denying that. One can't help but feel sorry for the poor fellow. He's a duke, an extraordinarily wealthy duke, and he looked like a gin drunk twitching in the gutter. Pathetic. This is an excellent vintage."

"Have some more." Neville refilled Cranmouth's glass yet again and signaled the waiter for another bottle. "I'm not asking you to bring the petition for a competency review, Cranmouth, merely to continue to serve in the capacity you always have. You are the legal conscience of the Rothhaven estate, the loyal servant of the family's interests. If Rothhaven is declared incompetent, you would simply carry on, though your direction would come from a guardian rather than from some difficult aristocrat in bad health."

Cranmouth didn't have to be told that the guardian would be Neville himself. Neville had been appointed guardian in several other cases, and was known to the court to be conscientious in the execution of his duties.

"You will bring the petition?" Cranmouth asked quietly.

"Of course not. I'll have Weatherby handle that part. He and I have cooperated on similar cases in the past. He brings the petition and asks to have me appointed guardian because I've shown myself to serve in that role effectively on other occasions. I also have a family connection to the Rothmeres."

Cranmouth's brows drew down. "You do?"

"My lady wife's sister had a liaison with the old duke. Our niece Sybil was the result, though a handy groom was found for her mama in time to prevent outright scandal. That makes my wife a relation to the Rothmeres of sorts."

"Not a close relation, Philpot, and not in any sense a court would recognize."

"Cut line, Cranmouth. My niece is a half sister to His Grace. That's family connection enough for benighted Yorkshire and you know it. When I am in charge of Rothhaven's affairs, I will take very good care of His Grace, you may be sure of that. I expect your fees will necessarily increase, because so much more of the estate work will be thrust onto your shoulders."

Neville was unwilling to be more obvious than that in a discussion with another solicitor.

Cranmouth studied his wine. He peered around the dining room, which was decorated with portraits of venerable judges in their robes and wigs, interspersed with various goddess-looking ladies. Justice and Victory, perhaps. The deities who truly ruled over the lives of solicitors were Hard Work and Whining Clerks.

Though an unhappy wife could make both of those afflictions look paltry by comparison.

Across the room, a waiter showed Sir Leviticus Sparrow to a table. Sir Levi was a conundrum, having married a very significant pot of money, and yet continuing his legal practice. He wasn't in York proper as often as he had been previous to his nuptials, and that was generally a source of relief in the legal community. Negotiating a contract with Sir Levi was a challenge. He was not merely conscientious, but rather, punctilious to a fault and took the job of zealous advocacy more seriously than most.

He nodded cordially to Neville and Cranmouth and conferred with the waiter.

"I'm doing well enough as it is," Cranmouth said. "I don't like the notion of standing back while you bring scandal down on a ducal family, Philpot. It's not the done thing."

Neville had not expected Cranmouth to fall in with a daring scheme at first mention. Phoebe had cautioned patience and persistence, and as usual, Phoebe had been correct.

"Nobody undertakes such a course enthusiastically," Neville replied, as a second man joined Sir Levi across the room. "For the present, all I suggest you do is have a glance at the old duke's ledgers and accounts. If you can find proof that regular payments were made to a private madhouse during the years corresponding to Rothhaven's absence, you will have evidence that supports my case. Does that sound reasonable?"

Evidence was dear to any lawyer's heart, objective proof that absolved a man of the distasteful uncertainty of—and responsibility for—a personal opinion.

"That makes sense," Cranmouth said. "And my father kept meticulous records for the old duke. Nothing less would do. Exactly how much extra work do you see my office taking on, should the present titleholder be found unfit?"

The bait had been taken, as Phoebe had known it would be.

"The additional work would be enormous, Cranmouth. A very great burden indeed."

"A notion worth contemplating." Cranmouth smiled and lifted his glass. "A health to your lady, Philpot."

"I am happy to share such a toast. When shall we revisit our earlier topic?"

"Give me a fortnight. The ledgers will have to be retrieved from the attics."

"Excellent." Within a week, Sybil's handsome swain should have proffered his proposal, and Neville could have a petition drafted to bring His Grace of Rothhaven before a board of competence examiners.

Truly, marrying dear Phoebe was the smartest thing Neville had ever done.

Chapter Twelve

Rothhaven as a lover was like a marching army: unstoppable, resolute, and—for Constance—liberating. He hadn't conquered her so much as he'd overwhelmed her with consideration. Even as passion had rendered her nigh insensate, he'd still been gauging her reactions and attuning his lovemaking to her responses.

And oh, the sensation of his voice, whispered in her ear...

"More, my lady?"

"Tell me if it's too much, Constance."

And the words that had sent her over the edge: "Let go. I have you, Constance. You can let go."

All of this, while their bodies were joined in a slow, relentless rhythm, and pleasure stalked Constance from within.

She *had* let go, of control, self-doubt, fear, fatigue, *everything*, except the man in her arms. Holding Rothhaven was like holding the sun in her heart. The darkness that had weighed upon her for years was supplanted with light, warmth, joy, brilliant colors, and—most of all—with hope.

When he'd loved her witless, he eased to her side and drew her against him. Constance cuddled closer, her head on his shoulder and peace in her heart.

"I want a special license, Rothhaven."

He hugged her with the arm he'd looped around her shoulders. "Robert, please, considering the circumstances."

Constance's *circumstances* included a pattern of blooming plum trees against a backdrop of blue-and-white Yorkshire sky, a sprinkling of fallen blossoms on the lush grass surrounding the blankets, and a joy so profound she finally understood why Quinn and Jane looked at one another as they so often did.

She smoothed a hand over her lover's chest. "A special license, please. *Robert*."

"Of course."

"Where?" Constance asked, fumbling about on the blanket to locate Robert's coat, then dragging it over her.

He tucked the coat around her shoulders. "Where shall we hold the ceremony?"

"And when? I want Althea's nuptials out of the way, but I don't want her to have to put off her wedding journey while we fuss about ordering flowers and waiting for Quinn to make another copy of the settlement agreements."

"You are eager to become my duchess?" He sounded so normal, so in control of himself, while Constance was drunk with affection and a complicated variety of relief.

"I am not particularly eager to become your duchess. We will be an eccentric couple, entertaining little, traveling even less. Most of our efforts will be absorbed with putting the Hall to rights. I am very eager to become your wife, though."

He kissed her ear. "And I am eager to become your husband, Constance Wentworth. You don't mention the effort we will expend finding your Artemis. Ensuring that your daughter thrives is more important to me than designing a damned gatehouse or completing an inventory of the library. Are you cold?"

"No." She was warm, for the first time in years. "You?"

"Not in the least, but if we remain in this state of delightful dishabille, I will soon be again comporting myself like a beast in rut. One doesn't want to impose."

Constance shifted about under his jacket, then straddled him, the jacket over her shoulders. "Yes, one does. One wants to impose if one's lover is willing."

He smiled not at her, but at her breasts, which he caressed in slow, considering strokes. "I learned not to notice desire. I taught myself to regard self-satisfaction as simply another aspect of personal hygiene, like brushing my teeth, until I could ignore the urge altogether."

He was already aroused, which made joining her body to his an easy, rocking slide of her hips.

"Ignore *my* urges at your peril, Robert," Constance said, setting up a rhythm.

"I suspect—I fear—I will be a demanding husband, Constance. Perhaps a bit obsessed at first."

"Good." She increased the tempo minutely, for already desire was routing self-discipline. "For I intend to be a very demanding wife."

He curled up off the blanket and seized her in an embrace that only ended when they were both limp, panting, and spent, he flat on his back, she sprawled on his chest, riding the rise and fall of his breathing like a happy little seabird on a sunny, joyous tide.

"We will be married here," Rothhaven said, making lazy patterns on Constance's back. "Vicar Sorenson can preside on short notice so that the weather will not thwart our plans. I want the staff in attendance, if you don't mind."

She loved the feel of his voice, loved the calm in all he said. Loved the scent of his skin, loved that he wanted to be married where they'd consummated their engagement.

"Right now, Your Grace, I mind the prospect of putting on my clothes. I mind that I must move. I mind that I must open my eyes, but at least if I make that great effort, I will behold my beloved."

"You will also behold a picnic basket that includes servings of Monsieur Henri's pear torte."

Constance opened her eyes. "I suppose we should keep up our strength. It wouldn't do to expire of bliss prior to speaking our vows."

He patted her bum. "I am marrying a practical sort of duchess. Good to know."

Being a duchess didn't sound so awful if it meant Robert would pat her bottom like that.

They took their time getting dressed, with kisses, laughter, and even some truly inane tickling making the process more protracted. They fed each other sandwiches and torte, and drank from the same flask of lemonade.

"You probably prefer yours sweeter than this," Robert said, sitting cross-legged opposite Constance on the blanket. "I avoid consuming too many sweets, just as I avoid strong spirits. I've found that both are correlated with a greater frequency of seizures."

They had much to learn about one another, and seizures were only part of it. "I did not avoid strong spirits,"

Constance said. "Even though gin ruined my father and eventually killed him, I have still been tempted by the oblivion to be found in a bottle. Althea has an occasional nip, but I don't gather drink is a problem for her."

Robert took the flask and jammed the cork in the top. "Is drink a problem for you?"

Nothing Constance could say in reply would drive him away, which gave her the courage to be honest.

"Drink *could* be a problem. I hope it never will be, but Jack Wentworth was my father. He was a vile, lazy, violent man, and ultimately, he was self-destructive."

"What could be more mentally unsound than a man in good health, one blessed with precious children, seeking to destroy his own life?" Robert murmured. "And yet I did contemplate that very course myself. Then you came along." His expression was alight with wonderment, with a bemused tenderness Constance had done nothing to earn.

"When I was younger," she said, "I told myself that as soon as I had pin money, I could find my daughter. Then I began the search, and Artemis was nowhere to be found. The drink helped me cope with that. The drink and the painting. I could be alone for hours, nothing but a canvas and my colors, and for a time, I could forget that a piece of my heart was missing."

"Tell me more about this missing piece of your heart," Robert said, passing Constance a sandwich. "What do we know of her early situation, what direction is your inquiry agent pursuing now?"

"The couple who took her in had no children of their own. They were clergy, both from large families. When Artemis was about seven years old, an influenza epidemic hit the town where her adoptive father was vicar. Both husband and wife died, and I wasted years pursuing the adoptive father's side of the family, only to learn that the wife's side took Artemis in. Her adoptive mother was one of eleven. My efforts have focused on finding the other ten siblings, in hopes that Artemis yet bides among them."

"If means and determination can find her, Constance, she will be found. Do we alert your family the ongoing progress of this quest, or wait to inform them when we have results?"

Constance hadn't thought that far, hadn't considered repercussions. "I am bringing scandal down on my family if I try to take a place in my daughter's life. I avoided involving Quinn in my search precisely because I did not want my scandal to touch him any more than it already had."

Robert took a bite of his sandwich. "If your sister should offer us her cook's services as a wedding present, we will accept. As far as scandal goes, I will inevitably fall to pieces at some social event. Half the neighbors or what passes for good society in these surrounds will see me again disoriented, disheveled, fumbling for words, and unable to control my movements. If I do not create that degree of spectacle, I will have a staring spell at a formal dinner or in the churchyard. More lemonade?"

"No, thank you. You are saying that a by-blow will pale in comparison to your disability?"

He went rummaging in the wicker hamper. "I have two half sisters, courtesy of my father's philandering. You may have met the one, Miss Sybil Price. Her parentage is probably an open secret—she looks nothing like the man who married her late mother. Nathaniel tells me some viscount or other is about to offer for her, and her irregular origins are no hindrance to that match whatsoever. This pear torte even smells divine. We ought not to let the last piece go to waste."

"Your smile is divine—also devilish."

He withdrew the torte and let the lid to the hamper fall closed. "So there's Miss Price, marrying a viscount, and her papa was an adulterous, dishonest duke. You could easily present Artemis as my offspring and not a soul would question that story."

"But that would be a falsehood bruited about to spare me from shame."

Robert kissed her, holding the pear torte aside. "The purpose of the falsehood would be to spare the child the worst repercussions regarding her origins, and to spare your family the admission that they'd failed to keep you safe. Your brother might appreciate the gesture, because his banks are built in part on his good name."

"I have been all too aware of the impact my past could have on my brother's business, which is most of the reason I've limited my search to very discreet inquires. This will grow complicated." More complicated than Constance had realized.

"For others, perhaps, but not for us," Robert said, holding up the slice of pear torte for Constance to take a bite. "We will offer the child whatever resources will ease her way in the world, on whatever terms you and she choose."

"She may not want anything from me, may not know I exist, or may hate the thought of me. She's still a minor. She will have family through the couple who took her in, and be very attached to them."

"Then she will acquire more family when we find her."

He was so confident, so unruffled in the face of complications, that some of Constance's anxiety where Artemis was concerned abated. She would find a way to discuss the situation with Quinn—eventually—and they would do what was best for the girl.

Constance spent most of the afternoon in the orchard

with Robert, eating and drinking, talking and kissing, and sometimes falling silent to lie by his side and contemplate the glory of Yorkshire in spring. When they left to wander down the hill hand in hand, Constance knew that whether she ever found her daughter, she'd found the man she was meant to love for all time, and the sooner she married him, the better.

* * *

"Nobody would blame you if you declined to attend services henceforth," His Grace of Walden said, "though your gawking neighbors would doubtless miss the spectacle your convulsions provide."

"Doubtless," Robert replied. He occupied the forward-facing seat in his own coach, Constance beside him. He recalled leaving his coach to take his place in the family pew, recalled indifferent singing, and then Sorenson reading the banns for Miss Sybil Price and William, Viscount Somebody.

Then, more swiftly than it had in York some two weeks past, the damnable peculiar feeling had risen up as Robert had reached for Nathaniel, who was goggling in Lady Althea's direction. The next thing Robert remembered was Walden and Nathaniel helping him to his feet and assisting him back into his coach.

His Grace of Walden sat on the opposite bench looking peevish and severe. He thumped the roof once, far harder than necessary to signal the coachy to quit the churchyard.

"Quinn," Constance said, "you are not helping matters. My intended is not a spectacle."

"He might well have been making a point with that

public display of infirmity," Walden said, regarding Robert with a brooding sort of curiosity.

Robert forced himself to sit up straight. "I do not appreciate being spoken of in the third person." Getting out that sentence had taken effort, enunciating, stringing the words into the proper order, adding the note of hauteur...no small feat this soon after a shaking fit, and still he'd come off sounding a bit drunk.

Walden held out his flask, perhaps a gesture of apology.

Robert shook his head. "Ill advised. Give me a quarter hour. I'll be fine."

"You won't ever be fine," Walden muttered.

"And you," Constance shot back, "will never acquire tact. Rothhaven has been honest about his malady. You're simply upset because you were for once unable to control matters, and you deal poorly with feeling helpless. Rothhaven, by contrast, has the strength of character to endure the same challenge without pouting or fuming."

Walden looked like he'd been kicked in the balls, poor sod.

"I'm feeling better already," Robert said, "and in a sense, it's best to get the churchyard debacle behind me. They've all seen me twitching and jerking, seen me dazed and undignified. They can have a good gossip, assure one another they will pray for my health, and get on with their impersonations of Christians."

Walden drank from his flask, an elegant silver vessel with a coat of arms embossed on both sides. "Does that mean we can anticipate a dinner party seizure? A Venetian breakfast seizure? A few seizures at the next summer fête?"

"Stop it," Constance snapped. "The falling sickness is a *sickness*, Quinn. It strikes where and when it pleases to."

Robert squeezed her fingers, though he could not recall taking her hand. "Be easy, my dear. Your brother is trying to understand a disability that has baffled mankind for eons."

"It sure as hell baffles me," Walden said. "I have heard of the falling sickness, but the reality surpasses the description. You could have hit your head on the bloody pew."

"I have hit my head, my knees, my elbows, my hips…The seizures are relatively painless, though the illness is not."

Walden took another draw from his flask. "Does your head hurt? Your brother said you have headaches."

Exactly when had Nathaniel said that, and why? "Mild headaches occasionally follow the convulsions, as does fatigue and some mental sluggishness. Are we not returning to Rothhaven Hall?"

Having the shades up allowed Robert to see where the coach was going, and passing the turnoff to the Hall engendered near-panic.

"We're going to Lynley Vale," Walden replied. "Constance will doubtless want to fuss at you, as will my duchess. You will bear up manfully under this display of tender concern lest I have to shoot you for being difficult with Her Grace."

Constance nipped the flask from her brother's hand. "When Quinn threatens to shoot you, it means he's worried for you. An allusion to fisticuffs is an expression of friendly affection." She tipped the flask to her mouth and passed it back. "He's actually a decent fellow, if somewhat indelicate about expressing his tender sentiments."

Walden capped the flask. "To quote a man who appears to have earned your esteem, Sister, I do not appreciate being spoken of in the third person."

Constance stuck her tongue out at her brother, Walden

became fascinated at perhaps the millionth sheep-dotted pasture he'd seen, and Robert allowed himself a smile.

"It was only a seizure, you two, and a relatively mild one. If I'm not to hide away at Rothhaven Hall for the rest of my days, I will occasionally fall prey to my illness in public. Life goes on."

And that was something of a revelation. The seizure in York had been embarrassing, the seizure in the church aisle unfortunate, but what life didn't include a bit of mortification or misfortune? Was avoiding either worth hiding away year after year?

Maybe not. When a man could leave behind his self-imposed prison, tool about the countryside with his coach's window shades up, contemplate marriage to the dearest woman in creation, and twit a hopelessly self-important peer, maybe the time to hide had finally passed.

"Are we expecting guests?" Walden asked, pushing the curtain on his side of the coach all the way aside. "Whoever has come calling drives a very modest conveyance."

Constance sat forward, the better to peer out Robert's side of the coach. "I'm not expecting anybody. That horse has come a distance, and on the Sabbath."

A gig sat at the foot of Lynley Vale's front steps, the bay in the traces dusty, its coat matted with sweat. The beast was more sturdy than handsome, as was the vehicle. Travel on the Sabbath was reserved for emergencies, and some of Robert's unexpected good cheer ebbed.

"Perhaps it's a friend of Stephen's," Constance said. "He has all manner of interesting associates."

When the coach came to a halt, Walden descended first, then handed his sister down.

"I'll see who it is," she said, trotting up the steps without benefit of an escort.

"Do you need assistance?" Walden asked, as Robert negotiated the coach's steps more slowly than Constance had.

"I can manage." Though in truth Robert wasn't quite as steady on his pins as he would have liked. "A seizure leaves me slow, mentally and physically, but the effects fade soon enough."

"Stephen has been training a horse for you. The beast is learning to stop and stand if the rider becomes at all tentative in the saddle. Revanche also stands on command. You tell him to halt, and he plants his hoofs as if Gainsborough were painting his portrait."

Walden was babbling, probably giving Robert time to get his bearings, and that was almost endearing.

"I doubt I will have the nerve to ever again sit a horse," Robert said, as the coach rattled off toward the carriage house, "but the thought is appreciated."

"With Stephen, one is often left to appreciate the thought. Why don't you use a damned cane?"

"I do, but some idiot forgot to bring it along when he stashed me into my coach." The steps had a railing on one side, which was fortunate because that railing spared Robert from taking Walden's un-proffered arm.

Robert had no sooner gained the front terrace than Constance came barreling out of the house.

"Robert!" She tucked into him, her arms tight about his waist. "Oh, Robert, Miss Abbott is here, and she's brought the most wonderful, wonderful news."

"Tell me."

"We've found her! We've found my darling girl, and she's living not thirty miles distant."

Robert embraced his beloved, the joy vibrating through her resonating with his own. He'd been the exile, the imperfect son banished to the shadows. To see mother and child reunited would heal that wound somehow, and make right so much that had been put wrong.

"I'm glad," he said, as Constance nearly squeezed the stuffing from him. "I could not be happier."

Walden watched this scene with a furrowed brow, then directed a groom to take Miss Abbott's vehicle to the carriage house.

* * *

"All over again," Quinn said, "I am the incompetent older brother who was too busy worshipping at the altar of mammon to notice that my own baby sister was in harm's way."

Stephen watched Quinn pace the length of the game room, a display of pique Stephen would never be able to indulge in. Over the Sunday meal, Quinn had been the gracious host, while Althea and Jane had shared hostess duties. Miss Abbott had joined the family at table, and for the eternity of the weekly feast, all the talk had been of the weather, the crops, and—when matters had grown desperate—the new posting inn being built on the northern end of York.

When the meal had finally concluded, Constance and Rothhaven had closeted themselves with Miss Abbott. Jane and Althea were swilling tea or stirring a cauldron in Althea's parlor, and the gentlemen, minus His Grace of Public Fits, had been dispatched by Her Grace to enjoy a manly game of cards.

In his present mood, Quinn ought not to be trusted with a round of darts.

"You feel inadequate as a brother," Nathaniel Rothmere

said as he prowled about the room opening cupboards and drawers like a snooping parlor maid. "At least you didn't leave a sibling stranded on the moors for years, dependent on a physician whose notions of good care included starvation, restraints, whippings, purges, and ice baths. Where the hell do you keep your playing cards?"

"In the drawer of the card table," Stephen said.

"Your card table has no drawers."

Quinn crossed to the table in question. "It's a puzzle table, with all sorts of hinges and hidden compartments. Stephen designed it."

"Press on the *fleur-de-lis*," Stephen said, from the depths of a comfortable reading chair. "The drawer will open. To see you feeling helpless simply breaks my heart, Quinn. Must be terribly frustrating."

That comment should have provoked at least a thunderous scowl. Quinn merely sank into a chair at the card table.

"You are not helpless, Stephen, but I take your point. Rothhaven's reserves of patience doubtless approach biblical proportions. To be afflicted with seizures, having no idea when they will strike, no control when they do . . . and to simply carry on. I am as impressed with his fortitude as I am worried for our sister."

Nathaniel slapped a deck of cards on the table. "Rothhaven will spoil Constance within an inch of her life. He will dote and fuss, he will build her a palatial dower house, he will kit out the Hall to accommodate her every whim and fancy. Are we playing cards or not?"

Stephen voted not, because weighty matters required discussion.

Quinn picked up the deck. "If Jane looks in on us, we must appear to be enjoying one another's company, or trying to."

Nathaniel angled a chair away from the table. "Jane or Althea."

Stephen shoved to his feet, collected his canes, and took the proffered seat. "I am an uncle again," he said. "Nobody thought to acquaint me with the details of Constance's situation. I can understand withholding the information from a moody boy, but I am more than of age and in a position to aid my sisters. The family continues to ignore the resources I could have brought to bear on the problem."

Stephen staged this pout in part to distract Quinn from his fraternal guilt, and in part because Nathaniel needed to become acquainted with his in-laws. For better or for worse and all that.

Wentworths didn't engage in polite sniping, they came out with fists swinging, verbally.

"What resources do you have that I lack?" Quinn asked, taking up the deck and shuffling.

"Tact, subtlety, a devious mind, charm, a sense of humor. What are we playing?"

Nathaniel took the third chair. "What are we drinking?"

"Help yourself to the brandy." Quinn finished shuffling and began dealing. "I wouldn't mind a tot. Stephen?"

"None for me." He'd cut back since coming to Yorkshire. Achieving true inebriation had honestly become difficult, requiring an alarming quantity of spirits. Jack Wentworth's fate suggested that less drinking, not more, would be a prudent choice.

"I longed to get drunk," Nathaniel said, retrieving the decanter from the sideboard and pouring two glasses. "I would dream of that mellow, semi-coherent benevolence, but didn't dare indulge because Robbie—Robert, rather, or Rothhaven—could not get drunk with me. And what if he had a fit while I was three sheets to the wind?"

Quinn passed out seven cards to each player and set the balance of the deck in the center of the table. "Your staff could not manage without you in even that situation?"

"I didn't want to find out, and then too, Robert does not drink but a single glass of ale or one serving of wine with a meal. I would have felt disloyal."

Quinn saluted with his glass. "Here's to sibling loyalty. What do you suppose Miss Abbott has to say that could not be said to the family members involved?"

"Constance is the girl's mother," Stephen replied. "Even if all Miss Abbott has to say is that the young lady has brown hair and a good singing voice, Constance deserves to hear that in private." Though Miss Abbott had driven out from York on a Sunday likely to impart more than such simple details. "Did either of you happen to notice Neville Philpot's reaction to His Grace's seizure?"

"Philpot's reaction to everything is usually to assess Lady Phoebe's reaction," Nathaniel said. "And Lady Phoebe is consumed these days with ensuring all goes well between Viscount Ellenbrook and Miss Price. What game are we playing here?"

"Quinn is a father," Stephen replied. "He forgets how to play anything but matching games."

Nathaniel arranged his cards. "We could play three-handed cribbage."

Quinn hadn't even glanced at his cards. "Stop being a barrister, Stephen. What do you know?"

"I don't know anything, but I suspect trouble is afoot. Lady Phoebe has the pew across from and immediately behind ours, and she thus had a fine view of the duke's difficulties. Vicar Sorenson confirmed that she was an irregular attendee. Rothhaven starts going to services, and lo, Lady Phoebe does too, dragging her devoted solicitor-husband with her."

Nathaniel drank half his glass of brandy at one go. "The entire congregation had a fine view of Robert's seizure, and I must tell you both, the situation bothers me."

"Bothers you how?" Quinn asked.

"Robert can go a month without so much as a staring spell, particularly in high summer, when he spends the most time in his garden. He's had three seizures that I know of in the space of little over a month. The other day, I'm fairly certain he had a staring spell as well."

Stephen didn't bother picking up his cards. "Are you implying that Constance has a bad effect on your brother's health?"

"Stephen," Quinn said, a note of quiet warning in his voice.

"No," Nathaniel replied. "But change can affect Robert adversely, and he's dealing with a lot of change lately. If I go through with my nuptials and remove to my own property, he'll have yet more change to deal with, and if he marries Lady Constance..."

"*When* he marries her," Quinn said, "she will aid him to adjust. Stephen, pick up your cards."

Stephen obliged, because Quinn was right: If Jane peeked in on them, they must appear to be passing a genial hour banished from the ladies' company.

"About Neville Philpot," Stephen said. "He bears watching. He and Lady Phoebe were not exactly aghast to see a peer of the realm shaking and twitching in the church aisle."

"Few people have seen an epileptic seizure," Nathaniel said. "One doesn't want to gawk, but it's hard to look away."

"They were gawking," Stephen said, "and, having been gawked at any number of times myself, I know the difference between compassionate gawking, curious gawking, and malicious gawking."

Quinn paused, his drink halfway to his mouth. "Theirs was malicious?"

"Delightedly so," Stephen said, "and I would put that down to small-minded evil, except that my man of business met me in York the other day to discuss some changes at my estate. He knows Philpot and had little good to say about him."

Nathaniel tipped his chair back onto two legs. "Philpot is successful."

"Philpot's family had money," Stephen said, "hence the union between Lady Phoebe and a mere solicitor. The wealthiest uncle on Philpot's side grew dotty, and dear Neville stepped in to have his uncle declared incompetent. Neville was appointed guardian of the old boy's means, and the family was all for that. By the time the uncle's will was probated, the means had largely disappeared. Citizen Philpot has made something of a cottage industry off of guardianships. An auntie here, a former business associate there."

"What has that to do with us?" Nathaniel asked.

Quinn's scowl said he grasped the connections, as Stephen had known he would.

"Rothhaven ended up convulsing on the walkway in York a fortnight ago," Quinn said, "and, as you know, Philpot witnessed most of it. Philpot saw today's display as well. Lady Phoebe carries a grudge against any who challenge her dominion over local society. You and Althea have done that, and now Rothhaven has found a duchess."

No announcement had been made, but anybody with eyes could see Constance and Rothhaven were besotted.

Nathaniel raised his glass, then set it down without drinking. "This explains a mystery that was costing me significant sleep."

"Say on," Quinn said. "The ladies won't leave us unsupervised indefinitely."

"Robert recently transferred to me and to my mother enormous sums of his personal money. The estate proceeds remain untouched, for they belong to the title, but he passed much of his private wealth into our keeping, asking only that we ensure his dependents are well cared for at the time of his death."

"Is he planning to die soon?" Quinn asked.

"Likely not," Stephen replied. "I suspect he's planning to be legally emasculated. If the money isn't in Rothhaven's possession at the time a guardian is appointed for him, Philpot won't have the opportunity to steal it. Has Rothhaven signed the marriage settlements yet?"

Quinn nodded. "For both Althea and Constance, and the funds remain in my hands. If anything happens to me, management devolves to you, Stephen, then to Cousin Duncan, and if all else fails, His Grace of Elsmore manages the money."

"The money is safe," Nathaniel said, "but what of my brother? A guardian could send him back into the keeping of some private madhouse, and none of us would be permitted to see him."

"He likely knows that," Stephen said, "and he's taking defensive measures, but defensive measures are insufficient to secure victory." Footsteps sounded in the corridor, so Stephen studied his cards and slapped a bored expression on his face. "Quinn, do you have any sevens?"

The door opened to reveal Jane and Althea, both looking happily intent on intruding on male pastimes.

"Alas no," Quinn said, mildly. "Rothmere, any threes?"

Chapter Thirteen

"She goes by Ivy," Miss Abbott said. "That threw us off the scent. I'd told all my contacts to scan the records for an Artemis Ivy, or Artemis, but her parents thought a pagan name less suited to the offspring of clergy than a common English name."

"Go on," Constance said.

To Robert, she sounded calm, but her grip on his hand was desperate. The tea tray sat before her untouched, so Robert poured out for the ladies.

"We knew she would not be a Wentworth," Miss Abbott said, "despite whatever name you gave her at her christening. James and Etta Wilson took her in, so we searched for Wilsons in every direction."

"And you found them." Robert poured three cups of good China black. "This being Yorkshire, and Wilson being an exceedingly common name in these parts, you found Wilsons in every village. How do you take your tea, Miss Abbott?"

Miss Abbott moved through life with an air of unshakable confidence. She did not walk, she marched, a stout cane in her hand, though she appeared to be free of every infirmity. She had tossed a glorified nod in Robert's direction when most women would have curtsied to an obsequious depth. Constance had asked that he remain present for this interview, and Miss Abbott had drawn her employer aside and held a whispered exchange first.

Very likely Miss Abbott had ensured that Robert's company was, in fact, what Constance truly sought, and not a capitulation to domestic tyranny. He held out the tray of tea cakes and the lady looked at him as if he were a stuffed canary that had started singing.

"You are a duke, sir."

"Lamentably so, and yet, I am able to manage a tea tray."

She considered the sweets and considered him. "A touch of honey will do, Your Grace. Thank you."

Never had thanks been more grudging. Robert rewarded her skepticism with a double serving of tea cakes.

He fixed Constance a cup of tea, plain, because later in the day she preferred it that way, and then prepared his own, also with just a drop of honey. Miss Abbott watched all of this, her expression unreadable.

"You were saying," Constance prompted. "The Wilsons had the raising of Artem—of *Ivy*—for seven years."

"But Mrs. Etta Wilson was not, of course, born a Wilson. I'd thought she was born a Brown, another common Yorkshire name, and she was, but in other regards I was in error."

A peal of thunder should have accompanied that admission, so portentous was Miss Abbott's tone.

"Etta's mother, Daphne Shaw, was the second wife of Mr. Abel Brown," Miss Abbott went on, "but Etta was born only four months after the wedding. Her mother had been widowed after conceiving Etta, and by agreement, Etta took her stepfather's name. Etta was thus born a Brown, though her full siblings are Shaws."

Constance ignored her tea. "You were looking for an Artemis Wilson, but you found an Ivy Shaw?"

"Exactly so. My apologies that it took this long, but as His Grace has pointed out, all of the names involved—Brown, Shaw, Wilson—are exceedingly common in the northern counties."

"And how," Robert asked, "did you eventually find her?"

"The past two weeks have been nigh frenetic, because I was able to put all available hands to her ladyship's project. Some of my agents are Americans, though most are from other parts of Britain. They have been inquiring at vicarages and posting inns as if searching for relatives on this side of the Atlantic or in this part of England."

Clever and plausible. "Your agents are female?"

"Yes, Your Grace, most of them. Fewer people suspect a female of being an inquiry agent. I also find women tend to notice what men miss and are more inventive and subtle about the job."

Said with the merest suggestion of condescension.

"Tell me," Constance said. "Is she well? Is she happy?"

"Ivy appears to be in blooming good health." Miss Abbott opened a satchel that could have doubled as a traveling valise. "She goes to market in Fendle Bridge every Wednesday with her uncle's housekeeper and attends services regularly. She is being raised in the home of the Reverend Whitlock Shaw, her nominal uncle, where she appears to be well cared for."

Appearances, as Robert knew, could be devilishly deceptive.

Miss Abbott withdrew a piece of paper from the depths of her satchel. "I thought you'd like to see this." She passed over a sketch, a thorough likeness of a girl who might well have been a very young Constance Wentworth.

"Did her hair stay red?" Constance asked, handling the page as if it were a holy relic. "She was born with bright red hair."

"Her hair is quite red."

Something about Miss Abbott's tone caught Robert's ear. "You never did answer Lady Constance's question: Is the child happy?"

The unfaltering Miss Abbott peered at her teacup. "She's at a difficult age."

"*I* am at a difficult age," Robert replied. "I'm at the age where I'd rather deal in plain speech and uncomfortable truths than endure polite dithering."

"Just tell us," Constance said. "If now is not the time to make myself known to her, I can be patient, but surely some funds, a finishing school, a governess, a competence—there must be something I can do."

The girl portrayed in the sketch had a bleak expression. She was pretty enough, though she would be prettier in a few years' time, and yet, her gaze suggested she did not look forward to whatever those years held.

"My agent chatted with the curate," Miss Abbott said. "Curates tend to be more forthcoming than vicars, happier to pass the time. He said Ivy has been a trial to her uncle, who is not the vicar in Fendle Bridge. Mr. Shaw is preparing to emigrate to New South Wales, where he hopes to have a congregation in one of the settlement colonies. Ivy has run away twice in an effort to avoid joining her uncle on his travels, but he is the guardian the family has chosen for her, the oldest Shaw brother. She is bound to go with him."

Constance pitched into Robert, her forehead against his shoulder. "Oh, God. New South Wales is full of felons, and she's just a girl."

Robert looped an arm around Constance's shoulders. "Can the reverend be persuaded to place his niece with other parties here in England?"

Miss Abbott closed the snaps of the satchel and set it aside. "He's the patriarch on that side of the family, which is how Ivy ended up with him. She is difficult, according to the curate, and her aunts and uncles were hoping Mr. Whitlock Shaw would be able to curb her headstrong tendencies."

Constance made a sound of inarticulate misery.

"Can the reverend be bought?" Robert asked. "If a sponsor were to step forward offering to generously fund his mission, would he be willing to see reason where his niece is concerned?"

"I don't know, Your Grace. His vocation is regarded as sincere, and he's been planning this journey for years. He might well not need a sponsor."

Constance wasn't in tears, but Robert could feel the emotions reverberating through her. Tremendous relief that somebody she'd long loved was still hale and whole. He'd felt that same relief when Nathaniel had finally fetched him home to Rothhaven Hall.

Dismay, because the situation was so fraught.

Anger, that Ivy's adoptive family should be a poor fit for her, at least at present.

"We must not despair," Robert said, kissing Constance's fingers. "You have never faltered in your determination to find your daughter, and now your persistence has been rewarded. Drink your tea before it gets cold."

He issued that order in part to provoke a flash of

resistance, but Constance saw through him. "Drink your own tea, Your Grace. Miss Abbott, does Ivy know of her origins?"

"I'm afraid she does."

If Miss Abbott was afraid, matters were dire. "Please explain." Robert did not admonish Miss Abbott to drink her tea, lest he suffer injury to his person.

"Ivy has apparently been told that the Wilsons took her in because her parents were not married and her mother was quite young. Mr. Shaw is concerned that those antecedents have resulted in a predisposition to bad judgment and wayward behavior."

Constance sat up straight. "Must I kidnap her?"

"My love, she might not take kindly to being kidnapped. If all about her are consumed with telling her what to do, how to speak, what to think, how to walk, and when to pray, she might be averse to replacing one jailer with another." *Exceedingly averse.*

"But she is *my daughter*." Constance rose and crossed to the window. "I can't lose her to the wilds of Australia now, not when she's a mere thirty miles from me and miserable. If she wanted to leave England, I could almost learn to live with that, but now? I want to order the grays put to so I can introduce myself to her before sundown."

"I wouldn't advise that, my lady," Miss Abbott said, downing her tea. "Mr. Shaw is reported to be old-fashioned. Today is the Sabbath, and even calling upon him without a proper introduction could set you off on the wrong foot. I've heard nothing to suggest his departure is imminent, or that he's an unreasonable man. You have time to consider today's developments and confer with your family."

Not much time, apparently.

"My family would be listening at the keyhole to this

discussion," Constance said, "except that Her Grace of Walden won't allow it."

Robert rose to join his beloved at the window. "They are concerned for you, as I am."

Constance's gaze went to the moors stretching endlessly to the west. "I am concerned for my daughter, Your Grace. I have ever been concerned for her, and now it appears she's to be dragged off to some colonial wilderness by a scripture-spouting martinet. Ships sink, foreign climes are full of diseases, and she does not want to go. I felt the same way every time Quinn dragged us south to London."

Robert took Constance's hand when he wanted to enfold her in his arms. "Miss Abbott, our thanks for all you've done. You will please accept Lynley Vale's hospitality for the night, and I'm sure Lady Constance will have more questions for you later."

Miss Abbott gathered up her walking stick and satchel. "I need not stay the night, Your Grace, but thank you."

"Stay anyway," Constance said, "please. I'd like an opportunity to discuss the matter with you further."

"Of course, my lady." Miss Abbott rose, curtsied to Constance, and withdrew.

"She's being diplomatic," Constance said, wandering back to the sofa and picking up the sketch. "Miss Abbott is not usually so delicate. Maybe you intimidated her. You did get a bit ducal. I was impressed."

"Maybe she's castigating herself for failing to make the familial connections sooner. Come here."

Constance stared at the sketch a moment longer. "Do you give orders when you're upset?"

He gave orders when he was determined. "I need to hold you when I'm upset." The notion of a young girl, forced to remain where she was unhappy, a loving mother unable to help, family nearby but of no use to her…Of course he was upset.

Constance put the sketch aside and came to him, slipping her arms around his waist. "How soon can we be married?"

"I have the special license, but I thought you wanted to wait until your sister had spoken her vows. Are you fond of shortbread?" The plate was half empty, though Robert could not recall anybody consuming so much as a single bite.

Constance eased away. "Miss Abbott pinched it. She has a sweet tooth. I suppose we'd best get on with the family conference."

"In a moment." Robert caught her by the wrist and stepped closer. "Do you know, I have yet to kiss you today?"

Her smile was wan, but it was a smile. "You should remedy that oversight immediately, Your Grace, for I grow difficult when deprived of your kisses."

* * *

"Make haste, you two," Stephen said, stopping just inside the door to the duchess's sitting room, "we must interrogate Miss Abbott while we have the opportunity. Constance and her duke won't be gone long."

Quinn and Jane exchanged a glance, which from long practice Stephen could decode easily enough: Do we ambush Miss Abbott without our brother's meddling assistance and attempt to intimidate her with ducal consequence, or do we allow Stephen to be the disagreeable meddler—a role he plays *so very well*—while we personify gracious, concerned reason?

All of that passed between them in the time it took Jane to rise and smooth her skirts. "Why exactly are Constance and Rothhaven calling on Vicar Sorenson now?"

"Because they need a letter of introduction from him, apparently," Stephen said. "Some of the girl's connections are clergy, and Sorenson is likely to be at least indirectly acquainted with them. Where has Lord Nathaniel disappeared to?"

"Wherever Althea has disappeared to," Jane replied. The look she sent Quinn this time was a bit harder to read. Had Stephen been forced to translate, the script might have read: Just as I could once be found wherever you were, before children, duchessing, and family became such a burden on my time.

Quinn offered Jane his arm, which was purely ridiculous when the distance to be traveled was down one sunny, carpeted corridor.

"Tell me, baby brother, how it is you know why our sister and her intended are calling at the vicarage? Have you taken to listening at keyholes?"

Stephen's leg was paining him only moderately today, but the situation with Miss Ivy Wentworth—to hell with those other names—grieved him sorely. He therefore opted for more honesty than he might have chosen in other circumstances.

"I am constitutionally incapable of listening at keyholes, but I am well aware of how chimneys connect from floor to floor in a well-built house. An unused guest room sits above the parlor where Constance and Rothhaven interviewed Miss Abbott, and when our little card game broke up, I happened to find myself near its hearth when they spoke to her."

He hadn't caught every word—Constance had likely got up to pace—but he'd heard plenty.

"Tell us what you learned before Miss Abbott joins us," Quinn said.

"And don't leave anything out," Jane added with a pleasant touch of dire duchess-threat.

Stephen first tended to the business of situating himself in one of the library's reading chairs. Fortunately, he didn't ache quite badly enough to prop his foot on a hassock. For Miss Abbott to see him impersonating a gouty bachelor uncle—which he nearly was, come to think of it—would not do.

Althea and Nathaniel arrived, and a footman was dispatched to summon Miss Abbott. Before her arrival, Stephen summarized the relevant facts for his family—uncle planning to emigrate, Ivy comporting herself like a headstrong Wentworth, dire measures under consideration.

All in all, a fine mess, and for once, Stephen was not to blame.

Miss Abbott arrived in the company of a footman who bowed and withdrew. Notwithstanding her escort, she'd brought her walking stick, along with her ever-present air of having business to be about. Stephen had met Wellington on several occasions, and His Grace had the same quality. The duke was not impatient so much as he seemed more interested in fighting the next battle than wasting time in civilian company.

"Miss Abbott, please do have a seat," Jane said. "I can ring for a tray if you'd like."

"No, thank you, Your Grace. I gather the family has questions."

"We are worried," Althea said, "as any loving family would be."

Quinn and Nathaniel were trying to look lovingly concerned and were mostly looking dyspeptic, which left Stephen the job of asking the actual questions.

"Is the girl safe for the present?" he asked.

"You ought not to have ambushed me like this," Miss Abbott replied, and her tone said she was using the singular *you*, meaning the rebuke was personal to Stephen. "This is a highly confidential matter and I do not discuss my clients' business with anybody."

"We're not *anybody*," Nathaniel said, assaying a smile that he likely meant to be charming, the clodpate. "We are all the family Lady Constance has, and prepared to use our collective resources to see her objectives met."

"We are most anxious to be of assistance," Althea added. "Constance is only newly engaged, and she and Rothhaven should not have to carry this burden alone."

"My brother's circumstances," Nathaniel began, as if embarking on a lecture before the slower pupils in the class, "are somewhat diffi—"

"I know your brother's circumstances, my lord. His Grace himself acquainted me with them by letter, including the situation in which he and Lady Constance met."

Well, damn. Posturing and charm would get nowhere with this woman. "Then you know much more than we do," Stephen said, "and while I respect your protectiveness toward my sister and her duke, we are protective of them as well, and of Ivy. Is there anything you *can* tell us without violating confidences? Anything a casual inquiry regarding Reverend Shaw might turn up?"

Miss Abbott palmed the head of her walking stick, which was carved to resemble—of course—a dragon.

"You will have those inquiries made, won't you, my lord? You'll go barging into a small Yorkshire village, a handsome, wealthy stranger asking awkward questions and expecting honest answers simply because you rolled into the square, your London coach pulled by matching grays."

Stephen laid his cane across his knees and shifted pieces on his mental chessboard. *Handsome*, was he?

"I will send my groom, Thomas Goodman, Yorkshire born and bred, riding a mule named George, whom Tom will stable at the livery because the poor beast will be tired after a long day's trot. Tom will put up at the drovers' inn outside the village, but stop by the church to give thanks for safe travels.

"Thomas will bump into the curate," Stephen continued, "then he'll enjoy a pint or two at the posting inn. If all else fails, he'll stop by the apothecary to buy a patent remedy or two for the severe rheumatism that so clearly plagues him. If market day in Fendle Bridge is Wednesday, Thomas will arrive on Tuesday afternoon, and tarry to enjoy the market. He will take particular care to flirt with the alewife, because all the friendly young fellows hang about her stall, and he will allow as how he's bound for Liverpool, and thinking of taking ship for the Antipodes. Need I go on?"

"You don't have a groom named Thomas Goodman," Althea said.

Because a sister's sworn duty was to un-horse her younger brother just as that good fellow had secured control of the conversation reins.

"I like that part about the mule named George," Miss Abbott murmured, brows knit. "A jackass or mule named for the king would be a winning touch in most livery stables, and certainly in the drovers' inns. I must remember that."

"A jackass named for the king would go over well in most London gentlemen's clubs too," Stephen said. "As for the villagers, the apothecaries hear all the sickness and sorrow in the neighborhood. They know who cannot have children as well as who has conceived inconveniently."

Stephen was gambling that Miss Abbott's sense of fair play would allow her to take a bit of pity on her hosts. She would not betray confidences, but in exchange for a few worthy ideas freely offered, she might relent *a little.*

"One must approach the apothecary as a supplicant needing aid," he added, "not simply as a nosy interloper."

Having patronized apothecaries since childhood, Stephen was intimately acquainted with the breed. Miss Abbott appeared to be considering his offering.

"You give me something to think about, my lord."

Quinn looked like he was about to drop ducal consequence on the discussion at the exact wrong time. Stephen thus decided to entrust Miss Abbott with the truth—a risky tactic, and not one he often used.

"Constance was bitterly unhappy as a young girl and made terrible choices as a result. She put herself at risk for serious harm, endured many hardships, and still has not entirely recovered from her youthful miseries. We would spare Ivy those same miseries if we possibly can, and spare ourselves the guilt of having failed yet another Wentworth relation when she desperately needs the support of people who mean well by her."

"Ivy's uncle means well by her," Miss Abbott replied, though she was stroking her dragon with the tip of one finger, which Stephen took to be a hopeful sign.

Also unintentionally erotic, which was of no moment whatsoever.

"He's not her uncle," Stephen said. "He's a fellow she doesn't obey willingly who's intent on dragging her off to Australia, where they have deadly spiders, snakes, crocodiles, fish that can eat a man whole, and foul miasmas by the dozen. If anything happens to Ivy's so-called uncle, what will become of her in such a place?"

Miss Abbott met Stephen's gaze, and he realized what had been bothering him about her—besides her confidence, brains, and air of iron resolution. She was *pretty*, beautiful even, though all her stomping about and thumping her walking stick, as well as her drab clothing and a severe bun, were intended to hide her looks. She was bloodstock trying to impersonate a mule, and mostly succeeding.

"Ivy is pretty, isn't she?" Stephen asked, quietly.

"Lovely," Miss Abbott replied in equally soft tones. "Has the most gorgeous red hair, and she's nearly taller than her uncle. Men hate that. Some men."

"A pretty girl," Stephen mused, "fourteen years old or nearly so, on her own in Australia, where she never wanted to be, where she never *had* to be... Anything you can tell us, Miss Abbott, *anything*, would be appreciated."

She looked around the room, taking in Althea and Nathaniel practically sitting in each other's laps on the sofa, and Quinn and Jane, equally connected but more dignified about their relationship, and then Stephen, alone in a reading chair, and—as always—clutching his cane.

"I can tell you this," Miss Abbott said. "Whitlock Shaw has no congregation here in England because he does not get on well with the bishops."

"Does he have a temper?" Quinn asked, seeking information any Wentworth needed to know about any parental authority figure.

"Not a temper, so much as convictions, Your Grace. Mr. Shaw detests everything high church. He blames the Church of England's corruption and greed for the rise of Methodism and dissenters of every stripe. He had a pulpit down near Manchester, but he fell out with the earl who held the living. The earl wanted to replace a plain window with stained glass, and Mr. Shaw refused. The dispute escalated, and Mr. Shaw was succeeded by a vicar willing to glorify God's house with man-made beauty."

"He lost his job over a window?" Jane sounded dismayed rather than impressed.

"Over a principle," Stephen said. "I take it that experience has left the reverend intolerant of aristocrats?"

"Exactly, my lord. Mr. Shaw has been heard to say that the colonies are the only hope for salvation on earth because they tend to be less infested with lords, bishops, and other moral pestilences. He believes the aristocracy embodies the deadly sins and all that's wrong with Britain."

"He's not entirely wrong," Quinn said.

"While you are entirely a duke, Your Grace," Miss Abbott replied, gently. "*Lady* Constance is marrying another duke. Had you been millers, yeoman, engravers, or teachers, Mr. Shaw would view you more favorably, according to what I know of him. As it is, the last people he's likely to allow near Ivy are a bunch of wealthy, titled strangers."

"Then we will be family rather than strangers," Jane said. "My father is clergy. His congregation is out in the West Riding. Surely that will mean something to Mr. Shaw?"

"I don't know, Your Grace. If your father supports the church's traditional thinking, it might be yet another strike against the Wentworths."

"Have you told Constance and Rothhaven what you're telling us now?" Stephen asked.

"Not yet, but I will. His Grace expressed a willingness to fund Mr. Shaw's ambitions, and I don't think that approach well advised."

Nathaniel rose, extending a hand to Althea. "Then Mr. Shaw is an idiot. My brother is obnoxiously wealthy. Shaw could build the first cathedral in the whole of Australia with Rothhaven's pocket change."

Althea took Nathaniel's hand and stood as well, though she'd been getting to her feet unassisted for as long as Stephen could recall.

"I don't think this Mr. Shaw sets much store by cathedrals, my lord," Althea observed.

They remained hand in hand, close enough to embrace. "He sets store by something," Nathaniel said. "We just have to deduce what it is."

They left, heads close together, apparently intent on further discussions of a private nature. Quinn and Jane withdrew on assurances that they would consider what Miss Abbott had imparted, and do anything in their power to aid Constance's objectives.

Leaving Stephen alone, unchaperoned with a relatively young, unmarried female who looked anything but pleased at the prospect of bearing him company.

"I am harmless," he said, gesturing with his cane. "They mean you no disrespect by leaving you here with me. The door will remain open at all times. You have only to holler for a footman or tug the bell pull should I teeter menacingly in your direction."

He didn't bother with a charming smile. Miss Abbott would cosh him on general principles should he be so foolish.

"That is a handsome sword cane," she said, glancing at the door. "Might I examine it more closely, my lord?"

Oh, she was a dear when she was trying to come across all hesitant and respectful. "I'll show you mine if you'll show me yours," Stephen said, holding out his cane.

She rose, closed the door, and traded him her sword cane for his.

Chapter Fourteen

"Weatherby, the case could not be simpler," Neville said, keeping his voice down amid the hum of multiple conversations. The club was busier than usual for noon on a Monday, and nobody could out-gossip lawyers.

Solomon Weatherby was both a neighbor in the country and a fellow legal practitioner in York. His wife, Elspeth, was one of few women Phoebe considered a friend. Neville did not consider Weatherby a friend, but he had been useful on several previous guardianship cases.

He was not being useful now. Not at all.

"Philpot, you know as well as I do that the cases appearing simple initially are the cases that become the most grievous messes all too soon. Missing heirs, complicated trusts, opinions from Chancery, secret weddings, mistresses bearing grudges... We see more drama behind the doors of the average courtroom than the public pays to see on the stages of Drury Lane."

Weatherby delivered this sermon while sawing away at his beefsteak. Took his victuals seriously, did Solomon.

"I have never seen such drama as I witnessed when His Grace of Rothhaven fell to the ground," Neville countered, "not two streets from here. The poor man commenced shaking and twitching worse than any case of Saint Vitus's dance you ever beheld."

Weatherby chewed a bite of steak, his mouth working vigorously. "I have never beheld a case of Saint Vitus's dance and I would hazard you ain't either. Besides, one can be physically infirm without being disordered in one's thinking, and God knows the reverse is also true. My own daughters are all too hale and fit, while they drive me to Bedlam with their chatter."

Neville took a long drink from his tankard, for good porter should not go to waste when a man faced a tedious discussion—or any other time, come to that.

"And what do my daughters chatter about?" Weatherby asked, gesturing with his knife. "Marriage. Marriage, engagements, flirtations, who is walking out with whom, and which callow nincompoop stood up with which featherbrained twit at the last assembly. And why, I ask you, is this topic of obsessive interest to them? It's not as if marriage has led their parents to anything approaching connubial bliss."

"Young ladies are a hopeful sort," Neville remarked, though his own hopes were feeling somewhat daunted at the moment. "I am prepared to generously compensate you for bringing this petition, Weatherby."

That compensation would flow outside documented channels, of course, as per usual when Weatherby brought petitions at Neville's suggestion.

"How much?" Weatherby washed down his steak with

a quarter tankard of good porter and held up his glass for a refill. He had once been a handsome young man. Now he was thick about the middle, and his nose had taken on the deep pink of the inchoate sot.

"I will pay you triple the last arrangement," Neville said, quietly.

Weatherby set his tankard down slowly. "What are you up to, Philpot? Rothhaven is a duke, and possibly well-to-do, but his ancestral pile is falling apart. The drive is a weed patch, the terraces crumbling, and the roof doubtless leaks in fourteen places. The old duke wasn't exactly a genius at investing, and keeping up those stately manors takes a fortune. As guardian, you will have to see to the Hall, and the whole time, Lord Nathaniel will be glowering over your shoulder demanding to inspect the accounts."

"And he will be permitted to see them." Those accounts would balance to the penny, and reflect efforts intended to safeguard Rothhaven Hall as an asset. The figures would not necessarily match what was paid to the tradesmen actually restoring the Hall. "If Lord Nathaniel grows too bothersome, his daft older brother will be sent to another private madhouse, and there's nothing his lordship can do about that. A guardian's authority is quite extensive."

Other diners arrived, the noise level in the room rose, and laughter erupted from a table by the window. Sir Levi Sparrow's wife was said to be in anticipation of a happy event, and that apparently occasioned a jovial crowd around his table, the good wishes and bad jokes flowing apace.

Weatherby waved his fork, another bite of steak speared on the tines. "Philpot, aren't you getting a bit ambitious? So Rothhaven has the falling sickness. He has a fit, he takes a nap, he wakes up, and he's still a duke who can likely recite Caesar's Gallic letters by heart. Find us a bit more porter, if you please."

Neville held up Weatherby's empty tankard and signaled a harried waiter. "Rothhaven's situation is far more complicated than a few seizures. We don't know how long he's been at the Hall, but for whatever time he's dwelled there, he's been unwilling to leave the premises."

"You said he had a fit in church. He apparently leaves the Rothhaven premises now, don't he?"

"That's only the second time he's attended divine services in my memory, and when the fit subsided, he was barely coherent. I witnessed the same sad truth when he took a fit right outside Cranmouth's office. In that state, His Grace can't stand unaided, he doesn't seem to recognize friend from foe, and I have it on good authority that he will soon be dwelling at the Hall without his brother to coddle him."

Phoebe really should have been an intelligence officer, for she missed nothing and saw connections others were blind to.

"Lord Nathaniel is off to join the navy, is he?"

"He's getting married, and he plans to dwell with his bride at Crofton Ford, twenty miles distant from Rothhaven Hall."

"The moment I file this petition, Lord Nathaniel will scrap those plans, and his bride will have nothing to say to it."

"Let him, for that will only put Rothhaven under the thumb of the same sibling who all but imprisoned him at the Hall in the first place. Our case becomes that much stronger." Phoebe had made that point too. "Lord Nathaniel stands to benefit the most by exacerbating Rothhaven's malady. Epileptic fits can be fatal, you know."

"Now you're a physician, Philpot?"

The waiter came with a pitcher and refilled both tankards.

"You can leave that pitcher here, boy," Neville said, "and a plate of buttered crab legs wouldn't go amiss."

The waiter tossed them a bow and moved away. Neville detested the untidiness of buttered crab legs, but Phoebe claimed Weatherby was partial to them.

"I am not a physician," Neville said. "Dr. Warner is prepared to serve in his usual role." Warner *looked* like a physician—dark-haired, tall, lean, handsome, and articulate, with a canny balance of a younger man's charm and a mature fellow's professional confidence. The judges liked him, as did the aging females he tended to collect as patients.

"And how many cases of epilepsy has Warner treated?"

"That hardly matters. The course of the disease is notorious enough."

Weatherby let out a slow, rumbling belch. "You don't anticipate any trouble from Cranmouth? He's at least the fourth generation in his family to serve the Rothmere interests. Even to Ebenezer, that ought to mean something. He must put on a case for the defense, and a case that holds up to scrutiny. Declaring a duke mentally incompetent ain't for the faint of heart."

Phoebe always said one mustn't be too patient or too understanding with the lower orders lest they take advantage of their betters.

"Scruples at this late date do not become you, Weatherby."

Weatherby smiled. "I bend rules, Philpot, as we all do. The solicitor who breaks rules can soon find himself without a practice. The prior cases you've brought to me were all heading for a guardianship eventually. My petitions might have been a few years premature, but I've also kept an eye on your management of the clients and their wealth. You bend rules too, but you've yet to actually break them—as far as the *available* evidence suggests."

A threat for a threat, because evidence could be manufactured, taken out of context, and twisted to assure a particular judicial outcome.

Neville fortified himself with another long drink from his tankard. Damned fine stuff, if he did say so himself.

"If you win this case," he said, "I will never ask you to bring another petition before a board of competency examiners. Cranmouth won't be a problem. I established that much before I even thought of approaching you. Cranmouth said he'd be joining us today, in fact."

"Then he's a fool. I can be seen having a meal with you—we occasionally share a table in the ordinary course—but I do not regularly break bread with Ebenezer Cranmouth. His clientele is too exalted for him to sit at the same table with a lowly squire's son from west of town. If the three of us are seen together, it will be remarked."

"When the dining room is this crowded, nobody will remark anything save whether their steak was properly cooked."

The crab legs arrived, adding their characteristic fishy odor to the scent of cooked beef and baked potatoes.

"These fellows ain't stupid," Weatherby said, glancing around the room. "The usual run of solicitor has worked hard, studied hard, and means to do good while doing well. You and Cranmouth have airs above your station. That catches up with a man."

Neville pushed the plate of crab toward Weatherby. "Is Ebenezer Cranmouth begrudging his daughters their every hair ribbon? Does he have to borrow the funds to keep his wine cellar stocked? Is his coach nearly as old as his firstborn?"

Weatherby seized the largest of the crab legs. "No need to be petty, Philpot. It's the damned marriage settlements that keep me up at night. My girls are lovely young women, but they haven't a serious thought between them and their mama's no better. I cannot expect a nabob to come along and fall in love with a chit who's neither bright nor wealthy nor beautiful."

"At least you've only the two," Neville said. "They are quite lovely."

Weatherby sent him a look that said he knew placatory platitudes when they were served up with the crab.

"Cranmouth's ears must have been itching," Weatherby said, gesturing with a crab leg. "Yonder he comes, and with a bee in his bonnet, if I'm not mistaken."

Cranmouth danced between tables and dodged waiters as if they bore contamination rather than good food.

"Philpot," Cranmouth said, nodding and leaning his walking stick against the table. "Weatherby. Might I join you?"

"Please," Neville said, pushing out an empty chair with his foot. "I've acquainted Weatherby with my concern for our mutual neighbor."

Cranmouth sat and hunched forward. "The poor fellow is barmy, all right, or the next thing to it. Your mutual neighbor, that is. A few years ago, he bought a certain property out on the Dales. He recently sold that same property to somebody looking to set up a home for navy pensioners. Do you know what price he commanded for a large home with outbuildings, home farm, stables, and twelve acres of park?"

Neville let Cranmouth draw out the pause.

"One shilling," Cranmouth said, banging the table. "He accepted one shilling in payment for the lot of it, furnished, as is, with all fixtures, livestock, appurtenances, and stores, in fee simple absolute. An uncomplicated property sale like this one is normally handled by my younger cousin. Had he alerted me to the peculiar terms, I would never have allowed such a failure of consideration to pass unremarked."

Weatherby picked up another crab leg. "The quality can be generous, and navy pensioners are a worthy charity. What else have you got?"

Neville peered into his tankard rather than let his interest in the question show, for there had to be more. There had to be.

Cranmouth was not given to smiling, but he smiled now. "Oh, yes, Weatherby. There is more. Given the recent upheaval with the ducal title, I was prompted to review some of the family's older files and ledgers. The property His Grace most recently sold has a very interesting provenance, one that goes back to His Grace's boyhood."

Thank the merciful powers. "Do tell," Neville said, "and shall we order you some sustenance?"

"Please. The tale is long and sad, and the ending, I fear, will be none too happy for my unfortunate client."

* * *

Rothhaven rapped his knuckles on the coach roof, then settled beside Constance on the forward-facing seat. "The courtesy of a night journey is appreciated, your ladyship."

"That sounds very formal, Your Grace. Perhaps I wanted to arrive at Fendle Bridge after dark to ensure we create the least possible stir."

Constance turned her head to gaze out the window, but of course, the shades had been drawn before Rothhaven had handed her up into Stephen's traveling coach. Rothhaven had given orders to have the crests turned, and the grooms and coachman were not in livery.

"We will create a stir nonetheless," Rothhaven replied, taking off his hat and setting it on the opposite seat. "The quality of the horses alone will draw notice."

Matched blacks, not a white hair upon them, the leaders full of fire, the wheelers bristling with muscle. Stephen knew his horseflesh.

"We'll change at a posting inn," Constance said.

"The inn, recognizing the coach, will put a Wentworth relief team in the traces."

Rothhaven's argumentative mood put Constance in mind of his behavior on the way into York. "Do you feel a seizure approaching?"

"No."

"Has the prospect of a coach journey out onto the Dales put you in such a foul humor?"

He swiveled his gaze to regard her, and by the dim light of the single coach lamp, Constance could see that her beloved was in a foul humor indeed. He might have been Quinn attempting to quell a sibling insurrection, so glacial was his expression.

"Constance, we might well fail."

Was he *worried*, then? "I've been failing my daughter since the day I put her into Etta Wilson's arms, Rothhaven. I expect Ivy will be wroth with me—if I'm ever introduced to her—and that more failure awaits me in the mothering department. She's my daughter, though, and I hope she will eventually see the advantages of attaching herself to a ducal household. In any case, her well-being must come first. I simply want to see her."

"You long to see her, though you hope for much more."

The coach was barely past the village, and the journey would last for hours. Perhaps rolling along in the dark, spatting and sparring, was a metaphor for marriage, but Constance believed in beginning as she intended to go on, even with the man she loved to distraction.

"If you cannot conduct a civil conversation, sir, I will ride up with John Coachman."

Rothhaven guffawed, the first such expostulation Constance had heard from him.

"You'd do it too, and probably take the reins from him before another mile's progress. Has it occurred to you, my love, that in addition to the fact that you and I are the aristocracy Mr. Shaw so detests, I am also afflicted with the falling sickness?"

"And why is that detail relevant?"

Rothhaven kissed her cheek, for no reason Constance could think of. "Some consider the falling sickness a curse, evidence of divine judgment, a mark of the devil."

"*Some* are ridiculous." Constance took off her bonnet and put it on the opposite seat next to Rothhaven's top hat. "I was poor, Rothhaven. Grindingly, wretchedly poor. I picked oakum, I carried hod, I ran errands all over York in my bare feet in wintertime and was glad for the coin. The same ignoramuses who think the falling sickness is a sign of God's disfavor think the poor are lazy and stupid. You never saw a harder-working, more resourceful, wily, self-disciplined, and determined batch of people than the nearly destitute. Before the hope gets kicked out of them, they are unstoppably ingenious and tireless in their efforts to survive."

"Is that why you were so determined to thwart Soames's awful treatment of his patients? Because you'd experienced oppression firsthand?"

"I had certainly been on nodding terms with despair by then. Soames was evil, treating people who should have been guests in his home like specimens or livestock."

Rothhaven turned down the lamp so the coach was all but dark. "I fault my father for many, many things, but he at least did not give Soames guardianship of me. I later learned that Soames was legally in no position of authority over any of us."

"He was confident that your families would not trifle with his experiments. Vile man. Is obtaining guardianship complicated?"

"That depends. If Shaw consented to give me guardianship of Ivy, that would simply be a matter of paying the lawyers and waiting for a judge to sign an order."

"And if he refuses to consent despite clear evidence that Ivy wants to be with me and would flourish in my care?"

"I do not kidnap minor females, Constance, and you cannot either. That is precisely the sort of eccentric behavior that will attract all the wrong notice."

The horses stretched into a canter, meaning the swaying of the coach grew worse even in this exquisitely engineered vehicle.

"I am compelled to agree with you," Constance said. "Those who go around kidnapping children are precisely the sort of people society looks upon unfavorably. Let's get comfortable, shall we?"

"I beg your pardon?"

"The benches, Rothhaven." She lifted the opposite bench to withdraw a pair of blankets. "They fold out to make up a bed, and we will be stuck in this wretched coach for hours."

"By rights, our families ought not have allowed us to share this coach."

Constance kissed him. "You are my family now, and I hope Ivy is soon to become family in the meaningful sense. Get up so I can find us some pillows."

He rose and switched seats while Constance retrieved pillows from under the forward-facing seat. The next few minutes were taken up with creating a bed from the folded-down benches.

"To gain legal authority over Ivy," Rothhaven said, "would mean bringing a petition in court, and if Shaw objects, proving Shaw unfit."

"Do you trust Cranmouth to undertake that assignment?"

"Not particularly." He pulled off his boots and set them aside. "Cranmouth might have alerted Nathaniel to the single apparently charitable donation my father made—year after year. Might have stopped some of my father's more dubious investments. Cranmouth chose not to. He is a cypher, loyal to Rothmere coin rather than to the Rothmere family. Now that I've concluded some real property transactions, I can look to replace him."

Constance unlaced her boots and set them beside Rothhaven's. "Quinn is similarly disdainful of toadies, as am I."

"Lord Stephen designed this arrangement?" Rothhaven asked, when they were stretched out side by side under the blankets.

"Stephen should have been an artificer. He likes solving puzzles. We have food and drink in the panel on your side."

"Good to know. Why, Lady Constance, how friendly you've become."

She'd snuggled up to Rothhaven's side, though with both of them fully clothed, snuggling was more a theory than a reality.

"Tell me about the legal process involved in prying Ivy away from Reverend Shaw," she said. "What does it mean to have him declared unfit as a guardian?"

Rothhaven looped an arm around Constance's shoulders. "It means scandal, of course."

"And scandal is no sort of recompense for a man who has voluntarily provided for my daughter for the past seven years, even if Ivy isn't particularly happy under his roof." Compared to Jack Wentworth, Whitlock Shaw was probably a prince among uncles.

"You make a valid point," Rothhaven replied, "and as to that, I am firmly opposed to any initiative that blights my family escutcheon. For good and sufficient reasons, the Rothmere family is already considered eccentric, and my objective over the next few decades is to rehabilitate that reputation. Dragging Shaw into court, when he might well be doing better than most bachelor uncles would do with a stubborn niece, is to be avoided."

"You are thinking of our children. I love that about you." Constance was growing fonder of rocking along in this marvelous coach too.

"I am thinking of my own peace of mind and yours as well. It's one thing to bring a by-blow to dwell under the ducal roof—men are expected to support their offspring, regardless of legitimacy—but it's quite another to bring a legal action in the courts against a family member who has been more generous than many would be."

"You're right." Which meant attacking Shaw's fitness would be a waste of time, and even if successful, such a suit could not put right all that Constance had put wrong. "What if she hates me?"

A masculine sigh redolent of resignation wafted through the darkness. "Ivy may know little of you other than that you gave birth to her. We must proceed delicately lest your daughter take you into needless dislike."

"I know that, Rothhaven, but I am hopeful. For the first time in years, allow me to be a little hopeful."

"Hope makes fools of us all." He rearranged pillows so Constance's neck was at a more comfortable angle. "I hoped for years that my family would retrieve me from Soames's madhouse. I would have given anything for an uncle to take me in when I was Ivy's age."

"Even if that uncle was dragging you off to the Antipodes?"

Another sigh, softer, more tired. "The settlement colonies are thriving, from all reports. Many sensible, sane, fit men are emigrating and taking their families with them."

Though Rothhaven would not be among them. Perhaps *that* realization had occasioned his initial sour mood. Shaw could take Ivy far, far away, and as long as Constance remained attached to Rothhaven, she could not follow her daughter to that distant, untamed land.

"We have Sorenson's letter," Constance said. "We have Ivy's best interests at heart. Shaw will listen to reason if he has any sense at all." That was a prayer, or as close to a prayer as Constance could fashion in her present state.

Rothhaven rolled to his side and spooned himself around her. "You want to be at your best if you are determined to meet your daughter. Try to get some sleep. The night will be long, and the ride bumpy."

Another metaphor. Constance closed her eyes, and managed to not sleep at all.

Chapter Fifteen

"I almost didn't recognize you," Robert said, sidling up to Lord Stephen in the innyard. "You even smell like a peddler."

"I smell like my stout four-footed companion of the road, George the Fifth," Lord Stephen replied, leaning heavily on a plain walking stick. "How is Constance?"

"Anxious, hopeful, determined, braced for heartache." As was Robert. "The facts in evidence regarding Miss Ivy and Reverend Shaw are discouraging. Have you learned anything?"

Stephen wore blue-tinted spectacles, just the sort of odd touch that made him blend in more effectively than if he'd worn no spectacles at all. Otherwise, his attire was that of a man recently down on his luck. His clothing was worn and wrinkled but fairly clean and well made. His boots matched, and his neckcloth was neatly tied though devoid of starch.

"The market opens at nine," Stephen said, gaze on the green across the road where vendors were setting up booths and unloading wagons. "The housekeepers descend early in hopes of finding the best produce. Shaw's housekeeper is a formidable female by the name of Mrs. Hodges. She does not suffer fools."

"Then you stand no chance with her."

Stephen tipped his hat to an older woman hustling past with a basket over her arm. "Why don't *you* try to charm her, Rothhaven?"

Robert had forgotten to tip his hat to the lady. Remiss of him, and one of a thousand mistakes he regularly made because in a madhouse, nobody wore a hat, much less used it for polite gestures toward passing women.

"All of my charm," Robert retorted, "is reserved for your sister. She's waited years for this day."

"So she has. What's your plan?" Stephen asked, casually propping himself against a hitching rack. "How do you see the morning unfolding?"

Robert had spent much of the jostling, bouncing night considering that question. "Constance wants to introduce herself to Ivy before any other steps are taken."

"Con is afraid the girl will be snatched away," Stephen said. "Afraid this will be their only chance to meet. What do you think?"

"That a mother's instincts are to be respected, though Constance is taking a great gamble. She doesn't mean to present herself to Ivy as her mother, though Constance and her daughter bear a close resemblance."

"The risk being," Stephen said, shading his eyes against the morning sun, "that if Shaw gets wind of today's doings, he could be a proper arse about the whole business. Trying to buy him off or flatter him then will only make the situation worse."

Constance emerged from the inn. She wore a modest walking dress of brown velvet, no piping, no lace, no ornamentation, and yet, the quality of the fabric and the workmanship proclaimed it to be a costly garment. Her beaded reticule caught the morning light, offering another advertisement of her social standing.

"Constance would be better off attempting to win Shaw's approval without a duke on her arm," Robert said.

"If you were not on her arm, Quinn would be," Stephen replied, a kindly observation, however grudging it sounded. "If Quinn weren't a duke, he'd still be a banker awash in wealth or a man who escaped the gallows. When people are determined to be hateful, they can find any number of excuses for their meanness."

"True enough."

"I happened to overhear the blacksmith's apprentice and his older brother enjoying their ale last evening."

The weight on Robert's heart became heavier. "And?"

"Shaw has put his house up for sale. He's booked passage to the Antipodes for himself and his niece in about one month's time. Nobody will miss him, but the whole village feels sorry for the girl."

"As do I, and I haven't even met her." Constance waved and stepped off the inn's front porch, her stride confident, her expression cheerful. Robert fell in love with her all over, for the thousandth time. "She smiles when a lesser woman would be cowering in her room, clutching her handkerchief, and praying for a miracle."

"A lesser woman would never have thrown in her lot with you, Rothhaven." Stephen took off his glasses and polished them on the sleeve of his coat. "Have I mentioned that breaking my sister's heart will considerably shorten your life expectancy?"

Despite all inclination to the contrary, Robert found himself taking a liking to Constance's younger brother.

"Nathaniel warned me that yours is a violent version of fraternal devotion. If you can tell me the name of the ship the reverend is traveling on, I can possibly buy it, and at least delay his departure."

"Impressive," Stephen said, putting his glasses back on. "I hadn't thought of that tactic, though if you delay Shaw's passage, you will infuriate a man already predisposed to righteous ire."

"Nothing will part him from his anger, if he's true to his type. By buying the ship, I might be able to give Constance a few more weeks with her daughter, particularly if Shaw's house doesn't sell and he grows short of funds."

"True," Stephen said as Constance drew nearer. "I can buy the house and be slow to finalize the sale."

"That would save me the trouble. Let's hope none of these machinations will be needed." Robert tipped his hat to his beloved, and this close, he could see the anxiety clouding her gaze. "Good morning, my dear."

Stephen pushed away from the hitching rack to tip his hat and bow. "I'm off to befriend a lonely alewife, or at least sample her wares." He paused, both hands resting on his walking stick. "You will have to fight for the girl, Rothhaven. I don't know how to advise you regarding tactics. Charm won't work, money won't work. In court Shaw will be the poor, sincere preacher whose true vocation is thwarted by a bellicose duke."

"Then what will work?" Constance asked, threading her arm through Robert's.

Stephen tugged down his hat brim and surveyed the increasingly crowded green across the street. "I wish to hell I knew. Mrs. Elizabeth Hodges is over by the tinker's cart, the tallish lady with the blue ribbon on her bonnet. She is Shaw's housekeeper. I do believe that's my long-lost niece at her side."

Robert covered Constance's hand with his own. "Shall I escort you to her?" He was tired from a night without sleep, tired from worry, tired from racking his brains for a solution. Constance would not march up to the girl and announce their relationship, but hiding that relationship from Ivy could be a greater error than announcing it.

That he was standing under the Yorkshire sun in a village square surrounded by strangers added to his burden, but if this was what Constance needed him to do, he'd do it willingly.

"She's my daughter," Constance said. "I'll manage this part. Will you wait for me?"

"Always."

She walked away, shoulders square, while Robert trailed behind more slowly. He'd keep a respectful distance, but like Lord Stephen, he was prepared to shorten the life expectancy of any who interfered with Constance in this most precious and fraught moment.

She was brave—God, was she brave—but courage cast out neither fear nor vulnerability. To stand as her champion, however imperfectly, was an honor. Once before, Robert had appointed himself her champion, and the decision had changed something in him for the better at a critical moment.

Across the green, Lord Stephen was keeping an equally careful eye on the proceedings.

He saluted under the guise of admiring the mighty oaks shading the green, and Robert returned the gesture. They might not secure a future for Ivy in the ducal home, but if the girl was willing, they would damned sure try.

* * *

Constance had grown up in a household where mortal fear was a frequent caller. Jack Wentworth had been a fiend, and his exalted authority as a father meant nobody intervened to keep his children safe from his violence. *Spare the rod*, the neighbors had said, smiling with pious resignation and shaking their heads.

Perhaps that's why Constance had been so determined to thwart Dr. Soames, not because she'd seen oppression firsthand, but because she detested oppressors and all who ignored the oppressor's evil. Jack had delighted in terrorizing his children, just as Soames had flattered himself that he was engaged in science rather than tormenting the afflicted people in his care.

And that—the ghost of Jack Wentworth, of his violence toward and disgust with his own children—had sent Constance into the arms of the first man to show her any personal regard.

How stupid she'd been, and how vulnerable. Seeing Ivy—tall, healthy, ready to enjoy a morning out on a pretty spring day—the last of Constance's sorrow over her childhood faded to mere sadness. Jack Wentworth's children had learned how to fight, to think for themselves, and to face any foe with head held high.

No matter the sheer terror they might be experiencing within.

The emotion Constance felt upon beholding her daughter had something of dread in it, and even touched the boundary of fear, but the overwhelming sentiment was profound joy. While Constance pretended to fish about in her reticule, she watched Ivy confer with Mrs. Hodges, point to a bookseller's stall, and pat the older woman's arm.

Mrs. Hodges nodded and strode off in the direction of a greengrocer's wagon, and the moment arrived for Constance to move her feet and make her daughter's acquaintance.

Rothhaven was ten yards off, admiring some sketches displayed by a caricaturist who'd set up his booth near the inn. Stephen was flirting with the alewife, a woman who looked to be twice his age and at least twice his weight.

Still Constance could not make her feet move. Ivy wound through the growing crowd to cross to the bookseller's, her stride confident, more than a few people smiling and nodding to her.

Move. Constance could only stand in the shade of an oak and gape in wonder at her daughter. A sensation like faintness welled, but no shortness of breath or weakness of limb accompanied it.

Rothhaven appeared at her side. "I'm in the mood to look over the bookseller's offerings." He put her hand on his arm. "Care to join me?"

She managed a nod.

"Breathe, my dear. You need not even speak to her, though she is a younger version of you to the life."

"She is?"

"Your hair was more reddish when you were younger."

That Robert could offer this conversation in such a nonchalant tone was fortifying. Constance took a firmer hold of his arm as they drew nearer to where Ivy stood, nose in a book, apparently oblivious to all around her.

"I hated wearing bonnets when I was her age. The sun was doubtless bad for my hair and my complexion. I didn't care."

"Tell her that. She has the look of a young lady who could use a pleasant encounter with a friendly stranger."

"Robert, I'm..."

"Afraid?"

Some, maybe. Afraid of losing Ivy, which was old business. "I am *awed*. Look at her. She's wonderful."

He stood very close, as if they were husband and wife exchanging a private word. "To feel that way about somebody is lovely, isn't it? That they are wonderful simply for existing. Such sentiment fills the heart with gladness. Perhaps all parents experience that joy, but I know I felt the same way about you when you sneaked me that cheese all those years ago. This female, I said to myself, is a wonderful human being, somebody with the courage to act on her convictions, and what kind, sensible, marvelously devious convictions they were too."

Rothhaven might as well have wrapped her in a hug, right before all these strangers. "Don't make me cry, or Stephen will deal with you harshly."

"I'm a-tremble with dread. She's reading Byron, by the way. Looks like she's enjoying all that clever twaddle too."

Constance dared a peek. "Reverend Shaw will never allow that girl to buy a book of Byron's verse."

Robert smiled down at her, his gaze tired and loving and utterly at peace. He winked, then sauntered off to lean against a lamppost.

Right. A pleasant exchange with a stranger it would be. Constance meandered over to the bookstall and picked up another of the volumes of Byron laid out on the table. She moved a few steps away and opened the book to a random page: *Love will find a way where wolves fear to prey.*

"Do you enjoy Byron?" she asked, pretending to peer over at Ivy's book. "I certainly do. He has the knack of being both sly and tenderhearted."

"Yes," Ivy said, closing the book and holding it to her middle. "Byron says the things most of us haven't words for, and he says them more clearly than we think them. You're my mother, aren't you? My first mother."

Ivy's expression was guarded, but far from wrathful. She looked curious, hopeful, and oh, so vulnerable. Constance's heart began beating so hard she put a hand to her sternum.

"I have the very great honor to be the woman you were born to. How did you know?"

"You look like me grown up, though you're prettier. Mama Etta told me who my real mother was. Constance Wentworth, from a wealthy banking family that lived far, far from the West Riding. She said you cried when you gave me up, and that you would find me one day. I'm leaving for New South Wales in a few weeks, so I figured you'd better find me soon. Did you cry when Mama Etta fetched me from you?"

Constance experienced the sensation of her heart breaking and mending in the same moment. *You're my mother, aren't you?* Of all the words to come from Ivy's mouth, Constance would never have anticipated that question. Never have expected her daughter's forthright curiosity to solve so many riddles and puzzles with simple honesty. Never have expected that Etta and James Wilson could have been so generous with the truth.

"I cried when I parted from you," Constance said, "cried for days, until I learned how to keep the crying on the inside, though I knew your Mama Etta and your Papa James would love you dearly. She cried the day you were laid in her arms." That memory became less painful with the telling, less bitter.

"Was my first papa a rotter?"

What an extraordinary, wonderful person Ivy was. What wonderful people Etta and James Wilson must have been.

"He was young and spoiled. You have his height and his beautiful hair. He did not survive to know of your birth."

"Was he a soldier?"

"He was the son of a wealthy York merchant. He died while at university." More than that, Constance could pass along at another time—she hoped. "Are you happy, Ivy?"

Ivy looked around, then stepped closer. "I am soon to be dragooned away to the Antipodes. Uncle Whitlock has quarreled with his bishop *and* his archbishop, and nobody in all of England wants him for a vicar or even a curate. The aunties despair of him. I don't want to go to Australia, but Uncle sends me to my room to memorize Bible verses if I argue with him. I'm through the Gospels already."

Such a mild punishment was a relief to Constance. "I don't want to see you go so far away."

"Mama Etta said you'd find me. She had a daughter when she was young, but the baby died, or so she was told. My aunties are scandalized that I know of such things, but they are easily scandalized, except for Aunt Flora. She says mendacity has no place in a child's upbringing. Are *you* happy, Mama?"

Mama. She called me Mama.

And what a question. What a dear, insightful, fraught question. "I have found the man with whom I'd like to spend the rest of my life, and that is a significant, precious joy. I have been searching for you, though, for much of the last decade, and right now, I am the happiest woman on earth. When I think of you being forced to emigrate, much of that happiness fades."

Ivy regarded her, the girl's expression puzzled. "You talk like a lawyer. Everything has a *but*. You are happy, *but*. You have found a good fellow, *but*. I am only happy to meet you, purely, entirely happy. Uncle Whitlock said you'd never come, and he was wrong. He's wrong a lot, but one doesn't tell him that."

"Ivy, if there were a way for you to stay in England rather than go to Australia, would you want me to pursue that opportunity?"

The woman in the bonnet with the blue ribbon, Mrs. Hodges, was looking around as if in search of Ivy.

"Stay? You mean like at a finishing school? Uncle hates finishing schools. He says they give young women airs and are not pleasing to the Lord."

I despair of Uncle Whitlock sight unseen. "I mean, would you prefer to stay, as in stay with me. In the household I will share with my husband. He is a lovely fellow and quite capable of supporting you."

Ivy considered the volume of Byron. "Uncle wants me to go to New South Wales and keep house for him. Mrs. Hodges says he's daft, but my aunties say I'd best resign myself to that course. They don't argue with Uncle either."

"I will argue with your uncle." *And he's not your uncle.*

"Best not, Mama Constance. Uncle digs in his heels and gets all martyr-y if you disagree with him. Let the women keep silent and all that. He'll pray at you and you can't shout at a man who's honestly praying. Nobody doubts Uncle's vocation. They just all wish he'd pursue it someplace else."

The temptation to spirit Ivy away, to bundle her into the big coach and gallop back to Rothhaven Hall, nearly made rational thought impossible.

Stephen, though, had set down his tankard of ale, and stood frankly staring at Constance, as if he were trying to communicate a warning.

"I believe Mrs. Hodges is trying to get your attention, Ivy."

Mrs. Hodges was looking about worriedly, her basket laden with cabbages and carrots.

"Well, drat," Ivy said, shoving Byron at Constance. "Uncle Witless must have finished his morning prayers early."

A short, round man attired in brown from head to foot was bustling down the church steps and heading straight for the green. He slapped a low-crowned hat on his balding head and tucked a black leather-bound book against his chest.

Why, he's only a little man. That thought was quickly followed by a frisson of unease, for little men could still claim a towering sense of self-importance.

"Will I see you again?" Ivy asked, gaze anxious.

"I hope so. I have a letter of introduction for your uncle."

Mr. Shaw approached Mrs. Hodges, who had apparently spotted Ivy. She pointed in the direction of the bookseller's stall and Shaw changed course.

"He hates for me to read anything," Ivy said. "Mrs. H sneaks me the newspapers when Uncle thinks they've been donated to the library. Don't leave me, Mama Constance, for he looks ready to preach on original sin."

Don't leave me. . . . The words tore at Constance's heart and stiffened her resolve.

She turned to Ivy. "Thank you so much, miss, for those directions, and how fortunate that Mr. Shaw is your uncle."

Shaw bustled up, coming to a stop beside Ivy. "That's Reverend Shaw, if you please, and who might you be?"

Good heavens. Had he no grasp of manners? "I am—"

"Don't bother telling me," he said, flapping a Book of

Common Prayer at her. "I can tell by looking at you that you're the wretched creature who gave birth to Ivy. Ivy, you are to go directly home and straight to your room. I'll speak to you later."

Ivy, stay. A touch on Constance's arm kept those words behind her teeth. Rothhaven was at her side, all languid grace and pleasant smiles.

"Reverend Shaw," he said. "I apologize for the irregularity of this encounter, here before the whole village, but we had heard that you make a priority out of morning prayers and thought to respect your piety by putting off the introductions. I am Robert, Duke of Rothhaven. I have a letter of introduction from Dr. Pietr Sorenson, our vicar."

He passed along a folded and sealed sheet of vellum and offered a goggle-eyed Ivy a bow. "Miss Ivy, good day."

That was clever, to acknowledge her as if she was more than a child truant from the schoolroom.

"I have little patience with dukes," Shaw snapped, glowering at Rothhaven and then at Constance. "And even less with strumpets." He spoke clearly, as if trying to make a spectacle in the middle of the market day.

"I have no patience with hypocrites," Rothhaven replied, pleasantly. "If our Lord can forgive Mary Magdalene for her failings, then who are we to cling to judgment when a young girl was taken advantage of by a worldly bounder?"

Shaw blinked, then widened his stance. "Forgiveness is a virtue, I'll grant you, but what of you, Your Grace. Easier for a camel to pass through the eye of the needle, than for a wealthy man—"

Ivy closed her eyes and took a step back.

"Excuse me," Constance said, "but might we move this game of scriptural battledore someplace more private? I had hoped to avoid airing family business for the entertainment of greater Fendle Bridge."

Shaw glanced about, not an ounce of chagrin in his bearing. Mrs. Hodges stood nearby looking ready to smite him with her cabbages, though, and some of the wind dropped from his sails.

"My home is humble," he said. "I am willing to hear you out there, but don't think you can waltz into Ivy's life, your corrupting influence already on display, and expect to be granted any access to the girl. She is impressionable and headstrong, and it won't serve for her to form attachments when she's soon to depart for the Lord's work in the colonies."

He strutted off, prayer book clutched in his pale hand, leaving Ivy to send Constance a miserable look before following in his wake.

"Not an auspicious beginning," Constance said.

"But a beginning nonetheless," Rothhaven murmured. "The whole village has remarked your resemblance to the girl."

"Ivy doesn't want to leave England."

"Then let's hope the reverend is willing to listen to reason." Rothhaven offered his arm, and Constance took it, ignoring the stares of the curious, and pretending a composure she did not feel.

Chapter Sixteen

"I am Sir Leviticus Sparrow," the fellow said, bowing to Jane. "I apologize for intruding on the household without an appointment, but my business with Lord Stephen is pressing."

"You are in his lordship's employ?"

Sir Leviticus didn't gawk, didn't take surreptitious inventory of the appointments in Lynley Vale's guest parlor. He was either exceptionally well bred or accustomed to commodious country houses.

"Lord Stephen first retained my services several years ago, Your Grace. I have had the honor of representing his lordship's interests here in Yorkshire since. His property and my wife's are within neighboring distance, not that we see much of his lordship in these parts."

Stephen was, despite all appearances to the contrary, a good judge of people. If he trusted Sir Leviticus, then Jane would at least give the fellow the benefit of the doubt.

"Please have a seat," she said. "I've rung for a tray, and if you rode out from York, you'll want some sustenance." The morning was only half gone, meaning Sir Leviticus had left York at dawn on a fast horse to be at Lynley Vale this early in the day.

Jane's guest made no move to get off his feet. "Perhaps His Grace of Walden can join us?"

"His Grace is away for the morning." Quinn, grumbling and muttering, had ridden out with Althea and Lord Nathaniel to call on the Lynley Vale tenants. Jane would have joined them on such a pretty day, but she wanted to be home in case any news came regarding the expedition to Fendle Bridge.

Constance might well be meeting her daughter at that very moment.

"Your Grace, while I don't wish to appear rude, I'm here on a matter of business."

Sir Leviticus had the look of a former military man. Lance-like posture, lean, tall, dark-haired, and exceedingly serious. He would take orders, but only from an authority he respected.

"Sir Leviticus, whatever has brought you here is apparently both urgent and weighty." Jane settled into a capacious wing chair. "All the more reason not to discuss your errand on an empty stomach. Please do *have a seat*."

He strode to the sofa, whipped out the tails of his riding jacket, and sat. "Perhaps I could leave Lord Stephen a note?"

Althea's butler, Strensall, appeared with an exquisitely arranged tray, complete with a vase of tulips. Consistent with Monsieur Henri's usual standards, the offerings would have fed a regiment of epicureans. Jane filled a plate with sandwiches, orange sections, two chocolate drops, and slices of yellow cheese flecked with caraway seeds, and passed it to her visitor.

"How do you like your tea, Sir Leviticus?"

"Plain will do, Your Grace."

Well, of course. "Eat. I make it a point not to interrogate my prisoners until I've lulled them into misplaced trust."

Sir Leviticus smiled—he was attractive when he wasn't being so serious—and Jane passed him a steaming cup of tea.

"I cannot violate client confidences, Your Grace, not even for such glorious sustenance."

"I will overlook the insult implied in your observation, sir. You are weary, thirsty, and hungry." He was also likely worried, and too much of a gentleman to burden a lady with his concerns.

He sipped his tea and closed his eyes momentarily. When he opened them, his gaze held lurking humor. "I meant you no disrespect, Your Grace."

"Of course you didn't, but when you imply Lord Stephen would hire a lawyer of less than sterling ethics, you insult his lordship."

Sir Leviticus commenced demolishing his food. "His lordship said you were fierce. Said you'd had to be."

"And now you redeem yourself by complimenting me. Lord Stephen has had to be fierce too. If he's being sued by some subcontractor or vendor, you could have informed him of that by letter."

Jane ought to have let the poor fellow finish eating before making that observation, but a lawyer riding hotfoot out from town did not bode well for Stephen's interests. Not even a lawyer who was probably former cavalry and who doubtless enjoyed a good gallop.

"Aren't you having any tea, Your Grace?"

Tell me why you're here. Jane could not make that demand and hope to get anywhere with Sir Leviticus. Anybody who'd endured several years in Stephen's employ would be a stout opponent in a battle of wits, and utterly loyal to Stephen. She considered strategy while she poured herself a cup of tea and stirred in a dollop of milk.

"Stephen once pointed a loaded gun at me," she said. "He thought he was protecting his brother. Mind you, at the time Stephen could barely stand unaided, he was years away from his majority, and his brother didn't need protecting—not from me anyway. If I were sent to my reward tomorrow, I could die secure in the knowledge that Stephen will guard with his life anybody whom he loves."

Sir Leviticus paused between sandwiches. "As you would die to protect him. I would expect no less, given how his lordship rhapsodizes about his family. My errand does not involve any looming threat to Lord Stephen's person or to his business interests."

Jane's stomach ceased roiling. Stephen had a temper, and as a younger man, he'd not always had self-restraint sufficient to match his passions. He'd fought duels, a notion that gave Jane nightmares, and if anything happened to Stephen, Quinn would not recover.

Jane would not recover. She had no sons, no brothers, not even male cousins, but she had Stephen whether he wanted her loyalty or not.

"He needs a wife," Jane muttered, and immediately hoped Sir Leviticus was too busy impersonating a plague of locusts to have heard her.

"The men who need wives are often the last to marry. Your tea will grow cold, Your Grace, and you should try the sandwiches. They are quite good."

Breakfast had been hours ago, and everything Monsieur

Henri prepared was scrumptious. Jane chose a butter-and-cheese sandwich, in deference to an expectant mother's unreliable digestion.

"I worry about Stephen, you know. He applies his considerable mental faculties to denying that the ducal title will become his, though all indications are that is exactly what will happen."

Sir Leviticus had the blue eyes of a man who hailed from the north, and they were trustworthy blue eyes too.

"Lord Stephen won't inherit that title anytime soon, Your Grace. You have years to find him a wife, and he has time to accustom himself to the notion of a spouse. He adores his nieces, as I'm sure you know."

"He does, doesn't he?" A comforting notion, despite the fact that Stephen was always careful to couch his affection in irascible tones. "The girls adore him too. He taught Hester how to pick locks and he's showing her how to build clocks."

"A fine skill for a duke's daughter to have."

"He reads to them," she said more softly, "and he changes all the knights in the stories into warrior maidens, and makes the dragons l-limp." Oh, *drat* the sentimentality that came with carrying a child.

"Your Grace," Sir Leviticus said, holding out a lawn handkerchief. "This is most unfair. I can battle opposing counsel on the most complex cases, recite the common law of contracts from end to end, and bear arms in defense of my country, but a lady's tears render me powerless."

Jane dabbed at her eyes, while mentally cursing motherhood, charming solicitors, and complicated family situations. She could not tell this stranger that Constance had gone in search of a daughter soon to be shipped off to the ends of the earth. Could not convey to him that

Rothhaven and Constance would allow only Stephen's assistance on that errand.

Could not tell him that Quinn hadn't slept for most of the past two nights, and probably wouldn't sleep until his siblings were back at Lynley Vale, and his prodigal niece under guardianship to a duke or two.

"I apologize for burdening you with this display," she said. "Lady Althea is soon to wed, and while we are overjoyed for her and for Lord Nathaniel, every change is an adjustment."

Sir Leviticus held up a plate of tea cakes. "My wife grows weepy from time to time. An occasional sweet seems to calm her humors."

Good Lord, how much had Stephen told him? Jane took a raspberry tea cake and found that it did taste particularly satisfying.

"I have not met Lord Nathaniel," Sir Leviticus said, topping up his tea. "I gather few people can claim that honor. Are the nuptials imminent?"

The tea, the sandwich, and the sweet were fortifying. Jane was supposed to be conducting an interrogation, after all. Quinn would expect no less of her, and she expected no less of herself. Why would a lawyer ostensibly in Stephen's employ come pelting out to Lynley Vale, when Stephen's interests were not in jeopardy?

"The happy couple has yet to set a date," she said, "and neither are they having banns called. We will probably come down to breakfast some morning and find ourselves with a new brother-in-law. Wentworths can be impetuous in matters of the heart. Tell me, Sir Leviticus, did you grow up in Yorkshire?"

"I did, Your Grace, but I was sent off to public school to get the accent beaten out of me. Headmaster was not entirely successful. Then it was off to Spain to chase Boney's minions back to France. Another tea cake?"

"No, thank you. Have you any legal dealings with the Rothmere family, Sir Leviticus?"

He set his teacup down a bit too slowly. "Why would you ask that, Your Grace?"

"Because I can think of no other reason for a well-to-do solicitor to race out from town, full of news about some matter involving Lord Stephen—or involving the family his sister is soon to marry into. I thus conclude that his lordship set you to spying, and your skulking about has borne fruit. If the evil tidings relate to the Rothmere family, I can assure you we are in His Grace of Rothhaven's confidence regarding the family history and we regard it as just that: history." She rose, more quickly than she should have. "In the past, of *no moment*. Do I make myself clear?"

Sir Leviticus was on his feet as well. "Your Grace, may I be blunt?"

"You shall be nothing but."

"Lord Stephen asked me to do a favor for His Grace of Rothhaven. I thought the request odd, but lawyers are often expected to handle matters requiring discretion. Might we sit?"

He'd taken her elbow, which was fortunate, because the occasional fainting spell was always possible when carrying a Wentworth baby.

"His Grace of Rothhaven's favor is the motivation for your call?" Jane asked, sinking back into her chair.

"Rothhaven's request came through Lord Stephen, by letter."

"Why would...?" Jane stared hard at the tulips gracing the tea tray. She could smell them, and in her present condition, the fragrance was too sweet, even a little *rotten*.

"His Grace would only ask a favor of another solicitor if he needed assistance his own attorney could not provide," she said slowly, wishing Quinn hadn't jaunted off on social calls. "Do I have that right?"

All charm fled Sir Leviticus's expression, leaving only astonishment. "I cannot confirm the particulars of a matter entrusted to me in confidence."

"Then allow me to conjecture: You've seen something, heard rumors, or otherwise come across alarming information of the sort the duke's lawyers would not hear, and time is of the essence."

Sir Leviticus remained standing, his posture militarily straight. "Your Grace, while I would never want to offend—"

Jane waved him to silence. "Lord Nathaniel Rothmere and Lady Althea Wentworth are to wed. Rothhaven might have enemies, but he also has allies, will he, nill he. You either tell me what you know, or I will have the footmen keep you here, stuffing you with sandwiches, until Walden, Lady Althea, and Lord Nathaniel return from their outing."

A tense silence ticked by, during which Jane's belly chose to inform her that she was hungry. She'd *just* eaten, and she was abruptly famished.

"My wife would get on well with you," Sir Leviticus said. "I don't suppose you like rabbits?"

"To eat? Actually, no. I don't care for most game."

"Rabbits as pets," he said, gaze on a drawing Constance had done of Septimus, the house cat. "I refuse to violate a confidence, Your Grace, but I can tell you that I and my clerks move in less rarified legal circles than does

Rothhaven's man of business, and I can discuss with you the law of guardianship as it relates to mental incompetence."

Jane sent out a silent plea for Quinn to gallop home, though he'd be gone for hours yet.

"You are telling me—or rather, *not* telling me—that you have evidence of somebody scheming against Rothhaven, and he's to be brought before a commission of lunacy examiners." Quinn had explained that process to her, one his banks occasionally became entangled in when a customer grew dotty. "Worse yet, you are telling me this plot is already afoot, and Rothhaven isn't even on hand to begin preparing his defense."

Constance would be devastated, Quinn would be furious, and Stephen would be plotting violent felonies. As for Althea and Nathaniel, Jane could not guess how they would react, and Rothhaven... If anything ought to cause an epileptic duke to succumb to seizures, a scandalous lawsuit should suffice.

"I can see why Lord Stephen holds you in such esteem, Your Grace," Sir Leviticus said, "but I cannot confirm your conjectures."

"You don't deny them either. I hardly know Rothhaven, but I would pit his sanity against that of any peer. His tenancies thrive, his investments prosper, his only sibling has nothing but respect for him. This petition cannot be allowed to go forward, Sir Leviticus."

He subsided into his chair. "I have not admitted to the existence of any petition, Your Grace."

His very posture, now that of a tired, unhappy man rather than a lancer preparing to charge, was admission enough.

The front door slammed and heavy footsteps sounded in the foyer.

Thank God. "Walden will demand to speak with you."

Sir Leviticus sat up. "I thought you said His Grace was from home?"

"He's back, and not a moment too soon."

* * *

"You'll want a tray for your guests, Reverend," Mrs. Hodges said, once she'd taken Constance's parasol and Robert's hat.

The tiny foyer was crowded, and the house smelled slightly of lye and tallow. The floors were nonetheless clean, the aging rugs recently beaten, and the corners free of cobwebs. The cleanliness would probably be a relief to Constance, though it meant little to Robert.

Soames's prison had been spotless.

"A pot of tea will do," Shaw said. "The *everyday*, Mrs. Hodges."

The housekeeper looked ready to mutiny at that blatant insult to newly arrived guests, but she bustled off toward the back of the house, while Ivy remained near Constance.

"Ivy," Shaw said, "to your room."

"But, Uncle..."

"To your room, and don't come down until you've copied at least an entire chapter of Matthew."

Constance patted Ivy's shoulder. "Do as your uncle says, Ivy. He and I have matters to sort out."

Ivy ran up the steps, and Shaw scowled after her. "Not a quarter hour after meeting you, and the girl is already inspired to further rebellions."

Constance swiveled a glittering gaze to Shaw. "Perhaps if Ivy had been allowed to spend more than a quarter of an hour with me, she might be more biddable."

Shaw bristled, clutching his prayer book to his chest as if it were his moral targe, deflecting arrows of disrespect.

"Might we continue this discussion someplace more private?" Robert asked.

Shaw marched down the corridor. "I cannot spare you much time. I am to lead a prayer group that meets every market day at the inn. I had allotted the remainder of the morning for quiet contemplation, the better to prepare for that solemn responsibility."

Robert would have bet his best microscope that the prayer group would be two venerable grannies and a gouty great-uncle dropped at the inn for safekeeping while their minders enjoyed the market and caught up over a pint of ale.

"My parlor is humble," Shaw said, "but you are welcome, despite interrupting my schedule and poor Ivy's peace."

"We apologize for that," Robert said, before Constance could raise a battle standard about the peace of a mother who had searched for years to find her daughter. "We want only what is best for the child."

"Pleased to hear it." Shaw settled his bulk into a reading chair near the hearth. That left a small, lumpy sofa opposite his chair, into which Robert assisted Constance. He took the place beside her, honestly grateful to get off his feet.

The night had been long, the day thus far fraught, and worry for Constance gave Robert's fatigue an edge of tension.

"You mustn't think that I don't love the girl," Shaw said, putting his prayer book on the low table beside his chair. "She is not to blame for the circumstances of her birth, and poor Etta was overjoyed when she and James took Ivy in. The girl has had a loving, Christian upbringing, and my sisters dote on her."

"I would like to dote on her too," Constance said, sitting forward. "Not spoil her, of course, but provide her some of the benefits I wish I could have provided in years past."

"Wealth," Shaw snapped. "Trappings of vanity, and sops to your conscience. You conceived her, my lady, but you didn't want the shame of raising her. You turned your back on her, and for that I do indeed judge you."

"I was fifteen," Constance began, in low, hard tones. "Not even out of the—"

"Well past the age of reason," Shaw retorted. "Old enough to grasp the consequences of your actions."

Well, damn. Robert cast around for a means of sending the combatants to neutral corners before Shaw ordered his guests off the property.

"Old enough to know right from wrong," Robert said, "but not old or wise enough to know a lying scoundrel when he made empty promises, and certainly not old enough to care adequately for a child, not without the support of family. Lady Constance's older brother, as head of her household, made the best provision for Ivy he could at the time, and placed the child with the Wilsons. He meant well, but I understand why his decision troubles you, Reverend."

"*Troubles* me? Sir, you refer to the *fate of a child* as if it's some…some mere trifle. Lady Constance's family has always had the means to provide for Ivy. The lady's elder brother acquired one of the highest titles in the land five years ago, and yet, her ladyship shows up only now, when Ivy must turn her sights to faraway lands and new opportunities. *I will not have it.*"

Constance's hands were fisted in her lap. "I started searching for Ivy as soon as I had the pin money to undertake that effort."

"Why not simply ask your brother what had become of his niece? He's rumored to be as rich as three nabobs. He could have waved his hand and located Ivy within a fortnight."

"If you knew the torment my brother went through," Constance began, "the risk my behavior caused to his business at a time when a fledgling bank was all he had, if you had any inkling how fragile a bank's reputation is regardless of how exalted its owner becomes... If you knew how vile the peerage can be when they believe somebody of high station has faltered... His Grace of Walden did what he thought was best for Ivy at the time. When I had the ability to act on my own initiative, I took it. I do not expect my brother to fight the same battle for me twice, much less at peril to his own interests.

"Moreover," Constance went on, rising to pace the faded carpet, "a small army of investigators and more than a little luck were required to find Ivy, because you have taken no legal steps to assume guardianship of her." Constance rounded on Shaw and came to a halt. "She's *my* daughter. Finding her was *my* responsibility, and now that I have found her, I don't intend to let her go."

Oh, blast and bedamned, that was the absolute wrong thing for Constance to say.

"And there," Shaw replied, shoving out of his wing chair and grabbing his prayer book, "is the headstrong, disrespectful, self-centered nature that I vow I will not allow Ivy to develop. A worse influence on the girl I could not imagine than an arrogant aristocrat who swans across the village green, no respect for the family who has raised Ivy from birth. You assume that pretty dresses and silver teapots should mean more to a young woman's well-being than a chance to serve God."

Constance sent Robert a desperate look, as if she knew she'd taken a sharp wrong turn but could not find her way back to the right path.

Shaw glowered at Robert, as if he too expected mediation, placatory gestures, something, from the duke who sat like a useless clod on the lumpy sofa.

The peculiar, half-asleep, pins-and-needles sensation skipped down Robert's arms and across his nape.

Say something. Do something.

"You abet this woman," Shaw snapped. "What have you to say for yourself, Your Grace?"

Robert heard the words. He deduced from Shaw's tone that he was supposed to reply. He perceived Mrs. Hodges coming through the open parlor door, a tray in her hands, and he knew that he was having a staring spell at the worst possible time.

"Yonder duke disdains to answer me," Shaw said. "You may return the tray to the kitchen, Mrs. Hodges. My apologies for putting you to the trouble. His Grace and Lady Constance will be leaving."

Shaw crossed his arms, barely possible given his rotund girth, and jerked his chin toward the door. Had Robert been capable of clapping, he would have applauded the reverend's sheer arrogance. A man who'd dismiss a duke so summarily was either brave or sorely misguided, possibly both.

And a man who'd disrespect Constance deserved transportation.

"Your Grace?" Constance said, resuming the place beside Robert. "Are you well?"

"Of course he's well," Shaw said. "In the prime of life and thinking his consequence would be enough to blind me to my Christian duty. I have asked you both to leave, and as Ivy's uncle, I warn you that further meddling in the girl's life will not be permitted."

Say something. Do something.

Constance put a hand on Robert's arm. "Rothhaven?"

Robert managed a nod, but from the worry in Constance's eyes, he knew his lapse had been obvious to her.

"Must I toss you from the premises bodily?" Shaw asked. "Our discussion is at an end."

Stand. Stand on your own two feet, and say something sensible. With Constance's aid, Robert rose.

"Matthew, chapter 22, verse 39," Robert said. "...*and thou shalt love thy neighbor as thyself.* Lady Constance seeks a chance to show her daughter the love of a mother who is far from perfect, but who has never faltered in her attempts to do the right thing by her only daughter. Who or what is it you love, *Reverend*, when you keep a mother and daughter apart, and drag that child away to someplace she doesn't want to go, the better to further your own ambitions?"

Robert had spoken slowly and carefully, his voice flatter than normal, and the result was a tone more arrogant than he'd intended.

Shaw lowered his arms. "How *dare* you? How *dare* you both? I could demand coin of you, I could threaten you with scandal, I could have called the magistrate on you for even approaching Ivy, and this is how you respond to reasonable reservations on my part? You insult me in my own home, and I have had enough. Mrs. Hodges, show them out. *Now*."

Constance was as pale as funeral lilies, though she appeared composed. "Rothhaven, let's be going, shall we?"

She kept her hand on Robert's arm, though she was escorting him more than he was escorting her. Constance was at the front door tying her bonnet ribbons when Ivy came thundering down the steps.

"You can't leave like this!" she said, throwing her arms around Constance. "I don't want to go to blasted Australia, and Uncle is wrong to toss you out."

Mrs. Hodges passed Robert his hat. "You'd best leave, Your Grace, my lady. The reverend might eventually calm down, but not if he thinks you've provoked the young miss to outright disobedience."

Robert braced one hand on the newel post and used the other to tap his hat onto his head. "If her ladyship writes to Ivy, can you see that the letter reaches her?"

"I will try, Your Grace. Ivy, for the love of God, get back to your room."

Mother and child hugged each other, for what might be the only time, and Robert had to force himself not to dwell on memories of his own mother hugging him desperately tight before he'd been packed into a traveling coach headed for "school." He hadn't seen the duchess again for more than a decade.

His mother had been overcome with tears, while Constance was dry-eyed and coherent, but he had no doubt their heartaches were of equal measure.

"Please, Ivy," Mrs. Hodges whispered. "You must not anger the reverend. Once he digs in his heels, there's no moving that man."

Constance stepped back. "I will write to you, I promise. This battle is not over, Ivy Wentworth."

The battle might well be over, and be resoundingly lost too, but use of the Wentworth family name had the girl smiling.

"Miss Ivy, a pleasure to have met you." Robert bowed over the girl's hand and then offered his arm to Constance.

She left Shaw's rickety little house, head held high, and walked beside Robert with all the dignity of a duchess.

"I'm sorry," he said. "I let you down. I should have disarmed Shaw's growing ire, and I did not."

"You could not. I know that."

I warned you this would happen. Robert kept those pointless, petty words behind his teeth. "I am still sorry."

"I met my daughter," Constance said, emotions roiling and seething beneath her words. "For years, that was the sum of my ambitions, and had you not spurred Miss Abbott's efforts, I might have never even seen Ivy."

The busy green came into view, and a wave of physical fatigue washed over Robert. "You could follow her to Australia." Those words needed to be said.

"Not without you," Constance replied, "and I won't ask that of you."

I'm sorry for that too. "I see Lord Stephen, trying to look harmless and bored. Shall we have him up to our sitting room?"

"That will cause talk. I will shop for a bit and then join you upstairs soon. You should probably rest."

Constance was being remarkably perceptive and considerate, though Robert felt dismissed. He felt, in fact, humiliated, inadequate, and unworthy.

"I do need a nap." He risked a buss to her cheek, and she caught him by the hand.

"*I* failed, Rothhaven. *Me*—Lady bloody Constance, mother without portfolio *or* daughter. I failed to heed common sense when a young man flattered me shamelessly. I failed to speak up when Quinn assumed I would not want to raise my own daughter. I would hate myself for that, but what did I know? I was fifteen, panicked, and ashamed. I failed to find Ivy when the whole situation might have been resolved years ago. I failed to approach Whitlock

Shaw appropriately and then made a bad situation worse. Your staring spell is not to blame."

How he loved her, and how she broke his heart. "My staring spell did not help, and there will be others."

"I knew you had staring spells, seizures, and a lovestruck brother when I agreed to be your duchess. I have not changed my mind, Rothhaven, and I shall not."

"I will try to buy the ship Reverend Shaw has booked passage on. That might slow him down for a short time. Passage to New South Wales isn't arranged in a moment."

Constance stroked his knuckles. "I adore you. You think like a Wentworth. Ivy calls the reverend Uncle Witless when she's wroth with him."

"We must not make the mistake of thinking him witless. I believe that is his worst fear, to be thought a fool rather than a conscientious man of God."

"You could well be right. I will report to Stephen, and you will rest." She kissed his cheek and strolled away, her every step conveying determination and courage.

Robert probably had another staring spell as he watched Constance's retreat, or perhaps he'd simply become lost in thought, as the saying went. He was too tired to care, but he would most assuredly ascertain whether passage for an additional female with an appropriate companion could be booked on the ship Ivy would take in a few short weeks.

And if so, he would make those arrangements as quickly as possible, before selfish ends obliterated his more honorable inclinations.

Chapter Seventeen

Constance pretended to read Byron under the enormous oaks of the green. When she could no longer support that farce, she examined hair ribbons, particularly the bright green satins and rich brown velvets that would flatter a girl with Ivy's coloring. When Constance had endured that torment as long as possible—Rothhaven needed quiet to rest—she wandered to the bench nearest the alewife's stall.

Stephen hobbled over, tankard in one hand, cane in the other. He made a convincing tinker, and wearing the blue-tinted spectacles and rumpled clothing, he also managed to appear older than he was.

"I take it matters did not go well." He remained standing, casually using the massive tree trunk for support. To any passerby, he'd be enjoying a patch of shade while perusing the market crowd. A few feet away, a lady would be doing the same on her solitary bench, while they politely ignored each other.

"*Matters* went horribly," Constance said. "Ivy is wonderful. If I try to explain the details to you now, I will end up marching back to Reverend Shaw's house and drawing his arrogant cork."

Stephen took a placid sip of his ale. "That's encouraging."

"Explain yourself." *Or I will draw your cork.* The violence of Constance's anger was both frightening—she never lost her temper—and inadequate. Ivy was bound for *Australia*, and nothing Constance could do or promise would change that.

She was angry with Reverend Shaw and—for no defensible reason—with Rothhaven.

"For too long," Stephen said, "you have been content to paint away your megrims, to have a nip or three on the bad days, and keep yourself to yourself. A daughter is worth fighting for, and that you want to plant Reverend Witless Show a facer doesn't mean you're a devil like Jack Wentworth. You are simply a mother frustrated beyond bearing."

"Witless Show? Is that what they call him hereabouts?"

"The alewives are a merry lot. Would it cause too much scandal if I shared that bench with you?"

Such a question meant Stephen's leg was paining him. "You had better not. Have you proper clothes with you or only the disreputable kind?"

"I have both. Did Rothhaven abandon you at your request, or must I have a chat with him about unmarried ladies and the behavior of a proper escort?"

"We are in *Fendle Bridge*, Stephen, not Mayfair. Any number of unmarried ladies are strolling the green without causing talk."

"And to think I have no use for life in the country

with all these fair damsels wandering at large. Where is Rothhaven?"

"Asleep, I hope." He'd been so apologetic, and yet his staring spell could not have come at a worse time. She'd been furious with him, and that was shameful, so she'd admitted what anger she could—anger at herself. She was still angry at herself.

"Your gallant duke is *asleep*?" Stephen took another sip of his ale, perhaps to buy time to marshal his own temper. "You lose the opening skirmish with Ivy's uncle, and Rothhaven puts his feet up, catches forty winks, and leaves you to wander brokenhearted among the yeomanry?"

"He had a staring spell as the discussion grew heated," Constance replied. "Reverend Shaw expected the gallant duke to curry the favor of a mere country parson. Shaw was instead treated to a cold, awkward silence. Rothhaven is unhappy with himself."

"*I* am unhappy with him. What manner of staring spell?"

"For a short time, he neither moves nor speaks. He appears to be asleep with his eyes open. I gather he could hear what was said around him, but he could not reply. Shaw took it as something like the cut direct, and I didn't help matters."

Stephen shifted his weight and set the tankard on the bench, so he could brace himself on both the back of the bench and his cane.

"You were in a towering fit of pique, and I wasn't there to see it. Have you considered next steps?"

"No."

Stephen waited with damnable fraternal patience.

"I can write to Ivy through the housekeeper, Mrs. Hodges. She appears to care for Ivy and she's patient with the reverend."

"A saint among women. I need to sit in the next two minutes or I will fall upon my arse, causing both talk and unnecessary humiliation. Go put Rothhaven out of his misery. He's doubtless castigating himself without limit for what was probably a doomed mission to begin with. I will nose around and see what I can learn about the larger picture."

For form's sake, Constance wanted to argue. To be ordered about by a younger brother who sounded unnervingly like their ducal sibling was annoying. Merely annoying, though, not enraging.

"Take the bench," Constance said, rising. "Can you transform yourself back into a prancing dandy and join us for dinner tonight?"

"Prancing, Con?" He slid onto the bench with a sigh. "I should live so long as to ever in my life prance."

"One can prance figuratively. Rothhaven asked me about emigrating to Australia." She made a production out of opening her parasol and adjusting it over her shoulder.

"You are tempted."

"His Grace cannot go with me, Stephen. He can barely tolerate coach travel at night, he regulates what he eats ruthlessly, and he must have rest and quiet, which are nearly impossible to assure on board a ship. I cannot ask him to travel that far away from his brother and familiar surroundings. Not yet."

"And you won't abandon him, though Ivy cannot stay here. I'm sorry, Con."

"I accepted his marriage proposal, Stephen. I knew what I was getting into."

"No," Stephen said, examining the handle of his cane, "you did not. Neither did Rothhaven. That is the nature of marriage—a vast and perilous unknown temptingly draped in promises of romance and erotic pleasure—and why you will not find me sticking my toe or any other part of me in parson's mousetrap. Away with you, or Rothhaven will fret himself into a twitteration thinking he's disappointed you."

He *had* disappointed Constance, and she had disappointed Ivy, and the reverend was a disappointment all around. "We'll hire a private dining room for supper and keep country hours—and Stephen?"

He looked up and for a moment, Constance recalled the vulnerable, furious boy he'd been, and how fiercely he'd fought for a scrap of dignity.

I am not the only one in the habit of keeping myself to myself. "Thank you. Thank you for everything."

He touched his fingers to the brim of his top hat, a jaunty tinker flirting with a lady far above his station, as jaunty tinkers were wont to do.

Constance crossed the street to the inn and climbed the steps to the inn's best rooms. She and Rothhaven were Mr. and Mrs. Rothmere here, only a slight distortion of the truth. She used her key to let herself into the sitting room and came upon her duke asleep on the sofa, boots off, shirt open at the neck, a pillow behind his head.

Constance refastened the lock, and when she turned away from the door, Rothhaven was regarding her.

"Don't get up," she said, taking the chair at an angle to the sofa. "I gave Stephen the bare outline of our call on Reverend Shaw. Stephen—properly attired—will meet us for a private dinner. He asked me what my next steps will be, and I hadn't an answer for him."

Rothhaven sat up and scrubbed a hand through his hair. "You must not despair, Constance. You have come far today, and Ivy herself welcomed you with open arms. For her to know that you did not willingly part from her, that you searched for her until you found her, that you want her in your life, will mean more to her than you can know."

He spoke from the bitter experience of a boy banished by his own father for an ailment that boy could not help.

"What was the worst part?" Constance asked, shifting to take the place beside him. "When you were trapped out on the moors in that awful place, what was the worst part?"

He tucked an arm around her shoulders, as if perhaps he thought better that way, and some of the misery in Constance's heart eased.

"Three demons converged," he said, "to nearly steal the spark of reason from my mind and the humanity from my soul. First, I was alone. Second, I had no idea if I would ever return to a life I could enjoy living. Third, I saw no point to my continued incarceration. I wasn't getting better, I wasn't serving a penance for a crime I'd committed, I wasn't earning somebody else's happiness with my misery. The suffering of those interned in Soames's hospital was entirely unredeemed, potentially endless, and utterly meaningless."

"And of those three horrors—the isolation, the lack of a hopeful future, the meaninglessness of your suffering—which was the worst?"

He took her hand in both of his. "The isolation. Then you came along, and showed me that I did not have to be alone. Soames's evil genius was that he managed to make a half dozen people feel alone while we literally took every meal together and dwelled under the same roof. You knew how to fight that darkness, and taught us how to fight it too. You saved my life, Constance. I want you to know that."

He was being kind, reminding her that she was more

than the failed mother of an adolescent bound for the ends of the earth.

"Thank you," she said, because thanks were in order.

"But you are still heartbroken, I know. Let's go to bed, shall we? You slept as poorly in your brother's coach as I did."

She could say no without offending him, could claim a need to think, or to draft her first letter to her daughter. Rothhaven would considerately leave her in peace and finish his much-needed nap in the big bed in the other room.

But Stephen's words repeated in her head: *You keep yourself to yourself....* And where had that landed her? Painting in her bare feet and hiding from the world. Simply touching Rothhaven, talking to him, hearing his voice, brought her comfort.

"I don't want to be alone right now," she said, turning her face into his shoulder. "I am more upset than I have ever been. I don't want to lose her just as I've found her, Rothhaven. I *cannot*."

He rose and drew Constance to her feet. "Dwell on the positive aspects of the situation for now. She won't leave for weeks, she is a wonderful girl, she wants to know you better, and we have many resources. You are tired and have had an overwhelming morning. Come to bed."

Constance went into the bedroom hand in hand with Rothhaven, and he undressed her as she let fatigue and sheer shock steal over her. She had met her daughter. Her lovely, delightful, stubborn, outspoken daughter. She could lose that daughter without ever seeing her again, and that was unbearable.

When Rothhaven had Constance down to her shift, he gave her a gentle push toward the steps beside the bed.

"You will join me?" Closeness with him, the man who knew her secrets, who shared her burdens, had become imperative.

"Not until I'm wearing less than you are, but yes."

Rothhaven peeled his shirt over his head, stepped out of his breeches, and neatly folded his clothing on the clothes press. Constance had seen him all but unclothed before, but this mundane display was more dear. She would see him like this often, moving around a bedroom in the altogether, preparing for sleep. His hair was tousled, his eyes ringed with fatigue, and yet, he was a splendid specimen—lean, muscular, well proportioned, and hers to love.

"Come to bed," she said, holding up the blankets.

Rothhaven climbed in beside her and spooned himself around her. He was mildly aroused, which Constance considered normal when a mostly healthy man contemplated sharing a bed with his lover. She drifted off on the thought that *this* was the tonic she needed.

Rothhaven's arms around her, his company, his warmth. The challenge of Ivy's situation was daunting, and it might never be happily resolved, but at least Constance would not face that pain alone.

* * *

You appear to have lost your shift, my dear.

Robert was unable to offer that observation aloud because Constance was kissing him. He'd awakened to find her straddling his lap, her breasts a feminine benediction against his chest.

"I didn't want to impose," he whispered, when she paused to nuzzle his ear. "Didn't want to bother you."

"You bother me. You bother me without ceasing." She

switched to his other ear. "I dreamed I was bothering you right back and awakened full of ideas."

"This isn't why I suggested we nap." Though Robert's masculine accoutrements thought Constance had lit upon the best idea in the whole world.

"We napped. Now I'm suggesting we move on to other agreeable activities." She rocked her hips, and *agreeable* became the most spectacular understatement in the language.

"Again, please."

She was a fiend, eventually sliding to his side to fondle him in ways that sent reason flying out the window. Her hand was an instrument of naughty, delightful inspiration, and her mouth…

"I'll spend," Robert whispered, eyes closed, hands fisted in the sheets. "If you don't cease this instant…"

She licked him slowly, like a favorite ice on a hot day, then desisted, only to straddle him again and sink down over his arousal on a single, sure glide of her hips.

"A moment," Robert rasped. "Please allow me a moment."

Constance folded onto his chest, her breath fanning across his shoulder. "I love being this close to you. Love touching you wherever I please."

"And I love touching you." Rejoiced in it, in fact. "For years I dreaded every tactile interaction with another person. You touch me, and I am saturated in pleasure."

She kissed his cheek. "Do you still own that awful place?"

"Gave it to a charity."

"Drat. I would have loved to help you burn it down." She began to move, igniting an altogether different sort of fire, and words became impossible. She raised herself off his chest, took his hands and put them on her breasts, then hung over him, panting while he tried not to lose his mind.

"You first," he managed.

"*You*..." She came at him harder without speeding up.

Robert held out, somehow, while she drove herself against him with all the passion and determination one courageous soul contained. When he could withstand the battering no longer, he bowed up to wrap her in his arms.

"Together, Constance."

She keened against his shoulder, a sound as much of grief as of pleasure, and he held her until she collapsed against him, then sank back with her against the mattress.

"Damn you," she panted, several minutes later as he smoothed his hands over her hair. "Damn you, Rothhaven."

As scolds went, that one was endearingly pathetic. "If you wanted a lap dog in your bed, you should have accepted a proposal from one of the Town dandies lusting after your settlements."

She lifted up enough to peer at him. "I did want to be in charge. For once."

"You want to be *in charge*, while I am *in love*." He brushed her hair back from her cheek, adoring the sight of her rosy and replete. "In charge ought not to signify, Constance. Not here. We will find a way for you to be together with your daughter. I promise you that. I am your ally in that fight, and I will not desert you."

Robert had no idea how to keep that promise, but he knew very well that he would not part a child from the mother who longed to be with her. When Constance again tucked close, Robert held her gently, as if she might break, as if he might soon have to let her go forever.

* * *

Unhappy couples in Stephen's experience all exuded the same combination of resentment, despair, and bitterness. Some went about it silently, some sniped and carped at each other before company, others pretended harmony in public, though never very convincingly.

The misery was obvious to him, no matter its form.

Happy couples, by contrast, exhibited variety in the joy they took in their couple-dom. Quinn and Jane, for example, had learned to hide most of their shared passion, and yet it smoldered beneath polite manners, parenting discussions, and exquisite social deportment. A casual brush of hands when Quinn removed Jane's cloak, and a spark would waft up on the marital breeze. Jane would smile and declare a need to retrieve a book from her private sitting room. Quinn would offer to help her find it, and off they went, chatting about some infernal bill in the Lords that Quinn was determined to see tabled.

Cousin Duncan and his Matilda were even more obvious. They could make a chess game into an erotic pavane without saying a word. At the conclusion of the game, Duncan would declare himself defeated and determined on revenge. Matilda would smile and note that the hour grew late. The combatants would wander up the steps to bed, ostensibly discussing queens adept at capturing unsuspecting knights.

Hardly subtle.

Rothhaven and Constance went about the whole business differently. Rothhaven seated Constance at the table, no little whispers or stolen touches tucked into his courtesies. Constance barely acknowledged his assistance, but when she took up the bottle of wine, she served her duke first.

"So what have you learned, Stephen?" she asked, filling Stephen's glass as well.

Rothhaven took his seat, to appearances quite the serious aristocrat, but when he gazed at Constance, his eyes gave away a fondness more palpable than attar of roses at close range.

"Half a glass for me," Rothhaven said, switching his full glass for Constance's empty one. "Your lordship, welcome. Your report would be appreciated."

Constance did as somebody told her to for once and poured His Grace only half a glass of merlot.

"I learned that Fendle Bridge is a typical English village," Stephen said, hooking his canes on the edge of the table. "Everybody lives in everybody else's pockets. Nobody has anything truly awful to say about Reverend Shaw, but they wish him good luck in the Antipodes rather enthusiastically."

"Any debts, scandals, or criminal issues in the reverend's past?" Rothhaven asked.

The merlot was passably good. "Alas, no. As the oldest son, he inherited the most from the parents. Two younger brothers now manage the engraving business in Leeds that Shaw came into upon his father's death. Shaw takes a share of the profits, while they do the work. Shaw tried his hand at teaching, but hadn't the patience for it as a younger man. His career as a vicar has been one unhappy patron after another."

"He doesn't fit in," Constance said, running a finger around the rim of her wineglass. "Having a half-grown girl in tow might help him fit in. Ivy will give her uncle Whitlock a domestic authority he otherwise lacks. He will appeal to the widows and spinsters more strongly for being a conscientious uncle, and despite being unmarried, he will have common ground with any parents in his congregation."

Rothhaven watched her fingertip trail around the top of the glass. "What do we know of the rest of Shaw's household, of his family members? Sometimes, a man will beggar himself for those he loves, when he won't spend a penny to save himself."

Constance sent him a complicated, fulminating glance, one that promised something other than a delightful search for a missing book.

"You said you doubt he can be bribed," she murmured.

"I doubt he can be bribed, for which I respect him, but I hope he can be reasoned with."

The food arrived, brought in by large, cheerful young women, one of whom managed to brush her breast against Stephen's shoulder while putting the platter of sliced beef roast and potatoes on the table.

"Perhaps I should give country life another chance," Stephen said. "Rural folk are so friendly."

"I did notice a Brown Bess behind the innkeeper's desk," Rothhaven observed. "Looked to be in good repair too, but then, the poor fellow has four daughters."

Constance began serving the beef and potatoes. "What else did you learn about Reverend Shaw?"

"I learned the name of the solicitor handling the sale of his house, learned that he's been talking of emigrating for years, and learned that Mrs. Hodges is a well-liked widow of very limited means." Nothing of real value, in other words, which was frustrating.

Stephen had taken up his knife and fork, intent on filling his belly with proper food for a change, when a soft tap sounded on the door.

"I'm not expecting anybody," Stephen said.

"Come in," Rothhaven called.

The young man who entered appeared somewhat familiar, though he was dusty and windblown and clutching a soft cap in his hands.

"Beg pardon for intruding," he said. "I'm Sample, from the Lynley Vale stables. I have a written message for Lord Stephen Wentworth and I am not to give it to any but he, posthaste."

"I am Lord Stephen."

"Can you stand, please, my lord?"

Bloody hell. Stephen reached for his canes.

"I am Lady Constance, and that is my brother. You may give him the letter."

"Does he limp?" Sample asked. "I was told his lordship is sore afflicted with a limp, but that he might not be dressed proper-like and lord-ish."

"You can see he's using two canes," Constance replied. "Please give him his letter."

Rothhaven remained silent, sipping his wine, or pretending to.

Stephen accepted the letter. "From my York lawyer." He slit the seal, foreboding making the wine in his belly roil.

A coin flashed through the air, which Sample neatly caught.

"Get yourself some food," Rothhaven said. "If his lordship has a reply, he'll find you in the common within an hour or so."

Sample bowed and withdrew, taking the scent of horse and road dust with him.

"What does it say?" Constance asked. "The news has to be important if Althea's groom came all the way from Lynley Vale."

Rothhaven patted Constance's wrist, the gesture so casual Stephen nearly missed it. The news was bad, but not bad for Stephen, which was worse in a way.

"Rothhaven asked for the use of the eyes and ears of my best lawyer," he said. "Sir Leviticus has heard something alarming, but it doesn't concern me."

He passed the letter to Rothhaven, and Constance was on her feet, reading over His Grace's shoulder.

"That vile, skulking, putrid parasite," she said. "Who the hell does this Solomon Weatherby think he is, to question your competence?"

"He's a neighbor," Rothhaven replied. "One who doubtless knows I had a full-on shaking fit at the church. He very likely heard of a similar episode in York right outside Cranmouth's office. Both times I suffered my usual disorientation after such a spell, and—worst offense of all—I am wealthy. Thus I must be put under guardianship, lest I be taken advantage of." He folded the letter and put it on the table. "I am sorry, my dear. So very sorry."

A beat of quiet ticked by, while Stephen resisted the urge to upend the table. "How can you sit there as serene as a bishop at a baptism when your very freedom is once more at issue? I am concerned for you, and I make it a point to never bother about anybody but family, which you might well not become. I am concerned for Constance and Althea, who will be caught up in your legal scandal even if you never speak your vows, and I am also selfishly disinclined to have a certified lunatic for a brother-in-law. *Bad for business*, Rothhaven. Very bad for business."

"Hush, Stephen," Constance said, "or I will make you hush."

Constance had enormous self-control. Stephen had no

wish to see that control snap in his direction. "I apologize," he said, "but the situation is dire."

She sank back into her chair. "We have faced dire situations before."

Rothhaven's reaction to a dire situation was apparently to enjoy his supper. "The difference this time," he said, spearing a strip of roasted beef from the platter in the middle of the table, "is that a young girl also faces a dire situation. Her well-being must take precedence over my own." He chewed his beef, then used the edge of his fork to portion off a bite of potatoes.

"I wonder if you aren't truly daft," Stephen said. "Thirty miles away, a lawyer as crooked as he is determined is plotting your downfall. If that happens, you won't be permitted to marry, you won't be allowed to oversee your own finances while your so-called guardian bleeds you dry. All the while, you sit there eating god-damned *potatoes* rather than *doing something*."

Constance had gone silent, which was more unnerving than her display of temper.

"My lord," Rothhaven said, considering a forkful of buttery potatoes, "do I tell you how to handle your canes? When to exercise your game leg, when to rest it? Do I presume to know the best means of ameliorating the pain it causes you?"

"My leg rarely hurts."

Rothhaven saluted with his potatoes. "If you say so. I, on the other hand, have epilepsy. Experience suggests I had best leave the tantrums to others."

Constance took a sip of her wine, her grip on the glass perilously tight.

"I am not having a tantrum," Stephen said. "When I have a tantrum, I destroy the room."

Rothhaven looked at him with faint humor leavened by a dash of pity, and Stephen knew he'd had his last room-destroying histrionic fit.

"Here is how I suggest we proceed," Rothhaven said. "Constance and I will finish our meal. You, my lord, will pen a reply to Sir Leviticus acknowledging receipt of his missive and thanking him for his diligence. I will return to Rothhaven Hall tonight and confer with my brother and His Grace of Walden to ensure that my financial affairs are in order, and my family well provided for. You, however, are needed here, for I suspect Constance will remain close to Ivy for the nonce."

Constance set down her wineglass. "I will go with you, Rothhaven. You shall not face this without me."

Rothhaven put aside his knife and fork and patted Constance's hand. "My dear, I fear I must. You cannot fight this battle for me. When I lose, you must be at as great a distance from me as possible."

Constance turned her hand over and laced her fingers with Rothhaven's. "You are saying that I must choose between you and my daughter?"

Rothhaven kissed her knuckles. "There is no choice to be made, Constance. If Reverend Shaw took umbrage at an arrogant duke, he will have no dealings whatsoever with one declared mentally unfit, nor will he want Ivy associated with such an unfortunate wretch."

"But you aren't unfit, Rothhaven. You are the most..." Constance fell silent, and a tear dropped onto the worn planks of the table. "This is so unfair."

Stephen had said the same thing, countless times, about an unreliable, aching leg. He would keep his miserable excuse for an appendage and be grateful rather than endure the pain Constance and Rothhaven were suffering now.

"I'm off to write a note to Sir Levi," Stephen said, pushing to his feet. "Rothhaven, I'm sorry."

He'd said that more today than he had in the previous five years, and the words grew more bitter with each use.

"I am not sorry," Rothhaven replied. "I have known more joy in recent days than any man deserves." He saluted Constance with his wineglass, and Stephen moved toward the door.

If Constance needed to cry, she also needed for her brother to leave the room. By the time Stephen closed the door, Rothhaven was at Constance's side, his handkerchief already in his hand. Stephen stood outside the door as the sound of quiet weeping commenced.

One of the buxom serving maids went by with two tankards in each hand. "Done so soon, sir?"

"No longer hungry. Where can I find paper and ink?"

"Ask the missus at the front desk. She'll charge you dearly."

Stephen remained by the door, listening to his sister's sorrow. Rothhaven's voice was a low rumble punctuating the soft weeping, a stream of steady reason at a time when reason struck Stephen as obscene.

Rothhaven's calm put Stephen in mind of martyrs, unconcerned about their worldly demise, fixed only on the honor of sacrificing all for their beliefs. Such steadfast purpose, such clarity, nearly defied comprehension.

And for a man facing a challenge to his mental competence, that selfless serenity could be a very great problem indeed.

Chapter Eighteen

Constance wept until her sides ached and her face burned. She wept until her eyes stung, and she wept even more than that because once unleashed, her tears were limitless. Through it all, Rothhaven held her in his lap, stroked her back, and murmured platitudes.

"You mustn't take on so. This too shall pass. Perhaps this is for the best."

Though she doubtless looked hideous, Constance sat up and glowered at him the second time he mentioned that last bit.

"This is not *for the best*, you dratted man."

"Perhaps not, ultimately, but better to face Weatherby now rather than after Ivy's ship has sailed. You can go with her, Constance, and perhaps you ought to." The actual threat, according to Stephen's lawyer, was from Neville Philpot, whom Weatherby would put forth as Rothhaven's proposed guardian.

Lady Phoebe was likely the hand guiding this whole charade, an aspect of the situation Constance would discuss with Rothhaven later.

She hopped off his lap before he could spew more sweet, selfless reason. "I gave Ivy up long ago, because I honestly never thought I had a choice. Quinn assumed I would be loath to bring down the scandal of an illegitimate child on my family, and he was right. I never questioned him, though, never asked for more time to think, never explored whether I might have lived quietly with Ivy somewhere on the Dales."

She paced away from the table, thoughts tumbling into one another. "I told myself the very sort of nonsense you're spouting now: *The hurt will fade in time. I did the best I could. Giving Ivy two loving parents is for the best.* The lies we tell ourselves lest we go mad."

Rothhaven rose and came around the table. "As far as the world is concerned, I *am* mad, or the next thing to it on a bad day. I cannot control my fits, then I am nearly incoherent for some time afterward. My memory is unreliable at times, I cannot enjoy the usual pursuits of men of my station—no riding to hounds, no drunken bacchanals during the shooting season, no drunken anything, in fact."

He closed the distance between them. "We must also count up the results of my little sojourn in Dr. Soames's care. I cannot dance, my French is provincial, I am uncomfortable in open spaces, I refuse to submit to the hovering intrusion of a valet. I never went to public school or to university and thus have no aristocratic associates. If Weatherby hadn't brought suit, somebody else eventually would have, for I fail spectacularly as a duke."

Constance leaned against him. "You succeed splendidly as a man."

He embraced her, the sheer comfort of his arms bringing her near tears again. "We've met Reverend Shaw, Constance. He sets very great store by his own standing. He might allow you a place in Ivy's life if you are *Lady* Constance, wealthy and penitent younger sister of a duke. If Shaw knows you willingly married a man at risk to be declared a lunatic, he will keep the girl from you. I cannot be Ivy's guardian if I myself am subject to a guardianship."

"I hate you for your common sense. I love you for your honor."

"I love everything about you, especially your stubbornness, but I refuse to be the reason you lose the daughter you've searched for all these years."

Rothhaven would have held Constance for the rest of the night, and she was sorely tempted to let him.

"I'm returning to Lynley Vale with you," she said, stepping back. "We should finish our supper first."

"Madam, the less you're associated with me from this point forward, the better."

She took her seat and poured Stephen's serving of wine into her glass. "A bit late for that, Your Grace. Eat before the food gets cold. Stephen will fret if we tarry too long at our meal, and his fretting is not to be borne."

Rothhaven sat at the head of the table. "At least write Ivy a letter. Tell her you've returned to York the better to consider options, tell her where to write to you."

"Now that is a sensible suggestion. Would you care for bread?"

"No, thank you." He put a bite of beef in his mouth, chewed, then set down his fork. "Constance, are you sure you shouldn't remain here? Lord Stephen would bide with you, and his charm might be able to do with Shaw what my consequence could not."

"Stephen has guile, a very different article from charm. I am coming back with you to Lynley Vale, and there's an end to it. I will write to Ivy, you will have the horses put to, and by the time we're ready to go, it will be dark enough to travel."

Rothhaven pushed his potatoes around. "I hate this. I hate that I am a burden to you."

"The man who made it possible for me to find my daughter before she sailed from England will never be a burden to me." Those words weren't helpful, but Constance was at a loss for what reassurances might serve. Rothhaven picked at his food, and the moment became unbearable.

"Rothhaven, I'm sorry, but I cannot retrieve the last part of your soul from the moors. Some corner of you still believes that you deserved to be shut away for all those years. You suspect you might have earned Soames's torments. You wonder in the privacy of your thoughts if perhaps a guardian isn't the penance you've incurred for longing to be happy."

He frankly stared at her, his green eyes unreadable. That wary, guarded expression put her in mind of the much younger man she'd met all those years ago in Soames's private madhouse.

Constance ploughed on, before she lost her courage. "I did not realize I had choices where Ivy was concerned. I won't make that mistake again. If I am to be your duchess, then I have choices and I am choosing to return to Lynley Vale with you. You have choices too, but please, please, never doubt that you are as entitled to happiness as any other man. More so, in fact."

"And if I consent to have a guardian appointed?"

Good God, she'd never considered he might simply cede the field. "You think Philpot will be easier to deal with if you yield the battle without drawing your sword?"

"Possibly." Rothhaven poured himself a glass of water

from the pitcher in the middle of the table. "When the lawyers are involved, negotiation is always an option."

Constance rose, the food having lost anything approaching appeal. "Philpot is a solicitor, true, but he's also a scoundrel, and his wife a greater scoundrel than he. I would not trust them to exhibit decency to an old stray dog."

Rothhaven took a sip of water. The wine was good quality and there was plenty of it, but he chose water and probably always would.

"I'll order the coach brought around," he said, "but you must feel free to change your mind at any time, Constance. Ivy is your daughter, and if she were my daughter, I would want her mother to think of her first."

"Which is why I love you, and why I'm off to write her a brief letter." Constance left the room while she could still resist the temptation to throw plates at the wall.

Rothhaven remained alone at the table, sipping his water.

* * *

Neville Philpot typically spent the week in York, returning to his country estate on Friday afternoon and spending the next two days enjoying the pleasures of rural life. The schedule deviated if Phoebe required him to serve as host at one of her gatherings, but she was quite capable of holding entertainments without him as well.

The day's developments were simply too promising for him to keep to himself, and thus Wednesday evening found him enjoying a glass of brandy while Phoebe presided over the after-dinner teapot and worked at her embroidery.

"And how has your friend dear Elspeth been keeping?" he asked. "Weatherby is forever going on about his girls, but he never mentions his wife."

Phoebe threaded a needle with gold silk. "If she can help it, Elspeth Weatherby makes little mention of her spouse. I believe their arrangement more cordial than devoted. What of matters in town? Any interesting news?"

Neville took a sip of his brandy, savoring the moment, for he so seldom felt of use to his wife. Of course, he provided well—a man ought not to marry if he couldn't provide for his wife and offspring—but Phoebe could have had her pick of good providers.

"What is that you're working on?" he asked, which was naughty of him. Phoebe had requested his report, and he was being dilatory.

Her smile said she knew his game and knew that it must end with good news. "This is an altar cloth. Just because our church is humble is no excuse for it to be plain. I really ought to be assisting Sybil with the finishing touches on her trousseau, but Sybil will have years to embroider her pillowcases, while the parish will gather again in a few days."

"Do you suppose His Grace of Rothhaven will make another attempt to attend services?"

Phoebe knotted her thread and began stitching. "One hopes divine services bring comfort to the afflicted, but I will never forget the sight of that poor man, utterly overcome, nearly frothing at the mouth. The memory will give me nightmares. That his family put him on display in such a manner is a shame and a disgrace. When, I ask you, did advertising bad blood become proper behavior?"

As best Neville recalled, Rothhaven had put himself on display, charging up the aisle after his brother had taken his place in the family pew.

"Perhaps Lord Nathaniel couldn't talk him out of attending," Neville said, "or perhaps his lordship knew the conversation would be fruitless. You will be relieved to know that Solomon Weatherby is drafting a petition to have Rothhaven declared mentally unsound."

Phoebe's needle stilled. "Mr. Weatherby is a conscientious man of the law. We must commend him for an effort to protect a vulnerable peer from further embarrassment. Have you offered to serve as guardian if the court should see fit to appoint one?"

"You know I have, my lady."

"Good of you. Your task will be thankless and burdensome, I fear, when His Grace apparently cannot leave the Hall without suffering a fit. And did you know, there's no physician in residence at the Hall?"

"No physician?"

Phoebe's smile would have done the cat in the cream pot proud. "I overheard old Everett Treegum complaining to the apothecary that his rheumatism had lingered longer this spring than last. If a man suffers rheumatism, he'll go to a physician for treatment if a physician is on hand, won't he?"

Treegum was the Rothhaven steward. Ergo, no physician at Rothhaven Hall. "My lady, you should have been a barrister."

"What duke lacks a personal physician, Mr. Philpot? What duke afflicted with a potentially fatal disease eschews the aid of those best positioned to abate his misery?"

She was the picture of womanly grace, plying her needle in the quiet hours of the evening, and yet, her brilliance blazed brightly for anybody with the sense to appreciate it.

"I don't suppose you'd be willing to read Weatherby's draft petition if I can get hold of it?" Neville asked, refilling his brandy glass. "I know your days are already quite full, but you have an eye for detail that Weatherby's clerks are sure to lack."

"I am always happy to help, Neville—you know that—and I do thank you for coming all the way out from town to keep me apprised of these developments. I fear for His Grace, I truly do. It's a wonder he hasn't come to grief already, racketing about a crumbling pile, nobody to look out for his best interests."

"Your generosity of spirit does you credit, my dear. I don't suppose generosity of the marital kind might extend to a husband who has missed you sorely of late?"

He always asked before visiting her bed. Phoebe was still regularly indisposed, and he would not impose unwanted attentions on her for the world. Weaker vessels were available for casual pleasure, and a considerate husband made frequent, discreet, use of them.

"I've missed you too, Neville. I know your clients must come first, but I do miss you."

That was a yes. That was a gracious, smiling yes, and Neville silently thanked whatever god had imbued the Duke of Rothhaven with an unsound mind. Perhaps the same god would grant Phoebe a child, and as long as miracles were under discussion, why not a boy child?

* * *

Robert felt as if he'd been caught in a whirlpool, a force that would drag him relentlessly to the darkest depths no matter how hard he struggled against the current.

A wheeler had come up lame on the journey back to Lynley Vale and what should have been a four-hour ordeal was taking all night. Constance dozed in Lord Stephen's capacious coach, while Robert held her and battled demons.

She had stated the blunt truth: He felt in some corner of his soul as if he deserved punishment. Perhaps not for having the falling sickness, but for being unable to fool the world into believing him hale and whole, as his father had fooled the world.

The falling sickness had taken the lives of royalty, people who'd surely had the best, most conscientious care available. The malady was not a sign of God's disfavor any more than crossed eyes or a stammer indicated celestial judgment.

And yet...Robert hated every mile spent in even the most luxurious traveling coach imaginable. Hated the anxiety that dogged him whenever he left Rothhaven's walls, hated having to limit his sweets, his spirits, even the amount of tea he consumed in the course of a day.

"I cannot smoke a damned cheroot," he muttered, "cannot get drunk, cannot ride hell-bent on the most sure-footed mount. Cannot waltz, cannot enjoy a pipe of hashish, cannot go for a swim in the river on the hottest summer days."

"You're awake," Constance said. She lay on her side facing him as the coach rocked along in the gray mists of dawn.

"So are you." The sight of her, even rumpled and tired, made him smile. "Did you rest, or did you feign sleep in hopes that I'd rest?"

She pushed the hair off his brow. "I promise you this, Rothhaven: I am a poor hand at dissembling. I slept some. You?"

"No sleep that I'm aware of." Which was bad, because regular rest was the foundation upon which all Robert's strategies for coping with his malady relied.

"You can sleep at Lynley Vale," Constance said. "I will

deal with the family, or put them off until you are feeling more the thing."

She was so confident of her course, or perhaps—contrary to her own words—she was good at *appearing* confident.

"Before I find a bed," Robert replied, "I will send for Cranmouth. He must be alerted to what's afoot."

"Mr. Cranmouth made an unfavorable impression on me." Constance sat up and rested against the seat back. "I met him on only the one occasion, and he managed to be both unctuous and dismissive."

Robert could recall little of that incident, except a towering sense of humiliation. "I don't care for Cranmouth much myself, but Nathaniel has never had a problem with him. Cranmouth's father either kept the old duke's secrets or didn't pry enough to learn them, which also weighs in Cranmouth's favor. I have contemplated changing solicitors, but wanted the marriage settlements tidied up first."

"The marriage settlements are quite tidy, Your Grace." She patted her thigh. "Get comfortable. We've a few miles to go yet. Can you sack Cranmouth?"

Robert laid his head in her lap, and something about that position was more restful than trying to make do with thin pillows and wadded-up blankets.

"If, immediately before a very serious legal proceeding, I sack the solicitors who have represented my family for generations, I will look somewhat foolish, won't I? Foolish or daft."

Constance stroked his ear, a peculiarly soothing caress. "If Cranmouth has never defended a client from a competency petition, isn't that a strong reason to turn elsewhere for at least this one case?"

The accumulated aches of thirty miles' jostling eased

under Constance's touch, and even some of Robert's mental tumult quieted.

"I might hire additional counsel," he said, "but I ought not to break ranks with Cranmouth. You are putting me to sleep."

"Fatigue is putting you to sleep."

Rather than argue, he let himself drift and had almost reached the sweet oblivion of true slumber when the coach swayed around a sharp turn.

"We're nearly there," Constance said, patting his shoulder. "Time to wake up and be ducal."

The near-occasion of sleep left Robert groggier than simply soldiering on through fatigue would have. He nonetheless assisted Constance to put the coach to rights. He was sitting beside her, properly attired and trying to mentally compose a note to Cranmouth, when the coach rocked to a halt at Lynley Vale's front door.

Robert descended from the carriage, feeling ancient, exhausted, and none too optimistic.

"You're home," Althea said, rushing past Robert to take Constance's arm before he could offer that courtesy. "Breakfast is waiting, and Quinn and Jane are most anxious to discuss matters."

"*Matters* must wait," Robert said. "Lady Constance is fatigued from her exertions, and our sortie to Fendle Bridge was not entirely successful."

Nathaniel, who was apparently already stepping into the role of host at Lynley Vale, waved the coach off to the carriage house.

"Did you meet the girl?" he asked.

Constance stopped her sister from dragging her into the house. "We met *my daughter*, your lordship. Ivy is in every regard a lovely young lady, though her circumstances are less than ideal. Thank you for asking."

The ladies continued on their way, heads close together.

"You deserved that," Robert remarked. "Constance is delightfully fierce when her protective instincts are aroused."

Somewhere down the drive, birds took up their matutinal songs. The sun hadn't yet cleared the horizon, but daybreak was imminent.

"Does Constance know what Lord Stephen's solicitor had to say?" Nathaniel asked.

"Of course, and her opinion on the matter would make a sailor blush. Let's walk a bit, shall we? After being cooped up all night, I find some fresh air welcome."

Nathaniel sent him a brooding look. "You want to wander down the drive, under the open sky, no fog, no mist, to obscure the horizon?"

A line of Shakespeare came to Robert: *This thou perceiv'st, which makes thy love more strong, / To love that well which thou must leave ere long.*

"Yes, Nathaniel, I do. I want to enjoy a pretty sunrise in the company of my soon-to-be-married brother. I want to clear my head with the fresh Yorkshire air. I want to give Constance a rest from fretting about me, and I want to put off, for a few moments, the ordeal of conferring with Walden and his duchess. Any more questions?"

"That woman is turning you into a duke."

Robert ambled along the crushed shells of the drive, enjoying the sound of his own footsteps, enjoying the birdsong, enjoying the golden light shining over the land rolling away to the east. So precious, this freedom, and he might soon have to part with it.

"*That woman* is becoming a duchess, but she will always also be a mother who regrets bidding her firstborn child farewell. Ivy is in the care of a bachelor uncle, a man of God who is determined to move his household to Australia. He has booked passage for himself and the girl on a ship due to leave next month."

"And this weighs on your mind more heavily than what Philpot and Weatherby are cooking up?"

Robert wandered over to a stone wall bordering a sheep pasture. Lynley Vale's flocks had yet to be shorn, though that work would start soon. He found a smooth patch and used the wall as a bench, the better to watch the sun come up.

"You have the right of it: The situation with Ivy weighs on my mind more heavily than the lawyers intriguing against us. A child who feels abandoned by her family exceeds what my conscience can bear. I have all but begged Constance to set herself apart from me, to emigrate to bloody Australia without me if that will reunite her with her daughter, but she refuses to go. My duchess will not abandon me, and I cannot make myself abandon her."

"Have you considered simply allowing Philpot to become your guardian?" Nathaniel shoved back to sit on the wall and posed that question casually—too casually.

"I did. You would prevent Philpot from his worst excesses, as long as you were extant. Walden would take a hand in matters, and my life would remain tolerable, at least in the opinion of most people. I would likely be confined to the Hall and its grounds, and some doddering old physician would suggest I be regularly bled, which would do exactly nothing to reduce the incidence of my seizures."

"You know that?"

"Soames bled me every day for a fortnight at one point. The seizures grew markedly worse the longer he persisted with his experiment. Alexander threatened to notify an uncle of what was afoot—an uncle who was a member of the Royal College of Physicians—and the experiment ended."

"And you would risk going back to that sort of life?"

"I am at risk for being *sent* back to that sort of life."

"No, you are not. You appear before the commission of lunacy, tell the examiners good King George sits on the throne. Identify yourself as Alaric Gerhardt Robert Rothmere, eleventh duke of Rothhaven. Tell them your date of birth, and that you dwell at Rothhaven Hall, and what day of the week it is. They dismiss the petition and there's an end to it."

Nathaniel, a brave, determined, tough-minded man, was afraid.

Robert was afraid too. Terrified, in fact. "And if I have a seizure in the midst of the festivities?"

"They suspend the proceedings until you're recovered, the same as they would if a lady witness swooned in the middle of her testimony."

A lamb rose from the grass and shook itself from head to tail. Another leapt up a few yards away and pronked and gamboled over to the first.

Such a sweet, happy scene. "A lady is permitted a fit of the vapors, Nathaniel. A duke is held to a different standard. I am honestly not as concerned about a seizure as I am about a staring spell. When Constance and I met with Ivy's uncle, the discussion was difficult. He is a man who craves respect, and at the height of one of his diatribes, I failed to respond sensibly. I failed to respond *at all*, in fact, and he took offense."

"Then he's a fool."

"He is the fool in authority over Ivy, and if I am declared a lunatic—and possibly even if I am not—the fool will sail away with her, perhaps never to be seen again."

The first slanting beams of morning sun crested the hill to the east, the gentle warmth palpable on Robert's face. Another benediction, like the birdsong, like the pleasure of a private conversation with Nathaniel, like the scent of lush spring grass and the sound of Lady Althea's fountain, splashing a few yards up the drive.

Life was so beautiful, given half a chance. For years, Robert had not seen the beauty, not tasted it or smelled it, not allowed it to touch his body, much less his heart.

Nathaniel pushed off the wall, and in the bright morning sun, Robert realized his brother was tired. He'd likely been up all night, holding a vigil not for the Duke of Rothhaven or for the Rothmere family patriarch, but for a brother he'd die to protect.

"Have I ever thanked you for all you've done for me?" Robert asked, hopping off the wall and dusting the seat of his breeches. "Ever told you how much I appreciate the years you managed the impossible without a word of complaint?"

"No, but feel free to embarrass us both with your effusions now."

Robert punched Nathaniel's arm, hard enough to convey affection, not hard enough to bruise. "If I fight this petition, Nathaniel, it won't be for your sake. You needn't feel guilty on that score."

Nathaniel strolled toward the house, though doubtless, in his mind he was strolling in Lady Althea's direction.

"Please tell me you have found some reason to fight Weatherby. I cannot bear to see you lose your freedoms now, Rothhaven. You have come too far, achieved too much—and oh, by the way, you are as mentally competent as any other peer, if not more so."

"There is that," Robert muttered, falling in step beside

his brother. "There is also the fact that Constance is depending on me. A lunatic duke cannot aid a lady to establish a relationship with her daughter. He is a flaming liability to her, in fact. A duke in full possession of his faculties might be able to help."

As one dark, uncomfortable mile had followed another, Robert had gradually settled on this conclusion. He might be able to tolerate the gilded cage of Philpot's guardianship, but what of Nathaniel, forced back into the role of champion but fighting Robert's battles without the weapons of familial authority?

What of *Ivy*? Sent to the ends of the earth when a mother with considerable resources longed to resume a place in her daughter's life, but could not—because Robert refused to contest a legal petition.

And what of Constance? Yoked to a half-duke, a man with all the standing of a peer and no more authority than a toddler confined to the nursery.

"I will fight the petition to the best of my ability," Robert said, "while planning for the possibility of defeat."

Nathaniel scooped up a few pebbles as he came to the fountain. "Tell me what to do, and I'll do it."

"Marry Althea at the first opportunity. My signature must appear on the settlements, before my authority to commit family resources is legally invalidated."

Nathaniel nodded and tossed his pebbles, one by one, into the splashing water. "Anything else?"

"I'll summon Cranmouth out to Rothhaven for a meeting. The sooner he starts preparing my defense, the more effective he's likely to be."

"Good thought. Walden will approve."

"Walden's duchess will approve. For now, I would approve of some food and a soft mattress."

Nathaniel resumed walking toward the house, which was bathed in morning sunshine. "You truly have become the duke, you know. Calm in the face of battle and all that. Wellington enjoying his breakfast steak while the French cannon pound away in the distance."

The worry in Nathaniel's voice broke Robert's heart. He seized Nathaniel by the arm and wrapped him in a hug.

"It will be all right, Nathaniel. I will manage, and you will be happy. Our womenfolk will allow no other outcome."

For a brief, wonderful moment, Nathaniel let himself be comforted, then he thumped Robert on the back and stepped away.

"Walden is a bit under petticoat government," he said. "Have you noticed?"

"I suspect all the best dukes are thoroughly under petticoat government, and a happier bunch of fellows—and governesses—you never did meet. Shall I ask Cranmouth to join us this afternoon?"

"That will suit. I never did much like him. Althea isn't too keen on him either, though I suppose needs must."

Chapter Nineteen

Althea and Nathaniel's nuptials were held on Friday morning in the Lynley Vale formal parlor. Stephen had been summoned back from Fendle Bridge, and it was agreed by some process to which Constance was not privy that a council of war would gather after the wedding breakfast.

"You aren't eating," Rothhaven said. "One must keep up one's strength, I'm told."

Constance fiddled with her wineglass, though for the first time in her memory, the siren call of alcohol had gone silent.

"One must rest too, sir. I find that activity best pursued when you and I share a bed."

At the end of the table, Jane raised an eyebrow at that remark, the gesture so subtle that Vicar Sorenson, seated at her elbow, likely hadn't noticed.

"And I," Rothhaven said very softly, "sleep better under the same circumstances. Patience, my love. The settlements have been signed, Cranmouth has been dispatched to research the legalities, and today is an occasion for joy."

Rothhaven's thoughts reminded Constance of a cabinet with many drawers, and when he closed the drawer marked *Construction of the Gatehouse* and opened the drawer labeled *Legal Incompetency Claim*, the gatehouse might as well be on an estate owned by some other duke in some other county.

Perhaps that was another legacy of time in Dr. Soames's care. "I wrote to Ivy again," Constance said. "Not knowing if she's receiving my letters is driving me barmy." *Wrong word. Wrong, wrong word.*

"Write to her anyway. Mrs. Hodges struck me as an individual blessed with a strong practical streak. If she can see a way to get your letters to the girl, she will. Keep copies."

"Because if the original never reaches Ivy, someday, the copy might." What a bilious notion. "Althea and Nathaniel look besotted."

"Are you as happy for Althea as I am for Nathaniel?"

Rothhaven's gaze as he beheld his brother—who at the moment was kissing the back of Althea's bare hand—was an expression Constance would have to paint to understand. Tender, wistful, proud, perhaps loving was the best way to describe it, but also a touch sad.

"For Althea, I am overjoyed. She and Nathaniel suit, and she was resigned to never suiting anybody, to settling. I am glad she didn't settle."

"Did you settle, Constance?"

Quinn heard that remark. He and Stephen were engaged in a lively discussion about exporting birds' nests to China, but a slight pause between Stephen's question and Quinn's reply suggested no privacy was to be had among family. Ever.

"Yes," Constance said, spooning up a bite of pear compote in cinnamon and clove sauce. "Yes, I did compromise. When I chose to believe Ivy's father's flattery and refused to tell Quinn the varlet's name. When I fled the protection of my family, when I took up the most menial and obscure occupation I could find. I compromised, and the result would have been tragic, had I not met you."

Rothhaven took her hand, and that gesture fortified Constance sufficiently that she could finish her declaration, even though the table had gone silent, and Jane looked quite severe.

"I compromised," Constance went on, "when I allowed Quinn to arrange for Ivy to be raised by the Wilsons. I most assuredly compromised when I sat like an agreeable statue in one Mayfair ballroom after another. I compromised and compromised and compromised, but no more. No more compromising, Rothhaven. I will have my duke, I will be the duchess who happily paints away her seasons on the Yorkshire moors, and I refuse to compromise."

God in heaven. Constance's entire family, plus Nathaniel and the vicar, were looking at her as if she'd sprouted horns and a tail. She put down her spoonful of compote and wanted to slither under the table. An apology tried to muddle forth, something about not meaning to air sad linen on such a happy occasion. She looked up and happened to catch Quinn's eye.

He was smiling, and Quinn smiled so seldom that Constance had forgotten the breathtaking warmth he could display. His daughters and his duchess were the usual recipients of his rare smiles, but he aimed the full-on version at Constance now.

He lifted his glass. "To not compromising on important matters, and if Rothhaven is to blame for your newfound sense of resolve, then I suppose we must thank him and welcome him—him *too*—to the family."

Heat stole up Constance's cheeks, even as a measure of joy pushed aside the worries plaguing her so sorely. Quinn had started the toasts that invariably accompanied any wedding breakfast, and as Jane stood to offer felicitations to the newlyweds, Quinn rose to fetch a fresh bottle of wine from the sideboard.

He passed behind Constance's chair and bent low enough to whisper in her ear, "Welcome home, my lady," then sidled on by with all the savoir-faire to which a bank nabob turned duke was entitled.

"What did he say?" Rothhaven asked.

"He said he loves me." Said he'd always loved her, and said he blamed himself for the whole sad business all those years ago. Silly man. Silly, dear, dear man. "You were right, Rothhaven." Constance took a taste of an exquisite dessert.

"I am frequently right. To which occasion do you now refer?"

"You said today is a joyous occasion."

"When I am with you, the occasion is always joyous."

And that was not flattery, that was Rothhaven speaking the truth, as he invariably did. Constance finished her sweet as the toasting and laughter rose around her, and a trickle of worry managed to wash back over her joy.

She was not being entirely honest with Rothhaven. She absolutely did intend to spend the rest of her life as his duchess, painting away the seasons, running his household, and raising his children—and also, God willing, her daughter—but she did not trust Cranmouth to adequately defend that future.

Not in the least, and thus she'd taken steps without

informing Rothhaven, steps he might well oppose. She lifted her glass yet again to the happy couple, and prayed that she and Rothhaven might also earn that appellation, sooner rather than later.

* * *

"I tell you, Sparrow"—Stephen tipped his hat to a pair of passing dowagers—"between true love, married love, and frustrated love, Lynley Vale should have a rose-colored miasma hovering over its roof. I had to get away." Stephen had also been entrusted with a letter to deliver for Constance, one she hadn't wanted anybody else to see. Miss Abbott had taken the missive, thanked Stephen, and he'd had no pretext for prolonging the encounter.

Regular constitutionals along the walkways of York had failed to produce another sighting of the lady, and perhaps that was for the best.

Sir Leviticus was doubtless slowing his usual gait, the better to accommodate Stephen's pace. He was astute like that, or Stephen would have sacked him years ago.

"Has the petition been served?" Sir Leviticus asked. "It's been a good week since I heard Weatherby's clerks complaining of his latest project."

Weatherby, along with Philpot, had apparently made a cottage industry out of guardianships for profit. If Stephen lacked patience with any variety of criminal, it was the criminal who preyed on the helpless and was paid to do it with the victim's own means.

"The petition was served the day after Lady Althea and Lord Nathaniel's wedding," Stephen said. "Cranmouth has been alerted to the situation, and Rothhaven pretends all is in hand."

"All is not in hand?"

"His Grace has staring spells," Stephen said. "I had no idea such an affliction existed. I was introducing him to a mount I'm training for his use and in the middle of a conversation, Rothhaven just...He went as still as a deserted cathedral. I babbled on, not even noticing the difference until, when I concluded my eloquence, he made no reply. Damnably awkward."

Sir Leviticus paused on the steps of his club. "More awkward than a shaking fit?"

"Yes, in a way, because he simply stares at nothing, says nothing, and generally comports with some people's notions of imbecility."

"Does Cranmouth know of this condition? If I were representing His Grace, I'd certainly find it relevant."

The lawyers' club was the usual dark, carpeted, wainscoted bastion of male self-importance, the majordomo as pretentious as any at Stephen's clubs in London.

"A quiet table, if any you have," Sir Leviticus said.

"Very good, sir. Follow me." The fellow collected two leather-bound menus and minced off with more dignity than the director of a state funeral. The scent of tobacco wafted from one of the reading rooms, while cooked beef perfumed the air nearer the dining room.

The whole place was tediously predictable, and Stephen's appetite for steak and ale abruptly fled. He didn't exactly miss London, and he certainly didn't miss Love Nest Vale, but he missed something and someplace.

Or someone.

"Oh dear." Sir Levi hesitated at the door of the dining room. "I suppose one ought not to jump to conclusions."

"Jump," Stephen said, remaining in the corridor and peering over Sir Leviticus's shoulder. "What do you see?"

"Weatherby, Philpot, *and* Cranmouth, all at the same table. Again."

"*Again?*"

"Yes, now that I see them together I'm reminded that they shared a meal a week or two ago. That made an impression at the time because they aren't typically social, at least Weatherby and Cranmouth aren't. Cranmouth takes his consequence from his ducal client, you see, and limits his associations accordingly. I am permitted to break bread with him by virtue of my knighthood, but I rarely do."

Stephen withdrew into the corridor. "Do lawyers opposing one another typically confer this early in the litigation?"

"Not in the usual course. Negotiations as the hearing approaches are common, but one needs guidance from a client before taking that step."

Rothhaven would not have guided Cranmouth to settle anything. Cranmouth's marching orders were to fight the petition by any and every legal means. Steak and ale did not qualify as courtroom weapons.

"Can you have somebody with acute hearing take a table near them?" Stephen asked. "I do not like what I'm seeing, and I suspect Rothhaven would hate it." While Constance would rid the world of a crooked solicitor or two. Or three.

The majordomo hovered a few feet away, tapping the menus against his palm. "If I might make a suggestion, sir?"

"Please," Sir Leviticus said. "I trust your discretion, Monmouth."

"Judge Framley takes his midday meal here without fail by one of the clock. I can seat him at the table next to Mr. Cranmouth's. I believe you and His Honor are on amicable terms."

"He's a retired judge," Sir Leviticus said. "We play the occasional hand of cards, and he is godfather to my eldest."

"And here is His Honor," Monmouth said. "Punctual as usual."

Sir Leviticus and the judge conferred, Stephen pretended to examine the portraits on the walls—why did half-naked goddesses appeal to a gaggle of staid lawyers?—and then Monmouth was leading the judge into the dining room.

"Why would the majordomo do that for you?" Stephen asked.

"You're asking if Monmouth is trustworthy, and he is. His loyalty is to the club, and if I had to guess, I'd say that Cranmouth, Philpot, and Weatherby are behind in their dues, rude to the staff, and parsimonious with their vales."

"Bad form," Stephen said, accepting his hat and coat from a footman. "Mortal sin, that. Have you ever defended a client accused of mental incompetence, Sir Leviticus?"

"No. Am I soon to have that honor?"

"You are soon to ride out to Rothhaven Hall with me and explore the possibility."

* * *

"So Cranmouth is telling you not to worry?" Lord Stephen asked, patting the gelding's neck. "Claiming you'll be home by supper following a pleasant chat with the commission members?"

After a week of riding lessons, Robert was still both amazed and terrified to find himself back in the saddle. The project had been necessary, both to provide an excuse to call at Lynley Vale every day, and to keep Lord Stephen from descending into a grand pout.

"Cranmouth tells me that I should be more concerned over a meeting with my steward than I am over this *mere formality*." Robert gathered up the reins as Lord Stephen took two steps back. For a man who professed to care about only his close relatives, his lordship certainly did hover near his riding student.

"If the lawyer tells you not to worry," Lord Stephen said, "then you should be very worried indeed. Though I have every faith in Sir Leviticus, *I* am worried, which is no credit to my masculine dignity."

"Walk on." Robert nudged Revanche with his calves. The beast obligingly shuffled forward, and the little boy who dwelled deep in memory gave a shout of joy.

"You have the natural seat of a damned cavalry officer," Lord Stephen said, backing away another two steps. The footing in the arena was sand, which had to be hard going for a man who relied on a cane.

"I am all but trussed into the saddle." The leather straps went over Robert's thighs, beneath the flap of his riding jacket. They had taken getting used to, for they prohibited rising from the saddle at the trot. His lordship had fashioned a mechanism that made the straps simple to get into and quick to release, and yet they held Robert snugly on the horse's back.

His lordship took another few steps back. "Some people trussed into the saddle bounce about like rabbits in a pillowcase. You must have ridden frequently as a child."

"Every chance I could. To the trot, Revanche." Another nudge, and the horse lifted into a steady, smooth trot. "I don't know where you found this fellow, but he's worth his weight in oats."

"Found him outside a knacker's yard, more or less. How is Constance managing?"

Robert rode a figure eight, which Revanche executed at a marvelous steady tempo. "Halt."

Just like that, motion ceased. Four hoofs remained planted in the sand, until Robert gave another nudge with his calves.

"If you are concerned for Constance," Robert said, executing a line that moved both forward and to the side at the same time, leaving a diagonal track in the sand, "you should ask her."

Lord Stephen perched upon a barrel in the center of the arena. "I hope to live to see my next birthday, Rothhaven. Con has that *come near me at your peril* look about her."

And yet, she clung to Robert whenever they found a private moment. "She is concerned for her daughter. Halt." Again, Revanche heeded the command, even though it had been buried behind normal speech. "Good lad, walk on."

"Con has been concerned for her daughter for years, apparently. What has changed?"

The challenge of navigating between Wentworth siblings was new, and Nathaniel was of no help regarding its perils. He was as puzzled by the Wentworth family dynamics as Robert was, though at least Nathaniel could cuddle up with his wife of a night for an occasional consultation.

"Constance cannot approach Reverend Shaw to renew negotiations until my situation is resolved."

"Your situation will be resolved by this time tomorrow, barring last-minute lawyerly posturing."

"Which one should never bar. Canter."

The horse lifted into a scrumptious, cadenced canter, circling the arena as gently as a breeze. The motion was magic, banishing worries and doubts with sheer bodily joy. *Dear God, I have missed this. Missed this freedom and pleasure…*

The next thing Robert knew, the horse was once again standing motionless, and Lord Stephen was hobbling over from the center of the arena.

"Your usual calm has deserted you, my lord. Is something amiss?" Robert patted Revanche soundly, for such joy should be rewarded.

"Rothhaven, you stopped listening to me." Lord Stephen spoke carefully, as if Robert held a loaded gun casually pointed at a live target.

"I beg your pardon?"

"You went around the entire arena three times at the canter, while I admonished you to sink your weight in your heels, and relax your elbows and all manner of whatnot. You ignored me."

The joy vanished like a candle snuffed by a stiff breeze. "I did not hear you."

Lord Stephen leaned against the horse, who was puffing slightly. "A staring spell?"

"Apparently so."

Robert sat atop his horse as a chorus of emotions tried to join him in the saddle: Terror galloped at the front of the pack, eager to drag him back to a boy's helplessness and confusion. Worry followed close behind, because this development must be conveyed to Constance, who had enough burdens already. Resentment—never far away—prepared to shove aside even the terror of falling, because the bloody illness had to taint every joy and hasten every sorrow.

"Well, then," his lordship said, fiddling with Revanche's mane, "I suppose we know the harness works."

"You are uncomfortable," Robert said. "I am sorry for that, but this is who I am. I have staring spells, I have seizures, and they are only the visible parts of my illness.

The memory lapses, muddled thinking, the fatigue...they are equally burdensome. That others have to deal with any of it vexes me exceedingly. Walk on."

A horse recovering from exertion should not stand. That commandment welled up from childhood, and Revanche was apparently happy to saunter forth.

"I've considered having my leg amputated," Stephen said, both hands resting on the top of his cane. "You must not tell my family I said that, or they will haul me before a board of examiners."

I am your family now. "If you can't end your life, you'll at least end your leg's life?"

"The bloody thing hurts, Rothhaven. *All the time*, and it will only grow worse as I age. I can delay the inevitable by living in a Bath chair, but would you rather have twenty years shuffling around with your canes or forty years in a Bath chair?"

Were Robert not on horseback, idly circling the arena, had he not just had a spectacular staring spell, Stephen would very likely not be sharing these confidences—these frustrations.

"So why haven't you made a date with the surgeon's knife?"

"I have, twice. Canceled both times. The surgeons, fellows who learned a lot on the battlefield and were confident of their craft, talked me out of it. Infection is inevitable, and even a severed limb can cause pain. One of them opined that the problem is not my shinbone—he had some Latin name for it—but rather my knee. What a cheerful topic this is. You'd best canter him the other direction, and then I'll fetch my mount so we can hack about the park."

The riding out had started two days ago, at the walk,

with short stretches of trot. "I want to canter up the drive," Robert said.

Stephen resumed his perch on the barrel at the center of the arena. "Do you really?"

"The worst that can happen is apparently that I will have another staring spell, in which case, if you don't instruct Revanche to halt, he will carry me back to the stable yard and halt himself."

They tested the theory, with Stephen instructing the horse to halt mid-canter in the second direction. Revanche nearly sat on his tail, so attentive was he to Stephen's command.

"Why aren't you quaking in dread?" Stephen asked when a groom had been sent for his horse. "Why aren't you leaving this arena, never again to return? You had a staring spell and didn't even know it."

The question had deeper significance, relating to Bath chairs, death, and tomorrow's looming ordeal.

"Constance has had a letter from Ivy," Robert said. "You will not interrogate her about it."

"A letter from Ivy is good, isn't it?"

"Not if the letter asks Constance to send coach fare, so the girl can run away again and this time run so far her uncle can't find her."

"And Jane wonders why I will never marry," Stephen said, opening the gate so Robert could ride through. "Marriage leads to children, and any fool can see what a lot of nonsense children are."

Stephen was the most devoted, doting uncle a niece ever had, and no sibling claimed a more loyal brother.

"Marriage per se does not lead to children," Robert said, leaving the arena, "and I venture to guess that you are not a monk." Nor was Stephen a coward, but he was terrified of the very sort of intimacy Robert so cherished with Constance.

"I am not a monk. That is an accurate observation."

The next few minutes were taken up with arranging his lordship in the saddle and stowing his canes. Then Robert and Stephen sent their mounts ambling down the drive.

"So why are you still determined to ride?" Stephen said. "That little staring spell frightened me nearly witless. Sorry. Frightened me half to death."

"Why aren't you living out your life in a Bath chair?"

"Because I am a fool? Because I am too stupid to exercise prudence? Because my family would hate to see me in such a reduced circumstance any more than they already do?"

Because you are brave, and you yet cling to hope. "It's not enough to placate a commission of examiners with regard to my competence. I hope that exercise is the formality Cranmouth claims it will be. I must be in a position to accept Ivy into the household I will share with Constance, and that means I walk, talk, *ride*, and comport myself as a man worthy of being entrusted with the welfare of a child."

Stephen's horse came to a halt, though nobody had given that command. "Bloody Jack Wentworth haunts us all."

Well, no. Jack Wentworth haunted his children, apparently. Robert was haunted by an entirely different sort of incompetent parent, and that too was a reason to persist with horseback riding.

"You do know this examination will be more than a formality?" Stephen asked, sending his horse forward again.

"I am aware of that. Sir Leviticus has schooled me thoroughly, at least in terms of the examiners' questions."

While Cranmouth, may his traitorous soul rot in whatever hell specialized in crooked lawyers, continued to make reassuring noises while doing nothing.

"What will you do about Ivy's threat to run away again?"

"I trust my duchess to address that situation in the manner she deems most appropriate."

"She's not your duchess yet."

"Yes, she is." Robert settled his hat more firmly on his head and sank his weight into his heels. "*Canter.*"

* * *

"How gracious of the Lord Mayor to offer use of the Mansion House for the hearing," Constance muttered. The crowd outside the York Mansion House had parted for Quinn's coach, but by agreement, the ladies would wait in the vehicle until the gentlemen rode up on horseback to hand them down.

"Rothhaven knows the spectacle he'll face," Althea said. "He won't face it alone."

"Neither will you, Constance," Jane said, pushing a shade aside to peer out the window. "I do believe our escorts approach."

A clatter of hooves on the cobbled street presaged Quinn, Nathaniel, and Rothhaven trotting around the corner. They made a fine picture, but Constance alone knew what it cost Rothhaven to travel even a few streets in a saddle devoid of extra straps and buckles.

Rothhaven dismounted easily and a groom from the coach came forward to take his horse.

"Where's Stephen?" Constance asked. Stephen hated to have an audience when he mounted or dismounted, but the occasion warranted a show of solidarity.

"He might already be inside," Jane said. "Crowds and canes are not a good combination."

"And yet," Constance retorted, "he manages to attend the theater fairly often."

She was being difficult, but then, she was furious. Weatherby had known when he'd petitioned for the Lord Chancellor to appoint this commission of lunacy that the hearing would be public. A jury of six local worthies had been impaneled, and all the witness testimony would be so much entertainment for them and for the good folk of York.

"Courage," Althea muttered as a footman opened the coach door and let down the steps.

Jane descended first, followed by Althea and, finally, Constance.

Rothhaven smiled at her, a private, sweet smile that she would have sworn was not for show. Rothhaven had no notion of theater, no use for farce or intrigue, and that thought inspired Constance to smile back.

"My dear, good day." He bowed and offered his arm.

"Your Grace." She curtsied, unwilling to be rushed, unwilling to deny Rothhaven one jot of the deference his station was due.

They processed into the Mansion House as if Rothhaven regularly parted unruly, staring crowds under a bright spring sun. Constance wanted to stop before the door and turn to raise her fist at the lot of them.

"Any more letters from Ivy?" Rothhaven asked.

"No."

"That worries you."

"Everything worries me."

"When this is over, Constance, we will turn our considerable resources to her situation."

Those resources had not been sufficient to buy the ship Ivy was to sail on. The owner, a widow, refused to part with the vessel that she and her merchant captain husband had traveled together on for years. Even Constance hadn't been willing to press her on the matter.

The Mansion Hall was the public residence of the Lord Mayor, often used for ceremonies of state and large social gatherings. On this occasion, what looked like a ballroom or banquet hall had been fitted out to accommodate the commission proceedings. A makeshift jury box sat off to one side, and a minstrel's gallery opposite the witness box provided seating for spectators.

The ladies were handed into the front-row seats in the gallery. The general public and the press would crowd in behind them and even hang about outside the open windows. Witnesses, members of the bar, and other worthy local gentlemen were permitted to sit in the banquet hall proper, rows of chairs having been set up facing the commissioners' table.

Rothhaven took his place at the counsel table, Cranmouth beside him, a quantity of bound volumes arranged on the table along with paper and pencils. At the opposite table, Weatherby pretended to read a law book, while a clerk at his side arranged ink and writing paper.

"Are you expecting somebody, Con?" Althea asked. "You keep watching the gallery doorway."

Blast all perceptive siblings to perdition. "Why would I be expecting anybody?"

"Because normally, you'd have your sketch pad out of your reticule by now, and yet, you're fidgeting instead."

Jane smiled pleasantly at Lady Phoebe Philpot, who'd arrived with Mrs. Elspeth Weatherby. Neville Philpot was conferring with Solomon Weatherby at the counsel table, and neither man's expression reflected the solemnity of the occasion.

"Where is Stephen?" Constance asked, quietly, because the gallery was growing crowded and journalists were everywhere.

"Stephen and Rothhaven were conferring late into the evening," Jane said. "I think they have common ground of a sort, and it's wonderful to see Stephen embarking on a friendship."

"Wonderful of Rothhaven," Constance replied, "to make the effort of forming a friendship with a contrary, self-absorbed in-law. I think I'm about to be sick."

Jane passed over a peppermint. "Duchesses do not get sick, not in public."

Althea took a mint too.

A slight commotion behind the counsel tables ensued as Stephen emerged from the corridor and offered a nod to Neville Philpot. A word or two might have been exchanged between Stephen and Weatherby, but then Stephen was moving across the room to take a seat beside Quinn.

"What was that about?" Jane murmured.

"I don't know," Constance said, the upset in her tummy growing worse. "I don't like it."

She stole another glance over her shoulder. The gallery and banquet hall were packed, the bailiffs were closing the doors to further spectators, and still Miss Abbott was nowhere to be seen.

Chapter Twenty

The trial was off to a splendid start, in Neville's opinion, in part because Lord Nathaniel Rothmere, as the Duke of Rothhaven's next of kin, had announced that Ebenezer Cranmouth would be called as a witness.

The result was, Cranmouth could not represent His Grace.

The duke sat through this development looking bored. He'd muttered his consent when asked if he waived the confidentiality every lawyer owed his clients, which was proof everlasting that His Grace's wits had taken wing. With His Grace's waiver noted in the record, Cranmouth could be questioned on any topic that bore a passing relation to Rothhaven's competence.

The three commissioners conferred for a moment to debate whether Rothhaven's waiver was valid in such a proceeding. When Lord Nathaniel added his waiver as well, they concluded that Rothhaven wasn't *yet* legally incompetent, so the waiver of confidentiality must be allowed to stand.

Lord Nathaniel offered Sir Leviticus Sparrow as counsel for the alleged disabled party, alas for the brave knight. Sir Leviticus had never once touched a competency case.

As Mr. Able Drossman, head of the panel of examiners, droned on to the jury about the differences between lunacy, idiocy, and imbecility, Neville risked a glance over his shoulder at Phoebe. Drossman was white-haired, fleshy-jowled, and smarter than he looked, though he was fond of his port and harbored judicial ambitions.

Phoebe smiled down at Neville with particularly gracious warmth, and he resisted the urge to blow her a kiss. Weatherby suggested that Cranmouth testify first, as the court's witness, and old Drossman was so pleased with that notion that he allowed Weatherby to start the questioning.

And wasn't that just lovely? Cranmouth droned on about the ducal books—for the *most* part quite tidy—though he did slip in the fact that never once had he been called to Rothhaven Hall until the last week or so. As a witness, Cranmouth struck a balance between wanting to aid the court and wanting to protect his client's privacy, despite any dubious waivers of solicitor-client confidentiality.

"And did there come a time when His Grace visited you at your office?" Weatherby asked.

Cranmouth darted a glance at the ceiling, then looked down, and then over at Drossman. The great Mr. Garrick, late of Drury Lane, could not have presented a more convincing show of hesitation.

"He did."

"And the nature of that call, Mr. Cranmouth?"

"His Grace signed the documents required to divest

himself of a commodious estate some distance to the northwest of York."

"Was there anything unusual about the transaction?"

Yes. Yes, indeed there had been, as Weatherby, Neville, and soon the whole of York would know. The Duke of Rothhaven had *given away* an entire functioning estate with a sizable manor house and home farm.

"Had the previous duke made any similar transactions?" Weatherby asked.

"I should say not. The previous duke was quite mindful of his assets."

"And after your appointment with His present Grace, can you relate when you next saw your client?"

The coughing, throat clearing, and foot shuffling in the room stopped, as if everybody knew exactly what damning testimony would follow.

"I next saw my client..." If he'd had a handkerchief in his hands, Cranmouth would have twisted it to shreds. "Is this really necessary?"

A splendid touch.

Drossman looked over his glasses at the witness. "As Mr. Weatherby has brought a petition, and the Lord Chancellor has decided the case has merit on its face, yes. *This* is necessary. Answer the question, Mr. Cranmouth."

"When next I saw His Grace, he was sitting on the walkway. His hat was in the gutter, his watch dangled from its pocket. His walking stick was on the ground. He appeared not to be himself."

Weatherby waved a plump, pale hand. "Elaborate for the benefit of the jury."

"His Grace did not greet me, did not say much of anything. He appeared confused and frightened, and when others approached to offer aid, he scuttled away. He would not allow me to help him to his feet; he would not speak to me. He relied on strangers to assist him and on Lady Constance Wentworth, who is no relation to him at all. He acted as if he had no idea who I was."

"Had he perhaps stumbled and hit his head?" Weatherby asked.

"I saw no sign of bruising. Lord Nathaniel and Lady Constance Wentworth both confirmed His Grace had suffered a seizure. Her ladyship and his lordship are present, if the commission would like to question them directly."

"The commission," Drossman said, "would like to conclude this matter in time to enjoy a noon meal at home. Get on with your questions, Weatherby."

"You said that His Grace's books were *mostly* in order. Did aspects of the Rothmere finances give you cause for concern?"

"Not recently, no."

"During the present duke's tenure?"

"Well, that is hard to say. The present duke, Robert, that is, was least in sight at the time of his father's death and for many years before. We all believed that Robert had pre-deceased his father, didn't we? Lord Nathaniel, in fact, believed himself for a time to be the duke."

The members of the commission on either side of Drossman were sitting up and looking interested.

"Are you implying that the present duke allowed his family to believe him dead?" Weatherby asked.

"I cannot say that, sir. *I* believed the present duke dead, and I assume Lord Nathaniel did as well. We were happily mistaken."

Such a sickly smile. Cranmouth truly belonged on the stage.

"Have you any idea where His Grace might have been for all those—"

Sir Leviticus was on his feet. "I must object. The query before the jury relates to the duke's present mental state, not the faculties he possessed years ago or where his father sent him to school."

"I withdraw the question," Weatherby said, "because I assume the panel can ask His Grace directly to account for his whereabouts. A man who imposes on his family the very great grief of his death as a jest in poor taste is not a fellow of sound mind."

Drossman put his glasses back on. "You will confine your role to that of counsel, Mr. Weatherby, and spare us your opining. Sir Leviticus, your witness."

Another lawyer rebuked, and that pleased the gallery *and* the jury.

Sir Leviticus established that the Rothhaven dukedom under the present titleholder prospered handsomely enough to make a charitable gift of even a large, remote estate. He also got Cranmouth to admit that Robert's father had appeared quite sound of mind in all regards, sound enough to vote his seat, oversee multiple estates, and supervise the upbringing of his children. The old duke had not, alas, been as proficient at managing the family's wealth. Cranmouth was convincingly reluctant to part with that confession.

Dr. Warner, looking handsome, calm, and helpful, testified next. Seizures, in his *expert* opinion, were difficult to treat, and if they appeared in childhood, they seldom admitted of a cure. Repeated seizures often resulted in diminished capacity over time. Confusion, hostility, and loss of the faculty of speech, such as Cranmouth observed in His Grace, were sadly common in persons cursed with epilepsy.

All very tragic.

Sir Leviticus forced Warner to admit that he'd treated

a grand total of five cases of epilepsy in his two decades of practice, and further, that seizures could result from many causes other than the falling sickness. Warner was therefore not in a position to diagnose His Grace with the falling sickness, much less do so by innuendo.

The gallery liked seeing the doctor put in his place as well, more's the pity.

Weatherby rallied, though, asking Warner if he was professionally familiar with the late Dr. Obediah Soames. As it happened, Warner had read the many august treatises on mental derangement Soames had penned, and had heard Soames's private madhouse described as a model of compassionate care for the insane. Soames's death had been a great loss to the medical community.

A great loss, indeed.

What would Rothhaven and Wentworth relations think if they learned that Soames's name had been passed along to Neville by no less personage than Lord Stephen Wentworth, and that his lordship's motivation had been to prevent a mésalliance between the Wentworths and not merely a family afflicted with madness, but the madman himself?

* * *

"And why did you purchase Dr. Soames's establishment?" Weatherby asked.

None of your damned business. Robert couldn't say that, but ye gods, he wanted to. What prevented him was the sight of Constance in the gallery, pale, composed, and doubtless ready to do Weatherby a grievous injury at the slightest provocation.

The truly relevant questions—What day is it? What

is your name? Who sits upon the throne of the United Kingdom? What is the sum of 23 plus 42 plus 4?—had been dispensed within the first two minutes of Robert's testimony.

"Not all of my memories from the years in Soames's care were bad," Robert said. "I formed fast friendships with the other residents, and I met my wife there."

Weatherby sent a sly smile toward the jury. "Are you married, then, Your Grace?"

"As it happens, I am."

The jury looked uncertain, while Weatherby appeared to have found a gold sovereign among his legal notes.

"Has the queen of the fairies accepted your proposal? Perhaps you married a madwoman while you were still a minor? Do favor us with the details, Your Grace."

Sir Leviticus rose and aimed a disdainful look at Weatherby. "I ask the commission to instruct Mr. Weatherby regarding his duty of civility toward the witness. Mocking one alleged to be disabled should be beneath the dignity of any decent person, and mocking a witness worse yet."

"Weatherby," Drossman growled, "stop baiting the witness. The noon hour approaches."

Weatherby merely smiled. "To whom are you married, Your Grace?"

"To the former Lady Constance Wentworth, who is present in the gallery. We met while I resided with Dr. Soames. Her ladyship briefly joined the domestic staff years ago. We renewed our acquaintance as our siblings courted, and her ladyship did me the great honor of accepting my proposal."

Her ladyship wasn't looking very honored at present, or rather, *Her Grace* wasn't. She looked ready to murder Solomon Weatherby.

"How is it you come to be married when we've heard of no ceremony, Your Grace? You must admit an invisible wedding is hard to credit."

Weatherby's tediousness would drive Robert daft in truth. "Dr. Pietr Sorenson married us by special license when we had occasion to request a letter of introduction from him. We did not want to detract from the attention due our siblings, who were also planning to wed and who have now done so."

Robert and Constance had also needed to travel to Fendle Bridge as a married couple, though the outing had made a poor wedding journey.

The gallery was abuzz, pointing at Constance, who bore that rudeness with enviable serenity.

"Well, congratulations on your nuptials, Your Grace." Weatherby sounded jovial, but his gaze had narrowed, "and on distracting the commission from my original question: Why buy, then *give away*, a prosperous property where you had been hospitalized for *half your life*?"

"Dr. Soames never called it a hospital, did he?" Robert replied. "Never had any of his guests certified as insane or incompetent, never had to comply with the legal requirement to have an independent physician evaluate the people forced to bide in his house. I gather he was solving embarrassing problems for well-to-do families, and my epilepsy—my very existence—was exactly such a problem for my father. What would you call Soames's establishment?"

Sir Leviticus had said that Weatherby polished his glasses when he needed time to think, and he was polishing his spectacles to a high shine now.

"I will ask the questions, Your Grace, and ancient history isn't what concerns me or the jury. Why buy a madhouse, for surely we can agree Soames was running a madhouse."

"I do not agree, Mr. Weatherby. He was operating a profitable venture of some sort, but entirely outside the laws pertaining to care of the mentally enfeebled. I bought the place to ensure that my friends there were freed to pursue more meaningful lives, and to that end, I aided them in their ambitions. I also met my duchess at Soames's establishment. Until she and I were reunited by recent circumstances, that property was my sole connection to her. She became dear to me years ago, and I thank benevolent Providence that we are reunited."

Elspeth Weatherby leaned over to whisper something in Lady Phoebe's ear, and her ladyship looked ready to smack Mrs. Weatherby with her reticule.

Constance, however, was smiling sweetly.

"So you *are* an epileptic?" Weatherby said. "You admit to that terrible infirmity?"

"I *have* epilepsy, much as Caesar, Napoleon, various European monarchs, Leonardo da Vinci, and Michelangelo were rumored to have epilepsy. As my own father certainly did."

A murmur coursed through the gallery, and looks were exchanged among the three men on the commission of lunacy.

"Is it your sworn testimony," Weatherby said, "that your own father, the previous duke, was an epileptic? On what do you base that claim?"

Thank heavens Sir Leviticus had demanded that Robert rehearse this as well as dozens of other lines of questioning.

"The times were less enlightened years ago," Robert said. "My father was made to feel ashamed of his condition, and feared that he would be exploited by *unscrupulous parties* if his seizures became public knowledge. He nonetheless managed his ducal responsibilities adequately, as we heard Mr. Cranmouth himself testify earlier."

Cranmouth was examining his pocket watch as if the secret to eternal life were written on its face. A few people in the gallery got up to leave, others took their seats, while Robert remained focused on Sir Leviticus. Robert's sense was that the tide had turned, and the case was going against Weatherby. But legal proceedings were the province of the devious, among whom Robert had never sought to number.

A clerk passed Sir Leviticus a note.

"Then your unfortunate malady is inherited," Weatherby said, his statement dripping with false pity, "and I'm sure Dr. Warner would tell us that what is inherited cannot be cured."

"My condition is not inherited, but rather, the result of serious head injuries sustained one after the other at the age of eleven. My brother, Nathaniel, has no symptoms of the falling sickness, as he would doubtless testify. He would further testify that I myself had no symptoms until after my boyhood riding accidents."

Robert offered this hearsay on behalf of his brother with an apologetic smile at the commission, who were at risk for missing their nooning, thanks to Weatherby's ridiculousness.

Sir Leviticus was re-reading the note in his hand, and that, along with a quiet and growing sense of dread, kept Robert from claiming a premature victory. Weatherby was not acting defeated, and Neville Philpot wasn't looking ashamed.

"Have you more questions, Mr. Weatherby?" Drossman asked.

"Yes, I have more questions. I am far from done with my interrogation. Have you a physician in residence at Rothhaven Hall, Your Grace?"

"I do not. I doubt any of the epileptic patients your friend Dr. Warner has treated have physicians in residence, and not one of those five people was declared mentally incompetent either."

A snicker went through the gallery. Nathaniel was trying not to smile.

Weatherby grabbed his lapels and drew himself up. "I respectfully ask the commission to caution His Grace. He is under oath and bound to answer my questions, not expound upon whatever speculation seizes his considerable fancy."

Drossman waved a hand. "No gratuitous speculation, please, Your Grace. Weatherby, are you almost finished? I vow I've yet to see anything approaching lunacy in these proceedings, unless it's the lunacy of lawyers alleging mental illness where it doesn't exist."

The commission only oversaw the proceedings. The jury made the actual finding, and the jury appeared amused by Drossman's observations.

"To the contrary, sir, this matter deserves our utmost consideration," Weatherby said, raising his voice to be heard over the whispers flying around the gallery. "We see here a man afflicted since his youth with seizures, and we have the unrefuted testimony of Dr. Warner that seizures can and do diminish reason."

Weatherby swept Robert with a pitying look. "His Grace was hospitalized for years, no matter the genteel fictions maintained to the contrary, and now we learn that despite these factors, a man of considerable means has no medical professional on hand to care for him. His family has provided no such medical professional, and some in attendance today regard this as a laughing matter."

Drossman dropped a pencil onto a sheet of foolscap. "I regard it as a serious matter, but that needn't mean it must become a lengthy matter. I'm sure the jury would agree. Get on with it, Weatherby. Sir Leviticus must have his turn to call witnesses, and he has ever been one for thorough prosecution of his cases."

"How did you arrive here today?" Weatherby asked, swinging his gaze on Robert as if the question was somehow of great import.

"I rode my horse. Revanche is a lovely fellow. Stands about seventeen hands, has a fondness for apples."

Lord Stephen smiled and saluted with two fingers, though his gaze remained watchful, as it had for the duration of the proceedings.

"You didn't take a closed carriage, one with all the shades drawn even on so fine a day?"

Robert sat forward and spoke slowly and loudly. "I rode my horse." Never had four words given a man more satisfaction, and yet, Robert had the sense he was being drawn into a trap.

"And isn't it true," Weatherby went on, "that you eschew strong spirits, abhor cheroots, and seldom eat sweets?"

"Quite true. I limit my tea and avoid coffee too. Those measures appear to reduce the frequency of my seizures, and my duchess cannot abide the stink of cheroots."

His duchess nodded graciously at the jury.

And at that precise moment, the vague dread swimming around in Robert's mind coalesced into certainty. He made it down the steps from the witness box and halfway to the counsel table before his knees gave out, and he commenced shaking on the hard, cold floor.

* * *

The moment Rothhaven's knees buckled, Constance bolted from the gallery, weaving past gawkers, bailiffs, and Quinn's outstretched hand.

"There, you see!" Weatherby said, pointing at Rothhaven on the floor as the last of the convulsions ceased. "The disease lays the poor man low before our very eyes. The infirmity in all its ruthless horror on display before this august commission and the good gentlemen of the jury. Can Rothhaven speak? Can he even sit up? Ask him who graces the throne of England now, and—"

Constance marched past Weatherby and crouched beside Rothhaven. "What I see in all its horrid ruthlessness is a greedy, swinish lawyer. You long to take up where Soames left off, reaping an enormous profit while cloaking yourself in the virtue of false compassion. You are a parasite and a disgrace."

Weatherby looked gratifyingly startled by those passing observations. The jury looked positively delighted.

Quinn joined Constance at Rothhaven's side, as did Nathaniel.

"Rothhaven," she said, "we'll help you to your seat."

Rothhaven met her gaze, and though she could read little in his expression, he did not seem afraid.

"Ready?" Constance asked, as Quinn and Nathaniel each took an arm.

Rothhaven nodded, and they soon had him in the chair next to Sir Leviticus.

"Might we have a brief recess?" Sir Leviticus asked. "I'm sure His Grace will be prepared to resume his testimony shortly."

"Very well," Drossman said. "A short recess. Mr. Weatherby, have you any other witnesses to call?"

"I do not, sir. A few more questions for His Grace—*if* he can answer them—and I will rest my case."

The three members of the panel left the hall, and the hum and buzz in the gallery rose to a roar. Weatherby and Philpot began a whispered conversation on their side of the room, and Constance took the seat beside her husband.

"Shall we offer him some water?" Dr. Warner had inserted himself into the small group around Sir Leviticus's counsel table.

"Are you daft?" Constance retorted. "For His Grace to try to consume food or drink this soon after a seizure would be most unwise. Be off with you and take your silly little black bag with you."

Warner had the good sense to simply bow and withdraw.

"Fierce," Rothhaven said, his hand landing clumsily on Constance's arm. "My duchess."

"You surprised me with that announcement, Rothhaven." They'd agreed to keep the news of their nuptials private until after the competency hearing, barring some exigent circumstance. "I'm glad you acknowledged me as your duchess. Weatherby's shock was delicious."

"And what about my shock?" Quinn growled.

"And mine?" Nathaniel added. "Althea suspected. I laughed at her speculations."

Jane and Althea soon joined the conversation, while Constance sat beside Rothhaven, his cool hand in hers.

"Sir Leviticus," Constance said, "might you call me as a witness rather than have Rothhaven return immediately to the witness box? The more time His Grace has to recover, the better."

"A fine notion," Sir Leviticus said, "but His Grace is still Weatherby's witness. Weatherby gets another go at him when the recess is over."

"Then you must delay the inevitable with an eloquent and protracted argument about some legal inanity."

Much of the gallery remained milling about, unwilling to give up their seats. Clerks, bailiffs, and Mansion House staff conversed in small groups, and Constance longed for a quiet room where Rothhaven might gather his composure.

"I can offer a dilatory motion or two," Sir Leviticus said, "but we run the risk of antagonizing the commissioners and the jury. Then too, if I admit that His Grace cannot answer simple questions now, I've all but made Weatherby's case for him."

"We need time," Constance muttered. "A half hour at least, an hour would be better."

"My lady—I mean, Your Grace—I'm very much afraid—"

"Robbie!" a man called from the open door to the corridor. "Robbie, you old devil, is that you?"

The fellow was youngish, lanky, and wore attire such as a clerk or tutor might wear. His boots were dusty and his cravat much in want of starch.

"You came," Constance said, popping to her feet and seizing the man by the arm. "You came. Thank God and Miss Abbott. You came. Sir Leviticus, may I present to you Mr. Alexander Fulton, maths instructor at the Greater Wilburn Friends Scholastic Academy, and friend to His Grace from years gone by. Did Mrs. Fulton accompany you?"

"Helen's in the gallery." Fulton squeezed Rothhaven's shoulder. "Robbie, my friend, what a pass, eh?"

"You just missed a seizure," Constance said. "His Grace is not at his best."

Fulton looked around the hall. "And the crowd doubtless

gawked all the while." He waved to his wife, a small, blond woman with vivid blue eyes. "Well, we're here now, and we can tell the lot of them what you put up with for all those years. Bloody Soames, beg pardon for my language. Helly still has nightmares."

"Mr. Fulton," Sir Leviticus said, "we haven't much time to prepare if you're to testify. A few questions, please?" They moved to the corner of the room, Mrs. Fulton joining them.

Weatherby and Philpot were also exchanging whispers, sending curious glances in Mr. Fulton's direction.

"You sent for...?" Rothhaven gestured toward Mr. Fulton.

"Alexander Fulton," Constance said. "Yes. I had Miss Abbott track him down, but I didn't mention it because I wasn't sure she could find him in time. I only let Sir Leviticus know I'd done so after today's proceedings began. Are you angry?"

"Impressed." Rothhaven kissed the back of her gloved hand. "Grateful." He sat up as the members of the jury, one of them finishing a meat pie, resumed their places in the jury box. The bailiffs began chivvying the crowd to their seats, and Constance wanted to bellow at them to cease their foolishness.

Rothhaven wasn't ready to testify again, not nearly. Every minute of delay at this point would aid him, though Drossman seemed bent on hurry, and Weatherby doubtless sensed the advantage he'd just gained.

"Where's Stephen?" Rothhaven asked.

"He's..." Constance looked about. Stephen was in conversation with *Lady Phoebe*. Dear God, what could he be about? "He's here, has been here for the whole proceeding."

"Good."

And then they were out of time, with the bailiff bidding everybody to rise, and Constance having no choice but to rejoin Quinn, Althea, and Jane in the gallery. The air had grown closer as the morning had progressed, and both Althea and Jane were wielding their fans before Constance resumed her seat.

"He's not ready," Constance muttered, as the commissioners shuffled to their places, and Sir Leviticus began to prose on about the need to suspend the proceedings in fairness to the allegedly disabled duke. Weatherby was spluttering before Sir Leviticus had concluded his argument, and Drossman's expression said he had no patience with the pair of them.

"Jane," Constance said. "Now, please."

"Very well." Jane fluffed her skirts, waved her fan a few more times before her cheeks, then cast the fan out across the room to land with a clatter between the counsel tables.

"Oh, dear heavens, the heat!" She raised her forearm to her brow, then fell into a dramatic heap at Constance's feet.

"My duchess has fainted," Quinn bellowed, a credible note of dismay in his voice. "I want a sedan chair, smelling salts, and a glass of hock, and I want them *now*."

Assuming the nearest tavern stocked German wines, a glass of hock would take a good five minutes to produce. Sedan chairs were an outmoded means of transport, and finding one—even for a duchess—would take a good quarter hour.

"Thank you," Constance whispered, gently patting Jane's hand.

Jane's eyes remained closed, but she squeezed Constance's fingers before Quinn scooped his duchess into his arms and recommenced making a fuss worthy of an upset duke.

Chapter Twenty-one

"Her Grace of Walden has suffered a grand faint," Sir Leviticus whispered. "Walden is putting on a performance worthy of Mrs. Siddons when the royal box is occupied. I suspect your duchess is directing the play."

"I'm sure of it," Robert said, resisting the temptation to smile. The same wily determination that had prompted a young maid to slip a wedge of cheese between clean sheets was still much in evidence, and thank God for it.

For her.

The morning had had a low point—the moment when Robert had realized he was about to have a shaking fit before half of York and the commission of lunacy itself—but a high point had been granted him too, when he'd announced, before the entire room, that Constance had become his wife.

"Are you ready to testify?" Sir Leviticus said.

"Best not. Not yet. Soon."

The sight of Alexander, full of his usual energy and cheer, Helen clearly as devoted to her husband as Alexander was to her, was another high point. They'd met at the madhouse, as Robert and Constance had.

Robert let his thoughts drift, as they were inclined to do after a seizure, and eventually tried a sip of water. That went down easily, an encouraging sign. A sedan chair was eventually procured for the Duchess of Walden, and that good lady left the Mansion House, her duke at her side.

The time gained had been precious, but not enough.

Sir Leviticus moved to have Alexander testify out of turn, claiming that the witness had traveled some distance, and could not tarry long in York. Moreover, his wife was with him, also prepared to testify, and she was in a delicate condition. Weatherby had no credible reason for opposing the request, though he snorted and pawed about irregular proceedings and inordinate deference to *certain parties*.

Alexander was sworn in, and Sir Leviticus had the first opportunity to question him.

"Help us?" Alexander said, as the topic turned to the care Soames had provided for his guests. "Nothing could be farther from the truth. Dr. Soames needed to keep us alive, because we were a source of enormous income for him, but he was keen to use His Grace and me for his little experiments."

"Explain," Sir Leviticus said.

Weatherby popped to his feet. "I must object. What went on years ago at some obscure facility is of no moment to the instant inquiry."

Drossman peered over his spectacles. "You were happy to characterize this place as a madhouse not thirty minutes ago, Mr. Weatherby. Let's hear what Mr. Fulton has to say."

Alexander went through the whole litany. The ice baths, the purges, the bleedings, the electric shocks—Robert had mercifully forgotten about those—the strange diets, and sleep deprivation. The whippings—one of Soames's early investigations—and the isolation.

"Soames needed us alive if he was to reap his filthy profits under the guise of medical care," Alexander said, "but animals in a menagerie are treated with more dignity than we were. I suspect he was trying to drive us insane in truth."

Interesting theory.

"And yet, you appear before the commission today," Sir Leviticus said, "articulate, sound of limb, and in possession of your faculties. How did you resist the lure of insanity?"

Alexander braced both hands on the front of the witness box and nodded toward the counsel table.

"*Him.* Rothhaven. He figured out how to thwart Soames's worst impulses and how to make us a family rather than a collection of rejected oddities. Things changed about the time Her Grace joined the staff. She and Rothhaven formed a team, and the rest of us joined on as best we could."

"What sort of team?"

"If Soames decided somebody had to go a week without food, the rest of us would save a bit back and find a way to share it. If Soames had somebody locked in their room as a punishment—or simply because he pleased to inflict that misery on the unfortunate party—we found ways to slip his victim books, a deck of cards, a newspaper. The diversion itself didn't matter half so much as the notion that we cared for each other."

"Go on."

"We developed a code, a tapping code. If somebody

was confined to quarters, they could tap on the wall at certain hours, and we'd hear them and tap back. We had signals for food, water, and so forth, and to alert each other to one of Soames's unannounced room inspections."

"You describe a very difficult existence, Mr. Fulton."

"One that should have driven us mad, *but did not*."

"Thanks to His Grace?"

"In large part. And then his brother came and fetched him, but Rothhaven promised us—we only knew him as Robbie then—promised us he'd see us freed, and he did."

Sir Leviticus glanced around the room. "Was this some dramatic rescue in the dark of night?"

"Dramatic to us, but pure common sense to His Grace. Soames was entirely motivated by greed, so His Grace simply dangled a sum of money before Soames, and Soames sold up and took the bait. Just like that, we were free. Greedy people are far easier to manipulate than the principled kind."

That salvo apparently went straight over Weatherby's head. Robert searched the room for Neville Philpot, but he, along with Lord Stephen, was nowhere to be found.

Thank God.

"Mr. Weatherby," Drossman asked. "Have you questions for this witness?"

"Of course not," Weatherby replied. "This witness is the next thing to a dilatory tactic, providing no insight into the Duke of Rothhaven's present state of mind."

"Not quite true," Alexander said, pleasantly. "His Grace and I are regular correspondents. He wrote me a character to help me find my present post. He gave his violin to my wife, and she became proficient enough to teach music at the same academy where I'm employed. Both of my boys have modest trusts thanks to His Grace, and I will use those funds to see them educated as gentlemen. His Grace of Rothhaven is not only sane, he's entirely decent."

"The witness," Weatherby said, "is opining about matters he is not qualified to testify to. The commission may excuse him with my blessing. I next call—or recall—Robert, His Grace of Rothhaven."

"Mr. Weatherby." Drossman crossed his arms and leaned forward. "I am cautioning you in advance that time is of the essence. Make your inquiries brief."

Robert rose on slightly unsteady legs. Constance had bought him precious time, but more time would have been better. He took his place in the witness box and decided not to ask for a chair.

"Now, Your Grace," Weatherby said. "I remind you that you are still under oath. Tell me, who sits upon the throne of England?"

The schoolboy answer came immediately to mind. "Good King George."

"Ah, but *which* King George?"

The question was simple. Just as the French throne had been occupied by one King Louis after another, England for more than century had been ruled by a succession of King Georges. German George, Farmer George, Mad George...Robert's mind refused to sort out the details.

"The royal one." That produced a snicker from the jury. "He's stout. He likes art. He spends like the entire national exchequer is his privy purse."

"Right about that," somebody called from the gallery.

"Would that be George the Fifth, then?" Weatherby asked, smoothly, too smoothly.

George the Fifth for some reason conjured an image of a mule. "George, to the best of my recollection. Not the fifth."

Weatherby aimed a jovial smile at the jury. "Please note that His Grace thinks some random fellow named George sits upon the throne. Tell me, Your Grace, what is your name?"

"Robert."

"But that's not actually your name, is it? You were baptized Alaric Gerhardt Robert Rothmere. Why don't you use your given name?"

There was a reason. Robert glanced at Nathaniel, who was looking stoic. "My father was Alaric," Robert said, though that wasn't the whole answer. "My mother preferred to call me by a name that would not result in confusion with the previous duke."

Weatherby made a face conveying that the slow top had made a lucky guess. "And what day is today?"

"The day of my lunacy trial." Someone in the gallery guffawed, and Robert cast around for the right day. A trial would not be held on Saturday or Sunday, meaning he had a one-in-five chance of guessing correctly.

"What day of the week is it, Your Grace? Surely you know the day of the week?"

The silence that followed started small and patient, then grew dismayed, and eventually tragic. Robert did not want to guess incorrectly—he was fairly certain the day was Friday, but it might be Thursday—and he was absolutely convinced a wrong answer would seal his fate.

Sir Leviticus rose. "Mr. Weatherby himself must grow forgetful, for this question was asked and answered by this very witness. Today is Friday, as His Grace recently informed us. Perhaps Mr. Weatherby intends to repeat his entire examination of the witness?"

Robert honestly could not recall answering the question previously, but Sir Leviticus's ploy had reminded Drossman of the passing of time.

"Sir Leviticus has the right of it, Weatherby. You are repeating yourself. Have you any more questions that you haven't asked previously?"

"Rothhaven knows not who sits on the throne of England. He knows not what day it is. I rest my case." Weatherby made a sweeping bow in the direction of the jury.

Robert clutched the front of the witness box. "George the Fourth," he said, a bit too loudly. "George the Fourth sits on the throne of the United Kingdom."

That late answer—accurate though it was—only reinforced that Weatherby had succeeded in seizing the momentum of the trial, and God alone knew what the jury would make of a duke who could not recall the day of the week.

"Your Grace," Drossman said, "you may step down. Sir Leviticus, you aren't putting on any additional witnesses, are you?"

"Yes, sir," Sir Leviticus said, as Robert took his place at the counsel table. "I anticipate the testimony will be brief."

"See that it is. The commission is in recess for the noon hour. The proceedings will resume at two of the clock *precisely*."

Robert knew exactly whom Sir Leviticus intended to call, but he doubted it would make any difference. The last five minutes had decided the case, and the next two hours were all the time that remained to him as a free man.

"All is not lost." That came from Constance, who strode across the room as though she herself were the Lord Mayor of York. "Far from it. I need some sustenance, Your Grace. You will please escort me back to the hotel."

Robert rose, fatigue dragging at him. "I would be honored. Sir Leviticus, my thanks for your efforts thus far, but it's not looking good, is it?"

"It's not looking bad, either, Your Grace. Juries exist precisely because laws require interpretation, and juries do not like greedy lawyers."

"Speaking of greedy nodcocks," Constance said, "where is Philpot?"

That was an answer Robert could give her, but not here. "I'll explain. Let's take some air, shall we?"

* * *

Whitlock Theodophilos Shaw was in a quandary, and praying hadn't relieved his puzzlement. From long experience, he knew that on the rare occasions when the Lord seemed to be turning a deaf ear, He was in fact instructing Whitlock to put pride aside and consult a nigh infallible earthly authority.

"Mrs. Hodges, will you join me for a cup of tea?"

She set the tray on Whitlock's desk and stepped back. "I have much to do, sir, though I appreciate the gesture."

Her tone was deferential, as always. Still, Whitlock knew a silent scold when one was aimed his way every hour of the day.

"I am in your bad books, madam. I know that. You don't think I should drag Ivy off to New South Wales."

Mrs. Hodges gazed around the study, which she kept immaculate without disturbing its sense of masculine comfort.

"Ivy doesn't want to *be* dragged off to New South Wales, and girls her age can cause a great deal of upheaval when their sensible wishes are repeatedly ignored. I know. I was a stubborn young miss once upon a time."

Whitlock could imagine her as a very young lady. She'd probably been quiet, observant, industrious, and too wise too soon.

"Please do have a seat, Mrs. Hodges. You might think I took Ivy's attempts to run away lightly, but she scared me witless. My sisters were good girls, biddable, never a moment's trouble. Ivy...I fear Ivy takes after the woman who gave birth to her."

"Ivy is a good girl." Mrs. Hodges sank onto the very edge of the chair opposite Whitlock's desk. "The only trouble she gives you is when you insist she part from everything dear and familiar, and travel thousands of miles so you can do the Lord's work. Has it occurred to you that the Lord might have given Ivy an assignment that differs from your own?"

Mrs. Hodges never raised her voice, and because she spoke quietly, her words had all the more impact.

"As a matter of fact, it has. Read this." He passed her a single sheet of folded vellum, watermarked with the Rothmere family coat of arms.

Reverend,

Greetings and felicitations to you and Miss Ivy.

I must risk offending you by hastening to address a matter that by rights ought to be handled with respectful delicacy. I suffer the falling sickness, and an attack has been mounted on my legal competence. The enclosed bank draft is made out to you, though I trust your judgment regarding to what extent and how the funds can better Ivy's situation. I know you will exert yourself to the utmost to safeguard her well-being. My only request is that you keep her mother, now my duchess, apprised of Ivy's general situation to the extent your conscience allows you to do so.

By the time you receive this, I might no longer

have the authority to provide for Ivy or to aid you in your travels, so please deposit the sum as quickly as may be. If you or any member of your family is ever in difficulties, please apply to myself, Lord Nathaniel Rothmere, or His Grace of Walden. If you wish at any time to call at Rothhaven Hall, you will of course be most welcome. A child should unite a family rather than occasion division. To my sorrow, I speak from personal experience. I wish you the best, and I remain your obed serv,

Rothhaven

"The sum was considerable," Whitlock said. "Enough to see me well established in New South Wales and to dower Ivy handsomely." More than enough. *Far* more.

Mrs. Hodges set the letter on the desk. "And you don't know what to do, because this duke asks for nothing in return, save that you keep Ivy's mother informed of her situation."

"The blasted man is clearly competent, and woe to him who thinks otherwise. Rothhaven was polite to a fault with me—except that odd bit, which is probably a symptom of his illness. I, on the other hand, was not my most gracious toward him or toward his lady wife."

Mrs. Hodges poured two cups of tea. "His duchess."

And that was the real conundrum. Ivy's mother was a duchess, not only willing but eager to acknowledge her illegitimate daughter. Such women did not exist in Whitlock's experience, and yet…

"Have some tea," Mrs. Hodges said, adding two lumps of sugar to Whitlock's cup. "You will not send that bank draft back, Mr. Shaw."

"I won't?" He'd considered doing just that.

"The money isn't yours to reject. By rights, that money belongs to Ivy, and heaven knows she might need it."

Mrs. Hodges added a dollop of milk to her tea and took a sip. How a woman could do housework all day and still have such lovely hands was a mystery.

"I am being arrogant," Whitlock said. "Dukes are supposed to be arrogant. Rothhaven is disappointing me terribly when he denies me the opportunity to scorn him. Still, Ivy has no need of fripperies and furbelows. Such indulgences only lead to vanity."

Mrs. Hodges set her cup down silently. "Ivy might need that money *to eat*, to buy passage home from whatever colonial backwater you drag her to. She might need that money to avoid a very sorry end. You are *mortal*, Mr. Shaw. You are no stripling, and your ambitions could well result in Ivy being stranded halfway around the world in a place where women are too few in number."

Mrs. Hodges rose and braced her hands on the desk. "If she has some money of her own, she will enjoy a measure of safety in this wicked world, safety women without means lack. Toss that sum back at the duke's feet, and if Ivy is lucky, she might end up keeping house for a short-sighted fool who thinks only of his own ambitions. If she's unlucky...you will have guaranteed her doom with your righteous, masculine pride, and she herself might soon be a mother without benefit of matrimony."

Mrs. Hodges sat, lifted her teacup, then set it back on the saucer untasted. "I will not apologize for speaking my mind when Ivy has nobody else to talk sense to you. If you would allow me to stay on until you take ship, I would appreciate it. I won't ask you for a character."

"I have upset you." That realization qualified as a

revelation, a glimpse into a vast, dimly perceived array of possibilities, for Elizabeth Hodges was as stalwart a soul as ever donned an apron and cap.

"Ivy's situation upsets me." This time the teacup made it to Mrs. Hodges's lips. "She's writing to her mother, you know."

"Writing to... *her mother*?"

"To Her Grace of Rothhaven. You did not forbid her from doing so, and Her Grace writes back."

If Whitlock had boarded a ship and put out to sea in stormy weather, he could not feel more unbalanced.

"Ivy is corresponding with the *Duchess of Rothhaven*, and you are only now informing me?"

Mrs. Hodges finished her tea and put the cup and saucer on the tray. "You are a good man, Whitlock Shaw, but you need a wife to curb your excesses and explain to you the human side of life. Her Grace was here little more than a week past. It's not as if Ivy has been penning her letters in secret for years. Read this."

She passed over another folded piece of vellum, also watermarked with a coat of arms.

"We are abruptly awash in ducal correspondence."

"Read it," Mrs. Hodges said, "and then I will convey it to Ivy. She apparently asked her mother for coach fare so she can escape you once and for all. This is the duchess's reply. It's not the reply I would have penned to my only child, but then, I'm a *penniless housekeeper*."

She rose with none of her customary energy and left the room, closing the door quietly behind her. Whitlock let his tea grow cold, and sat with the letter in his hand, mentally vowing that he would find a way to tell Elizabeth Hodges that she was much more than a penniless housekeeper.

That discussion would take some thought and planning.

A lot of thought and planning in fact, given that Whitlock was supposed to take ship in little more than a fortnight.

He smoothed out Her Grace of Rothhaven's letter and began reading.

* * *

"I want you to know something," Rothhaven said, as he and Constance were shown to a private dining room at the Duck and Goose.

"I want the jury to know many things," Constance replied. "For instance, if they find against you, I will have Quinn and Jane ruin the lot of them unto the nineteenth generation." She would do no such thing, of course. Reverend Shaw detested high-handed aristocrats for reasons, and a tendency to abuse wealth and power for personal satisfaction was probably at the top of his list.

And in that much, oddly enough, Constance agreed with him.

Rothhaven held her chair for her as the serving maid closed the door. Luncheon was already laid out on the table, but Constance had no appetite.

Her husband leaned close to whisper in her ear. "I *loved* being able to tell the world that you are my duchess. I *love* that you sent for Alexander and Helen. I *love* that you put that vile excuse for a physician in his place. I *love* you."

Constance rose and wrapped her arms around him. "I love you too, so very much, and I am furious on your behalf."

He stroked her hair, and some of the ire drained out of her. "We shall contrive, Your Grace," he murmured. "That business with Her Grace of Walden fainting was splendid."

"I think Jane enjoyed using the fiction of female frailty to control an entire courtroom. She was very convincing, wasn't she?"

"*Walden* was convincing. Let's eat, shall we?"

He was so calm, so at ease when Constance was ready to rip up at all of York, and most especially at Lady Phoebe Philpot, who had no doubt authored this entire drama.

"I could manage some bread and butter," Constance said, resuming her seat. "A cup of tea wouldn't go amiss either."

"This is not the prisoner's last meal, Constance." Rothhaven sounded amused, which exceeded the bounds of savoir-faire by several leagues.

"Today has been far more than merely trying, Rothhaven."

He poured himself a glass of water, poured her a glass of ale, and sat at the head of the table. "It has been a challenge. Nonetheless, please recall that certificates of lunacy can be overturned, and if Weatherby prevails, Philpot will have to deal with you, Nathaniel, Walden, and my own efforts to limit his schemes. Speaking of schemes, I have taken a measure of which I doubt you'll approve."

"Say on. I have also taken a measure that I doubt will merit approval." *Another* measure.

"I sent a modest sum to Reverend Shaw while I still had control of my assets."

Constance paused, a piece of bread in one hand, the butter knife in the other. "Why would I disapprove of such generosity?"

"Because Shaw could take offense at my hubris, because funds make it easier for him to decamp to New South Wales, because I did not consult you before I sent him the bank draft."

Rothhaven grasped that a failure to consult his wife could *be* a transgression. That such a man stood accused of incompetence was an injustice of mythic proportions.

"We haven't exactly been in each other's pockets this past week," Constance said.

He touched her arm. "You are not wroth with me for my high-handedness?"

"Eat something, Rothhaven. I can sustain myself on anger and determination, but you haven't that luxury."

He served himself some beef and barley soup, which—now that Constance got a whiff of its aroma—looked tasty.

"Shaw might well return the money," Rothhaven said. "I might have made matters worse."

"Then he returns the money, but I don't know as matters can get much worse. I wrote back to Ivy and told her that under no circumstances was she to quit her uncle's protection."

Rothhaven filled a second bowl with soup and set it before Constance. "Did you, now? Told her to stay put when she'd all but begged you to rescue her?"

The best part, the very, very best part of loving Rothhaven was that he had from the first been Constance's friend. An honorable, kind, decent, tolerant friend. He greeted her announcement as pleasantly as if she'd informed him of a decision to have some new dresses made up.

"This whole legal mess," Constance said, "with Weatherby and Philpot, is driven by Lady Phoebe's mean-spiritedness."

"Very likely. Philpot does not need my money, but he needs to keep his wife happy. Sir Leviticus made it plain that Philpot married up, and his bride has never let him forget it."

The soup was good. Being able to air these thoughts

with Rothhaven was wonderful. "Lady Phoebe has been denied children." Constance had only worked this out on the coach ride back from Fendle Bridge. "She is angry and ashamed because she has been denied motherhood."

"My guess is, she would find reasons to be angry and ashamed if she had ten handsome, healthy children."

"Perhaps, perhaps not. Lady Phoebe feels entitled to have children, and she has been thwarted in that regard. I feel entitled to march into Ivy's life and be her mother. There is no such entitlement."

"Go on."

"I am responsible for heeding the flattery of a scoundrel, for allowing him liberties, for trusting him."

"You were little more than a girl yourself, Constance. Very much at sixes and sevens, and your brother was not as mindful of you as he should have been."

Rothhaven set aside his empty soup bowl, and buttered two slices of bread. He fashioned a sandwich from the sliced beef and cheddar on the plate at his elbow, and passed Constance half.

"All true, which is why I can forgive myself, but from Ivy's perspective, Etta Wilson was the woman who loved her and raised her. If Etta Wilson were alive, would I be dreaming of Ivy coming to live with me?"

"Etta Wilson has been gone for some time."

"But Whitlock Shaw stepped in—a bachelor of modest means—and provided for Ivy. He's seen her reasonably well educated, and he clearly cares for his niece. His siblings look up to him. I love Ivy, I would cheerfully die to protect her, but I don't actually *know* her anywhere near as well as Reverend Shaw does."

"So what did you tell her?"

"What somebody should have told me when I was

meeting an arrogant varlet in the mews, and thinking myself misunderstood and ignored by my family: Ivy should respect that her family has her best interests at heart. She should speak with her uncle honestly from that place of respect. She should realize that her whole life stretches before her, and many girls would envy her the adventure of seeing new lands. I told her that fleeing the safety of her uncle's home is patently foolish and ungrateful. If she doesn't like New South Wales, she can return to England in a few years, but for now, she must... I am about to cry."

Rothhaven was on his feet and around the table in an instant. "Cry, then. You are entitled to that much at least." He squeezed her shoulders and passed her his handkerchief.

"I want to be a good mother, not a pathetic, empty-hearted, selfish g-grasping harpy. Being a good mother is hard."

"But you are my dear duchess," Rothhaven said, returning to his seat, "and you are bound by honor to do the right thing. Unlike many people, you have the courage to act on your convictions. Setting that example for Ivy will stand her in good stead for the rest of her life."

Constance dabbed at her eyes. "You always know what to say. Thank you."

"Eat your sandwich. This difficult day isn't over, but I am so proud of you that I could post a notice in every newspaper in the realm. Promise me, though, that you aren't giving up on having Ivy share our home because your husband is the subject of a lunacy petition?"

"I am not. I am trying to protect my daughter from yielding to dangerous and foolish impulses. Perhaps that's why I've finally found her, because she needs me now for that very purpose."

Rothhaven made another sandwich. "An interesting perspective. Do you truly think Lady Phoebe is driven by frustrated maternal ambitions?"

"Among other afflictions of the spirit. She is very proud, more than a bit vain, and no longer young. One can almost pity her."

Rothhaven saluted with his glass of water. "I commend your generosity of spirit, but the sad truth is, Lady Phoebe can see me declared an idiot, plunder much of my fortune, and bring scandal down on both your family and mine, and that will not relieve what afflicts her."

"I suppose not. She has a sort of falling sickness of the heart—no known cure—but perhaps that's justice, for she has certainly inflicted substantial grief on others."

Rothhaven drained half the glass and waited for Constance to finish her second half sandwich. "Duchess, you will have reason to remonstrate with me."

"I will?"

"I have been a naughty duke, but like certain young ladies, I find myself faced with circumstances that prompt me to act with less than strict prudence. You asked about Neville Philpot's whereabouts, and it happens I can answer that query with some degree of certainty."

"Rothhaven, explain yourself."

Chapter Twenty-two

"We need to wrap this up quickly," Sir Leviticus said. "Drossman wanted the whole business finished before noon."

"In other words," Robert replied, "I inconvenienced him with my seizure." *How very inconsiderate of me.*

The gallery was filling with journalists and spectators. Clerks and bailiffs bustled about, and across the room, Weatherby sat at his table, pretending to read a treatise. Constance was once again ensconced in the gallery between Lady Althea and Her Grace of Walden, while Walden himself, looking like the Wrath of Yorkshire, stood near the door of the gallery.

"Your Grace," Sir Leviticus said softly, "where is my witness?"

"Weatherby is probably wondering the same thing." And where was Lord Stephen?

A commotion at the back of the gallery suggested both

questions were about to be answered. Lord Stephen, cane in one hand, the other wrapped through Neville Philpot's arm, made a gradual progress through the milling crowd.

He stopped just short of Weatherby's table, handed Philpot into a chair, then found a seat near a back corner.

"Your witness, Sir Leviticus," Robert said. And not a moment too soon. Drossman and his confreres resumed their seats, the jury filed into the box, and the room was called to order.

"Sir Leviticus," Drossman barked, "call your final witness."

"I call Neville Philpot, proposed guardian of the person and property of Robert, His Grace of Rothhaven."

Philpot rose, tugged down on his waistcoat, and marched for the witness box. Something about his air was overly determined, as if the box lay across snowy moors and boggy fens rather than ten feet away.

Philpot swore to tell the truth, then let out a stentorian belch. "Sorry, Pet." He offered a little wave in the direction of the gallery. "Nothing like good French brandy and good Yorkshire ale, aye?"

The gallery appreciated that remark, and the jury looked amused.

Drossman looked anything but. "Get on with your interrogation of the witness, Sir Leviticus. We don't have all day."

Because a man's future should be decided as hastily as possible?

Sir Leviticus rose. "Mr. Philpot, what day is it?"

"How should I know?" Another belch. "I'm a solicitor, not a bloody calendar."

"So you don't know what day it is?"

"It's a fine day to down a few pints, that's what day

it is." He beamed at the gallery, impressed with his own cleverness.

"Who sits upon the throne of England, Mr. Philpot?"

"Not me. Mad George, or one of them Georges. Bloody idiots the lot of them, and expensive. England could set up a whorehouse in every village for what we're spending on the royal foolishness."

Weatherby had dropped any pretense of reading his treatise. The two commissioners on either side of Drossman were frankly grinning, and Drossman's brows had lifted nearly to his hairline.

"Philpot, are you drunk?" he asked.

"Never say it, Dross, old boy. Pet would lock me out of the bedroom for a year if I were disord...disorb...hang it, drunk in public." Philpot pulled a face and the gallery erupted into laughter.

Sir Leviticus seemed the only attorney who did not regard the situation as amusing. "Mr. Philpot, do you believe yourself competent to handle the finances of an entire dukedom if His Grace of Rothhaven should be in need of a guardian?"

"Me? I'll handle those finances right into m'pockets, good sir. I adore a fat pigeon, and know exactly how to pluck 'em. Keeping Pet in the style she deserves ain't cheap. No, t'isn't." He winked at his wife, blew her a kiss, and emitted yet another fume-y burp.

"So it's your practice to fleece your wards?"

"Not fleece, exactly. Help myself to a bit of the extra. I do my dooty by 'em, but I take a wage for myself, so to speak. I say, a man could use a chamber pot, if one's handy?"

Sir Leviticus sent the jury a pointed look. "Mr. Philpot, please tell me the sum of 23 plus 42 plus 4."

"Say again?"

Sir Leviticus spoke slowly. "Add 23 plus 42 plus 4."

"In my head?"

"If you please."

Philpot sketched figures in the air with his fingers. "How about 93? I always did fancy 93. A very good year."

"Divide 66 by 11."

"Divide it yourself. I need a chamber pot, another pint, and some rum buns. A wench or two wouldn't go amiss either. Sorry, Pet."

Drossman folded his arms. "Sir Leviticus, I believe you've made your point."

"Pet's mad at me," Philpot informed the room at large. "Look at her. Spittin' mad but always a lady, that's my Pet."

Lady Phoebe rose and departed, while Philpot blew her kisses and waved. "Might I have another ale now?"

Drossman heaved up a sigh. "You may step down, Philpot. Mind you do so carefully."

The warning was lost. Philpot exited the witness box, neglected to recall that two steps were involved, and went sprawling onto the floor. He lay there for a moment, then rolled to his back.

"Damned fine ale, it was," he murmured. "I think I wet myself."

Sir Leviticus spared him not a glance. "I move to dismiss with prejudice the complaint brought against Robert, Duke of Rothhaven. In the alternative, I ask the jury for a verdict denying the petition. A man afflicted with the falling sickness might be slow to answer a few questions immediately following a seizure, but under no circumstances would justice be served by entrusting that man's welfare and fortune to an admitted criminal parading about as a guardian."

"Hear, hear," the jury foreman called.

The gallery was whispering, laughing, and pointing, while Philpot began gently snoring on the floor.

Drossman conferred briefly with the other commissioners, then motioned the bailiff to call for order.

"As chair of this commission, I hereby dismiss with prejudice the petition brought concerning Robert, Duke of Rothhaven. Your Grace, the falling sickness cannot be used as grounds to question your competence again. This commission is adjourned."

The commissioners left, Weatherby packed up his books and tried to slink away, though a journalist or two was already calling his name.

"You lot," Robert said, gesturing to Weatherby's clerks. "Get Philpot off the floor, find his coach, and send him home."

The older clerk grimaced. "Perhaps he ought to tarry in town for a bit, Your Grace. Lady Phoebe might do for him if we send him home now."

"Get him home," Robert said, "before my duchess takes a notion to have him sent to prison."

Lord Stephen watched as one clerk took Philpot by the boots, and the other under the arms.

"I have a hard head," Lord Stephen said, "but drinking that man under the table challenged even my considerable abilities. Devious of you, Rothhaven, and a marvelously effective strategy."

Sir Leviticus tidied up law books and treatises as Philpot was hauled away. "I can have him criminally charged. At the least he ought to be forbidden to do any further legal work."

"Yonder solicitor won't fare well in prison," Lord Stephen observed. "Perhaps that's the fate he deserves."

"Philpot will be in a prison of his own making at home with Lady Phoebe," Robert said. "His punishment will be to stare at the locked bedroom door every night, knowing he's been a fool for love." Or for some version of love.

Lord Stephen propped a hip on the counsel table. "And what is Lady Phoebe's punishment, for much of this mischief can be laid at her dainty feet."

"Philpot will stare at the locked door," Robert said, "and her ladyship's penance is to be on the other side of it, with only her incurable pride for a bedfellow. None of this had to happen, but she would not reconcile herself to her lot. They must forgive each other and themselves, or bitterness and regret will drive them mad."

"Rothhaven!" Constance flew from the doorway and bundled into his arms, hugging him fiercely. "How splendidly you managed that. Brilliantly. Sir Leviticus, have you ever seen the like?"

"Never, Your Grace, and if luck prevails, I will never see it again."

"Nor I," Lord Stephen said. "I am off to swill willow bark tea in hopes of warding off a sore head. Congratulations on your nuptials, Con."

Her Grace of Rothhaven stuck her tongue out at her brother. "Jane will see you married now. Best get back to Italy, or Persia, or wherever bachelors go to hide from true love."

"Persia sounds tempting." He bowed and withdrew, or tried to.

"Lord Stephen!" Robert called.

He stopped, half turned, head cocked as if listening to far-off birdsong.

"Our thanks. Our sincere, hearty thanks. I owe you, and I always repay my debts."

He shrugged. "We're family now. Debts don't come into it. Visit me in Persia."

"Will he really go?" Robert asked, feeling a profound wave of fondness for his new brother-in-law.

"Who knows," Constance said. "Take me home, Rothhaven. Take me home now, and tell my family they are not to call for at least a week."

He hugged her, though such affection drew stares and whispers. "An entire week?"

"That will buy us three days... and nights."

"Home, then," Robert said, and for the first time in years, he could say those words, knowing that with Constance at his side, Rothhaven Hall would actually become a home. Not a comfortable prison, not a place full of distant memories, not a mere dwelling, but a home.

Though of course the Wentworth family gave them only two days and nights of privacy before descending en masse.

Epilogue

"Your family takes getting used to," Rothhaven said, closing the door to the walled garden.

Jane's and Althea's voices faded, Nathaniel's and Quinn's deeper tones beneath them, as Constance took her husband by the hand and folded into his embrace.

"They worry for us. Our marriage has begun under unusual circumstances."

Rothhaven draped his arms across her shoulders and kissed her nose. "Our marriage began years ago, Your Grace. When we were both feeling angry and helpless. Look at us now."

The hearing had been three days past, and since then both Constance and Rothhaven had slept a fair amount, wandered the grounds of the Hall hand in hand, and shared simple, quiet meals. The reality of life free from lawsuits, intrigues, and family dramas was seeping into Constance's soul by slow degrees.

"Will you let me paint you this afternoon?" she asked. "You did commission a portrait from me, if you'll recall." And she could paint him for hours. He had the gift of a stillness that was yet vibrant, the lively intellect and observant mind evident even in his contemplative silences.

"If you must paint my likeness," he said, "I will bear up manfully under the strain. I might require a short nap at some point."

"I do adore our short naps."

A maid appeared on the terrace steps. Harris was young, new to the staff, and had the falling sickness. Her brother had signed on as a footman.

"Excuse me, Your Graces. You have a caller." She passed over a silver tray with a single card on it. *The Reverend Whitlock Shaw.*

"Oh, dear." Constance had given herself one week to rejoice in vanquishing Philpot's scheme. She had promised herself to hold the sorrow of Ivy's impending departure at bay for seven days, and then she would face the next ordeal squarely. That promise was neither consistently nor easily kept.

"Put our guest in the family parlor," Rothhaven said. "Send up a tray with all the trimmings. Some of Monsieur Henri's pear torte wouldn't go amiss."

The maid bobbed a curtsy and withdrew.

"I am nervous," Constance said, resting her forehead against Rothhaven's chest. "Why is he calling on us?"

"I invited him to, more or less."

"You did? Just told him to drop 'round for tea?"

"In so many words. I told him that family ought not to be divided by a child's circumstances, as my family had been divided by mine. Perhaps he's here to toss our money back in our faces."

"Oh, God."

Rothhaven took both of her hands and kissed her knuckles. "If Shaw is in a taking we will hear him out, apologize for overstepping, and try again. Family doesn't give up, Constance. Our family doesn't, not over a silly thing like pride. *You* certainly didn't give up when you were searching for your daughter."

Constance leaned into her husband, drawing strength from his sheer rationality. "Right. Family doesn't give up. I am terrified, and I don't know what to do."

This tendency to blurt out feelings was all Rothhaven's fault. Nothing dismayed him, nothing shook his common sense, and very little inspired his temper. He was in every way the opposite of the man who'd raised Constance, and thank the heavenly powers for that.

She paused only to peek at her appearance—tidy but informal—before preceding Rothhaven through the door of the family parlor.

"Reverend Shaw." She dipped a curtsy. "Welcome to Roth—*Ivy*." Rothhaven came up on Constance's side, and that alone prevented her from rushing across the room to hug the stuffing out of her daughter. "Welcome, and Mrs. Hodges, a pleasure to see you again. A tea tray is on the way, so let's please sit down. Did you travel all the way from Fendle Bridge this morning?"

Nobody moved, and Constance's attempt at gracious chatter died. Ivy wore a pretty green dress that reached to just above her ankles, a nearly-grown-up dress, and she carried a reticule trimmed with a ribbon the same color as her dress.

The sight of her, the sheer, wondrous, dear, amazing sight of her…Constance blinked hard, longing for her paints, completely at sea.

"Girl," Reverend Shaw said, "have you misplaced your manners? Greet Their Graces."

Ivy bobbed at the knees. "I don't know what to call you now. You are a *duchess*."

"Call me happy to see you," Constance said. "Very, very happy. You didn't run away. I am proud of you for that, not that it's my place to be proud of you." An ache started in Constance's chest, unshed tears, perhaps, unspoken hopes colliding with inevitable heartbreak.

"Uncle and I talked," Ivy said, staring past Constance's shoulder. "Mrs. Hodges says we will talk some more."

God bless and keep Mrs. Hodges. "Sometimes talking takes more courage than riding into battle, I'm told." *Please, may I hug you? Please, oh please....*

"Uncle said we must talk with you and His Grace too." This occasioned a shy peek at Rothhaven, who was trying to look harmless and not quite succeeding. He had that *listening intently, adding up every word, and coming to fourteen accurate conclusions* look about him.

"Reverend Shaw is a wise man," Constance said. "Might we continue this discussion over tea cakes and shortbread? I'd also like you to try some of our pear torte. My sister's chef refuses to part with the recipe, so we all try to stay in his good books."

That observation had Mrs. Hodges smiling at the reverend, for some reason, and he held her chair for her. Rothhaven seated Constance, then held a chair for Ivy—who blushed the roaring pink of an embarrassed redhead.

Constance managed the tea tray with Rothhaven's assistance, but the ordeal was nerve-racking. She wanted to grab Reverend Shaw by the lapels and demand to know why he was paying this call, and she wanted to simply stare at her lovely, precious, blushing daughter.

"Elizabeth and I," Shaw began, clearing his throat, "Mrs. Hodges and I, rather, have discussed Ivy's situation at some length, and I do value Elizabeth—Mrs. Hodges's—insights keenly. I read your letter, Duchess, the one in which you admonished Ivy not to embark on a path of dangerous folly. I could have told the girl the same thing fifty times over, complete with citations from Proverbs—I doubtless have, in fact—and she doesn't listen to me. She *listened* to you."

"My duchess," Rothhaven observed, "has a way of getting to the heart of matters. I ignore her at my peril."

"Mrs. Hodges has the same effect on me, sir. In any case, Ivy doesn't want to go to Australia, and I have come upon a reason to delay my own departure indefinitely."

"Have you?" Constance asked, as the ache in her chest acquired a quality of yearning. "You've found a reason to remain in England?"

"Mrs. Hodges has long held my esteem, and I am delighted to learn that my respect for her is reciprocated. I have reason to hope that a courtship will end happily for both of us, though Mrs. Hodges has admonished me that we have much to discuss before that happy day."

"They are sweet on each other," Ivy said. "I have to sing as I move about the house, lest I come upon them engaged in shocking familiarities."

"Ivy, hush," Mrs. Hodges said, smiling, "or I will tell your mother about the time I caught you waltzing about the upper hall in your nightgown."

"Perhaps another time," Constance said. "For the present, I am pleased to hear that Ivy might be in England a while longer." Heartbreakingly pleased. I will tell *your mother*....

Reverend Shaw set down his teacup. "As long as I'm to

bide in England for the foreseeable future, and as long as Ivy is desperate to see you, I thought perhaps..."

"Yes?" Constance didn't recall reaching for Rothhaven's hand, but his grip on her fingers was snug.

"I want to visit here," Ivy said, "if it's not too much trouble. Uncle thinks opening a girls' school might be God's plan for him, or Mrs. Hodges's plan for him. He says other girls haven't mothers as sensible as my mothers have been, and those girls need guidance and moral examples if they aren't to make featherbrained decisions."

Rothhaven topped up the reverend's teacup. "It's been my admittedly limited experience that people who have not used up all their patience raising their own children are often marvelously understanding and tolerant of other people's children. Don't you agree, Reverend?"

"Mrs. Hodges has observed that very same thing, Your Grace, and witness her kindness toward Ivy. She is also of the opinion that funds available to me for the Lord's work in Australia might go twice as far here in England if devoted to a girls' school. The north hasn't many, and thus our girls must travel all the way to the Midlands or farther."

Rothhaven—who had provided the funds under discussion—made encouraging noises, served up pear torte, and generally acted as a competent host while Constance knew a joy too magnificent for tears.

Ivy was not to go away, she wanted to visit at the Hall, and nothing, nothing on earth, could be better news than that.

A tap on the door suggested the kitchen had sensed when more torte was needed, but the maid Harris again announced guests.

"Their Graces of Walden," she said. "Her Grace forgot her gloves."

Well, no. Jane had doubtless spotted Reverend Shaw's coach drawing around to the carriage house, and promptly decided to investigate, towing Quinn, Althea, and Nathaniel with her.

Rothhaven made the introductions, presenting Mrs. Hodges and the reverend to Jane, Quinn, Althea, and Nathaniel in turn. Through the endless bowing and curtsying, Ivy sidled closer and closer to Constance's side.

"And this," Rothhaven said, turning to Ivy, "is our dear Ivy. She has expressed a desire to visit at the Hall, and we are negotiating that happy prospect with her uncle. Should we perhaps move into the garden on such a fine day?"

The familial herd decamped to the walled garden, which was approaching its peak glory. Constance found Ivy walking on her left, Rothhaven on her right, and, without asking permission, she joined hands with them both.

"I am so happy at this moment, I am at risk for bursting into song."

"Please don't, Mama Constance—I mean *Your Grace*—or Uncle will suggest we sing hymns, and his braying is the epitome of a joyful noise."

"I like the other better," Constance said, daring to loop an arm around Ivy's shoulders.

"Mama Constance?"

"Yes, that. I like it very well indeed." She gave in to temptation and hugged Ivy, a quick squeeze that the girl tolerated good-naturedly.

Ivy was as properly awed by Rothhaven's flowers as any visitor would be when surrounded by so much fragrance, color, and beauty. She skipped ahead and began investigating the plantings in each bed.

Constance stood on the steps beside her husband, letting joy wash through her as Althea and Mrs. Hodges discussed the best way to dry meadow mint, Jane and the reverend took the bench near Saint Valentine's statue, and Quinn and Ivy took turns flicking pebbles into the birdbaths. Nathaniel was picking a bouquet of tulips, probably for his wife, and Monteverdi chased a butterfly among the rosebushes.

"You will paint this," Rothhaven said, "and we will hang it in the family parlor."

"Is that a request?"

"A prediction."

"First, I will paint you."

Nathaniel passed Ivy a pink tulip, occasioning another blush, and Constance's heart beat harder. "Thank you, Rothhaven, for this."

"Thank you, Constance, for this."

She rested her head on his shoulder. "You know, I once wanted nothing so much as to pass through life unseen, to slip quietly from one shadow to another. I wanted only peace and privacy, and someday—maybe—to know my daughter was well and happy."

"I wanted to hide as well, to be left in peace while I waited for the next seizure. I wasn't very ambitious, was I?"

"And now?"

"Oh, I think eight is a nice number."

"Eight?"

"Children. Ivy will make a superb big sister. Nathaniel will try to out-uncle Walden and Lord Stephen, and Her Grace will teach our daughters how to climb trees. Althea will commiserate with you as she deals with the same challenges regarding her own offspring."

"What a gorgeous family portrait you paint, Rothhaven. I should have luncheon served out here."

"And have guest rooms made up for Reverend Shaw, Mrs. Hodges, and our daughter."

Constance was so busy being happy and enjoying the sheer pleasure of cuddling with her husband that she at first missed Rothhaven's choice of pronoun.

"Our daughter?"

"Why not, if Ivy will have me as an honorary step-papa? I would hate to be the only Your Grace underfoot when you are Mama Constance and Walden and his duchess will be Uncle Quinn and Aunt Jane. Doesn't seem fair that I alone should be saddled with a title when the family is together."

The only reply Constance was capable of was to hug him and hug him and hug him, until Jane hooted at the sight, Quinn muttered, Nathaniel and Althea kissed, the reverend and Mrs. Hodges began applauding, and Ivy tossed her tulip at the happy couple.

LOOK FOR STEPHEN'S STORY IN

HOW TO CATCH A DUKE

AVAILABLE SPRING 2021

KEEP READING FOR A PREVIEW.

Chapter One

"I have come to ask you to kill me, my lord."

Abigail Abbott had surprised Stephen Wentworth from the moment he'd met her several months ago. May she ever bask in heaven's benevolent light, her unexpected call renewed his delight and amazement.

"Miss Abbott, while it is my greatest joy to accommodate a lady's pleasure *wherever* that quest may lead, in this instance, I fear I must disappoint."

"You are the logical party to execute this errand," she went on as if he hadn't spoken. "You are in line for a dukedom and thus too highly placed to face repercussions should you be charged criminally. You'll see the thing done properly."

The butler had shown Stephen's guest into the library, which was a breach of etiquette. Miss Abbott should have been received in the formal parlor, which faced the street and thus afforded a lady's reputation greater protection.

Bless all conniving butlers. “Might we sit, Miss Abbott? My knee is—as it were—killing me.”

She glowered at him down the length of her magnificent nose. “I importune you to commit murder, and you jest.”

Stephen used his cane to gesture at a comfortable wing chair set before the blazing hearth and waited until Miss Abbott had seated herself before he settled onto the sofa.

“Your faith in my abilities is flattering, Miss Abbott, but my family takes a dim view of violence toward women—as do I. I cannot, alas, accommodate your request.”

She popped out of her chair and paced across his new Axminster carpet, gray skirts swishing. “And if I were a footpad trying to snatch your purse, a brigand menacing your person? Then would you send me to my reward?”

She moved with all the confidence of a general marching to war at the head of a vast army, though her attire made for very odd battle finery. Stephen had never seen her dressed in anything but gray frocks or dark cloaks, and the severity of her bun would have done credit to a particularly ascetic order of nuns.

Everything about Abigail Abbott was intended to disguise the fact that she was a stunningly well-built female with lovely features. Such attributes made her merely desirable, and Stephen had come to terms with desire years ago—for the most part.

What fascinated him about Miss Abbott was her wonderfully devious mind, and how her penchant for guile waged constant warfare with her unbending morals.

“Why would a professional inquiry agent with very few unhappy clients need to die?” Stephen asked. “From what my sister has said, your business thrives because you excel at what you do.”

Miss Abbott had been a very great help to Constance up in Yorkshire. To see Miss Abbott in London was both a lovely surprise—to see her anywhere would be lovely—and worrisome. If the Creator ever fashioned a woman who did not need any man's assistance, for anything, Miss Abbott was that formidable lady.

"My situation has nothing to do with my profession," Miss Abbott replied, resuming her seat. "Might you ring for a tray?"

"Is that how you go on with your lovers? Issue commands couched as questions? *Sir, might you apply your hand to my*—"

"My lord, you are attempting to shock me." Her expression was so severe, Stephen was certain she was suppressing laughter. "As a dilatory tactic this is doomed to fail. I am very hard to shock, and I am also quite hungry. A tray, if you please. In more genteel circles, this is called offering a guest sustenance. Hospitality, manners. Need I explain further?"

"Tug the bell pull twice," Stephen said, gesturing again with his cane. "I have been taken captive by the sofa. *You* are being dilatory, madam, evading a simple question: Why must you die? I would be desolated to think of a world without you in it."

He offered her the God's honest truth, at which she sniffed.

"You are doubtless desolated eleven times a day." She gave the bell pull a double yank and sat back down. "I am not asking you to rid the world of my presence in truth. I must convincingly appear to die. I have some means, and I can make my way from England easily enough once I've been officially expunged from the race."

"My dear Miss Abbott, had you wished to terminate

your existence in truth, you would have done so by now. Never for a moment did I think you expected me to actually take a life."

A scintilla of the starch suffusing her spine eased. "I should have been more clear. I know you are not a killer."

"I am, as it happens. A killer, though that's old business." Old business she should at least be warned about before she awarded Stephen any points for civility. "I generally avoid violence if I can do so without compromising my honor."

"And when you cannot?"

What an odd question. "I keep my affairs in order and make sure my family remains untroubled by my actions. If your work has not forced you to flee for your life, then who has inspired you to take the grave step of asking for my help?"

Miss Abbott stared at her gloved hands, then she consulted her pocket watch, which looked to be a man's article, heavy and old-fashioned. As stage business went, the watch was badly done, because the ormolu clock on the mantel was in plain sight and kept perfect time.

Stephen let the silence stretch, unwilling to trick Miss Abbott into any admissions. She'd resent the manipulation, and besides, she was tired, hungry, and unnerved. To take advantage of her in a low moment would be unsporting. Far more interesting to put her back on her mettle and engage her when she could bring her usual trebuchet of logic and the boiling oil of her asperity to the battle of wits.

The tray arrived, and without Stephen having to ask, Miss Abbott poured out. She apparently recalled that he liked his tea with a mere drop of honey. She used far more than a drop in her own cup, and she made short work of two toasted cheese sandwiches and an entire sliced apple.

"Don't neglect the shortbread," Stephen said, sipping his tea.

"You're not eating, and the food is delicious."

"Not much appetite." Stephen had an enormous appetite, but a man with an unreliable leg ought not to push his luck by carrying unneeded weight. He was nowhere near as well disciplined when it came to his mental appetite for solving puzzles.

Still, he had learned some manners, thanks to the ceaseless efforts of his family. He waited until a mere half sandwich remained on the tray before he resumed his interrogation.

"Have you committed a crime?" he asked, starting with the usual reason people shed an identity.

"I have committed several crimes, as do most people in the course of a week. You, for example, are likely behind on the longbow practice mandated by the Unlawful Games Act of 1541. Very bad of you, my lord, considering how much interest you take in weaponry generally."

A footman came for the tray, and Miss Abbott's look of longing as he departed made Stephen jealous of an uneaten half sandwich.

"We will not be disturbed again," Stephen said. "For you to resort to sixteenth-century legislation for your obfuscations means, my dear, that you are very rattled indeed. Miss Abbott—Abigail—you are safe with me, as you knew you would be. I cannot help you if you refuse to apprise me of the nature of the challenge you face. Who has presumed to menace you?"

She had taken off her gloves to eat. She smoothed them against her skirts now, one glove atop the other, matching the right and left finger to finger. Why should that image be vaguely erotic?

"I have apparently angered a peer," she said. "Infuriated him, though I haven't done him any wrong."

Why come to the brother of a *duke* for aid unless...? "A *marquess* is after you?" They were few in number, particularly if the Irish and Scottish titles were eliminated from consideration. "An English marquess?"

"I think so."

"You *know* so, but how do you know?"

She tucked the gloves away into one of those invisible, capacious pockets sewn into women's skirts.

"Do you promise not to repeat what I tell you, my lord?"

"You are exhausted and afraid, so I will overlook that insult you imply."

Her head came up, like a dominant mare sensing an intruder in her paddock. "I am *not* afraid, I am vexed past all bearing."

She was terrified, and that was a sufficiently unlikely prospect that Stephen himself became uneasy.

"Give me a name, Miss Abbott. I cannot scheme effectively on your behalf unless you give me a name."

She had the prettiest gray eyes. All serious and searching, and those eyes were worried. That some fool had given her cause to worry made Stephen vexed past all bearing. He'd not enjoyed a rousing fit of temper for some time, and the prospect of putting some fool marquess into his place appealed strongly.

"You won't believe me."

"If somebody had told me a mere marquess had blighted the confidence of Miss Abigail Abbott, *that* I would have found hard to believe. The ranking imps of hell could provoke you to brandishing your sword cane, and for the massed armies of Britain you might slow your stride a bit. St. Michael the Archangel might inspire you to a respectful pause. But a marquess? A lowly, human marquess?"

Her hands bunched into fists. "He has tried to kill me, twice. Before he tries again, I will simplify matters by having you commit an arranged murder."

Like an arranged marriage? "Who is this vexatious marquess?" Stephen mentally began sorting through Debrett's. This one was too old, that one too young. Several were on the Continent, a few were simply too decent or too arrogant to resort to killing a female of common origins.

Females were easy to ruin, and a female inquiry agent with a tarnished reputation would be ruined indeed.

"Stapleton," he said. "He's an idiot. Arrogant, wealthy, nearly ran off his own son, God rest the earl's randy soul. Stapleton has made his daughter-in-law's life hell. You needn't die. I'll kill Stapleton for you and the world will be a better place all around. Shall I ring for another tray? You're still looking a bit peaky."

About the Author

Grace Burrowes grew up in central Pennsylvania and is the sixth of seven children. She discovered romance novels in junior high and has been reading them voraciously ever since. Grace has a bachelor's degree in political science, a bachelor of music in music history (both from the Pennsylvania State University), a master's degree in conflict transformation from Eastern Mennonite University, and a juris doctor from the National Law Center at George Washington University.

Grace is a *New York Times* and *USA Today* bestselling author who writes Georgian, Regency, Scottish Victorian, and contemporary romances in both novella and novel lengths. She enjoys giving workshops and speaking at writers' conferences.

You can learn more at:

GraceBurrowes.com

Twitter @GraceBurrowes

Facebook.com/Grace.Burrowes

Looking for more historical romances?
Fall in love with these sexy rogues
and darling ladies from Forever!

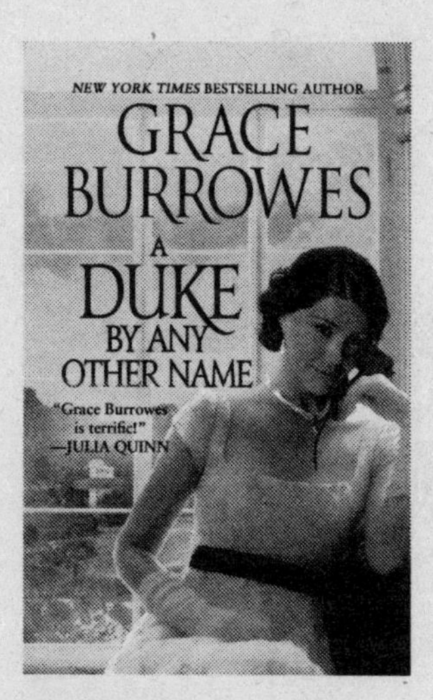

A DUKE BY ANY OTHER NAME
by Grace Burrowes

Lady Althea Wentworth has little patience for dukes, reclusive or otherwise, but she needs the Duke of Rothhaven's backing to gain entrance into Society. She's asked him nicely, she's called on him politely, all to no avail—until her prize hogs *just happen* to plunder his orchard. He longs for privacy. She's vowed to never endure another ball as a wallflower. Yet as the two grow closer, it soon becomes clear they might both be pretending to be something they're not.

THE TRUTH ABOUT DUKES
by Grace Burrowes

Lady Constance Wentworth never has a daring thought (that she admits aloud) and never comes close to courting scandal... as far as anybody knows. Robert Rothmere is a scandal poised to explode. Unless he wants to end up locked away in a madhouse (again) by his enemies, he needs to marry a perfectly proper, deadly dull duchess, immediately—but little does he know that the delightful lady he has in mind is hiding scandalous secrets of her own.

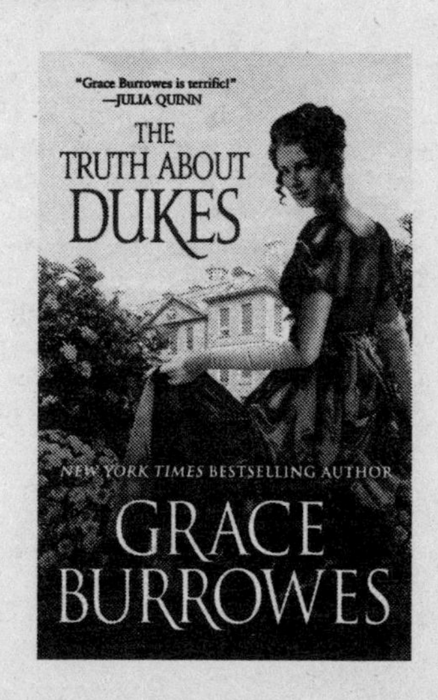

Follow @ReadForeverPub on Twitter and join the conversation using #ReadForever

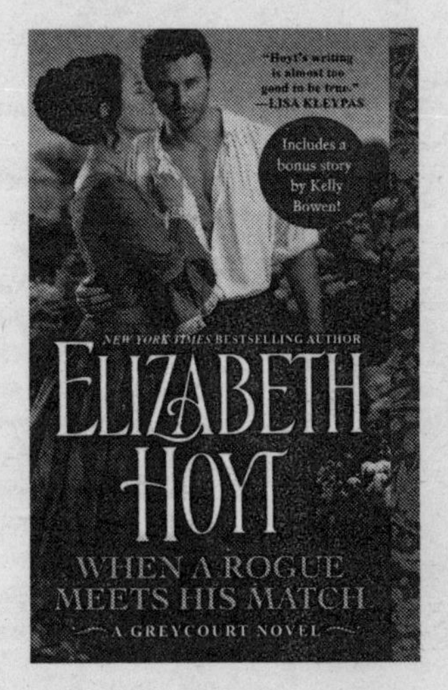

WHEN A ROGUE MEETS HIS MATCH
by Elizabeth Hoyt

After clawing his way up from the gutters as the Duke of Windemere's fixer, ambitious, sly Gideon Hawthorne is ready to work for himself—until Windermere tempts Gideon with an irresistible offer. Witty, vivacious Messalina Greycourt is appalled when her uncle demands she marry. But Gideon proposes his own devil's bargain: protection and freedom in exchange for a *true* marriage. Only as Messalina plots to escape their deal, her fierce, loyal husband unexpectedly arouses her affections. But Gideon's last task for Windemere may be more than Messalina can forgive... Includes a bonus story by Kelly Bowen!

Discover bonus content and more on read-forever.com

Connect with us at
Facebook.com/ReadForeverPub

A GOOD DUKE IS HARD TO FIND
by Christina Britton

Next in line for a dukedom he doesn't want to inherit, Peter Ashford is on the Isle of Synne only to exact revenge on the man responsible for his mother's death. But when he meets the beautiful and kind Miss Lenora Hartley, he can't help but be drawn to her. Can Peter put aside his plans for vengeance for the woman who has come to mean everything to him?

ANY ROGUE WILL DO
by Bethany Bennett

For exactly one season, Lady Charlotte Wentworth played the biddable female the *ton* expected—and all it got her was society's mockery and derision. Now she's determined to take charge of her own future. So when an unwanted suitor tries to manipulate her into an engagement, she has a plan. He can't claim to be her fiancé if she's engaged to someone else. Even if it means asking for help from the last man she would ever marry.

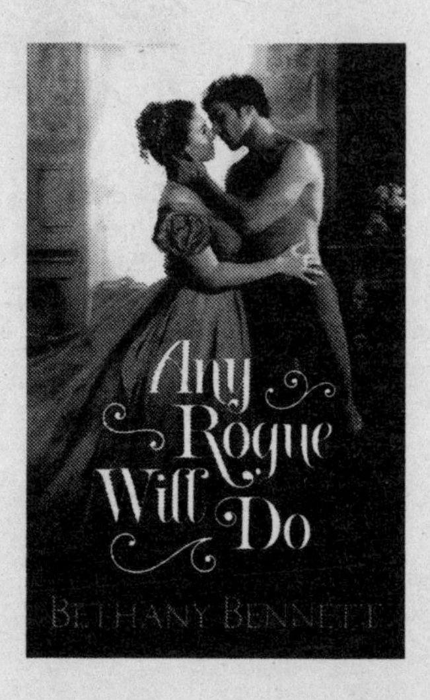

Find more great reads on Instagram with @ReadForeverPub

THE HIGHLAND LAIRD
by Amy Jarecki

Laird Ciar MacDougall is on a vital mission for Scotland when he witnesses a murder—and then is blamed for the death and thrown into a Redcoat prison to rot. He never thought he'd be broken out by a blind slip of a lass and her faithful hound. He soon learns that Emma Grant is just as fierce and loyal as any clansman. But now they're outlaws on the run. And as their enemies circle ever closer, he will have to choose between saving his country or the woman who's captured his heart.